To Bernadine —

I hope you enjoy the read.

Carol Sigwin Hicks

"I wish they would only take me as I am."

—Vincent Van Gogh

The Color of Acceptance

A Novel

Carol Siyahi Hicks

Author of *Gifts from the Garden*

Copyright © 2022 Carol V. Hicks. All rights reserved. No part of this book may be reproduced in any form without written permission of the publisher.

Printed 2022 in the United States of America.

Please note: This book is a work of fiction. Names, characters, corporations, institutions, organizations, events, and locations in this work are the products of the author's imagination or, if real, used fictionally. Historical terminology related to Blacks and People of Color in the 1940s to early 1970s is used in this work for historical accuracy.

Acknowledgments:

Special thanks to the Dunedin Writers Group and Jon Michael Miller—and to Vicki Perez, Abi Karaa, Lee Huntington, Rebecca Arno, Polly Perkins, David Farrell, Sven Midelfort, and Bob Bingenheimer.

CONTENTS

~I~ MOON SONG 1
1945-1946—San Miguel & San Felipe de Jesús,
Southwest New Mexico

~II~ NEW DAY DAWNING 20
1946 - 1963 – Merrick, Long Island

~III~ THE FOOTHILLS.. 51
1965 – Hattiesburg, Mississippi, & Oberlin, Ohio

~IV~ LOVE THAT BINDS 97
Summer 1965 – New York City & Long Island

~V~ ADVENTURE IN A FOREIGN LAND.............. 125
1965 – 1966 – Istanbul, Turkey

~VI~ COMING HOME 197
1966 – Istanbul & Merrick

~VII~ DISCOVERIES IN A FAMILIAR LAND 211
1966 - 1967 – Oberlin & Merrick

~VIII~ NO MOUNTAIN TOO HIGH 247
1967 – 1971 – New York City & Chicago

~IX~ INTO THE UNKNOWN 358
1971-1972 – Chicago to New Mexico

Moon Song

~I~
MOON SONG

1945-1946—San Miguel and San Felipe de Jesús, Southwest New Mexico

1
April 6, 1946

The distant howling of dogs nearly shattered her resolve. *It's the moon,* she thought. *It brings out the wolf in them.* Trembling, she tightened her hold on the basket woven with sweetgrass and love. As she quickened her steps, the newborn stirred in her sleep.

* * *

"Forgive me, Mother Mary!" Elena whispered as she crossed herself with one hand and with the other laid the carrier on the steps of the old mission in San Miguel.

Passing clouds briefly dimmed the full moon's luminescence that threatened to uncover some truth. In the shadows Elena pulled aside the worn blanket that had been hers as a child and her mother's before her, the blanket woven and appliquéd with care by her grandmother Maribel in San Cristobal de las Casas in southern Mexico.

Under the colorful cover the baby girl lay attentive now, but quiet. The fragrance of the newborn mingled with the perfume of the basket's grasses and wafted up toward the hesitant girl bent over her. Looking at her mother who was just a child herself, the infant wore an expression of sweetness and acceptance that startled the beautiful Elena.

"I can't," she said, her voice husky, "I can't keep you. You'll be better off without me. Forgive me little one, please forgive me."

The clouds passed, and the light of the full moon burst from darkness and flooded the steps above where she huddled. With a sense of urgency she bent her kerchiefed head to kiss her daughter one last time. Weeping as she closed the carrier lid, she slunk down the mission stairs in silence just as the moonlight struck.

Running across the grounds, she reached an opening in the wall some seventy feet from the mission steps. Hidden now and leaning against the archway's cold bricks, she was determined to stay until the child was found and she knew her baby was safe. Elena comforted herself with the thought that momentarily the priest would open the mission door.

"Mother Mary, please let him be quick," she called softly into the receding night.

No sooner had she whispered her prayer, than she saw to her horror the approach of a four-legged creature moving from the shadows. In the light of the moon she could see now that it was a dog.

"Please Mother, let it pass!"

But the wild dog had lurked, watching for several minutes. With determination it moved slowly up the mission steps. The dog was half-starved, and the basket offered the smell of something warm and inviting. Batting its nose against the wicker, it sniffed the contents before trying to raise the lid that wouldn't budge. Unsuccessful and frustrated, the creature lowered its head like a battering ram and drove it against the carrier using the weight of its mangy mid-sized body. Toppling onto its side, the container slid a few steps to the cobblestone landing. The lid was ajar now, the mongrel poised to extract the contents.

Then Elena heard her baby cry. Gasping, she ran toward her daughter.

Moon Song

Excited now, the dog took a wide stance and knelt to grab the wailing infant in its jaws.

At just that moment the mission door opened. Orange light from inside flooded the scene before the aging priest. He was not a tall man, and he leaned on a walking stick. Hearing a child's scream, he stopped. Spotting the basket beside the snarling animal, he inhaled a gamy scent that rose from the creature.

"Get back!" the priest shouted as he stepped forward forcefully.

The dog growled.

Elena stopped half the distance to the mission and partially hidden from the moonlight by a tree's cast shadow. The kerchief fell from her hair, her dark tresses tumbling about her face. Freezing in place, she feared that her movement might further excite the dog to snatch the newborn. She felt her heart race as her breathing grew rapid. Adrenaline flooded her body.

Breaking into a sweat, she struggled to restrain herself from running to her daughter. Then a cry rose in Elena that demanded release. A cry of a mother to her child. A cry that said, "I'm here! You're mine! I'll not let anything harm you!" She had to cover her lips with her hand to stifle the animal-like sound that fought to escape from the well of her belly, that place that had sheltered and nurtured her baby, that place of hope and longing.

Just when she thought she could mask her cry no more, she watched in amazement, then gratitude as the priest lunged down the stairs toward the animal baring its teeth. It was as if a Mayan God possessed Father Martino as he brandished his staff and a warrior's cry. As the canine crouched in readiness to spring toward him, his rod came down hard against the beast. Yelping in pain and surprise the animal retreated, saliva dripping from its mouth. Some thirty feet away the dog growled again as the priest righted the container and peeled back the lid.

"Shoo, you miserable cur!" he yelled, raising his stick again, shaking it ominously. The creature yelped and retreated into darkness.

Elena cupped her ear. Standing still, hoping not to be seen, she listened for the barest whisper of a sound from her daughter. "Sing to me, little one," she moaned. Hearing nothing she wept, struggling to muffle the primal sound resurfacing in her. She crept closer, still hidden in the shadows. Then she detected the Father talking to her baby and strained to catch his words. Too far away, she couldn't discern what he was saying as he moved the wraps to reveal an infant no more than a few days old.

As Elena strained to understand her little one's plight, the baby let out a short, loud cry. Then the child stopped. The silence thundered. Elena choked. She took a step forward to leave her cover and claim her daughter. But then the Father put down his walking stick and placed one hand under the infant's bottom and another under her head, lifting the swaddled, dark-haired, olive-skinned baby from the basket.

Elena watched as he held the child to him, soothing and warming her. Closer now but still in shadow, Elena thought she saw her little one move. She caught her breath as she watched the priest with her girl child. The Father's gentleness with the infant comforted Elena as she stood motionless.

"You must be frightened and half-frozen, you poor child," he said aloud as he held her tiny form against his nubby robe, warm from his body. Grabbing the carrier and leaving his staff behind, he labored up the steps and entered the mission holding the newborn.

While Elena was too far away to catch what Father Martino said, she knew her child was alive. Retreating to the opening in the mission wall, she shook as she covered her face with her hands and sobbed. Her long hair fell away from her face as she raised it to the sky.

"Mother, what have I done? I almost killed my child! Please forgive me! Watch over and protect my little one, Mother Mary, I beg you!" she pleaded as she made the sign of the cross.

Pivoting, her shoulders bowed, she began to move slowly away. She knew in her heart that she might walk in another direction, but she never could reverse the tragedy of this night. She hesitated. She still could change her mind. She looked back.

"I cannot!" she cried, turning her back to the mission and sighting the moon that seemed to follow and expose her. "Get away!" she shouted as she shook her fist.

2
Dawn's Early Light

The moon gave way to the early rising of the sun. Fearful of discovery, Elena quickened her pace as Carmen's street came into view. Soon she tapped softly on her childhood friend's bedroom window. As she started to speak, Carmen put her finger to her lips to quiet her. Then the heavy-set, dark-skinned teenager reached down and pulled her best friend up and through the window into her room.

"You okay?" Carmen whispered into the room's shadows as she looked at Elena covered with dust, her face swollen and stained with tears. "And the baby, is she okay?"

"I think so," Elena said as she shook her head in affirmation. Then she started to cry. Carmen took her in her arms and stroked Elena's hair.

"There there, Elena, it'll be okay. Rest now and tell me what happened."

Elena gradually quieted. The small room, draped with sarapes and filled with Carmen's family pictures and the aroma of just-lit candles, seemed to fold comfortingly around Elena. She wiped her eyes and sat on the bed beside her short, sturdy friend.

"This is so difficult Carmen. I never imagined how hard," her voice trailed off as she struggled to check her emotions. "I left my baby on the mission steps as we planned." She swallowed forcefully to keep from choking on her words and memories. "And then…then…," she hesitated, recounting all that had happened. "I think she's okay. I didn't hear her cry after the Father picked her up. But I was too far away and don't know for sure." Elena broke down, sobbing on her teenage friend's shoulder again.

"There there," Carmen crooned. "I'm sure she's fine. We'll find a way to check on her. Don't worry. Come get in bed with me and try to sleep. You're shot Elena. You only had your baby six days ago, and you're not well yet."

Indeed Elena looked as if she might faint. She was young and strong, but giving birth in the abandoned shed in the field behind Carmen's house, with only Carmen to help her, had been a harrowing and dangerous ordeal. Then the uncertainty and fears she had harbored about leaving her child at the mission and finally witnessing the wild dog's threat to her newborn, bled the last of her energy and resolve.

Seeing concern on Carmen's face, Elena reached for her hand. "Thank you Carmen, for being my friend," she said, a weak smile breaking like a small light across her face. "I don't know what I'd do without you."

Then tears welled in her eyes again as she wept for her daughter, herself, and her family, whom she loved and had tried hard not to fail. She knew they had always wanted her to be strong and chaste. They hoped she would be the first to pursue her education past high school and in some manner follow in the footsteps of her independent female forebears. Having sought to please her family throughout her life, she realized now she didn't have the strength to face their disappointment.

But what she realized even more fully was that if she kept her child, the girl indeed would have been ostracized. She would suffer for her mother's mistakes and ultimately bear the scars of her mother's transgressions.

Oh my poor dear child, she thought. *This would have been no way to start your life. Carmen was right. You'll do better without me. God willing, a loving family will find you and give you a chance to make your life on your own terms, free from the baggage of mine. Forgive me that I couldn't bear to name you, little one. But know I'll carry you always in my heart. You'll never know how much I love you, and always will!*

Carmen squeezed Elena's hand as she tried to rescue her from the sorrow into which she saw her descending. "Elena, you're my dearest friend. I'd do anything for you. Rest here now. It'll be fine. The worst is past. You'll see."

3
One Year Earlier

Elena was just fifteen when she met Mario. It was in early May. She was on her way home from the school for children of Mexican descent. He came riding across the field on his sleek chestnut horse. Startling and nearly running over her as he galloped from the field onto the road, she fell.

Stopping to see if she were hurt, he extended his hand, pulling her up to where he could see her full form. Two years older than she, Mario caught his breath as he eyed Elena's womanly body, her large dark-brown eyes, full lips, olive skin, and long, nearly black hair that played about her face in a most appealing way. She looked up at him with equal astonishment and delight.

After that Mario chased after her, insisting that she see him secretly. Often they met in a grove of live oaks some distance from where the farm workers toiled in the fields. Talking as they walked, he would take her hand in his. Elena thought she would die from the ardor his touch stirred in her. She had never had a boyfriend before and never been in the company of someone as educated and fine as Mario. Still she worked hard to keep some physical boundaries with him, as she was a devout Catholic determined to stay a virgin until her wedding day.

Mario, however, tall, blue-eyed, and Hispanic-Anglo, was not only physically attractive to her, but also attentive and persistent. Many of his words and gestures demonstrated an interest in Elena beyond purely physical attraction. What she had to say and how she felt appeared to interest him, showing a tenderness that moved her.

One day under the oaks and amid the stir of leaves and blades of grass, the inevitable occurred. He was kissing her. His hand found her breasts. She was lost in desire. Before she knew it they were half-naked and entwined on the ground. She no more could have stopped what happened than a stream could help swelling from too much rain.

When it was over she lay in his arms torn between fulfillment and shame.

They met several times after that. Mario always was glad to see his dark beauty—until late July when she came to him with the news that she was pregnant. As he urged her to get an abortion, she looked at him in horror and told him she never would do this. He saw her only once more, when he returned to offer her money and the name and number of an abortionist scrawled on a piece of paper he had folded neatly and placed in the pocket of his expensive trousers.

Shocked by what he wanted her to do, Elena again refused. He was Catholic too, she cried, how could he ask her to do such a terrible thing? "Help me Mario, help our baby!" she sobbed.

"I can't," he answered, a flash of hidden feeling in his voice. Then he pulled himself up and responded sternly, cold now. "We're from different backgrounds. My parents would never allow it. It could never work." As he renounced her, she thought she glimpsed emotion touch his face.

"Mario!" she called.

Swiftly he turned away and kept walking, his movements stiff, resolute.

She stopped, struck. What had she been thinking? That a rich family like Mario's would welcome a poor Mayan girl, daughter of former farm workers, a girl who would give herself up in an oak grove to a boy to whom she clearly was so ill-suited? As she watched him leave, she saw all her hopes for her and her baby's future vanish with him.

Knowing that her family would be shocked by her actions, she felt certain they would cast her out. Believing she had no one now—save for her best friend Carmen—she ran to the girl's house and told her everything.

"So why can't you tell your mother? You really think she'd disown you?" Carmen probed.

"My mother? You've got to be kidding. You know she comes from a long line of independent women. You've heard the legends of my grandmother's heroism during the Mexican Revolution—how she fought to guarantee workers' union rights and peasant land rights and worked for social justice for Mayan women like herself. Then she was forced to flee Mexico with her young daughter. You know the stories."

Carmen watched Elena as the intensity of her reply grew.

"And you know how my mother told me that Grandmother Maribel despised the wealthy landowners in Mexico *and* America. My mother said if I ever did what I've done now, she'd whip me until there was nothing left of me, then throw me out! Do you think for a minute she'd accept me and this baby, this child of a rich landowner's son? Mario represents everything my family despises. How could I be so stupid? I thought he loved me…"

Her passion spent and emotionally exhausted now, Elena moaned, "What am I going to do, Carmen? What am I to do?"

"Let me think on this. For now, stay here tonight. I'll run and tell your mother you're here and not to worry, that you'll be home in the morning. It'll give us time to make a plan."

By morning they had decided to try to hide her pregnancy, assuming nature cooperated and didn't cause her to show too much.

"Remember my cousin, how small she was?" Carmen coaxed. "She only looked like she was putting on weight from eating too many tortillas." She laughed, trying to cheer Elena. But Elena was too sad and frightened. "Maybe you'll be lucky like that," Carmen said. "We'll let out your skirts, and no one will know."

"I doubt I'll be so lucky," she replied. "But let's say I am, and I manage to keep my mother and sister from seeing me naked. How and where will I have this baby?"

Carmen fell silent. Pondering her friend's question, she bit along the side of her fingernail before looking up. "That shed in the field behind here. It's quite large, and no one ever goes there anymore. There's even a cot back there where the old shepherd used to sleep."

Elena gasped. "And then what?"

"I can help you with the birth."

"Carmen, you can't be serious."

"Remember when my sister had her baby at home and the midwife came? Well I watched everything she did and even helped her. I can do this. I know I can."

Elena shook her head. "And what then? You can't hide a baby forever. Where will we live? How?"

Carmen hesitated, chewing on her lip. Then she responded. "You can take the baby to the orphanage. Someone will adopt it, it'll have a home, and everything will be fine."

"The orphanage in San Felipe de Jesús? Carmen, you can't be suggesting that."

"And you think that you, when you're sixteen, will be able to take care of yourself and a child all by yourself? And what about how your baby will be treated? People will call it a bastard," Carmen retorted. "Elena, you're not thinking."

She flinched at the specter of her child as an outcast and grew quiet. At last she said, "If I did this awful thing, then everyone would know anyway, wouldn't they?"

"Not if you left the child at the mission door where Father Martino would find it. He would take the baby to the orphanage, and no one would ever know."

"Abandon my child? Carmen, I could never do such a thing!"

"Just think about it. What choice do you have? And the baby will be better off with a family who can take care of and love it. It'll be free to make its own way in the world without ugly labels. Think about it Elena."

Hanging her head, Elena felt exhausted from the events of the day and the consequences of what her friend was describing. She could no more imagine giving up her unborn child to strangers than she could envision no one guessing she was pregnant nine months from now.

"It'll work out. Don't worry," Carmen said. "I'll take care of you. Now lie down and rest. I'll get us cool tea and food from the kitchen. Then I'll run and tell your mother you're here. Rest Elena. It'll be fine."

4
Nine Months Later

Ultimately Carmen managed Elena's birthing surprisingly well. After Elena's baby was born, Carmen buried the bloody linens and afterbirth in the field so no one would find them. Caring for her friend and the newborn in the shed she had prepared for them, she brought Elena fresh bedding, food, soap, and water for washing her and the baby, as well as strips of clean cloth to diaper the tiny girl. As her breasts filled with milk, Elena nursed her child and watched with a mixture of sadness and satisfaction as the infant suckled contentedly.

But the nursing soon brought Elena closer to the infant she knew she must give up. Crying now each time she nursed, she dreaded the day she would take her daughter to the mission.

"That miserable Mario," Carmen said one day, almost hissing the words. "If he was any kind of man, he'd marry you. Him and the whole high and mighty Santorez family can all just go to hell!" There was fire in Carmen's black eyes as she spoke of the anger in her heart for the spoiled Hispanic-Anglo boy from the family that owned most of the county.

"Our families for more than a generation broke their backs in their fields. Who do they think they are anyway?" Carmen huffed, turning away in disgust. "You know as well as I do that Mario's family would no more have taken a poor Mayan girl into their home than do the hard, sweaty work they farm out to others."

Elena waited for her friend to quiet. "It's difficult for Mario," she started to say.

"Difficult?" she turned sharply toward Elena. "You still defend that snake? He seduced you, stole your virginity, and then took a hike, abandoning you and your baby. He's not worthy to be in the same room with you. He's nothing but a damn creep."

Elena said nothing.

"Then, *then*," Carmen continued, "he had the nerve to tell you to get an abortion. You said you'd never do it. But he'd have you be damned for all eternity so he wouldn't have to look at what he did. Difficult? He doesn't know the meaning of the word!"

Downcast, she knew Carmen was right. But she had loved Mario, her dark-haired, blue-eyed, Hispanic-Anglo boyfriend. She remembered how he had made love to her so sweetly that she forgot about the sin she was committing and what might happen later. Now she pulled herself up short, chastising herself for harboring tender feelings for someone who ultimately rejected her.

More importantly, however, time was running out, time with this little one she so loved. Soon she must take her to the old mission and put her in Father Martino's care. *Mother Mary,* she prayed, *please help me through this and protect my baby. I beg you Mother, please watch over her.*

5
April 6, 1946, Following Father Martino's Rescue

Back in his office behind the sanctuary, Father Martino put the child on the crude table he used for a desk and unwrapped her.

The little one appeared to watch the priest as he worked, this man who was only five-foot-six, but squarely built. Although he was in his fifties, he looked old beyond his years. He wore a long brown robe and had a nest of thinning hair wound around an ample bald spot at the crown of his head. His skin was dark and badly weathered from years in the often-brutal New Mexico sun as he traveled throughout his parish ministering to his parishioners' needs. Despite the strength of his jaw and the stubborn set of his mouth, there was a certain softness of expression in his eyes that only could come from a kind heart and a life focused on God and the relief of human suffering.

The child seemed comforted by his presence. As he worked, he noticed that she was swaddled in multiple layers. This included a beautifully woven, but worn blanket with unusual colorful, hand stitched appliqués. They looked like a family insignia of some kind, he mused. He would take a closer look later.

Turning his attention back to the child, he hummed softly to reassure her. Removing her wet diaper, he examined her face, torso, and limbs. Miraculously she appeared to be physically unharmed, and only her face was cold. The careful swaddling may have helped, he thought. "But Mother Mary was watching over you little one," he said aloud as he shook his head. "How close you came to your death."

The baby girl with no name didn't cry when his hand covered her head and he muttered a prayer to the Virgin Mary. He asked for forgiveness for the baby's mother—whoever she was—and gave thanks for sparing the life of the infant.

Opening his eyes from prayer, he gazed with wonder at this girl child. She had a calmness about her that he couldn't explain. Having been through a harrowing experience, she now was being prodded and prayed over by a man who was a stranger to her. Despite all this and the discomfort she had to be experiencing, she seemed to watch him with a serenity he had never witnessed before in a child.

There's something special about this little one, he thought as he wrapped her back up before taking her to the cot in the corner of his office. There he secured her in the middle of the platform and banked her with blankets he rolled and placed beside her so she wouldn't fall onto the tile floor.

"Be still my child," he called softly to her, "I'll find you dry diapers and something to eat. I'll be back soon."

The baby fell asleep as the priest shuffled to his room to find clothing that he could tear and make into diapers. Then he hobbled to the kitchen farther down the narrow hallway from the office and his bedroom. As he entered the kitchen, the door creaked. Walking across the cold rude tiles, he opened the door to the outside and breathed in the fresh air. He raised the lid of the box the delivery boy had filled with two bottles of milk and brought them inside with gratefulness.

"Thank you Mother Mary for this food for the child."

After pouring milk into a cooking pot, he reached over and pulled some small pieces of wood from a pile beside him, stuffed the kindling into the cast-iron cooking stove, and ignited the wood. Then he went back outside to retrieve his staff while the milk heated, its aroma filling the kitchen.

Back inside and after checking on the sleeping girl, the priest cast about for something with which to feed her. Cursing himself for throwing away an old baby bottle he had found at the back of a kitchen cabinet a few months ago, he wondered what he could use.

Then he saw a pair of new rubber gloves one of the women who cleaned for him had left behind. Starting another pot heating, he poured water into it to sterilize the gloves. To enable the infant to suckle, he poked a pinhole at the end of one of the fingers after filling a glove with warm milk. Smiling with satisfaction at having solved an urgent problem, he bowed his head again, thanking Mother Mary for giving him the solution.

In just a couple of hours he had found everything the child needed, awakened and bathed her, wrapped her in a crude diaper, suckled her with warm milk, and burped her. As he laid her down again, she cooed before falling into a deep sleep. For several minutes he stood there watching her, as if standing guard. And he smiled.

6
August 1946—Another World

Kay stood with the child in her arms. The four-month-old girl rescued by Father Martino looked up at her new mother-to-be with an expression that only could be described as acceptance. In the nursery of the Orphanage of Our Blessed Mother in San Felipe de Jesús, children wailed all around Kay and her charge. But as Kay, just thirty, stood there with the baby, she found herself wondering how with such commotion, this little one could exhibit peacefulness. She thought too about how this child's life would be bound to hers forevermore.

Taking the baby's outstretched hand in hers, she said aloud, "Gabrielle." Kay didn't know where the name came from. Suddenly it entered her head and spilled from her mouth. Knowing that she didn't fancy the name Maria that the nuns had been calling her, Kay wanted the child to fit into *her* family, an Anglo family, and for her to not think of herself as different from others as she grew up.

She was an Andersen now, Kay thought, even convincing herself that the baby resembled her with her dark hair and full lips. But the little one also had slanted blue eyes and olive skin. In truth the child looked nothing like Kay. The baby was of mixed heritage and had a look all her own.

When the Sister returned to the nursery, Kay told her that she had decided upon a name. "I'll call her Gabrielle," she said with certitude.

"Ah," said the young Sister Angelina, "the Archangel Gabriel, divine messenger of God."

Kay thought about that for a moment. "Yes I will call her Gabrielle, but with the 'a' pronounced as in 'to gab' and with the emphasis on the last syllable," she said, correcting the young Sister. But not to be rude, she then acknowledged, "Maybe she *is* bringing a message to me. She's such a peaceful baby, so full of love."

As Kay gazed at Gabrielle, her hazel eyes warmed. The baby was a miracle to her. For almost four years now she had longed for another child. After the birth of her daughter Ruth, the doctor had told her she could have no more. But she wouldn't accept it. She kept trying with her husband Arthur for a second child, but the doctor was proven right.

Finally accepting her fate, Kay applied through various agencies to adopt. Most required large sums of money, which they couldn't afford. But then she discovered the Catholic orphanage in this New Mexico border town that had more children than they could manage well. They only required a donation as generous as the family could make and the assurance of good care for the adopted child.

The moment she saw the wide-eyed, dark-haired baby girl, she knew this was the child God intended her to have. Reluctantly she gave the baby to the bespectacled Sister Angelina so she could sign the papers that the Reverend Mother Juanita put before her. The Reverend Mother then handed her the legal papers she would need to show that she indeed was the rightful mother. Kay's arms trembled as she took the child back, now hers and her husband Arthur's from this moment on.

"Would you like this?" the plump middle-aged Mother Juanita asked Kay as she removed a woven object from a desk drawer.

"What is it?"

"It's the only possession the child has." She passed the handwoven and appliquéd blanket to Kay.

"I don't understand."

"The baby was wrapped in this when Father Martino saved her from a wild dog," she said, going on to tell Kay the story of how Gabrielle was found. "You can see from the weaving and the appliqué that the blanket is Mexican in origin, Mayan actually. Do you want this for the child?"

Kay was startled by the danger her baby had suffered. "Oh my poor child!" she gasped. She stared for a moment at the blanket and then at her newly adopted daughter. *What good would it do to confuse the child?* she thought. *Better that she believe she was born to us. I remember the adopted children when I was growing up and how everyone thought less of them for how they were born. I'll not put my daughter through that.*

Saying nothing of this she answered the Reverend Mother simply. "Thank you, but she'll not need it now." Rising, she thanked the stalwart Reverend Mother and exited the room.

Talking to her child as she carried her down the long corridor to the entrance, she deposited into the rude wooden collection box as large an offering as her family's modest means could provide. Then she walked down the stairs and stepped into the waiting taxi. As the dust swirled around the car on its way to the airport, the infant fell asleep in Kay's arms, the baby's breath slow and sweet amid the stale air of the taxi.

Later that day Kay and Gabrielle boarded an airplane for Long Island. As the plane took off, Kay thought how her child was speeding toward her family and a new life hundreds of miles away. She thought too about how baby Gabrielle would never have to know of her abandonment, the wild dog, and the truth of her ancestry. No, she reflected, she would protect her from this. She was an Andersen now, an Andersen from Long Island.

Alone, the Reverend Mother sighed, smoothed the unusual blanket and stared at it for a moment as if trying to decide something. She had been concerned about Father Martino and how he was taking the news of Maria's adoption, given how attached to her he had become. Looking at the blanket again, she tucked it into her robe before exiting the office.

Meanwhile, deep inside the mission, Father Martino knelt in prayer. His shoulders drooped as he covered his face with his deeply veined hands. Although he struggled to sequester his emotions, he was distraught that he never again would be with the radiant child he visited frequently these past months, held, played with, prayed for, and grown to love. The priest felt smaller and older as he sank under the weight of his loss.

"Forgive me Mother Mary," he muttered, "as this should be a happy day for my little Maria. She has a family now and a kind woman to love her. Please watch over Maria and bless her precious life."

A knock roused him. Using his walking staff to help him to his feet, he wiped his eyes as he hobbled to the door and opened it.

There stood the Reverend Mother Juanita flushed and perspiring. A taxi waited for her on the dirt road. Wiping her brow she pulled out something from inside her robe. It was Gabrielle's baby blanket.

"I thought you might like to have this back Father."

The priest stared at the object, then took it between his hands.

"The new mother didn't want it. The child will be fine, Father. We've said prayers for her." The Reverend Mother's broad and aging face was kind as she looked at her longtime friend. He nodded as he gazed somewhere beyond her.

"Are you all right Father? I know how much you love little Maria."

The Father hesitated, then composed himself. "I'll miss her, I admit. But I'll be fine, knowing that the child will have a home and parents who will love her. You're most kind to come here and bring the blanket. Thank you Reverend Mother. But I'm forgetting my manners. Would you like to come in? Let me get you something cool to drink."

"The taxi's waiting," she said, gesturing toward the car, its motor humming. "Another time perhaps? Take care Father." She reached toward him, patted his arm, then turned her ample body, leaving Father Martino with the keepsake and his thoughts.

I'll save this, he mused as he watched the taxi drive off with the good woman. *Maybe someday Maria will want it. I'll keep it for her along with the scarf I found on the grounds the morning Maria came*

Moon Song

to me. Maybe there's a connection and it'll help my little one. I'll hold onto them, just in case.

~II~
NEW DAY DAWNING

1946 - 1963 – Merrick, Long Island

1
1946 - 1949

Arthur stared at the baby Gabrielle. He wasn't happy with Kay's persistence about adopting a child. Ruth had been born to them four years ago. On numerous occasions he had argued that he saw no need for a second child, which he believed they couldn't afford. "We have too many mouths to feed now," he would say. But Kay just got that stubborn look on her face, and he knew he was fighting a losing battle.

As he stood over the crib, he gazed at his new daughter as she slept. "She's so different from Ruth, darker hair and skin...and her features. When will we tell her she's adopted?"

Kay turned toward him with an angry demeanor. "She's *not* so different. In fact she resembles me, her hair and lips especially."

Arthur shook his head. "Anyone can see she's not born to us."

"You're wrong," she shot back. "And no one must know. I'll not have her shamed by other children. I saw too much of that when I was growing up. You must promise me you'll tell no one—not her, not anyone. Promise me!"

Finally he acquiesced with a reluctant nod of his head. At just that moment Gabrielle opened her eyes and seemed to smile as she gazed into the blue-gray of Arthur's. Something in him stirred. "Jesus," he muttered. He didn't like to show his soft underbelly, not when he was sober anyway.

Arthur was not a tall man, five-foot-eight perhaps, but he was well built and nine years his wife's senior. Although just thirty-nine, his dark hair had thinned and his hairline already was receding. He had a pleasant, if not exactly handsome face however, and a ruddy complexion.

"Daddy," a small voice came from behind him. Feeling a tug on his pant leg, he turned to find Ruth peering up at him. He smiled at his blonde-haired, blue-eyed child who had a certain determined look on her pretty face. "Kin I see too?"

"Of course baby," he said as he lifted the four-year-old and held her in his arms.

Ruth gazed at the bundle of blankets with the small face looking in her direction. "Is this baby?" she asked.

"Yes dear," he said, covering his dislike for Gabrielle's swarthy appearance. Not wanting an altercation with Kay, he responded, "This is your new sister. Her name is Gabrielle."

"Gabel," she said, then repeating "Gabel" with certitude.

Arthur grinned at Ruth.

Pulling back the blankets, she found Gabrielle's hands and legs moving as only babies could, with a certain uncoordinated glee. Ruth giggled and reached for the infant's hand. Gabrielle grasped it enthusiastically.

"This is baby sister," Ruth said, "Gabel...." She shook Gabrielle's hand about and laughed as Gabrielle cooed.

At that moment, Arthur realized that his battle over this child's place in their family had been lost. Kay and Ruth's acceptance of her prevailed. He saw that he would have to acknowledge her as his child, although he swore she never would be the daughter to him that Ruth was.

* * *

One day, when Gabrielle was just three years old, Kay walked with her into a nearby neighborhood. Coming from the opposite direction was a teenager with his mangy, mid-sized mutt. Gabrielle stopped, her eyes opened wide and terror-filled. Then she started to scream as she clung to her mother's skirt.

"Gabrielle!" she shouted. "What's wrong? It's just a boy and his dog!"

But she kept shrieking. Her mother picked her up and turned toward home, her daughter clinging to her as she cried uncontrollably. Kay was beside herself as she tried to understand what had happened and worked to calm her child. Then it hit her. It had to be that distant memory Gabrielle harbored, Kay thought, the one of the wild dog that threatened and nearly killed her on the steps of the old mission in San Miguel. "My God," Kay muttered. "There there Gabrielle," she said, kissing her little one's face and stroking her hair to calm her. "There there. It will be all right. Mommy's got you."

2
1951

As a kindergartener at the Tabor Avenue Public Elementary School, Gabrielle charged down the hall from her classroom to the girls' bathroom. Her skinny limbs churning at top speed, her dark, short-cropped hair punctuating her movements, she was just thirty feet from her destination when a shout brought her to a halt.

"STOP! RIGHT THIS MINUTE!" a woman's voice blasted from down the hallway. "STOP I SAY!"

Her heart pounding, Gabrielle turned to face a wall of angry sound.

"Get over here THIS MINUTE!"

She hesitated, frightened. *What'd I do? Why's she mad at me?*

"THIS MINUTE I SAID!" The woman stamped her foot as she motioned to the child.

Gabrielle hurried to her as fast as her increasingly limp legs would carry her. She knew she must have done something terrible, but had no idea what.

"Just what do you think you're doing?" demanded Miss Leaper.

The tall, thin woman peered down at her with such a look of utter loathing that Gabrielle was struck dumb. Miss Leaper undoubtedly saw what she had decided was a disobedient child, but she also clearly noted that the girl looked different from the mass of Anglo children that composed the school's homogenous student body. She seemed to not know exactly what was different about her, but it was evident that she didn't like it. She glared at the trembling youngster with a look of utter disdain.

Gabrielle wanted to answer the angry teacher's question, but she couldn't get her lips to form the words. Looking down at her feet, she hoped that this woman, who seemed to grow more ominous by the second, would go away.

"Well if you won't talk to me, then maybe you can explain yourself to my class," the scowling woman said, dragging her by the ear into the classroom.

Three dozen first graders watched as Miss Leaper summoned the kindergartener to the front of the room.

"Get me the stool," the woman barked to a student as she continued to pinch Gabrielle's ear until the child thought she might faint.

"Sit!" the teacher ordered.

Released from the woman's grip, Gabrielle climbed onto the stool, her small body trembling as she struggled to hide how scared and embarrassed she was. Miss Leaper wiped her pinching hand on her skirt, as if trying to rub off something nasty.

"Now you can tell my class what you were doing running down the hall."

Gabrielle hesitated.

"NOW I said!"

Gabrielle pulled back as the severe woman with the dark glasses and tightly-pulled-back nondescript hair moved her face toward her. The teacher was so close that Gabrielle could smell the soap the woman bathed with this morning and feel a force that made her shudder.

"Goin' ta the Girls Room."

"The Girls Room?"

"Yes ma'am."

"Speak up girl, you're making me mad." Miss Leaper's eyes darkened with something that looked to Gabrielle like hate.

"Yes ma'am."

"Yes ma'am what?"

"Yes ma'am, I was goin' to the Girls Room."

"Well that doesn't explain why you were running," the teacher said, her burly brows rising and falling as she burrowed into the child's space.

"I...had ta go," Gabrielle replied defensively.

"Had to go what, where?"

"The bathroom..." Her voice trailed off.

"That still doesn't explain your running, girl." Miss Leaper leaned in farther.

"I waited too long...I had ta...GO," Gabrielle blurted out in frustration and embarrassment, her face turning bright red.

Giggling went up around the room, which Gabrielle suddenly became more aware of behind the looming presence of Miss Leaper. Some of the first graders looked to be enjoying her misery, while others just stared open-mouthed at the spectacle.

"You think that's any excuse for running in the hall?" The teacher pulled back sharply and started pacing back and forth in front of the class.

"Couldn't help it," Gabrielle replied half-pleading, half-defiant. Then she closed her eyes as the pain in her bladder intensified.

"COULDN'T HELP IT?" Miss Leaper shouted, spinning toward her as she spoke and seeming to relish the pained look on the kindergartener's face. Then the teacher's dark presence dropped down on her again, dropped like that big limb from the mulberry tree behind Gabrielle's house one night during a thunderstorm.

"Couldn't...couldn't..." Gabrielle's voice trailed off.

"No excuses girl. No running in the hall PERIOD!"

All Gabrielle could think of was *What if I can't hold it? All the kids will see! Why's she doin' this to me?*

"Did you hear me, girl?"

"Yes ma'am," Gabrielle said.

"Do you understand?" her tormentor asked testily.

"Yes ma'am."

"Yes ma'am what?" Miss Leaper said, her brows furrowing as she spoke.

"Yes ma'am I understand," she replied, clenching her laced fingers more tightly. Gabrielle, however, didn't get what it was that she had done wrong.

"You don't sound very sure to me girl," the woman said, at once sensing her thoughts and growing tired of this game. "I think you'd better sit here awhile until you understand a little better."

"But ma'am..."

"Don't 'but ma'am' me girl. Now I have a class to teach."

For another fifteen minutes that seemed to Gabrielle like hours, she sat on the high stool in front of Miss Leaper's class as the teacher wrote numbers on the blackboard and grilled her students about addition and subtraction.

The students, however, seemed more interested in watching the kindergartener and whispering to each other when Miss Leaper turned her back. Gabrielle tried not to notice when several smirked at her with her sagging olive-skinned face, her sweaty brow, her tightly folded hands, her skinny legs, her plain hand-me-down dress, and her sturdy brown oxford shoes.

Soon this sea of strange and inhospitable faces taunting Gabrielle became a blur. The pain inside her had intensified to the point that her whole body hurt. All Gabrielle could think about was how she was going to keep from peeing on the stool and that she just wanted her mommy.

She closed her eyes and sang inside her head the song she whispered at night to cover the sounds of her parents fighting.

"Hush little baby don't say a word, momma's gonna buy you a mockingbird..."

"GIRL!" Miss Leaper's voice shattered her concentration.

Gabrielle flinched, leaking a warm wetness into her underpants.

"GIRL, I SAID!" the woman yelled. She appeared now to Gabrielle as a spider taking renewed interest in her prey.

"Yes ma'am?" Gabrielle mustered. Frightened, she looked down quickly hoping that her secret hadn't revealed itself.

"What have you learned girl?"

"Uh...not ta run in the hall ma'am?"

"Under NO circumstances, right?"

"Uh, yes ma'am."

"Yes ma'am what?" The spider played with her catch.

"Yes ma'am...I'm not ta run for nothin'."

"For *anything*, you ignorant child! Get back to your class girl, and don't EVER let me catch you running again!" The harsh voice of Miss Leaper cracked before she turned away with a seeming loss of interest now.

"No ma'am," Gabrielle answered, sliding off the stool that had a small wet spot on it, which she deftly wiped with the underside of her dress as she jumped to the floor. Then she walked as fast as she could out of the classroom and down the hall to the Girls Room.

Bolting for the nearest stall, she latched the door before sitting on the toilet and letting the hot liquid pour out of her. She didn't know whether she was more angry or hurt. Then her small body started to shake.

Sitting there, her fists and teeth clenched, Gabrielle made a vow: No one was ever going to make her feel squashed like that again. As she shuddered, her body gave in to the full weight of her emotions. Her legs buckled as she got off the toilet. Her tongue felt thick and her jaw trembled. Overwhelmed and torn between rage and humiliation and unable to decide which feeling to own, five-year-old Gabrielle cried.

3
1955

Nine-year-old Gabrielle gazed at the massive rose window high above the sanctuary. The stained glass mostly was deep blue, her favorite color. As the morning sunlight filtered through the glass, she witnessed the revealing of images of Jesus, the Holy Ghost, the Virgin Mary, the Cross, and Christ's disciples.

Lost in the beauty of the window, she suddenly winced. She heard her father striking a sour note on the organ in the first refrain of "Onward, Christian Soldiers." The discordant note rose awkwardly into the sanctuary's vaulted ceiling like fingernails on a blackboard. Although Arthur was half-hidden behind the organ, she thought she saw him start at his own mistake. This was only the Sunday school he played for, but for a man who once wanted to be a concert pianist, this was not a happy episode. Before the hymn was done, three more misplaced notes tore through the children's high-pitched voices.

At the hymn's conclusion, the Reverend's voice rose amid the organ's trailing sound. Gabrielle watched her father's shoulders sag as he temporarily shut the organ down and removed his hands from the keyboard. Knowing that the mistakes would happen again, she also recognized that he seemed not to be able to help himself. *What was it made him drink this time?* she fretted, shaking her head.

The Methodist minister was talking about redemption. "The Bible says that if you come unto Jesus as a little child, you will be saved. Let us rejoice and be glad, for ours is the Kingdom of Heaven!"

Gabrielle knew that Arthur had turned to God many times and believed in Jesus. But this didn't change the direction of his life. *Maybe he doesn't believe enough,* she thought. As the preacher directed the children to their Sunday school classes, her father played "Nearer My God to Thee." The organ music faded behind the shut door of Gabrielle's classroom. Ten fourth graders sat in the middle of the choir robing room. They were surrounded by the dark-blue vestments and morning sunlight that streamed through the windows and bathed them before coming to rest on the wooden floor.

As the children sat in a circle, perched on metal folding chairs like small birds in their feathered best, Mrs. Garry welcomed them. "Children, it's good to see you this bright winter morning!"

Gabrielle smiled back at her as did the other children, except for Robert. He squirmed in his chair and pulled at the stiff collar and black tie his mother always made him wear. Robert clearly didn't think it was good to see any of them on this winter morning.

"Well who wants to share what they found that shows how much God loves us?" the teacher asked.

A silence filled the room vibrating with light. Seeing that the woman looked a little lost in the void of no response, Gabrielle cleared her throat. Although she brought something to share, she hated speaking up in a group. As Mrs. Garry's discomfort weighed on her, however, she dug deep and cleared her throat again. "I do Mrs. Garry," she croaked.

"Oh good Gabrielle," she sighed her words. "What do you have for us?"

Gabrielle opened her pocket New Testament, a gift to the children from the church. They were supposed to bring it each Sunday to get accustomed to using it. Sometimes she forgot to bring it, but not this morning.

Somewhere in the book of Luke, Gabrielle found what she was searching for. It was a dried hollyhock bloom that she had picked and pressed carefully between the Testament's pages in late summer. It was a pink-violet flower, a color Gabrielle liked especially well.

Removing the flower from the book, she held up the pressed bloom for the other children to see. The light from the window passed through it, now translucent and glowing with color like the stained-glass window in the sanctuary.

"That's beautiful Gabrielle," Mrs. Garry said. "Was there something you wanted to tell us about it?"

Gabrielle wanted to describe the happiness she experienced when she looked at the flowers in her mother's garden, or climbed the old mulberry tree behind the house, or watched the sun go down as it burned itself into a pink-orange sky.

She could say how whole she felt when sitting with her toes dug into the sand, watching the ocean crash to foam at the boundary between land and water. Or tell about the incident that occurred earlier in the winter when the cross of bright light tore through the night sky and warmed her heart on that lonely evening in her and Ruthie's bedroom.

The incident occurred after the usual cycle of their father's drinking and her parents' shouting subsided. Their quarrels always were about alcohol and money. Sometimes, however, she would hear her name amid the litany of Arthur's gripes. One of these nights, Gabrielle rose from her bed in the darkness. She tiptoed across the cold wooden floor and past her sleeping sister to peer out the window into the backyard.

Drawing back the white Swiss-dotted curtains, she stared into lighted darkness. The mulberry tree reached black and leafless into the night sky. Through its branches the moon radiated light so bright that she could clearly see the white picket fence defining the next-door neighbor's back property and the forms of the bushes, dried plants, and the swing set in the neighbor's yard.

Gazing at the face of the full moon glowing in the winter sky, she thought how peaceful and beautiful it appeared, how perfect and whole. Staring at the luminous surface of this lonely sphere of matter floating in the cold blackness of space, she thought that the moon seemed to focus on her and the white-blanketed earth outside her window.

As she observed this celestial body, its light appeared more intense, tearing at the hurt inside her. Like the feeling the setting sun gave her or the peace she experienced when visiting the beach and watching the ocean surge against the land, she felt the moonlight pour through her veins and explode inside her heart. She had the sense that her body was taken over by a light so warm and powerful that she thought she might transform into something new. It was a sense of kindly invasion, of acceptance, of love even.

Tears welled in her eyes and traveled her cheeks, causing the orb's shape to erupt in her vision into a kind of cross of white light. It tore through the black sky and joined the hot light coursing through her body.

    Stepping back from the window, she fell to the floor. Gazing about the room she watched moonlight filter through the curtains. Shaking her head she glanced again around the chilly bedroom filled with her sister's heavy breathing. She stood and stepped cautiously back to the window and pulled the curtain aside.

    Staring into the winter sky she saw the moon as it had been before, whole, white, peaceful. The swing set, the picket fence, the mulberry tree, the shrubs and other plants stood as she saw them earlier, stark under the moonlight. All was the same as it had been and as it should be.

    But Gabrielle herself felt different. At nine years of age, Gabrielle knew in that moment that there was something beyond her that was so large and loving that she had no words or thoughts that could contain it. She didn't know if this feeling was the result of her yearning and loneliness, her wanting something that was powerful enough to take away all the chaos and hurt in her young life, or if this was something more deep and mysterious. She didn't know exactly what she had experienced except for a kind of huge awareness of a connection to something vast and seamless.

    As Gabrielle climbed back into bed and pulled the covers about her, she closed her eyes. She acknowledged a warm glow that still embraced her. Before leaving her last threads of consciousness as she glided toward sleep, she remembered thinking that at this moment she didn't feel so alone and afraid. Falling asleep she drifted toward a place that was neither earth nor heaven, moon nor stars. That night she didn't have one of her frequent nightmares. Rather she seemed to float through a kind of protective space until she was ready to return to the warm breath of her body and the start of another day.

Gabrielle flinched as Mrs. Garry repeated the question, "Was there something you wanted to tell us, Gabrielle?"

But the words caught in Gabrielle's throat. All that escaped was the small sound of "no."

4
1956

"Whataya doin' Gabby?" Gabrielle's neighborhood friend Betsy Boatman asked.

"Nothin' much," ten-year-old Gabrielle replied as she stretched the phone cord as long as she could before returning to the phone cradle in the kitchen.

"Ya wanna come over? My dad's takin' mom and us kids down ta the docks to go snapper fishin' and he said you could come too," Betsy said.

"Sure, that'd be great! I gotta ask my mom. Just a sec."

After forty-five minutes, during which time Gabrielle finished her chores, she grabbed sunglasses and a hat and ran across the street to where Mr. Boatman had his car loaded. Already in the back seat of the family station wagon was Betsy's nine-year-old brother Ralph. He was banging his foot impatiently against the back of the driver's seat. Looking sourly at Gabrielle and Betsy, he yelled, "We ever gonna get outa here, poop heads?"

"Shut up Ralph! *You're* a poop head!" Betsy fired back before tossing her bag into the car trunk. "What a pest," Betsy grumbled to Gabrielle.

With everyone in the car, Mr. Boatman backed out of the driveway and headed south of town to the docks. As he drove, Gabrielle looked at the back of his prematurely balding head and listened to him chatter about how it appeared to be a good day for fishing—a little overcast and not too busy. The greyness of the day indeed was keeping traffic down, which he said should make the fish a little less wary.

Soon he had the bamboo fishing poles out and was baiting the lines with live squid. He handed the strung bamboo poles first to his slender, blonde-haired wife Mable, then to Betsy and her. Ralph strung his own, waving the bait in Gabrielle and Betsy's faces every chance he got.

As their lines dangled in the water for a couple of hours, she and ten-year-old Betsy talked and watched the boats pull in and out of the docks. Gabrielle noted that most were fishing boats, but some were cabin cruisers and other pleasure boats. Enjoying watching these vessels and the people in them, she couldn't help but wonder what it would be like to ride around in a pleasure craft.

Only twice had she been on a boat, old rowboats hauled in a chain of them along the southern coast of Long Island by a small tugboat. The tug left the rowboats all day far out in the bay and then rounded them up before dark. Her dad had taken her, along with his fishing buddy, in the hope of a good haul of flounder and fluke. It was the only thing she could remember ever doing with her dad when her mom and Ruth weren't along.

The only two snappers she and the Boatmans caught all day lay in a bucket on the dock. Gabrielle thought how forlorn they looked and felt sorry for them. The kids caught a catfish and what Ralph called a dogfish, but they threw them back. Gabrielle thought that the "dogfish" was about the ugliest thing she had ever seen. Before tossing it into the water, Ralph grabbed it and chased her and Betsy with it, until Mr. Boatman intervened and made Ralph get in the car until he could behave.

When they were done fishing, Betsy's father drove them to the frozen custard stand about a mile away. There the Boatmans treated the three kids to chocolate and vanilla custard. Sitting in the car in the parking lot as they ate their cones, the girls fought silently with Ralph in the back seat.

As the three children settled down some, Gabrielle noticed a very large woman walking beside their car on her way to the ice cream stand. Gazing past Betsy and Ralph at the woman, she noticed Ralph stop licking his ice cream as his eyes widened. Then he lifted his left pointer finger in the woman's direction. "Geesh! Looka that big fat nigga lady, willya?" Ralph screeched, snickering as he spoke, not caring that the woman could hear him through the open window.

"Gadzooks," Betsy joined in, "willya lookit that wiggly nigga!"

Gabrielle then watched as Betsy's whole family laughed until they about dropped their cones. Even Mr. Boatman was bent over the wheel and half snorting.

Gabrielle blushed with embarrassment and shock as she saw the woman turn her head toward them while she tried to keep a poker face. But Gabrielle could tell from the pain in the woman's eyes that she had heard their ridicule. Upset, Gabrielle scrutinized the Boatmans. She wondered how Betsy's parents could encourage this. What did they find so funny? She sort of got the fat part, although she didn't see that as cause for making fun. But she didn't know what "nigga" meant.

As the laughing went on, Gabrielle's stomach started to churn. She felt sick. There was something about this woman that the Boatmans disliked. They didn't know this woman, but still they didn't like her. *Was it somethin' about being fat?* she wondered. *Was it that the lady looked different? She's heavier and darker than us, but I'm darker than Betsy or any of her family. I don't understand. Do they make fun of me behind my back?*

Gabrielle's stomach heaved as she reached to crank down the window. Lowering it a little, she stuck her nose up close to the opened glass to breathe fresh air. As the Boatmans guffawed, she felt increasingly raw inside and struggled to keep from losing her stomach. She had never heard anyone being called "nigga" before and couldn't understand why the Boatmans used that word.

But Gabrielle knew that something had been stolen from that woman—and that something important had been taken from her too. She felt it in her gut. As her neglected ice cream melted, collapsing into its cone and sullying her fingers, she realized that she too might be the target of ridicule and exclusion just because she looked different from the people around her.

5
1959

"Be careful with those!" Mrs. Bealey called from the kitchen.

Gabrielle quickly separated the porcelain cups that had just tinged as she tried to return them to the hutch. "Sorry," she answered.

"No problem Gabriella." Mrs. Bealey liked to call her young friend "Gabriella" for some reason. To Gabrielle it was an expression of endearment.

Maureen Bealey was the stepmother of Ruth's best friend Dorothy, who lived next door. A year ago, when Gabrielle turned twelve, Mrs. Bealey hired her as a mother's helper.

Always trying to earn money, Gabrielle made a bit of a pest of herself with the neighbors by always trying to sell them something to generate a little cash. But once she started babysitting, she stopped making rounds of her white middle-class neighborhood where every Cape Cod-style house had two bedrooms and one bath and looked like every other house, save for paint colors and landscaping.

Nearly every weekend she had a job watching three young children who lived in an adjoining development that had replaced the cornfield behind her family's southern Long Island house. Since she was only eleven at the time, she mostly had just watched the kids when their mothers were home and needed a break.

Thirteen now, Gabrielle was pleased with Mrs. Bealey's job offer. She thought with delight about having more money to save and for things she couldn't buy with just her fifty cents a week allowance—extra chocolate and ice cream and non-hand-me-down clothes, especially important to a new junior high school student. But she also took a shine to Mrs. Bealey and enjoyed being around her beautiful things.

It wasn't long after she started her mother's helper job, though, that the Bealeys moved across Merrick to an upper-middle-class part of town. To keep the arrangement going, however, Mrs. Bealey picked Gabrielle up after school on Thursdays, when Dorothy had after-school activities.

Gabrielle's face radiated pride that first day, when she saw Mrs. Bealey in her shiny new Buick waiting for her outside the front entrance to the Baxter Avenue Public Junior High. She noticed with pleasure that students who also waited to be picked up looked surprised that such a fine car came for the olive-skinned girl from what they apparently assumed was a lower-class family.

"Hi Mrs. Bealey," she beamed as she opened the passenger door and climbed into the seat beside her.

"Good afternoon Gabriella," the woman responded, smiling warmly at her now-thirteen-year-old friend with her dark ponytail, her big pile of books, and her violin case. "Why don't you put your things in back."

"Oh right," Gabrielle said, reaching behind her to unload her stuff. She smiled as she took a last look at the gawking teenagers by the school entrance, a couple of whom had called her names when they passed her in the halls.

Seeing them brought back an incident a week ago, when one of them yelled "spic!" She didn't know what that was, but she knew the word was said in malice. Her feelings hurt, she told her mother about the incident and asked the meaning of the word.

Kay had looked hard at her daughter and saw how hurt she was. "Has anyone called you this before?" she asked.

"No."

Releasing a long sigh, Kay said, "It's a name unkind people have called Italians and also Spanish-American people."

"Why would anyone call me that? I'm not either of those."

"You mustn't pay any attention to them. Only stupid people say such nonsense. It has nothing to do with you and who you are. Just ignore them."

But the hurt lingered. Seeing the kids' surprise at her leaving school in an expensive, spanking new car, however, gave her a thrill. As Gabrielle turned back toward Mrs. Bealey, she gave her mentor a big grin.

As Mrs. Bealey smoothed her just-beginning-to-gray brown hair back with one hand and adjusted her tortoise shell eyeglasses with the other, she restarted the car while inquiring about her young friend's day. Always Gabrielle would chatter about school and avoid talking about her family. But just being asked about her day gave her the attention she craved and made her feel important.

When she couldn't connect with Mrs. Bealey during the week, she would try to talk to her mom. Often though, Kay was too overwhelmed with her own life to listen. So Gabrielle played her violin to assuage her hurt, her confusion and fears about how mocked she felt at school and about the turbulent evenings in the Andersen household.

Then there were her recurrent nightmares, especially the one where she was trapped in what she first thought was a cave. Soon she saw it as a huge mouth, swollen and swallowing all sound so no one could hear her cries. Then she would remember the light she saw four years ago when the moon exploded in her mind's eye. It was as if something was watching over her and would help her if she just didn't forget what she saw and stayed true to what she believed.

Gabrielle still was talking when they pulled into the Bealeys' driveway. "Well now Gabriella," Mrs. Bealey said, turning toward her, "what do you say we go in and have a snack before we get to work?"

The teenager smiled in acknowledgment of their Thursday ritual, one in which she drank tea from gold-rimmed porcelain teacups and savored something nice to eat before starting to clean. This time it was pound cake with vanilla ice cream and strawberries arranged on china plates. Gabrielle delivered them to placemats on the mahogany dining room table set with cloth napkins and sterling silver forks and teaspoons.

"Remember Gabriella, the fork goes to the left of the plate, the spoon to the right, and the napkin gets folded like this," she said, rearranging her place setting as Gabrielle copied her on the other side of the table. "You picked the correct fork though," she added encouragingly.

Soon I'll get it just right, Gabrielle thought as she watched Mrs. Bealey set her slightly plump body gracefully onto one of the damask-covered dining room chairs.

Studying how her mentor shook open her cloth napkin in one movement before laying it neatly across her lap, she sought to do the same. It remained folded, however, and she had to flick it repeatedly to get it to unfurl and lie across her legs. She thought she saw Mrs. Bealey muffle a kindly smile as she watched Gabrielle struggle with the napkin and turn red with embarrassment as she frantically tossed the white linen about in the air.

At last the deed was done, and it wasn't long before they finished every last crumb, berry, and spoonful of ice cream on their plates. Her former neighbor took her napkin from her lap one last time, daintily dabbed the corners of her mouth, and placed the napkin beside her plate. Gabrielle obediently followed suit, then cleared the table and washed the dishes.

As she picked up her cleaning supplies, she looked at the downstairs baseboards she would wipe today in addition to the usual dusting and polishing of all the wood furniture. Having a lot to do in two hours, she got right to work. She knew this would give Mrs. Bealey time to make her teaching preparations for her next day's art lessons at a nearby elementary school.

As Gabrielle cleaned, she remembered the first time she saw the Bealeys' new home and how she hardly could contain her excitement. It seemed to her the opposite of her family's house, which held so little beauty and lacked any semblance of order. She thought how their house reflected her family's spare budget and the disarray of their lives.

The Bealeys' house made her think of her Great Aunt Etienne's Brooklyn brownstone where they visited regularly. It was here that she first was exposed to a finer way to live and the privileges of money. She thought about her great aunt's furnishings, antiques passed down generation to generation, the artwork that hung on every wall, and the objects she brought back from her regular travels throughout Europe, Asia, Africa, and across the U.S. The mementos in particular entranced Gabrielle and her sister, especially the birdcages from Thailand, kimonos from Japan, and inlaid boxes from Egypt.

"Yes my dears," Etienne had assured the girls as she smiled warmly at them, "someday family pieces will come to your mother and her sisters, and you all will have your pick of my jewelry and keepsakes from abroad."

After Etienne died, however, Gabrielle couldn't remember why she and Ruth never pressed her for her travel stories. All they had now were a few keepsakes, their imaginations, and hundreds of photographs documenting such adventures as their Great Aunt riding a camel, hiking in the Swiss Alps, and traveling onboard a steamer crossing the Atlantic.

"Why did we never think to ask Auntie Eti details about her travels?" Gabrielle queried Ruth one day.

Ruth shrugged. "I don't know. Maybe it was because the grownups were talking with each other all the time. Or we were too caught up playing with her stuff and pretending we were Japanese princesses. Or we were too young to think to ask. I don't know. It's too bad, isn't it?" Gabrielle nodded.

Turning her attention to the task at hand, Gabrielle set to work polishing and dusting. She worked gingerly around porcelain figurines, the gold clock on the fireplace mantel, and a stone sculpture of a turtle.

"Mrs. Bealey?

"Yes dear." The woman stopped as she was walking through the living room.

"I was wondering about this turtle. This wouldn't be something you made, would it?"

"It was my first attempt at sculpture," she answered, moving closer while adjusting her glasses. "Goodness that was a long time ago. I was taking college art classes. Working in three dimensions was new to me. But this was the piece that convinced me that art would be my path forward."

"How did you know?"

"I'm not sure exactly. It just felt so right to chisel away at this block of white marble. I didn't set out to make a turtle. But at some point the stone told me what it was meant to be. And I had to obey."

"Wow. Was it very hard to carve?"

"It was. But with every stroke, I got more confident. And when I finally finished it, I swore I would keep it with me always as a reminder of what bent me toward art and ultimately to teach it."

"Golly, I hope something like that happens to me. I think and think about what I might be when I grow up, but I keep changing my mind. When I was little I wanted to be a cowboy." She laughed, as did her older friend. "Then I wanted to be an astronomer. But I don't know. It's all very confusing." She shook her head.

"Gabriella, you're barely thirteen! Most of the students I went to school with didn't even declare a major until their junior or senior year in college. So don't worry about it. When the time's right, you'll know what you're meant to do. You'll see."

Gabrielle turned these words over in her mind as she stared at the turtle, then went on with her cleaning. In this house she found work to do, order, and a love of beauty. Of greater consequence to her, however, was the warmth and generosity of spirit that was reflective of Mrs. Bealey and her view of life.

From her mentor came love, the friendship and guidance of a caring adult, and the promise of something finer than what Gabrielle presently knew. And Mrs. Bealey professed to love teaching Gabrielle about good manners and the finer points of life, as Mrs. Bealey's mother had taught her. Soaking up everything she said, Gabrielle always was anxious to learn more. She was all hugs and smiles when she was around this woman who responded in kind. Mrs. Bealey even confessed once that she looked forward to Thursdays as much as Gabrielle did.

"Gabriella, Gabriella," she would call her, herding her out through the front door and back into the car to take her home. And all the way back, Gabrielle chattered about school and classmates and what she was going to do this weekend. And Mrs. Bealey just listened and smiled.

* * *

Her father came home just as he had every night for as far back as Gabrielle could remember. It seemed to thirteen-year-old Gabrielle that he dragged with him a kind of lingering dissatisfaction with life and the smell of the failed cure-all of alcohol. She knew from Kay's remarks to Arthur that home was not his first destination after work. It was the Club Fifty bar a few blocks from their house. There she imagined he found the promise of whisky and commiseration about his thwarted desires in life and his hatred of his accounting job at a Brooklyn firm.

She couldn't help remembering an incident she witnessed one day when Mrs. Bealey drove her home. They got talking and drove a block too far before turning and passing by the bar her father frequented. About to avert her eyes, Gabrielle stopped and noticed, to her horror, a familiar man stumbling out of the pub and weaving in her direction. It was her father. Gabrielle stared in shock, fighting back tears. *Oh Lord, please don't let Mrs. Bealey see my dad!*

As Gabrielle recalled this, she watched her father plop down in his easy chair as he did most nights, drop his briefcase on the floor, remove his suit jacket and tie, and toss them onto the sofa beside him. His face, it seemed to her, wore an expression of weariness and dejection. Almost immediately he started snoring.

All this left Gabrielle conflicted. She was angry with her father for drinking again. But she also felt sorry that he never became the concert pianist or scientist he dreamed of being.

"How many times," Gabrielle said to Ruth, "did he tell us how the Depression kept him from going to college?"

"Yeah," Ruth said, "and he had to drop out of high school to go to work as an office boy to help support his family."

Gabrielle thought about that for a minute. "That's where he said he got stuck doing office work and never saw the chance to leave for something better," she said as Ruth nodded.

Marrying a college-educated wife seemed to Gabrielle to only remind him of what he had missed. His drinking and his fear of never having enough money—a common dread of many who lived through the Great Depression, Gabrielle came to understand—she thought were the main sources of her parents' conflicts. Their arguments often started at the dinner table and went on long into the night, as she and her sister struggled to study and sleep.

Through all this she felt grateful for what sisterly bond she and Ruth shared. Being four years apart, however, didn't make for as close a relationship as it might have been, especially as Ruth entered her latter teenage years.

"Ruth, can I come too?" was Gabrielle's recurrent request when her sister went out with her older friends.

"You're too young," she would chastise her. "Stop bugging me Gabel."

As thirteen-year-old Gabrielle began to ponder what it would be like to start high school as a freshman this next year, Ruth—unbeknownst to their father—already was talking to their mother and to her high school guidance counselor about college. Gabrielle saw Ruth's actions as a kind of triumph that gave Gabrielle hope for her own future.

On more than one occasion the girls heard Arthur object to the idea of their obtaining a higher education. Kay, however, insisted that they have the opportunity if their grades were good enough. She even attempted to substitute-teach English at a nearby high school to put away money for Ruth's schooling. The girls hated to see their mother abandon this when she found herself ill-suited to deal with student disciplinary problems.

But Kay soon afterward took a job at a nearby bookstore. She told the girls that while their father finally acquiesced to her working, he still insisted that college was out of the question. "I'm not giving up though," she assured them.

Then one night at the dinner table, Kay raised the subject again with Arthur. He lifted his eyes from his spaghetti dinner and glared at her, then at the girls for a long time before blurting out, "Why do you want to go to college? To have educated babies?"

Appalled, their mouths dropped open.

"Arthur!" Kay chastised him.

"What?" he retorted, growing angry. "You of all people, Kay, should get it. You couldn't even hold a substitute teaching job. Now all you can do is be a bookstore clerk. What good did all that education do for *you*?"

Arthur returned to his preoccupation with his dinner. He didn't see Kay grab her food-laden dish and hurl it across the table past their wide-eyed daughters. It barely missed Arthur's head as it shattered against the wall, strands of spaghetti oozing serpentine-like, the tomato sauce trailing like blood staining the wall and the girls' consciousness. The incident registered in slow motion in Gabrielle's mind, unaccustomed to witnessing her mother in an act of physical violence.

"Mom!" the girls shouted in unison.

Kay put her hand to her mouth, as if only now realizing what she had done. Then she broke into tears and ran from the room.

Arthur just sat there, his mouth gaping.

In the weeks after "the incident," the girls talked about their father's comments and concluded that they largely would be on their own if they wanted to go for higher education. Ruth at least would get some help from their mother. Gabrielle decided it was unrealistic to think her mom would be able to help Ruth and also give her financial support. So Gabrielle bent herself to the need to work very hard over the next few years to win a scholarship and earn as much money as she could.

"I don't care what dad says," Ruth told Gabrielle. "I'm going to college."

Gabrielle, tight-lipped, shook her head in agreement. "Good for you, Ruthie. One way or the other, I'm going too."

* * *

Over all the years of her childhood and despite her mother's assurances to the contrary, Gabrielle continued to feel different from everyone around her. Her hair was almost black, straight, and thick. She was five-foot-nine, taller and more slender than any female in her family, and her skin was olive-toned, growing darker in the summers. Her lips were fuller than those of anyone in her family and her nose longer. Her eyes were vaguely Oriental in their slant and strikingly blue—bluer than Arthur's. But more importantly, deep within, she *felt* that she didn't fit.

Although her father never directly said anything to her, she saw every day that he loved Ruth more than her. He frequently told Ruth how beautiful she was, but never said this to Gabrielle. Her hurt and doubt about herself were accentuated by whispers and furtive glances from girls in the gym locker room when she entered and dressed—and muffled taunts from passing students in the hallways, "You speak *Inglés?*" and "*Cha cha cha*, eh?" And then there were the proms, to which no boys asked her, and the parties to which she received no invitations. These jabs and her father's reticence toward her had created wounds and longtime scars that tore at her self-esteem.

Her tranquility as a baby now seemed buried irretrievably deep. Her mother continued to brush off her daughter's queries about her lineage. As Gabrielle's questions lingered, she could find no answers and no peace. Carrying a persistent hurt, she sensed she was being discriminated against—perhaps even by her father—but without an explanation as to why. She knew that her mom and dad tried to be good parents, but life was tense and sadly lacking in acknowledgment in the Andersen household. And her father's alcoholism and insecurities made their nights almost unbearable.

Gabrielle typically fell asleep each night with her fingers in her ears and a pillow over her head. Although she loved her parents, she dreamed of herself in some other place…or even in another time. Always it was far far from southern Long Island and the screaming and crying on the other side of her bedroom door.

* * *

While still an eighth grader, Gabrielle met a girl in her history class who had just transferred to their school. She noticed how isolated the new student seemed, appearing to know no one and wearing extremely thick eyeglasses that made her eyes look strange. So Gabrielle decided to wait for her as she gathered up her books.

"Hi, I'm Gabrielle," she said, walking over to the slender, brown-haired student. "You're new here in town?"

The girl looked up, her green eyes trying to focus from behind her heavy lenses. "Yeah. Just moved from Brooklyn. My name's Adrienne."

"Well Adrienne, I'm glad to meet you. If you need help with anything, just let me know. It must be hard to start over in a new place."

"Yeah. You're the first person to introduce herself. Thanks." She half-grinned, looking long at Gabrielle.

"You on your way to English now?" Gabrielle asked.

"Yeah."

"Me too. Guess we should mosey that way so we're not late."

"Yup."

As they walked, Adrienne chatted about Brooklyn and the school she left behind, while Gabrielle just listened and smiled. After English class Gabrielle took her to the cafeteria, where they fetched food from the steam table before sitting by the windows.

"So how'd you wind up here?" Gabrielle asked.

"My dad's been wantin' to move here for a long time. He thinks the schools are better and it's a healthier place for kids to grow up—and less likely to get teased or into trouble!" She giggled.

Gabrielle smiled. "They do have about everything you'd ever want to study here," she said, "and really great girls' athletic stuff, orchestra and band, drama stuff, lotsa clubs…about everything."

"I thought Brooklyn was fine too, but my dad had other ideas. So here I am," She sighed, attempting a smile.

"Where in town do you live?" Gabrielle asked.

"I live real close. Just a few blocks. You?"

"Up north. It's a bit of a hike for me every morning."

"You don't take the bus?"

"If I lived a tenth of a mile farther away, I'd get bussed. No, I have to walk. Quite a trek with all my books and my violin too!" she laughed.

"You play violin?"

"Guilty," Gabrielle chuckled.

"I play flute."

"No kidding?"

"Yeah."

"You could play in band *or* orchestra—or both!"

"I'm gonna look into it."

"What else you like to do?" Gabrielle asked.

The girls' conversation showed Gabrielle that they had a lot in common. It wasn't long before Adrienne shared with Gabrielle that she was very farsighted and astigmatic, making it necessary to wear "Coke-bottle" glasses. This made her eyes look small and rather odd. Gabrielle had never seen anyone who wore glasses like these. *It makes her a little different,* Gabrielle thought, *like me.*

Soon Adrienne joined the orchestra, which made Gabrielle happy. And it wasn't long before they became close friends. She loved Adrienne's zany sense of humor and how direct she could be. Adrienne was the best friend she dreamed of and never had before. The first time she acknowledged this she cried.

At school they hung out, studied, and played music together. Gabrielle thought that Adrienne was the best thing that had happened to her in a very long time. Appreciating that her friend was so accepting of her, she noted that Adrienne didn't seem to care that she looked different from other kids. Nor did Adrienne press her about why she never invited kids to her house and why she talked so little about her family. So when they had a sleepover, it always was at Adrienne's.

One day, as they walked down the school corridor between classes, three guys passed them, going the other way. "Taco!" one of them mumbled, "beaner" shouted another as they passed Gabrielle. "Beady four-eyes!" the third lobbed, catching a glimpse of Adrienne.

Adrienne glanced at Gabrielle and saw hurt. Immediately Adrienne swung around and shouted, "Assholes!"

Turning back to her friend, she saw Gabrielle's mouth drop open. "What?" Adrienne said.

Then Gabrielle laughed harder than she had in a very long time. "You're really something," Gabrielle said as she got hold of herself. "Thank you Adrienne!"

Later that day Gabrielle admitted to her friend that she had heard similar jibes any number of times in the hallways, as well as tittering and glances in her direction in the girls' locker room.

"Well it just makes me mad," she replied looking earnestly at Gabrielle. "You never talk about this."

"No. I get that I look different in some ways. I guess we both do. You think I look Mexican or somethin'?"

"I don't know. You do look unusual. You could have a little Mexican in you. What does your mother say?"

"I've asked her any number of times. She just keeps saying there must be someone in our family far back who looked like me."

Adrienne studied her. "What do *you* think?"

Gabrielle hesitated. "I don't know. Either it's true or they're protecting me from somethin'. It does trouble me. I try not to dwell on it. But I think that's why I don't get invited to parties and proms—and get called out in the halls." She dropped her gaze.

Adrienne looked hard at her, then put her hand under Gabrielle's chin, raising her head. "You just keep holding your head up, girl! Look at you. You're gorgeous and smart—and the only one I've met since I left Brooklyn who makes any sense to me. Anyone who makes fun of us is a creep and just plain stupid. Listen to me. You're not less You're more!"

6
1963

One night, after seventeen-year-old Gabrielle had slept several hours, her dreams took her to a place she didn't recall her subconscious venturing.

In her dream she was in a space where brown-skinned women in long gowns floated by peacefully. While there she was embraced by a dark-haired woman with white skin and taken high up into the air. Gabrielle felt that she missed someone. A man was it? Something about him gave her a feeling of tranquility and joy.

She awoke abruptly. The images still in her mind, she threw her covers back, rose, and walked to the window. Pulling the curtains aside, she saw a friendly moon illuminate her backyard and the familiar mulberry tree with its three trunks that had been her special place since early childhood to climb, sit quietly, and think.

It was just a dream, she told herself. *Just a dream. But it seemed so real. If I told Ruth she'd say, "Gabel, you're always having crazy dreams. Remember when you said you dreamed mom picked you from a tree as if you were a peach, brushed you off, then tossed you in the air like a ball and caught you before hiding you under a bush. Just another of your crazy dreams sister. You're just crazy daisy. Go back to bed."*

"Ruth's right," Gabrielle said aloud. "It's just a crazy dream." Shivering, she returned to bed. But she couldn't sleep. Then she remembered the night the moonlight lit up the sky before coursing through her body. Just thinking about it brought a sense of comfort to her and the lingering belief that she was loved and accepted by something vast and seamless.

A week later she woke in the night following the same dream about the women and the man. Sitting up in the darkness, she trembled, her body chilled, her face wet with tears. She couldn't help thinking that the dream meant something she was supposed to understand.

The next morning she found herself alone at the dining room table with her mother.

"Mom?" Gabrielle hesitated.

"Yes dear?"

Gabrielle paused, then persevered.

"Mom, I had such a strange dream again last night."

"You do have some odd ones. What kind of dream dear?"

Observing Kay, Gabrielle noted how her lined, round face was drawn from another difficult night with Arthur, deepening the dark circles under her eyes. This gave her mother a certain weariness of expression that made Gabrielle feel sorry for her and think the better of burdening her mother with her concerns.

"Uh, it's nothing Mom, nothing really."

She stared at her daughter. "Gabrielle, if you have something on your mind, something that's troubling you, I'd like to hear it."

Discerning the stubborn set of Kay's jaw, she knew there was no point in keeping silent. So she told her mother the story of her latest dream in as much detail as she could remember.

When Gabrielle finished, she noticed that Kay had an odd look on her face.

"Mom?"

Kay appeared almost frightened, but she quickly composed herself. "Sorry dear, I was just responding to what a strange dream you describe and how much it's disturbing you. I'm not sure why you have so many odd dreams." She picked at an imaginary spot on her apron.

"Mom, what do you think it means? It seemed so real."

"That's the way dreams are sometimes, Gabrielle. You had a peculiar dream is all." She reached over and patted her daughter's arm. Pushing herself away from the table, she stood. "Now pick up your breakfast plates and help me do the dishes. It's best not to dwell on these things dear. Just get on with your day and try to forget about it."

But Gabrielle couldn't forget. It haunted her. She believed the dream held a truth she had to understand, perhaps a clue to something in herself that she needed to find.

* * *

This latest dream of Gabrielle's occurred in the spring of 1963 as she prepared to go to Oberlin College on a scholarship. The dream reoccurred several times more that spring and summer. Each time it unsettled her. She thought and thought about it, looking for some analogy to her life. But she never could find a meaning that made sense to her. And then, in the excitement of getting ready to go to college, the dream simply stopped.

"Adrienne," she exclaimed, "I can hardly wait till it's fall! It's *our* time to fly. You at NYU and me at Oberlin. Wow!"

Adrienne laughed. "Some kinda crazy, no? It'll be so cool."

"Beyond cool," Gabrielle countered. "Time to make a life that's all ours. The only thing not cool is that I'll only get to see you in the summers and maybe Christmas. I won't be able to afford to come home Thanksgiving or Easter."

"Yeah. Bummer. But we can call and write," Adrienne said hopefully.

"Sure thing."

"And we're both gonna waitress at one of the Jones Beach restaurants in the summers, right?"

"Absolutely."

Kay smiled at the transition she saw in her daughter who had grown light of heart and step. She clearly had worried about Gabrielle's dreams and her months of brooding and now appeared to believe that her daughter had moved past that.

Kay also showed sadness at the impending loss of the presence of the child she had come to love, delight in, and rely upon. As Ruth had left home for college in Boston four years ago, now Gabrielle was following in her footsteps. Kay's nest was about to be empty, and she surely was downcast.

But Kay didn't wear her melancholy and helped Gabrielle shop and pack a trunk to ship to Ohio. Just before Labor Day Arthur stated again his opposition to supporting the girls' college education and refused to see Gabrielle off. So Kay went alone to take her to the bus and waved goodbye as the bus got ready to pull away from the station. Waving back, Gabrielle watched her mother smiling bravely and dabbing at the corners of her eyes. Hurt that her father declined to see her off, she managed a smile for her mother's sake and waved some more.

Leaning back into her seat, she worked to dispel the pain inflicted by her father's rebuff. She strived to let it go like the Long Island suburban towns rushing by her window. Then came a new world as she gazed up at city buildings and changed buses to take her through New Jersey, Pennsylvania, and eventually Ohio.

Having never been anywhere other than a small part of the Northeast as her family visited relatives, she felt the beginnings of excitement and happiness as she looked out at a world she never saw before. The breadth of the open expanses of rolling land was new to her. She loved the green pastures, the hills, and the long stretches of forests and fields. Soon she would be in Ohio to begin a new chapter in her young life. She could hardly wait.

~III~
THE FOOTHILLS

1965 – Hattiesburg, Mississippi, and Oberlin, Ohio

1
March 1965
Road to Hattiesburg

"Dirty nigga lovers!" the men yelled, beating on the sides of the bus.

Just weeks after the "Bloody Sunday" Selma march, with emotions running high, Gabrielle found herself and her fellow students caught in the very situation they had hoped to avoid. Warnings were out that buses carrying Northern civil rights workers would be easy targets for the anger some harbored as the winds of social and political change shifted and stirred around them.

Gabrielle's eyes grew wide with panic. Clutching at the back of the bus seat in front of her, she smelled her own fear. Sweat ran down her arms as she felt the hair rise on the back of her neck.

Her bus had stopped to refuel outside Batesville, Mississippi. Looking out at the unexpected mass of white faces and flailing arms on the other side of the bus windows, she recognized the face of a mob, its aspect distorted with shouting and hatred. She caught the eye of a man who was not more than five feet from where she sat. She stared at him in disbelief and with a question written across her nineteen-year-old face: *Why? Why do you hate so much?*

It was as if he read her mind. As he watched her, his eyes hardened. Then he mouthed the words, "Bitch! Nigga-lovin' bitch!" as he moved to go nose to nose with her. Without warning he rammed her window with a rock clutched in his fist.

She heard the glass crack and jerked back in her seat. A guttural sound rose from her. Then she experienced pain and saw blood dripping from her face. As she felt it, she pulled glass from her cheek.

Then everything started to rock as scores of men pressed against the sides of the bus.

Thrown against the window, she suddenly was up against the visage of the man she had recoiled from. Emboldened, he opened his mouth wide and laughed. She went pale, blood flowing now from her wound.

Then the bus tipped the other way.

As she slid along the seat away from the man, the driver revved the engine and jerked the bus into gear. Startled, the mob parted in front of them and inadvertently gave the driver an opening. He gunned the engine. Not a minute too soon, the vehicle rocketed away from the mob.

Silence fell like stones.

When sound returned, it came in punctuation marks rising all around them.

"Shit!"

"Good God!"

"Do you believe this shit?"

"Man oh man…"

"They wanted to kill us!"

"Damn!"

Gabrielle was speechless. All she could think was, *My God, what have we gotten ourselves into?*

Then came a voice from across the aisle. "You okay? Here, take this," said the Oberlin student who offered his handkerchief and a thermos of water. "Here, let me help you," he said as he crossed the aisle and ministered to her wound.

"Is it very bad?" she asked.

The Foothills

"Hard to tell. It doesn't look very deep, but it's maybe two-and a-half inches long. Thank God it didn't get your eye. But it was close. Not sure if you'll need stitches." He peered closer.

"I think I got out all the glass in your cheek. Just put your head back and hold the handkerchief on the cut till the bleeding stops."

"Uh, thanks...Rick is it?"

"Yes. You're welcome. Some kind of crazy back there, no?"

"Horrid," she said. "Was anyone else hurt?"

"I don't think anything serious, but everyone's shaken up. I'm just thankful for the driver's quick thinking. We could have been pulled out of the bus and beaten like students before us. I'll let you rest. Let me know if you need anything."

But she couldn't relax. She pressed the cloth more firmly to her face, hoping to quell the bleeding and the pain. Still frightened and suddenly exhausted, she couldn't help but replay in her mind old news reports. This made her think of the battered freedom riders and civil rights workers like them, committed to the job they were traveling toward.

She thought about how it was just over nine months since three young civil rights workers—James Chaney, Andrew Goodman, and Michael Schwerner—had disappeared at night as they drove their car along Highway 19 in Neshoba County, Mississippi. She found it hard to believe that it was a full two months before their remains were found in an earthen dam in that same county. She shivered as she remembered reading reports of how the three young men had been terrorized by the county sheriff and two carloads of KKK members, then shot to death. The report said that Chaney, who was black, also suffered severe beating and mutilation.

Despite the horrors of these young men's fates and the rampant dangers bussed volunteers suffered on their way south, their buses firebombed even, Gabrielle thought how Sam, her friend at Oberlin College, had urged her to go to Hattiesburg.

"When you look into the eyes of the people you'll come to know," he said, holding her in his arms and looking down into the blue pools of hers, "you'll be certain that there's nowhere else you can be. I know how passionately you care about this struggle. If you back away from it, you'll be backing away your whole life."

Gabrielle believed he was right. The abduction and murders of the civil rights workers, the brutality of "Bloody Sunday," the history of oppression, and the bitterness and strife that she knew lay before her, had frightened her and made her hesitate. But something about the Civil Rights Movement resonated in her at a profound level. She knew that in part it was the political consciousness of the times. Partly it was her passion for justice and her identification with those who looked different from others. But in some measure the Movement went deeper yet—to something personal she couldn't understand, let alone explain.

Yes, Sam was right she concluded. She couldn't turn away. If she did, her beliefs meant nothing. Her young life meant nothing. She would go, she decided, no matter what the consequences.

Gabrielle's bus wasn't far into Mississippi. It still was some distance from Hattiesburg in Forrest County, which was in the southeastern part of the state. She made herself think about what the city would be like. This was the place where she and her fellow students from six Midwestern colleges would spend their spring break working for three civil rights organizations: Delta Ministry, an interdenominational effort unprecedented in U.S. history; a coalition of major civil rights organizations operating in Mississippi—COFO, the Council of Federated Organizations; and SNCC, the Student Nonviolent Coordinating Committee.

She continued to try to turn her attention away from her cut face by considering the job ahead of them, canvassing black neighborhoods and documenting residents' experiences with past voter registration attempts. The volunteers' charge included disseminating information about Negroes' rights and the support available to them to increase success in registering. The volunteers also would document which blacks planned to register and what their knowledge of the procedures was.

The Foothills

As she thought this, Gabrielle removed Rick's handkerchief from her cheek. The cloth was soaked in blood and the wound throbbed, though bleeding had slowed. She hoped it would heal without infection and stitches. Reclining the back of her seat farther, she tried to rest before reaching their destination. Her hurt, however, was a constant reminder of the horror of the mob's hatred and the viciousness of the attackers. Every time she tried to close her eyes to sleep, she trembled. All she could see was the attacker's face and the ugliness and threat wielded by his and the mob's hatred. She thought how such acts happened with frequency to blacks who stood up to them.

Ultimately she realized how desperately caught up she was in this conflict for racial equality—and how the mob's victimization of her only brought her closer to the people she came to stand beside, capturing her attention and her heart. While she might not know what it was to be black, she knew what it was to be different.

To not feel different was what she wanted for those whom some tried to say were worth less than others. She identified with a people discriminated against by virtue of a happenstance of birth in ways she couldn't fully explain. She had grown passionate in her desire to help when she saw the news clips of the demonstrations, learned the reasons for them, and listened to speakers from the movement who came to Oberlin. It was not a great leap from there to her decision to go to Mississippi. Her mind drifted to circumstances that led to her presence on this bus heading deeper into the South.

Gabrielle's Sam had preceded her on his own journey south just weeks before, when he participated in the third Selma, Alabama, voting rights march. It was March 21, 1965, when Sam joined civil rights marchers walking fifty-four miles along U.S. Route 80 from Selma to the Alabama State Capitol in Montgomery. It was a time of intense feelings on both sides of the conflict and violence against demonstrators. She feared for Sam's safety.

She understood that for Sam, there had been nothing to think about. He simply had to be there. He hadn't asked her to join him. Three days before the start of the march, he just stuffed his backpack with a change of clothes and a toothbrush and headed toward the Oberlin College chapel. There the bus would pick up Sam and his friend Nate.

Standing outside his off-campus room, she watched Sam leave. She studied his tall, slender form, the back of his curly blond hair, and that distinctive walk he had, quick and full of purpose. Then she replayed how they had lain together all night, fully clothed, but with their bodies pressed against one another. She felt the warmth of his arms and kisses, the tickle of his blond mustache and beard. As if in some sacred circle, they lay there without succumbing fully to the ardor they felt. They slept lovingly, guardedly, as if afraid to sink from this place a little above earth before being asked to do something selfless, to lay something down inside themselves for the good of others.

Gabrielle was to join a Selma sympathy march, set to also begin on March 21st and conclude March 25th. The word was that over a hundred Oberlin students and townspeople had signed up to walk the same number of miles from a northern Ohio meeting point along US 75 South to the Ohio Statehouse in Columbus. She knew there was considerably less danger in her commitment compared to Sam's, but it was important to call attention to the cause.

Gabrielle saw Sam as a self-described revolutionary who flirted with Marxism and anarchism. At twenty-one, he distrusted the government and all established institutions of American society. He was suspicious of the motives of politicians, businessmen, clergy, people of wealth and establishment influence, in fact anyone who wasn't downtrodden or fighting for the oppressed. Passionate, highly intelligent, and well read, poetic in both spoken and written word, he was a leader among the more radical students on campus.

While liberal politically, she wasn't entirely comfortable owning Sam's radicalism. Still, barely nineteen, she found herself hopelessly drawn to him. Although she shared his determination to work to change what clearly was wrong, she didn't agree with all his methods. She noted with concern that while he didn't practice violence, he also didn't rule it out. Yet two years older than she, well-traveled and accomplished as an organizer, writer, and speaker, Sam represented something she was reaching for in her life: a clear sense of her identity and a consuming purpose. He seemed to know exactly who he was and why he was here. Troubled by the nagging uncertainty she felt about her origins, she longed to experience the clarity that Sam represented. She struggled with how to get there. Sam riveted her. Feeling quite helpless to resist him, she sought to study and know him better.

As she looked back, she remembered how they met at a campus political rally six months before. A member of the Southern Christian Leadership Conference was speaking at Oberlin's Finney Chapel. Sam stood beside her. Later he confessed that he couldn't help but notice her, seeing her as a stunningly ethnic-looking woman with her dark hair and skin and intense, slanted blue eyes. After the rally ended, they stayed behind and talked. Five hours later, he walked her back to her dorm and kissed her on the cheek before leaving her. It was almost a brotherly kiss, but it made her heart race. She had never met anyone like Sam.

To Gabrielle's mind, that was the start of a strange and troubled relationship. She was powerfully drawn to him. *Love was it?* she asked herself. But although he was endlessly seductive with her, he never made love to her. She knew Sam's reputation. He had many women friends, all of whom he had slept with at one time or another. Except for Gabrielle. As she pondered the enigma of their entangled lives, she harked back to a conversation they had a month after they met. She remembered him saying that he saw in her an innate innocence and goodness of heart. *Is that what this is about?* she wondered.

His withholding behavior infuriated her. She wanted him to be the first man she gave herself to. There was no one who captivated her as Sam did. But his seeming refusal to sleep with her made her hate her virginity and her innocence. Yet there was no one but he that she would lose them to.

While she didn't follow him to Alabama, she prepared for the Selma sympathy march to Columbus instead. Rising before dawn to a wintry chill as the sun slept behind the city of Oberlin's buildings, Gabrielle and scores of others gathered in their winter coats and hiking boots in front of the steps to the old post office building on Main Street.

Waiting for the first light of the sun, the crowd witnessed dawn brushing the sky and buildings with a softening pink wash. Getting word that the TV cameras had arrived, a local civil-rights activist, a black man in his twenties, walked up the steps to the microphone and called out to some hundred people, white and black, congregating in the square below.

"We're here today to bear witness to the struggle for freedom taking place hundreds of miles to our south in Selma, Alabama! Our brothers and sisters are marching into terrible danger. They're marching against ignorance, prejudice, and hatred."

"Yes brother!" someone called.

"Our white brothers and sisters," the activist continued, "have joined hands with our Negro brothers and sisters who have been grievously wronged by a white establishment set on denying them their God-given rights!"

Gabrielle shouted support with others as they raised their fists.

"This system of racial prejudice and injustice must be brought down!" he shouted.

The crowd cheered louder and shook their fists again.

"You and I can't be free if all of our nation's people aren't free! Those of us here today take a stand against the oppression of blacks, as Oberlin did throughout its abolitionist history. Today we march in solidarity with our fellow protesters in Selma!"

"Yes brother yes!" another voice came from somewhere in the crowd.

"Those of you coming with us will board the buses here and drive to a meeting place south of Mansfield where we'll join other freedom marchers," the activist said. "Then we'll walk together over fifty miles until we reach the Ohio Statehouse in

Columbus. We'll stop overnight in churches along the way and hope to end our march around the time the Selma march concludes. Walking together in Selma and across the nation, we'll make our stand for freedom! Brothers and sisters, together we will overcome!" The crowd cheered.

A white woman in her forties, a scarf covering her hair, came forward from the throng and walked to the microphone. Her lips parted, and out of them flowed the music of "We Shall Overcome." Her rich contralto tones seemed to Gabrielle to echo against the old post office and float over the gathering, now silent under the spell of her voice and the power of the song's words. And then a middle-aged black man in the crowd began to croon with the singer. Soon more people joined him. They clasped arms and swayed. Their voices grew louder as more people participated and the fervor for the cause grew. When the song ended, the crowd went silent, save for the punctuation here and there of people weeping.

The woman singer stood there as the speaker moved closer to her and clasped her hand. Then they lifted their joined arms and said together into the microphone, "And now brothers and sisters, let's march!"

A deafening cheer came from the crowd as they elevated their interlocked hands, black and white, young and not so young, before heading for the buses. Gabrielle's excitement swelled as she felt the power of the protesters' convictions and the history they would make as part of thousands upon thousands marching not just in Alabama and Ohio, but all across the country. "We *shall* overcome," she whispered, saying the words like a prayer.

The smarting of her cheek brought her back to the present. She struggled to refocus as she gazed out the window. Enshrouded in darkness, all she could see was an occasional light hitting the windows of the bus rushing toward Hattiesburg, a place she imagined held yet unknown dangers.

2
Arrival in Hattiesburg

It was long after dark when the bus arrived in Hattiesburg. The driver left the thirty-two exhausted and frightened students at the civil rights office. It was in an old spartan place with a linoleum floor, plainly paneled walls, and bright florescent lights.

A heavy-set man with undistinguished features and mousy-brown hair, came to greet them and escort them to where several blacks and two other white people stood waiting for them. One of the greeters noticed Gabrielle's face and took her to the restroom to wash her cheek, apply ointment, and bandage her cut. When she returned to the group, someone already was speaking.

"We know you're tired," the man said, "so I'll keep it brief. Like you, I'm from up north. My name's Jim Dunning, an organizer for Delta Ministry. I'm the guy responsible for you greenhorns while you're down here. So if anything goes wrong, you have a problem with anything, you see me. I want you to meet my friends and colleagues, Skip, Susan, Richard, Phil, Robin, Tom, and George." He gestured toward them as he spoke their names. "They're also here to help you and will take you to stay with your families tonight."

Gabrielle surveyed the people whose names they just heard. They had faces that had witnessed things she wasn't sure she was ready to see. Looking at the demeanor of her thirty-two fellow students, she saw exhaustion and uncertainty.

"We heard about your bus being surrounded, and one of you was cut," Jim was saying, pacing as he spoke and glancing toward Gabrielle. "That kind of thing goes on all the time here. You know about the young men who disappeared down here not long ago. This is a dangerous place right now, so you have to listen to what we tell you and do what you're told. Your life may depend on it, and the lives of those with you. If you don't think you can do this, you better get back on that bus now before it leaves. Is that understood?"

The Foothills

Some heads nodded.

"I'm asking *everyone*," Jim halted in mid-step, turned toward them, and repeated. "Is that understood?"

"Yes!" the students replied in unison.

"Okay." He resumed his gait. "Tomorrow morning we'll start work. You'll need to be here by eight-thirty. One of the people I introduced you to will be the one responsible for getting you to and from your sleeping quarters. They and others will take you to your voter registration canvassing job each day."

He stopped moving about and turned to face them directly. His speech slowed, as if to emphasize the importance of what he was about to say. "You're not to travel by yourself or without your escort to the neighborhoods where you'll work—or to anywhere else. The whole time you're here, you'll be in the Negro part of town. You'll sleep here, eat here, work here. Going into the white section is putting your and others' lives at risk, so you're not going to do that. Is that understood?"

"Yes," the students said, shaking their heads.

"Say it louder!"

"Yes!" they shouted in unison.

"Good. I'm glad you're here." His face seemed to soften. "We need your help, but we also need you to be careful. I'm going to read the list of your names that your schools sent and tell you who you're riding with tonight and in the coming days. Becky Adams, you ride with George. Ray Fink, you're with Tom...."

As the pairings continued, Gabrielle wound up with three other students in Tom's 1950 Chevy sedan. Only one of them—Rick Dressel—was from Oberlin. He was the one who ministered to her in the bus. Gabrielle noted that he was about her height, had dark curly hair, a black mustache, and a nice smile. She recalled noticing him at campus rallies. But she didn't really know him.

Their black driver, Tom, appeared to her to be middle-aged. Born and raised in Hattiesburg, he said he was a bricklayer by trade. As he shook the students' hands and smiled in greeting them, she felt the strength and roughness of his hands.

"I'll bet you're tired. I know I am," he admitted as he started up the car engine. "I know you've had a long day, and Jim gives quite a speech, don't he?" Gabrielle and the other students laughed with him. "Jim can be a little tough," he drawled, "but he has to be. He's really a great guy, and he knows his stuff. You'll learn from him if y'all pay attention and do what he says."

The rest of the ride was mostly in silence, except for a series of goodbyes as he dropped the students at their respective houses. Tom left Rick and her for last, delivering them at Mike and Edith Brown's home.

The family's porch light threw illumination into the yard, which otherwise was totally dark. Gabrielle noticed there were few, if any, streetlights in this part of town and only dirt roads. Dogs barking from several nearby houses terrified Gabrielle, a response she had to dogs as far back as she could remember. But as Tom's car doors slammed and his two charges got their bags from the trunk, she worked to calm herself before he led them up the stairs to the house. The wooden dwelling appeared to Gabrielle to be decades old and was covered in chipped paint. Without knocking, he led them through the front door, the screen door slapping shut behind them.

As they entered, she saw a tall black man and four young children watching television and playing with a calico cat. The man and his children sat crowded on two mismatched sofas with fraying covers. The stocky man stood up.

"Hello," Mike said, brushing off his well-worn overalls and running his hand over his short hair as his looked at the Northerners. "You're later than I thought you'd be."

"Bus got delayed around Batesville," Tom intervened. "Buncha whites circled the bus, tried to cause trouble. Hurt this here young lady. And Jim of course gave the kids a li'l speech. Y'all know how that goes."

Mike laughed, but then he looked soberly at Gabrielle's bandaged face.

"But where's my manners," Tom said. "This here's Gabrielle Andersen and Rick Dressel. They're from Ohio. And I'd like y'all," he gestured toward Mike's family, "to meet Mike Brown and his children, Bessie, Boo, Johnny, and Tater." Johnny looked to Gabrielle to be about nine years old, Bessie about the same. Boo

The Foothills

and Tater she guessed to be five or six. As Boo and Tater smiled shyly at the Northerners, the two older children studied them from across the room.

"Where's Edith?" Tom asked.

"She's in back with li'l Rosie," Mike said. "What's the schedule tomorrow?"

"They've to be at the office by eight-thirty, so I'd better fetch them about eight," Tom drawled. "That okay?"

"Fine," Mike said. "I guess we'd better let you go, so we can get these two to bed."

"Rick, Gabrielle," Tom said, "I'd better get a move on. I'll see you in the mornin'." And with that, he was gone.

As the screen door closed, Gabrielle turned toward a short, skinny woman who had just entered the room. A scarf covering her hair, the woman Gabrielle judged to be in her late thirties held a baby of eight or nine months on her hip.

"Hi, I'm Edith…," she began, then said, "My stars, what happened to you girl?" Mike filled her in as Edith handed the baby off to him before taking Gabrielle by the hand to the kitchen sink. There she pealed the bandage back, cleaned it again, and applied a different ointment to help the healing. "This here stuff I'm putting on is somethin' my grandmother concocted a long time ago. Works great to keep infection down. But that's a bad cut. If it's not a lot better soon, we may have to have a doctor take a look. It's sure to leave a scar, a shame on such a pretty face," she concluded, shaking her head. "Damn crackers!"

Taking the infant back from Mike, Edith hefted her onto her hip before introducing Gabrielle to "li'l Rosie." The child cooed as Gabrielle bent to get a closer look.

"What a beautiful baby," she remarked to Edith.

The woman smiled. "She's a honey alright." Turning to her husband she asked, "Have you told them where they're sleeping and about the john and all?"

"Not yet. Tom just left."

"Damn, I wanted to give that scallywag somethin' for Martha," she responded. "Well next time. Gabrielle, you'll sleep with me and Rosie in the bedroom. Rick, you'll be sleeping with

63

Mike and the other children in here. You'll wash up in the kitchen. I got a towel for each of you. The john's out back. The flashlight's by the back door. Mike'll show you, Rick. Gabrielle you come with me."

Gabrielle followed Edith and Rosie into a tiny room barely large enough for a double bed and a small dresser. A gingham curtain separated the bedroom from the main living area.

"I know you're tired, hon," Edith said to her, then examined her more closely. "Are you okay? I see some caked blood I missed around that bandage on your cheek. I better take a look at it in the morning and see if it needs doctoring."

"Thanks Edith.

"It's getting late, and you traveled straight through. The bed's made. I'll lay Rosie down with you while I get the other little ones to bed. Then I'll turn in too. But let me show you to the john first."

She followed Edith out back, where Edith gave her the flashlight before leaving.

After opening the door to the outhouse, Gabrielle shined the light inside. Large spiders hung in the corners, and insects she had never seen before scurried in different directions. Gabrielle had only used an outhouse for a week at Girl Scout camp several years ago, and she didn't much like it. Taking a deep breath, she went inside, careful to steer clear of the critters by not sitting on or leaning against anything. As quickly as she could, she was out and back inside the house.

Washing up in the kitchen sink, she removed the caked blood Edith mentioned from around the bandage. Turning to go to her room, she noted Tater and Boo giggling and watching her from the doorway.

"Hi," Gabrielle said smiling, then wincing as her cut smarted and Tater and Boo ran away.

Pulling the cord that hung from the bare bulb in the center of the bedroom ceiling, Gabrielle undressed in the dark. After putting on pajamas and crawling into bed, she tried not to disturb Rosie who was asleep in the middle of it.

Lying on Edith and Mike's lumpy bed, she listened to Rosie's breathing and to the children and their parents in the next room. She thought about the experiences of the day as she tried to wait for Edith before going to sleep.

After a while her mind drifted back, back to when she was five years old, back to the house of her parents.

"Hush little baby don't say a word,
momma's gonna buy you a mockingbird,
and if that mockingbird don't sing,
momma's gonna buy you a diamond ring..."

She remembered how she sang this song so loudly inside her head that she thought she would burst. She had thought that if she could just fill her mind with the song, she wouldn't hear her mother and father out of control, their shouting barreling through the house like a runaway train. Now she internalized the words to chase away the images of the mob that had threatened their bus and the angry man who smashed her window and scarred her face.

HUSH LITTLE BABY DON'T SAY A WORD...

Shivering at her childhood recollections and the horrors of the day, she labored to expunge them further from her mind by attuning herself to the noises in the next room. They proved to be comforting sounds of the children as their parents coaxed them to bed. In synchrony now with the gentle, warm breathing of little Rosie beside her, she drifted into a sleep so deep that she didn't awake until Rosie cried just as a rooster crowed at morning's first light.

3
On the Job in Hattiesburg

"Good morning!" Jim said.

"Good morning," the group sang back.

"These men and women," Jim said, pointing to his colleagues, "will go over the forms you'll fill out for each interview you do. They'll give you your assignments and drop you off in your designated areas. I want you to listen up and follow what they say *exactly*. Our voter registration drives depend upon the information you'll collect. So it's got to be accurate—and complete."

He paused, looking meaningfully at them. "By your presence here, you are part of a defining moment in America's history. It's the time when we'll decide what kind of society we're going to be and what we'll stand for." He began to pace. "This battle for the rights of *all* of our citizens is being fought now in the South. But the consciousness of the whole nation is here, at least in part because you middle-class college kids from the North are down here." Turning toward them, he stopped.

"In the two weeks you're in Hattiesburg, you're going to see things you've never seen in your privileged lives. And make no mistake, your lives are privileged, whether you think your family is well-off or not." The students exchanged glances as the cadence of his thoughts resonated.

"You'll see black people and white people, poverty like you've never witnessed, fear, bravery, prejudice, and ignorance like you've never seen." He began walking again.

"Remember to show respect for the Negroes and our helpers whom you'll meet." He stopped momentarily, looking into their eyes, then paced again.

"Know that our black brothers and sisters have terribly difficult lives. They have to be heroes to register to vote and walk to the ballot box, something that you and I've taken for granted. But after your time here," he said, pivoting as he measured his words, "you'll *never* take this liberty for granted again. So show respect. Show it by doing your job the best you've ever done anything. The people of Hattiesburg depend upon it. Our nation's *future* depends on it."

He stopped, as if gathering himself before looking at them with an intensity that sought their very souls. "What happens here helps define the nature of the conscience of the United States of America! You and the brave Southern Negroes and whites who risk everything for freedom and justice for all this land's people...they who are willing to do whatever it takes to do the right thing...it's all of you who will lift up our country to something better. You'll help raise it to a place where all men and women, created equal in the eyes of God, will be able to live their lives without the bondage of ignorance and prejudice.

"Today, by your being in this place and dedicating yourselves to this mission, you're helping to untie the ropes of oppression and to build a nation that's truly free." He paused before saying softly. "I thank God for all of you here today."

When Jim finished, the room ached with silence. Gabrielle felt nothing but awe of this man and his colleagues and of the mission entrusted to them. *I can only hope that our work to gather and disseminate information will help increase black voter registration and change history,* she thought. *God I hope so.*

Jim's helpers moved to split the group into six and review their instructions. Robin gathered several students, including Gabrielle and Rick, who studied the forms and discussed their assignment with her. A slender brown-haired woman of twenty-one who had dropped out of college to devote full time to the Civil Rights Movement, Robin impressed Gabrielle as a strong, serious person who wore a look of determination that she liked.

After answering their questions, Robin shepherded her group of four to her vehicle to deliver each group of two to the blocks where they were to work today. Upon leaving them, she promised to fetch them for lunch before transporting them to other neighborhoods.

* * *

Holding their clipboards, Rick and Gabrielle gazed down Magnolia Street. The lone non-blacks in an all-black neighborhood, they remarked how they felt their skin color in a way they never had before. Everywhere they looked, they saw black faces observing them from porches and yards and out of windows, faces mirroring curiosity, caution, fear.

"I think I know now how James must have felt, that student from Kenya. Do you remember him?" she asked.

"Yeah," he said, shaking his head.

"I feel really weird right now," she continued, "kinda exposed, vulnerable I guess…more different than I've ever felt. Here we're the minority."

"Yes, but Gabrielle, I suspect you're feeling more vulnerable since being attacked and marked by that bigot. Does it hurt very much?"

She nodded. "I try not to think about it."

"Has anyone checked it this morning to make sure it's not infected or needing stitches?"

"Edith did last night after one of the people at headquarters treated it, then she looked at it again this morning. She said it probably was too late to stitch it, so she put on a special ointment and these little cross-bandages to keep the cut closed. Does it look very bad?"

"I wouldn't worry about it," he replied. "Anyone would know you've been injured is all. Well, guess we better get to it. We've only got three hours till our next assignment."

They turned and approached a modest wooden house, the first on their list. A black man casually dressed and, Gabrielle guessed, in his thirties, sat reading a newspaper on his porch stairs. He glanced up as they approached.

"Good morning sir," Rick said.

No reply.

"Uh, good morning," Rick tried again. "We're from Delta Ministry, COFO, and SNCC. We're here as part of a survey…"

"We just need a few minutes of your time sir," Gabrielle chimed in. "Would that be okay?"

The Foothills

The man just stared at them. He seemed to want to assess them as harmless, this dark-haired white guy and this tall, eager, unusual-looking young woman with a bandaged face. They kept calling him sir in their Northern accents.

"Where're y'all from?" the man finally spoke.

"Uh, Delta Ministry…" Rick repeated.

"No," the man interrupted. "I mean where in the North y'all from?"

"Oh," Rick said, relieved to finally be starting a conversation with the man. "Oberlin, Ohio. At least that's where our college is. Actually I'm from Delaware. My name's Rick." He extended his hand to the cautious man who remained sitting on the steps as he shook Rick's hand less than enthusiastically.

"I'm Joe," he replied.

"And I'm Gabrielle," she interjected. "I'm from Oberlin too, but New York's where I call home," she said smiling and extending her hand to the man.

He hardly touched her hand in response as he observed her bandaged face.

"Uh, Mr. Green, er Joe I believe?" Rick said, looking down at the name on his clipboard." Joe nodded in response. "Could we take a few minutes of your time to ask you some questions?" he continued.

"What fer?" he asked, putting down the newspaper and folding his arms tightly across his chest.

They explained about the survey and how important it was to voter registration to learn what he could tell them.

"Well," he drawled, "I guess the sooner I answer your questions, the sooner y'all will leave."

They gulped. This was not the reception they'd hoped for.

Then the man laughed. "Aw shucks, you two sure are wound tight! Bwah-ha-ha!"

Relieved, they laughed too.

As they chatted, Joe told them he was a brakeman for the B&O Railroad. As such, he said, he had traveled a lot and hoped to move north with his family when he had the money. He was born and raised in Hattiesburg, he said. "I love my family, but I hate this damn town," he continued, spitting into a nearby bush, "...'specially since we niggers been gettin' uppity." He laughed. "I travel and see how it is up north. Then I come back here and can't drink at white folks' fountains, gotta eat separate from white folk, ride in the back of buses. Ain't right!" he smacked his fist into his other hand.

"No, it's not, Mr. Green," Gabrielle said, her eyes reflecting shared indignation, "it's not right!"

His statements caused the first incident of overt racism she had witnessed as a young child to flash through her mind—the day her friend, Betsy Boatman and her family took her to a frozen custard stand where the family hurled insults at a black woman walking by their car. Memory of the humiliation the woman endured saddened and angered Gabrielle again.

She thought that over the past year she had come to understand that this incident, coupled with her own awareness that she herself was different, had been the start of her political consciousness. From this grew her passionate desire to end discrimination, racism, and injustice in whatever forms they manifested themselves.

Returning to the present where Joe and Rick were engaged in conversation, she shook off the memory and experienced a sudden sense of clarity. While there was any breath left in her, she knew that she had to do her part to help right injustices to which she had become a witness.

As this realization gripped Gabrielle, she caught a glimpse of a white Ford with large dents along the side, racing toward them as it kicked up dust along the dirt road. Turning fully toward the car, she heard its tires screeching as the driver revved the engine and laid on the horn. Three white men yelled from the open car windows, "Nigga lovers! Bitch!"

A loud crack rang out as she saw to her horror, the barrel of a rifle protruding from the rear car window.

"Get down!" Gabrielle yelled as adrenaline rose in her and her mouth went dry. On her way down, she yanked Rick to the ground as Joe dove beside them. She could hear her heart pounding so loudly that she thought it would tear loose from her chest, fear paralyzing her body. Then came Joe's voice above them as he stood and watched the Ford disappear down the road.

"Damn crackers!" he cursed, his nostrils flaring in anger. "Y'all okay?"

"Yes," Gabrielle muttered, trying to move and calm her racing heart, terror still choking her.

"I think so," Rick said, unsteady as he got off the ground and pulled Gabrielle to her feet. "Should we call the police?"

Joe snorted. "You gotta be kiddin'! Them white cops would just harass us and never bother them crackers!"

"You think they'll come back?" Rick asked, looking toward the road.

"Probably...but not right away," he said, talking louder as he grew more angry. "They're cowards, them crackers. Probably come back sometime at night." He looked again at the two of them. Then he glanced up and saw a bullet hole in the porch column beside him.

"Damn!" he said, turning back toward Gabrielle and Rick. "Y'all may be afraid, but y'all can go home in a few days or weeks or whatever. We...we gotta stay here. We got no place to go. Some night maybe they'll come back and put a brick or bullet through my window—or burn a cross in my yard...or worse...just because I was settin' here on my porch talkin' with you white folk." He stopped, checking the street.

"They know who y'all are and why y'all are here. That puts me in league with you. Maybe you better go. It's not good them seein' y'all here with me. Better not chance them comin' back," he said as he rose, starting up the porch steps before pivoting toward them. "I wish you luck." His voice carried a momentary softness before rising in anger and resolve.

"You can tell SNCC and those Delta people I'll be at the polls. Y'all kin bet on it! I understand what you're doin' here, you see, and you can bet I won't be kept from showin' up to vote. No way! Now get goin' and watch yourselves." Giving them one last look, he opened the front door and disappeared into the house.

As Rick and Gabrielle watched Joe leave, she knew they should get out of there. But her whole body felt as if it were made of concrete. They just stood speechless for what seemed an eternity. Suddenly Gabrielle didn't know what they were doing here. They were supposed to help make things better, but they just had put Joe and his family in harm's way. She felt stupid—and guilty. And at that moment, Gabrielle just wanted to go home.

* * *

"Why didn't anybody warn us?" Gabrielle grilled Robin when she picked them up for lunch. "How could you let us put that family at risk? Why didn't you tell us to go inside, stay out of sight?" Gabrielle had her fight back now.

"And what difference would that have made?" Robin flashed at Gabrielle. "You think that just 'cause you're inside means they don't know you're there? You really think you can sneak around in an atmosphere like this and not have your every move tracked?"

"How can you be so sure?" Gabrielle snapped.

"Because I've been here for a year, and I know how these bigots work. These people are deadly serious, and they hate our guts, every Negro and every white joining up with them," Robin retorted.

"So what good do we do when we put these people in danger like this? What's the point?" she shot back.

"Look Gabrielle," Robin said, leveling her voice as she acknowledged Gabrielle's genuine concern, "I know how you feel..."

Gabrielle gave her a look of disgust.

Robin stopped in mid-sentence, then continued. "No, I *do* know how you feel. I went through the same thing when I first arrived. I couldn't see how I could ever do anything useful. It was like when you'd do good in one way, you'd wind up doing harm in another. I almost turned around and went home."

"So why didn't you?" Gabrielle persisted.

"Because I finally realized that's all part of getting involved in a revolution. That's what this is, you know. A revolution. Revolutions aren't pretty. People get hurt, often the ones you're most trying to help. But most people understand the risks. They know they might get hurt. But when you've suffered humiliation as long as these people have and you finally see some hope, you pick yourself up and do what needs doing. It gets very simple. And sometimes what's simple can be brutal."

As Robin finished speaking, her shoulders slumped. Seeing now how this place and these events weighed on Robin, Gabrielle was sorry she had been so belligerent with her. But she just couldn't help it. Deeply troubled by the possibility of harming the people she came here to work beside, she had a fierce need to understand what she had stumbled into. Gabrielle had never been able to tolerate not understanding something. She would probe and prod until she grasped what she needed to know. And so it was now.

4
The Lord's Day

"Can you believe our time here is half over? This week sure flew by," Gabrielle said to Rick at the Browns' breakfast table.

But before Rick could respond, Boo turned to Gabrielle, "You want your bacon?"

Gabrielle started, having been concentrating on Rick and their conversation. "Oh sure Boo, go ahead and take it. I'm full anyway."

Just then Edith walked back into the room after putting Rosie down for a nap. She returned just in time to see Boo balancing Gabrielle's bacon on his fork as he moved it from her plate to his.

"Boo!" Edith shouted. "Have you no manners at all boy? What have I told you? If I told you once, I told you a hundred times. You don't bug folk for their food! Now put that back boy!"

"Oh no," Gabrielle said defending him. "Really, I don't mind. I was done and it was just going to waste."

"Boo you put that back!" Edith persisted. "I'm not havin' one of my own acting so unmannerly. And this being the Lord's day too!" Edith glared at him.

Quickly returning the coveted bacon, he lowered his head.

"If it weren't the Lord's day, I'd send you to your room boy!" With that, Edith left to check on Rosie before attending to Gabrielle's cheek with fresh bandages. "It's still red around the cut, but it's healing. Probably will scar."

Gabrielle shook her head. "Thanks for the bandaging."

An hour later all nine of them—the Browns, Gabrielle, and Rick—had piled into Mike's pickup truck and the car of their friends next door. The Browns and their neighbors all wore their Sunday best. This included Edith's yellow straw hat with a bright blue silk cornflower on it.

Rick and Gabrielle rode with the neighbors behind the Browns' truck. They laughed watching the kids bounce around in the bed of the truck as it negotiated the potholes in one of the many dirt roads in the Negro part of town. They waved at the kids, and the kids waved back. Then the two boys got into a fistfight, and Mike stopped the truck, got out, and separated them.

"If I have to come back here again," they could hear Mike shout, "y'all will be grounded for a week! You'll be two sorry boys. Now try to remember this is the Lord's day. Show some respect!"

The boys hung their heads and were quiet the rest of the way.

In a few minutes they pulled up in front of a small white church. Paint was fading from the clapboards, but bright red hibiscus flowers bloomed on a dozen or more bushes planted along the front of the church and beside the sign declaring this to be "The Saving Grace Baptist Church of Hattiesburg."

Gabrielle and Rick were the only lighter-skinned people amid scores of blacks in colorful clothing and women in spectacular bonnets. Together the parishioners surged through the double doors into the nave with its white walls, red fabric-covered seat cushions, and deep-purple curtains framing tall windows. A small but lovely stained-glass window loomed high above the altar. It bore a picture of Jesus, pale as he hung dying on the cross. A white dove, with gold rays radiating from it, hovered above Christ's head. He had a look both of such agony and resignation, such sacrifice, that Gabrielle thought it must be the most beautiful rendering of Jesus she ever saw.

The sight of the stained glass window took Gabrielle back to the church where she grew up, the Maple Avenue Methodist Church on Long Island. Although this Hattiesburg church was very different from hers back home, just being in a house of worship again comforted and excited her. And while this one had no organ, it had a piano, on which a man was playing "Onward Christian Soldiers." She smiled, as she just was thinking about her dad performing that hymn for her old Sunday school. *And the hymn seems so fitting right now*, she thought.

The minister entered the sanctuary as the hymn trailed off. He was a big man, whom Gabrielle guessed to be in his mid-thirties. He wore flowing purple-and-white robes and carried a well-worn, white leather-covered Bible. Everyone stood as the choir and congregation let loose with "Rock-a My Soul in the Bosom of Abraham."

The sound that rose from the congregation on that warm, early spring morning in Mississippi lifted Gabrielle's spirits so high, she didn't ever want to come down. The whole sanctuary swayed with voices in song, moving bodies, waving arms and hands, joyful faces. She had never witnessed church music sung this way. Seeing so much passion and conviction in the congregation's musical expression, she felt nothing but awe and reverence. The worshipers continued through one more hymn before Reverend Jonas's large, low voice brought the fold to silence.

"This is the Looord's day!" he called.

"Yessir the Loord's day...," people responded. "Lord have mercy!"

"And what do we say to the Lord?"

"Thank you Lord, thank you!"

"We thank the Lord this morning for his children from Ohio..."

"Yes Lord..."

Gabrielle blushed, glancing briefly at Rick who was staring at his knees.

"Who came here to be with us in this time of trouble…"

"Trouble Lord, trouble…"

"To bear witness…"

"Yes Lord…"

"To the birthing of our freeeedom…"

"Freeeeedom Lord!"

"And the release that comes with justice…"

"Justice!"

"For all God's children…"

"All!"

"We thank them, Lord…"

"Thank them!"

"For their courage…"

"Courage…"

"Because we need their friendship…"

"Yes Lord!"

"Their presence and help in this terrible time!"

"Need Lord…terrible!"

"Our Negro sisters and brothers have been taken down, taken down by the oppressive hand of prejudice and injustice…"

"Lord Lord…"

"Made to feel small and unworthy of what the Constitution of the United States of America says are our rights…"

"Our rights, yes Lord!"

"But we will not be kept dooown!"

"No Lord no!"

"We will not be made less!"

"No Lord no!"

"Because we are *all* God's children, and we have a job to do!"

"Yes Lord!"

"This time when we go to the polls, more of us Negroes will stand in line to vote than at any time in our history. Can I hear an Amen, brothers and sisters?

"Amen Brother, Amen!"

Gabrielle felt the fervor in the room rise. She experienced it herself, the ardor for freedom, the call to a sacred battle. Rick looked at her, smiled, and took her hand. She thought they were comrades now. And they were in league with every person in the room—even some of the older members of the congregation who looked uncomfortable with the call to equality. Perhaps they feared for the safety of their children and grandchildren, she thought. Perhaps they had seen their people's struggles beaten down too many times. She believed that not everyone there embraced the cause with the same passion as Reverend Jonas, but it would be hard to know it by the chanting going up throughout the sanctuary on that Sunday in early April.

5
Shantytown

Monday was a slap in the face after the bright light of the Lord's day.

The pair was dropped off in the poorest neighborhood they had seen since they arrived in Hattiesburg. They smelled it before they saw it. It reeked of raw sewage and rotting garbage. They were in a shantytown of one-room tarpaper shacks with no electricity or running water, not even glass to cover the windows.

"My God, Rick," she whispered as she stared at the worst poverty she had witnessed in her young life. "My God…"

Too taken aback to respond, he just shook his head in disbelief.

A gaunt Negro woman in a torn dress and mismatched shoes with no ties, was bent over a wooden washtub in the dirt yard in front of a shack. Two skinny young children in tattered clothes ran to their mother and clung to her legs as Gabrielle and Rick approached.

"Ma'am…ma'am…," Gabrielle said gently as she approached them.

The woman looked slowly from her children toward Gabrielle and Rick and started when she saw they weren't black. A look of horror transformed the woman's face as she took her hands from the washtub and placed them on her children, pulling them protectively behind her.

"Ma'am," Gabrielle spoke even more softly now, "ma'am, we just want to talk to you for a minute."

Not responding, the woman just kept surveying Gabrielle with that same terrified stare.

"We're from Delta Ministry, COFO, and SNCC, ma'am. We just want to ask you a few questions. It would help people a great deal…" Gabrielle's voice trailed off as the woman backed away. The mother then folded the skirt of her dress around her runny-nosed barefoot children, seemingly to shield them from the threat she believed the strangers posed.

"Ma'am," Rick echoed Gabrielle, "ma'am please…"

But the woman raised her hand now, as if to ward off a blow. Backing up the steps to her shack, she brushed her children up and in through the doorway, which she shut without so much as a word.

They stared at the closed door, then at each other. "Sweet Jesus," was all Gabrielle could say.

6
The Goodbye

At the end of their second week, they said their goodbyes. Hugging Bessie, Boo, and Tater, she kissed baby Rosie. Johnny considered himself too old for that "sissy stuff," so she and Rick just shook his hand. They hugged Edith too and took Mike's hand, which he offered when Gabrielle was trying to decide if he would accept a hug.

"Now y'all take the rest of this sweet potato pie with you," Edith said as she wrapped the remaining pie in aluminum foil for their bus ride home.

"Edith, you're too good to us," Rick exclaimed.

"I'll say," Gabrielle chimed in. "That has to be the best pie I ever ate!"

"Aw go on now," Edith demurred, lowering her gaze.

"Honest Edith," she said, "I don't know how you make such great pies."

Rick and Gabrielle walked out onto the porch where Tom stood waiting. He took their bags and placed them in the back of the old sedan he was driving to the civil rights office. There the bus would take them and their fellow volunteers' home. Gabrielle watched through the car's rear window as Johnny, Mike, and Edith who was holding Rosie, stood on the porch and waved. Yelling as they ran along the dirt road behind Tom's Chevy, Bessie, Boo, and Tater followed until the car rounded the corner.

* * *

The bus ride back to Ohio was long. There were no more incidents of angry whites surrounding the bus, just the seemingly endless road and a lot of time to think. On the way to Mississippi two weeks earlier, Gabrielle remembered how the students had begun the trip exuberant, talkative, fearful, uncertain, but full of expectation and sense of purpose. Going home now, she observed that they were more thoughtful in their conversations and frequently quiet.

This experience was far different from the northern freedom marches in which Gabrielle and her fellow students had participated. With those, they marched from conviction, but without any direct experience of what they were fighting for and with a degree of safety they were stripped of in the South. There were hecklers on those northern marches and the occasional threat, but nothing like what they experienced in the Deep South.

Hattiesburg was an education beyond her imagining. Suddenly all those news reports, those faces on television and in the papers, took on a stark reality from which she couldn't turn away. It no longer was some nameless person barred from lunch counters, threatened, or disallowed from polling sites. It was Mike and Edith, Tom, Joe the brakeman, Reverend Jonas, the frightened woman in the shantytown. And someday, if things didn't change, it would be Bessie, Boo, Tater, Johnny, and Rosie as well. Sam had been right about that, she thought.

Never had Gabrielle seen the kind of poverty that they witnessed over the weeks on their rounds of Hattiesburg's black neighborhoods. Most of the people she met possessed little, and some literally had nothing. Yet many kept their hopes alive, nurtured their faith, and practiced kindness and charity toward one another. Gabrielle felt reverence when she thought of the people she had come to know.

If it doesn't destroy you, adversity can make you strong, she acknowledged. *Hopefully it also will deepen your capacity for humanity along the way.*

Gazing across the aisle at Rick, she smiled as she watched him sleep while cradling the remains of Edith's sweet potato pie. What a good friend he has become, she thought. At another time, in other circumstances, she could almost imagine something more between Rick and herself. If Sam were not in the picture, perhaps she could love him in another way. But Sam was present and very much on her mind as their bus moved closer to Oberlin.

As the students' bus passed the Mississippi border and entered western Tennessee, Gabrielle watched the last of the Mississippi countryside fade from view. With its passing, she felt the danger to herself and the others lessen. It wasn't that the more northern states didn't have their share of prejudice, discrimination, and racial strife—they surely did. But it generally seemed less overt.

Her mind rushed back to the time when she herself had felt the sting of injustice, discrimination, and humiliation at the hands of a first-grade teacher when she was just a kindergartener. Of course she knew she was too young at the time to associate Miss Leaper's victimization of her with something like ethnic or racial prejudice. But the teacher's actions had left scars, scars not unlike the physical one she now bore. These scars would continue to be reminders of the horrors of bigotry. Beyond what she witnessed and endured, she could hardly imagine what marks racial hatred would leave on Hattiesburg's black children, but undoubtedly they would linger and prove more painful.

She believed that the episode with Miss Leaper and then with the Boatmans when she was ten, followed by the social dismissal of her and the name calling in junior high and high school, helped her to understand something of what it was to be victimized by people in power and to have no good way to fight back. She saw clearly that these occurrences had a profound impact upon her. And after Hattiesburg, she knew she never would see the world quite the same way again.

Gabrielle's Hattiesburg experiences shook her to her very core. They had brought home to her on a piercingly raw level, the true terror of segregation. And it sharpened her commitment to civil rights. At nineteen, Gabrielle knew that she had to commit to work in any way she could for justice and equality for all people. Tears filled her eyes as she owned the realization that her life would be diminished if she didn't fight for what was right when she encountered injustices or hard choices along her life's path.

In time she fell into a restless sleep. She didn't awaken until the bus crossed the Ohio River, passing from Kentucky into Ohio. They were officially in the North. They were almost home.

7
Return to Oberlin

Dropping off the civil rights workers at their respective places, the bus finally entered Oberlin. She felt the safety of the trees and tidy homes, the familiarity of the landscape, the warmth of the sunshine streaming through the bus windows.

"Well Gabrielle, we're home," Rick said from across the aisle.

She smiled at Rick, who still hugged the last of Edith's sweet potato pie. Turning to gaze out the window, she watched as the bus came to a stop beside the campus chapel. Anxiously looking for Sam, she saw no one waiting. *Of course, how would anyone know we're back?* she thought. Just the same, she couldn't help feeling disappointed. She longed to see him. There was so much she wanted to tell him.

"Gabrielle!" Sam's voice sounded cheerful over the phone.
"Oh Sam," Gabrielle exclaimed.
"I heard you were back. So how was it?"
"I hardly know where to begin. Where are you?"
"I'm over at the Student Union doing a little rabble-rousing," he said.
"I'm not surprised."
"So when can you get over here?"

She was exhausted, but anxious to see him. "Why don't you walk over toward my dorm—and I'll walk toward you. I think I'd rather move around a bit. I've been sitting so long in that bus."

"Okay, I'm on my way."

She checked herself briefly in the mirror. Her bandaged cheek was an eyesore, but it was what it was, she told herself. After smoothing her hair, she ran down the stairs and out the dormitory door. It was a perfect early spring day, the grass greening, foliage beginning to show on trees and bushes, a gentle breeze in the air. But Gabrielle barely noticed all this new life as she walked toward Sam.

Taking note of his quick, distinctive walk, she knew it was Sam even before she saw him clearly. She had to restrain herself from running to meet him. And then, there he was, his blue eyes sparkling beneath his tussled blond curls.

"So how's my girl?" Sam asked, his arms about to enfold her as he pulled back to get a good look at her. "Geesh, what happened to your face?"

"It's part of a long story," she sighed.

"Well you're still one beautiful woman Gabrielle."

"Exhausted you mean," she managed, trying to ignore his assessment of her while melting under his gaze. She watched his eyes before turning her head so he wouldn't see how much she wanted him.

"Should we find a place to sit?" he asked.

"No," she responded. "Let's walk."

Putting his arm around her shoulders, he steered her from the main path and back toward a cluster of trees.

The Foothills

"How have you been?" she asked.

"Great. I've been busy helping organize another group to go to Mississippi. I think we'll have eight for the next bus south."

"Wow. That has to be a record."

"It's been a lot of work."

"Are they all Oberlin students?"

"Six of our students and two from town."

"That's good. You're getting more townspeople involved then."

"Yeah. That's been a struggle too, but it's good. So tell me about Hattiesburg—and your bandaged face."

Taking a deep breath, she told him the story of the mob rocking her bus and how she was attacked. He looked at her with concern. "It's a miracle it wasn't worse," he said.

"Yes," she replied, "but I couldn't have begun to imagine what Hattiesburg really was like," she said. He was silent, waiting for her as she gathered her thoughts. "The poverty," she continued, "the fear, the warmth of the family I stayed with, the commitment to civil rights. It was so intense, emotional. I'm not sure I'm really all here yet...."

"I know what you mean," he said, drawing her closer.

"I don't think I ever experienced being really unsafe before," she said. "It made me realize what a sheltered and privileged life I lead. We had to be vigilant every minute, always aware of what was around us. It made me think how harsh the reality of life is there and that maybe I've been living in a dream. I kept asking myself how this all came to be. Is this really America? The experience was almost surreal, like I was on a knife edge between two different realities...."

"Yes," he said.

"And not being black. I never felt so damned white."

He laughed. "I know what you mean."

"Here we were, in an all-Negro community...and for the first time, we were the minority. I felt so conspicuous, vulnerable." He looked squarely at her now. "I just wanted to blend in, but I couldn't. My lighter skin became a...a... embarrassment," she said, searching for words. "I just wanted people to stop looking at me, especially when someone would stare at me and I'd see nothing in their eyes but fear. It was awful," her voice drifted. "How did we become so different, so far apart? Aren't we all just people after all? People trying to survive? People having families, people working, wanting more for their children…people angry, loving?"

He pulled her around to face him. Holding her firmly by the waist with one arm, he brought her face to his with his other hand, giving her a long passionate kiss. When their lips parted, her eyes were closed. Tears escaped and trickled onto her temples, which had the little veins he once confessed to love that were just below the surface of her olive skin.

Opening her eyes, she stumbled as her feelings cried for release. All the joy and sadness, all the revelations of the past weeks rushed to this moment where she acknowledged so much love—for Sam, for the people she had left behind in Mississippi, for the confusing, maddening mill of humanity. Tears streamed down her face as she sobbed.

Sam was at a loss. He put his arms around her, but his embrace was less passionate. It was a dutiful embrace almost, and she stiffened as she pulled away.

"I…I don't know what's come over me," she said between sobs as she glanced away from him. "I…I…I guess I'm just tired… It's been a long, hard couple of weeks."

"Maybe I should take you back to the dorm, give you a chance to rest," he said.

She thought he looked relieved that she seemed to be calming down. "Yes, that would be good," she said, gaining control of herself.

She hadn't seen Sam for a couple of days. Her encounter with him left her even more confused about the nature of their relationship. His passion at their last meeting, followed by his lack of ability to deal with the intensity of her emotions, baffled her. She decided she was too emotionally exhausted to think about it anymore. As she concluded this, Shirley, a student on Gabrielle's dorm floor, knocked on her door before poking her head in.

"You've got a call from a guy."

The Foothills

"Did he say who he was?"

"Nope."

Gabrielle slipped on shoes and walked to the phone in the hall.

"Hey Gabrielle."

"Is this Rick?" she responded, brightening.

"It sure is. I haven't seen you since we got back. How are you doing anyway?"

"Fine...fine...not really," she confessed.

"You want to get together?"

"That'd be nice," she said.

"I'll come get you. How about an hour?"

"Perfect."

"Just tell me, did you see the doctor about your cut?"

"I did. He confirmed it was long past time for stitching and put on new ointment and bandages. He said to expect a scar."

"Well, I'm glad it wasn't infected."

They sat under an old hickory tree in a secluded part of campus and talked nonstop for nearly four hours. Missing lunch and the sounds of hickory leaves rustling above them, they only were mindful of the intensity of their shared weeks in Mississippi. Rick was wrestling with many of same thoughts and emotions that haunted Gabrielle. It was cathartic for them to open up to each other. She found him easy to converse with and felt none of the tension and confusion she felt every time she was with Sam. Everything between Rick and her seemed straightforward. Being with him was so blessedly simple.

"Did you ever finish that sweet potato pie?" she asked, grinning.

"You know, I ate all but a tiny sliver. I just couldn't bear to see it gone. It's sitting on my desk like a shrine to pie-hood," he laughed.

She loved his laughter. It started somewhere in his toes and rose through his whole body before spilling out his impish mouth. She couldn't resist it, joining in until their sides ached as they lay on the ground holding their stomachs, washing away tension from the past weeks.

"Thank God for you," she said, sitting up and smiling at her dark-haired friend.

"Well, I do what I can." He smiled. Standing, he reached down for her, pulling her easily to her feet. He hesitated, studying her for a minute, then looked away. Sensing his reticence to disturb the exuberance of the moment, she saw something different in his gaze and in his turning. She knew that Rick was well aware of her love for Sam, having seen them together on more than one occasion and from what she had revealed about him during their bus ride back to Oberlin. It gave her pause, wondering what he was feeling.

"Well ol' girl," he said, lightening up again, "classes are starting, and I have work to do."

"Me too," she said, brushing aside her thoughts, her spirits lighter now. "Rick," she said, becoming serious for a moment, "thank you. Thank you for…everything."

He seemed to struggle to stay breezy. "Sure ol' girl."

As she turned toward the dorm, she thought about his calling her "ol' girl." She couldn't figure out why he tagged her with that, but she kind of liked it. It had the ring of intimacy without anything serious attached to it. She decided it was a badge of their friendship, which she genuinely was coming to cherish.

It was odd, she thought, that they could become so close in such a short time. But then she noted that it seemed akin to what she had read about soldiers on the battlefield who formed a bond that was said to be like no other. Frequently they became closer than family or lifelong friends. In a way, she thought, they *had* gone to war together, the war for the heart and conscience of a people, of a nation.

8
Last Term, Equivocation, and Dr. Martin Luther King, Jr.

At the end of her sophomore year, Gabrielle was busy with a full load of classes, a part-time campus job in the cafeteria, and volunteer work at the new tutoring center on the edge of campus.

In addition she had taken up sketching, inspired by a beginning drawing class she was taking. Unexpectedly she found a budding talent she didn't know she possessed. Every chance she got, she drew. Soon she was bringing to life her memories of Hattiesburg—the people, the houses, the streets, the church, the stunning hats and faces of the church women.

Pouring her feelings about her Hattiesburg experience into her sketches, she created pictures that rendered her passion and compassion in ways that her words couldn't. A fellow student in her art class, Hermine, took note of this and stopped Gabrielle in the hall one day. "I love the emotion you communicate through your sketches. What was your inspiration for them?"

After telling her briefly about her weeks in Hattiesburg and how it affected her, Gabrielle said, "I guess you could say that drawing has given me an outlet for processing what I lived through in Mississippi."

"Your drawings are so unusual. You show your skills as an artist while conveying emotion," Hermine noted. "Are you an art major?"

She paused in thought. "It's interesting that you ask me that, as I've been considering it."

"Well I hope you do. What you create inspires me to find ways to convey more feeling in my own artwork."

"I appreciate your saying this, Hermine. Thank you," she responded as they parted to go to their next classes.

While her art began to flourish, she found her relationship with Sam growing more frustrating. This saddened her, because her bonds with both Sam and Rick played important roles in growing her political awareness and her desire to express it. She saw both of them frequently. But Sam frustrated her. He could be loving, then cold, unreachable even, leaving her to question why she still cared so much for him.

While her love for Sam stagnated, her friendship with Rick deepened. They became almost inseparable. They studied, hung out on campus, and went together to the tutoring center on the edge of campus that Rick had helped establish. The center worked to assist grammar school kids from town with their reading and math skills. It was an extension of their commitment to civil rights that went beyond demonstration and voter registration and now included education and one-on-one work with underprivileged children falling behind at school.

Gabrielle found tutoring difficult. She wasn't a born teacher, and she struggled along with her literacy student Jeremy. She found it hard to not get emotionally involved in this eight-year-old black boy's challenges. He barely read at a first-grade level, had been held back twice in school, and was older than his classmates by two years.

While she noted that he was making progress, she wished she had more months before she returned home for the summer. Furthermore she had signed up for the Junior-Year-Abroad Program. This meant she wouldn't return to Oberlin until her senior year. Jeremy needed more time, and her departure was imminent.

"I worry about what's going to happen to him when I leave," she told Rick as he drove them back to campus after picking up books downtown. "I may not be much of a teacher, but he *is* starting to improve. There just aren't enough volunteers. If Jeremy isn't able to read to at least an acceptable level before school starts this fall, I don't know what will happen to him. He's already lost two years. What's to become of a poor child who keeps getting left back and who can hardly read?"

Rick was silent as he drove. Then he said, "I'll tell you what. I've been thinking that I might not go back east this summer or even return to Mississippi as I've been considering. I've gotten so involved in the tutoring center here, and I'm seeing some real progress with these kids. I don't need to go home and earn money

The Foothills

this summer like you do. I'd like to stay here and work full time at the center over the summer. If so, I can take Jeremy on if you want, and assuming he wants me to."

It was Gabrielle's turn to be silent. Then she said, "I hardly know what to say. Lucky Jeremy. Of course he'll want you to. You're a born teacher. With your help Jeremy will have a chance."

"Well I can try anyway."

"Thank you Rick. I know how much you already have on your plate right now, and I know how much kids like Jeremy need our help. You're really something." She leaned across the stick shift of his VW Beetle and kissed him on the cheek. Blushing, he turned his head, looked at her, and smiled broadly beneath his dark mustache.

"So when are you leaving?" he asked, changing the subject. He shifted into overdrive. The motor hummed.

"In two weeks. The term's going by so quickly."

"And then you're off to Denmark in the fall?"

"That's the plan. But it's starting to feel like a selfish thing to do."

"What do you mean?" A car honked. Rick's attention had pivoted from driving to what Gabrielle was saying. He swerved into the next lane. "Damn!" He lifted his foot from the accelerator and downshifted.

"Sorry. My fault," she said.

They sat in silence for a couple of minutes.

"Rick, look at the work we've been doing. I mean there's so much more to do."

"Well of course there is. But there are others who can help," he said. He increased his speed and shifted back into overdrive. "We need to get more people involved. And you should go to Denmark like you planned, see the world a little."

"It feels selfish."

"It'll give you another perspective Gabrielle, and that's always good. It will educate you in ways you can't begin to imagine. You won't get that staying at Oberlin. It's one of the best experiences you can have in your life, living in another culture among people who have a different way of looking at things than Americans do."

"Then why aren't *you* going abroad next year?"

"Because I've already traveled and lived overseas, and I'll travel more later. Where I need to be right now is here."

She looked hard at him. "How can you be so sure?"

"I just am."

"Why isn't this where I should be too?"

"If you have to ask that question Gabrielle, then this isn't where you need to be." He accelerated.

* * *

It was June 1965. Sam was graduating, and Gabrielle opted to stay on after the end of classes to attend the ceremonies. But what most prompted her to delay her departure was the announcement that Dr. Martin Luther King, Jr., had accepted Oberlin's invitation to speak at graduation. She couldn't believe that she actually would see and hear this icon of the Civil Rights Movement.

Rick and Gabrielle arrived early to graduation so they could get as close to the front as possible. By the time the ceremony began, the site, which had to be moved outdoors to accommodate the expected crowd, was packed with people and news media. At the appointed time Oberlin's president, wearing his ceremonial academic robe, hood, and tasseled tam, rose and walked to the microphone. Acknowledging that Dr. King needed no introduction, he said he wanted all in attendance to know more about this man he revered.

"Dr. King is a man apart," he began. "Born in 1929 to a long line of Baptist ministers, he grew up in Jim Crow Atlanta. In 1944, when he was just fifteen years old, he became a student at Morehouse College, later graduating with a sociology degree and earning a divinity degree from Crozer Theological Seminary.

"In 1955 he achieved a PhD in systematic theology from Boston University, the same year he led the Montgomery Bus Boycott. Two years later he helped found the Southern Christian

The Foothills

Leadership Conference and served as its first president. That very year, in front of the Lincoln Memorial, he delivered his first national address on voting rights before tens of thousands of people." The president paused, looking intently at the crowd that made not a sound.

"A year after this speech, at a signing in Harlem for his new book, *Stride Toward Freedom*, a woman walked up to him. Quoted as saying, 'I've been looking for you for five years,' she drove a seven-inch letter opener into his chest, barely missing his aorta." Gasps rose from the audience.

"Rushed to the hospital, his surgeons later told him that had he sneezed, his aorta would have been punctured and he would have died. While in the hospital, Dr. King issued a statement affirming his nonviolent beliefs and that he felt no ill will toward his perpetrator.

"He's been imprisoned dozens of times for civil disobedience and trumped-up charges and helped organize nonviolent protests, including the 1963 March on Washington where he gave his 'I Have a Dream' speech.

"Last year he was internationally honored with the Nobel Peace Prize for combatting racial inequality through nonviolence. Earlier this year he helped organize the Selma to Montgomery marches that, I'm proud to say, some of you in attendance joined. I could go on and on about this extraordinary man. I'll conclude by saying that it's my great honor to present to you Dr. Martin... Luther... King...Jr."

The crowd rose with deafening applause as Dr. King took the speaker's platform. Local police accompanied and stayed with him for protection. As Dr. King turned to shake the president's hand, Gabrielle noted that while this giant of a man was not tall, he carried himself with a presence that dwarfed the taller people around him. As he turned toward the audience, the applause swelled and didn't subside until he gestured gently for the crowd to come to silence. As he started to speak, Gabrielle's heart raced with expectation.

From his first word, she was spellbound. The resonance of his voice, the clarity, the brilliance of the way he expressed his thoughts, the intensity of his convictions, all of these riveted her. He described the social revolution that gripped the nation, working to sweep away the old order of slavery and racial segregation with a vision for freedom and human dignity. We can no longer live in isolation, he said—what affects one, affects us all. We must think in terms of brotherhood, not just nationally, but globally.

"We must all learn to live together as brothers—or we will all perish together as fools," he said. "…All mankind is tied together, all life is interrelated, and we are all caught in an inescapable network of mutuality, tied in a single garment of destiny. Whatever affects one directly, affects all indirectly. … I can never be what I ought to be until you are what you ought to be. …This is the interrelated structure of reality."

Gabrielle hung on every powerful, incisive word. Dr. King went on to acknowledge that while changes in our nation's laws have created progress in breaking down legal barriers to segregation, social and economic reform have a long way to go. "Let nobody give you the impression that only time will solve the problem. …Somewhere we must come to see that human progress never rolls in on wheels of inevitability. It comes through the tireless efforts and the persistent work of dedicated individuals. …In the final analysis, racial injustice must be uprooted from American society because it is morally wrong."

He spoke with passion about the importance of change through nonviolence. "I am convinced that violence ends up creating many more social problems than it solves. …Unborn generations will be the recipients of a long and desolate night of bitterness. …It is possible to stand up against an unjust system with all your might, with all of your body, with all of your soul, and yet not stoop to hatred and violence…realizing that this is the approach that can bring about that better day of racial justice for everyone."

Challenging graduates, he concluded: "Let us stand up. Let us be a concerned generation. Let us remain awake through a great revolution. And we will speed up that great day when the American Dream will be a reality."

The Foothills

When he finished, the audience erupted first in total silence, then in thundering applause. Rick grabbed Gabrielle's hand as both wiped tears from their eyes. Dr. King was awarded an honorary degree of humane letters by Oberlin College, and the graduates received their diplomas. But of greatest significance to Gabrielle was how Dr. King had woven a spell that left the call to his challenge ringing in their ears.

His presence rendered her speechless and detached from her intent to find Sam, though he was leaving in the morning. She hardly heard him when he promised to call or write when he arrived in Greenwich Village for the summer. They would get together when she was home on Long Island, he said as she left to find Rick again. It was not Sam, but rather Dr. King's presence and the beauty and passion of his words that filled her in ways she couldn't have anticipated.

When she found Rick, now at the back of the crowd that lingered, she observed him pensively. "Never before have I heard such an orator," she said. "He speaks to more than the head or even the heart. He speaks to our very souls. Did you feel it?"

"Yes."

"He touched me in ways I couldn't have imagined. What he said was a call to battle to right what has gone terribly wrong— and to do it wholeheartedly with malice toward none. It's not an easy calling, but a right one. Violence does only beget violence, as hatred begets hate. It's our time to change this, isn't it?"

"I believe it *is*. It will take sacrifice."

"Yes. This is a truth I believe we have to follow, Rick. How can I go abroad after hearing what Dr. King described today?"

Rick studied her. "Let's walk a little," he said, taking her arm as they turned in silence before speaking again. "Remember that Dr. King also cautioned that change is a long process," he said finally. "You only will be abroad nine or ten months Gabrielle. So much will need to be done after that, and you'll find all kinds of ways to play a role. This is work that will take decades.

"You might remember Dr. King's words when he said that our responsibility as citizens of this nation is to a brotherhood not only with our fellow citizens, but also with those of all the world's nations. He shared how visiting India affected him and how it affirmed to him the power and importance of nonviolence. I too strongly believe that we have a responsibility to learn to be citizens of the world. Living in another country for an extended period of time educates us in ways we can't experience when we remain at home."

He stopped, released her arm as he turned toward her, then stared deeply into her eyes. "You will be of more help to the Movement—or the revolution as Dr. King calls it—if you educate yourself about a whole host of differences from those you've encountered in America. You can't imagine how this will change your ability to affect change. Don't equivocate anymore Gabrielle. You've dreamed of going abroad for a very long time. You had that dream for a reason. Go and claim it. Go and learn things you'll never learn if you stay at home. And come back ready to take your commitment farther than you now can envision."

They walked for several more minutes in silence before Gabrielle stopped. Regarding him thoughtfully, she nodded her affirmation. Then she turned and hugged him.

"Thank you," she said.

* * *

She had one last tutoring session with Jeremy before she left campus for the summer. He did better with his reading than at any time during the months they had worked together.

"Jeremy, that's wonderful," she exclaimed. "I'm so proud of you." She reached over and gave him a big hug. He was a shy boy, and the embrace caught him by surprise.

"I have good news for you," she said immediately, wanting to get past the awkwardness she sensed he was feeling. "You know Rick who works with Michael?"

"Yes ma'am." He fidgeted in his chair, his dark brown eyes cast downward.

The Foothills

"He's agreed to keep reading with you this summer after I'm gone. He's a great guy and a wonderful teacher. Would you like that?"

Jeremy, who was small for an eight-year-old, shifted in his chair. He looked up at her briefly from under his long lashes and answered, "I like working with *you*, ma'am."

"But you know I have to leave for my summer job. I need to earn money so I can keep going to college."

"Yes ma'am." His face fell. He looked at his hands, folded in his lap.

She persevered, "You do want to continue to work on your reading, don't you?"

"Yes ma'am." His voice had grown smaller.

"I'm really sorry I can't be here after today, but you'll like Rick and you'll learn a lot from him. He's a special person—like *you* are."

He looked at the floor now, trying to hide his embarrassment.

"Would that be okay with you?"

He hesitated, "I...I guess so ma'am."

"That's good," she said, struggling to stay upbeat. Then she turned and picked up two books from the table beside her and placed them on her lap. They were *The Family Under the Bridge* and *The Little Engine That Could*.

"Jeremy," she said, laying one hand on the books and the other on his back between his shoulder blades. As she touched him, she thought how small and fragile he felt. "I would like you to take these," she continued, retrieving her hand and firmly gripping the books. "They're a present from me to you. I remember them from when I was about your age," she said smiling. "I hope you'll like learning to read them. They're great stories, and the books have beautiful pictures. They were mine when I was a kid. I had my mother send them. They're yours now."

She picked up the books and gave them to him. He put his hands over them, but he didn't know what to say. She turned to look at him very directly.

"You can do anything you set your mind to. I know it. Keep reading. When you can read well, you'll come to love it—and a whole world will open to you. Don't ever give up, no matter how hard it gets. Can you do that?"

He was quiet as he struggled with his thoughts. "I guess so ma'am."

"Good." Gabrielle gave him another hug. This time he put his hand lightly on her arm as she held him. "I will never forget you. And I'll write to you and look for you when I return. Goodbye for now Jeremy."

Not waiting for him to respond, she rose quickly and left the room. So he wouldn't see her cry, she raced out of the building as she struggled to hold back tears.

Rick followed, catching up to her. Without hesitation he drew her to him, embracing her gently, lovingly as she let herself go and wept.

In time she pulled back from him. "It will be a long time till I see you again," she said, drying her eyes.

"Yes," he responded.

"A year and a half."

"Yes."

"Promise you'll write to me, let me know how you're doing—and Jeremy."

He smiled. "And certainly Jeremy."

~IV~
LOVE THAT BINDS

Summer 1965 – New York City and Long Island

1

Living at home for the summer, Gabrielle was set to soon start her six-day-a-week waitressing job at the Jones Beach theater restaurant. With a little time on her hands and on a whim, she hopped the Long Island Railroad to New York City to surprise Sam at his Greenwich Village apartment.

It was a sultry June afternoon as she arrived perspiring and anxious at the door to Sam's building. She gazed at the return address on the envelope of the letter he had sent her. Holding his seductive words tightly in one hand, she brushed her long hair back from her face with the other. As she did this, she felt the scar on her cheek, no longer bandaged. It still was red and raw, speaking to her in ways she hadn't foreseen. A daily reminder to her of the civil rights war the nation was waging, it had become a testament to the promises she made to it.

Looking up at Sam's building, she could hardly wait to see him. She drew her hand across her brow and the top of her lip, wiping the sweat with her fingers. Drying them on her simple blue cotton dress, she then smoothed her hair. Suddenly she felt somewhat faint. Then she panicked. *I should have called,* she admonished herself. *What was I thinking?*

But she was here, and Sam was so close that she almost could feel him through the brick walls and the four stories that separated them. Drawing in her breath, she tried the door to the building. It was unexpectedly open. Grimacing at the odor of urine and grime, she hesitated in the lobby. As she recovered her composure, she started up the stone staircase. On the fourth floor, amid walls laden with graffiti, she found his apartment: 4f.

Raising her hand to knock, she froze in hesitation. Her heart pounded so loudly, she was afraid Sam would hear it before her hand ever hit the door. *Why am I so nervous?* she asked herself. *It's Sam after all, and he'll be so glad to see me.*

With that, she rapped three times. She waited. No answer. She knocked again. Then hearing him moving toward her, she saw his eye in the peephole before he unlocked the door. Her heart raged. Her lips parted in anticipation of him. The door opened partially. She gasped. Her heart nearly stopped. It wasn't Sam. It was an attractive woman, maybe twenty-five, in a short white terry robe. Her wet hair was partially wrapped in a towel. Her face was rosy as from the heat of a bath. Gabrielle hoped that she had the wrong address. Looking down at the envelope again, she affirmed "4f," matching this apartment number.

"Beth...," a man was saying.

Gabrielle's breath caught. It was Sam's voice. Before she could do anything, she saw him appear behind the flushed woman, his hand sliding around the woman's waist as the door opened wide. And then he saw Gabrielle. His welcoming smile collapsed as he observed her and her startled face.

"Gabrielle...," he said, his voice fading in the air thick with astonishment.

She couldn't respond. Shock and dismay stifled her voice. Emotion flushed her face. For an agonizing moment they all just stood staring speechlessly at one another. Then the robed woman turned her face quizzically toward Sam's, sinking further into his arm as she started to say something.

Before Gabrielle could hear the woman's voice, she turned and ran down the stairs, now a blur as she hurried along the aging risers, through the stench, and out the building door into the din of the street. Pausing only a moment, she started to run. She dashed past the neighboring apartment buildings, the greengrocer, a flower shop, past a barking dog, a baby crying, the honking of automobile horns. But she heard and saw none of them. She ran until she had several blocks between her and Sam—and that woman.

In a little park she collapsed on a bench. Sitting there, staring straight in front of her, she saw nothing but the image of Sam and the woman in the doorway. Tears streamed down her face as her mind and body writhed in agony from his duplicity. People glanced at her as they walked by with a look that spoke wonder at what had overtaken this lovely young woman in her pale blue summer dress and sandals, her bare toes peeking vulnerably from under the straps. But no one stopped. And Gabrielle was aware of no one and nothing but this monstrous feeling of betrayal and the racing of her heart.

* * *

It was a long train ride home. She was relieved to find no one in the house. Not wanting to explain her swollen face and red eyes, she yearned to crawl into bed in solitude. After climbing the stairs to her bedroom, she slipped off her shoes, threw the bed covers back, and crawled under them while still wearing all her clothes. Pulling the linens tightly around her, she hugged the pillow to her belly.

It wasn't that she was blind to Sam's wandering eyes. She knew the stories about him. But she just had never seen him in such an intimate situation with another woman, and it rocked her. There was something in his and this woman's easy familiarity that told Gabrielle that this was more than a passing romance.

What a fool I am! she chastised herself. *How could I be so blind, so stupid?*

All the tender feelings for Sam that she had nurtured these past months collapsed around her. Her sense of disillusionment with this man—who fought so ardently against social injustice, but who could act so dishonorably toward her—was overpowering. *What a hypocrite!* she cried until her exhausted body fell into a fitful sleep. She didn't hear the phone ringing downstairs.

* * *

"Gabrielle...," her mother said as she shook her gently.

"Huh?" she muttered, struggling to awaken.

"It's nearly noon. You need to get ready for your first day at work. And a Sam somebody called twice and wants you to call back."

She slid deeper under the covers. The last thing she wanted was to talk to him. *How can I ever believe anything he says again?* she thought.

"Dear..."

"Ugh," she blurted out as she sat up, still wearing her street clothes from the day before.

"Gabrielle!" her mother exclaimed, noticing her clothes and puffy face. "What's going on?"

"Mom, I don't want to talk about it."

"But..."

"No Mom, I just can't. And if that Sam person calls back, I don't want to talk to him—not now, not *ever*!"

Her mother's mouth opened in surprise as Gabrielle bounded out of bed and down the stairs to the bathroom.

2

Exiting the bus at the Jones Beach Marine Theatre at Zach's Bay, she followed the cement path to the theater restaurant. As she approached it, she could hear the actors rehearsing for the evening performance of *South Pacific*. This was opening night for the summer season, and anticipation hung in the air.

But Gabrielle was oblivious to the excitement surrounding her. Feelings of betrayal and disillusionment dragging at her heart, she careened between sadness and anger. *How could I be so wrong about someone? How didn't I see this? How could he mislead me like that? Didn't he love me?* Leaving the walkway, she entered the outdoor restaurant tent. *What were all those words he wrote to me, all that tenderness he showed? Was it just an act and I another conquest? I was so naïve and stupid!* She wiped her eyes with the back of her hand. *Ugh. I have to get to work. I can't let anyone see me like this.*

But someone had seen her. She caught a glimpse of a handsome young man who stood watching her from the kitchen alcove. Dressed in a starched white cook's uniform, he appeared saddened by her demeanor. As she walked toward the locker room with her gym bag slung over her shoulder and her waitress uniforms draped over her arm, she noticed him as he turned and disappeared into the kitchen.

Opening a steel locker door in the waitresses' changing area, she hung up her uniforms—one for the dinner crowd and one for cocktail waitressing after the show. Removing her street attire, she stood in just a bra and panties before preparing to hide her curvaceous body in a shapeless, turquoise polyester dress, a starched white apron, pantyhose, and black "granny" shoes with fat two-inch heels. These made up the waitress uniforms for all of the Jones Beach restaurants.

Required to anchor or net any loose hair, she pulled it back from her face and secured it tightly in a bun at the top of her head, making sure to tuck in all the strands. While this was not the way she usually wore her hair, preferring it loose and natural about her face and shoulders, pulling it back created a look of elegance.

The style accentuated her long neck and the loveliness of her olive-toned skin and drew attention to her almond-shaped blue eyes and full lips. She looked quite stunning despite the scar she wore and the fact that she had been crying and used no makeup. But what heartened her was how her appearance also gave her a certain austere aura that she hoped would discourage inquiry.

"Hey Gabrielle!" shouted her longtime buddy Adrienne. "Are you ready for the big day?" As she entered the locker room swinging her gym bag and uniforms, Adrienne grinned, her character-filled face shining amid the chaos of her long brown hair.

"Sure," Gabrielle said without enthusiasm. Then involuntarily a smile graced her face as she gazed at Adrienne's wide, crooked smile and absorbed the exuberance of her friend's personality. "God, it's good to see you," she said. "And look at you. What happened to your old glasses?"

"You mean those Coke-bottle jobs? My dad did some research and found this place in Germany that makes special glasses for people like me by putting high-index prescriptions into wider, thinner lenses. I can see just as well now, but I don't look like a freak show anymore. Pretty snazzy, no?" Adrienne tapped her glasses.

"You look great. You're going to have *so* many boyfriends when you go to school in Spain."

"Well girl," Adrienne started to exclaim in her usual flip manner, but then she took a good look at her friend. "What the hell happened to your cheek?"

For the next few minutes Gabrielle told her the story.

Adrienne shook her head in acknowledgment, but also noticed her friend's swollen eyes. "Okay, give. What else is going on?"

"Drat," she muttered. "It's Sam. I went to New York to surprise him in his new apartment. Well turned out…there's another woman."

"What?"

"When I knocked on his door, this woman in a short robe opened it…"

"Oh for Christ's sake!"

"Sam was right behind her, his arm around her waist…"

"The rat."

"We all just stood there. No one knew what to say."

"Geesh!"

"It was so awkward. It was awful, Adrienne!"

"Well I guess."

"The woman was about to say something to him. I just couldn't bear to hear her voice. So I ran out of the building…."

"Damn. The bloody creep."

It felt good to Gabrielle to hear her friend's condemnation of Sam.

"What did the woman look like?" Adrienne asked, her indignation turning to curiosity.

Love that Binds

Gabrielle sighed. She really didn't want to relive the scene, but she knew her longtime friend would hound her until she told her everything.

"She was older than we are—I'd say mid-twenties."

"Ah. The 'older woman.'"

"Well I guess."

"Was she pretty?"

Gabrielle looked as if she had been struck. "Attractive unfortunately. She'd just washed her hair. Her face was flushed from bathing."

"Or something," Adrienne muttered.

"What?"

"Oh nothing...go on."

"It wasn't so much how she looked, but the familiarity of the two of them. I felt so...on the outside...like some stupid hick."

Adrienne looked sympathetically at her. "Gee Gabrielle, I'm sorry. But it's better you found out about the creep now rather than later. Imagine if you got more involved with him and then this happened. I'd say good riddance to bad rubbish!"

Gabrielle wished she could feel that way. She knew Adrienne was right. But somewhere in her heart she still loved Sam, even though she was furious with him and didn't ever want to see him again.

"Well what are you going to do now?" She looked quizzically at her best friend.

"Do? I don't know. Try to forget him I guess. You know I'm set to go to Denmark this fall."

"Yeah, a change of scene is just what you need."

"I'm just not sure I want to go there now."

She turned quickly from her locker to Gabrielle and glared at her. "Why the hell not?"

"Because that's where Sam went."

"What?" Adrienne looked exasperated.

"Remember he spent a summer there? He worked in a special program on a family farm and loved it."

"Vaguely, but I thought you mainly were going because a grandfather who died before you were born emigrated from Denmark."

"I was, but Sam's experience played a part in my choice too."

"So?"

"So right now I just don't think I want to have anything to do with anything he did."

"So you'd scrap your Junior Year Abroad just because of what that creep did?"

"No, although I was thinking about it before all this happened. So much is going on politically right now Adrienne. I hope that going overseas is the right thing for me to do."

"For God's sake Gabrielle, you planned to study abroad as long as I've known you, long before you got involved in the Civil Rights Movement. This is your big dream! You said that since you were in grammar school you imagined yourself traveling the world. When in your lifetime will you have the chance to do something like this again?"

Gabrielle said nothing.

"We'll never be as free as we are now Gabrielle. Think about it, and don't be a dummy. Go and live your dream. The Civil Rights Movement's been going on for a long time, and it'll still be here when you get back. Learning about other cultures is important. We've been planning this living abroad thing since we were thirteen. You're going to Denmark, and I'm going to Spain. You're not copping out now."

Gabrielle was surprised by the intensity of Adrienne's rebuke. She was more accustomed to her friend's flip and zany side than to such seriousness and conviction from her. Adrienne's words had their impact, but Gabrielle still wasn't sure.

"Well we're not going to have a job and the money to go anywhere if we don't get hopping," Adrienne added, looking at the clock on the locker room wall and hurrying into her uniform. "Shit. How I hate this frumpy uniform and these God-awful shoes," she exclaimed. "They'd make Brigitte Bardot look like a cabbage reject, left in the patch as too ugly to take to market."

Gabrielle had to laugh.

"Well, that's more like it," her friend said approvingly. "Now let's get to work and rake in those tips to send us on our way!"

* * *

"Wow, will you look at the activity going on in the restaurant tent," Adrienne observed as she watched busboys dragging tables and chairs into place.

"And the music. Is that Rodgers and Hammerstein?"

"I wish we could see one of these musicals," Adrienne said. "The productions are so lavish I hear, and being outdoors and on a floating stage in Zach's Bay to boot."

"I wish we could too. You know how many people come for these performances?"

"I've heard as many as eight thousand," Adrienne responded.

"You've got to be kidding."

"No. This theater's a huge deal. Guy Lombardo's a big part of the attraction. He's a producer and his band plays throughout the performance—and after. So we get the restaurant crowd early and the drink crowd afterwards when people dance to his band in the cocktail tent. The cocktail work should be easier and the tips better."

"I'll look forward to *that*," Gabrielle confirmed with a grin.

"I'll never forget those skimpy tips we got at the Boardwalk Restaurant last summer," Adrienne grimaced. "Those people had no idea how hard everyone worked to serve a nice meal and that we waitresses earn less than minimum wage. Now we'll have the time pressure to deal with too to get customers out the door to catch the show."

"Yeah. I guess that's the gig," Gabrielle acknowledged.

Although it was early, the wait staff gathered for instructions before setting up for opening night. The maître d', Luis, was dressed in his crisp white shirt and black pinstriped suit that sported a bright red carnation on his lapel. He wore unique footwear of white dress-spats with a small yellow-diamond pattern that capped blackened alligator-skin high-top shoes. Gabrielle had never seen anyone don such footwear, which seemed out of place while being strangely elegant.

Luis was dark-skinned and had thinning black hair combed straight back and pomaded to an oily sheen. He was the oldest of the many Cubans comprising the entire male restaurant staff and the bartender, Charlie, a graduate school student in his twenties. The waitresses were young college women like her, working their way through school.

"My name ees Luis. I am the maître d' and your boss. Thees ees my dining room, and I answer for eeeverything that happens here." He stopped, looking meaningfully at the wait staff. "I watch eeevery staff closely and inspect eeeveryone's work. I tolerate nothing but theee beest, and I make sure that ees what our customers get. Tonight ees opening night," Luis spoke dramatically in a heavy accent. It was a strange articulation using elongated vowels indiscriminately, Gabrielle noted, perhaps a cross between Cuban and something totally indescribable, creating a sense of mystery about his origins.

"The restaurant critics weell be heeere," he continued stretching his words. "Goood reviews mean goood business. And happy customers leeeave beetter tips," he winked and chuckled.

"You are aall experienced wait staff, or you wouldn't be heere. Wee'll take a few minutes to review table setups and standards I expect from eeeach of you. I want you aall to look closely at thees table," Luis motioned elegantly to a round table set with a white tablecloth, shining tableware, sparkling glasses, and starched cloth napkins raised in the middle to look like little tents. "Wee'll start from the center," he said, picking up the salt-and-pepper shakers, which clinked between his fingers. They should neever have food or naasty feenger marks on them." Luis made a face full of disgust at the idea of grimy shakers.

Luis's grimace tickled Gabrielle, and she had to cough to cover a laugh. Luis glanced quickly at her before talking for nearly an hour more, covering the entire table, bar, kitchen, and busing setups. He made clear he would tolerate no lower standard than his. Anyone caught cutting corners would suffer the consequences. Repeat reprimands would result in firing. It was as simple as that.

"Wee'll have a fuull house tonight. People weell arrive in less than two hours, and weee have work to do to make thees place shine." Luis clapped his hands for punctuation and floated off regally in his unique footwear to meet with the kitchen crew.

Following periodic inspections, adjustments, and then a final review by Luis, the restaurant opened promptly at five o'clock. All dining room staff stood at attention at their stations, their hair and uniforms smoothed and neat, their nametags straight, smiles on their faces.

Dozens of people crowded behind the maître d' station. Gabrielle noted how unperturbed Luis was as he seated each party gracefully, pulling a chair out for the person he quickly sized up as the "lead lady" at each table. He placed menus in each person's hands with a flourish, bowed and gestured, snapped his fingers for the busboys to pour ice water, and signaled the station waitress to come for the drink order. Then he returned to his station to seat the next party.

As Gabrielle waited on the bar line to fill her customers' drink orders, bartender Charlie worked at top speed. Although he was dressed very East Coast with his starched white shirt, black tuxedo tie, and slicked-back blond hair, she thought he would look more at home on a beach with a surfboard under his arm than behind a bar at a nice restaurant.

"Charlie," Gabrielle said as she picked up the correct setups to hand to the bartender, "I need two whiskey sours—up—and two Shirley Temples."

"Comin' right up," Charlie chirped as he poured sour mix and whiskey into a shaker with ice and filled exactly two whisky sours into her setups and not a drop more.

After delivering the drinks and taking the family's order, Gabrielle started another party before rushing into the kitchen to pick up salads for both tables. The kitchen already was bursting with activity. Pots clanked. Dishes clinked. The Cuban cook staff sweated and yelled back and forth, trading Cuban phrases and occasional laughter. The smell of a mixture of foods and steam rose hissing from the grill. And the vats of hot sauces and soups bubbled and popped.

Gabrielle gave her food orders to Marco, who was in charge of relaying them to the chefs. Scooping up salads and dressings, she arranged the plates on a large aluminum tray, lifting it carefully with both hands onto her shoulder before delivering it effortlessly to her customers.

She was luxuriating in her early success when Luis quickly filled her other three tables. Neither of her first two parties had their main courses yet, and now she had three more tables to start.

Before getting any more drinks, she hurried to the kitchen to pick up her first party's main course. The decibel level in the kitchen had risen at least two notches since the last time she swooped in there. The line to pick up main courses now was long. Across from her, the handsome young man she had noticed when she first arrived at the restaurant was dishing up seafood creole. Sensing her anxiety, he looked over the warming rack at her nametag. "Gabrielle is it? What a lovely name."

Managing a smile, she answered politely, "Yes. And your name?"

"Rafael," he said enunciating gently. "What do you need? Maybe I can help you."

The waitresses in front of Gabrielle glared at her. "Uh thank you," she responded, "but I'd better wait my turn." Giving him an appreciative look, she saw him smile, showing his bright white teeth.

As she and a server named Ethel exited the kitchen, Ethel said of Rafael, "Oooh, he's cute. But watch out for those Cuban guys. They sure know how to sweep a girl off her feet."

When the theater warning bell rang and the customers rushed to pay their bills, exiting the restaurant for the theater, the large dining room looked like a battle zone. Dirty dishes and used napkins lay everywhere. Gabrielle and Adrienne collapsed in chairs at their stations.

Love that Binds

"Oh my aching feet," Gabrielle sighed, longing to pull off her shoes and rub her feet. "I didn't remember how much they could hurt."

"Tell me about it," Adrienne echoed. "Oh for a pair of sneakers."

Their reprieve was short, however, as they had to clean up and prepare the dining room for the next day. Then they helped ready the cocktail tent for drinks and dancing after the show. All this took two-and-a-half hours. They had another hour until the after-show crowd descended. Allowed one of three entrees for their dinner, Gabrielle thought the seafood creole looked good.

Rafael served it up for her. "So how's your first day so far?" the twenty-five-year-old asked as he expertly arranged the food on her plate.

"Hectic."

"A typical opening night. You'll get used to it," he said, wiping a few creole drippings from the edge of her plate with his napkin. As he handed her the dish he said, "There's an opening night party after work at the Havana Grill in Bellmore. Everyone from work will be there. Are you coming?"

"I don't know."

"You'll enjoy it! Why don't you come."

Glancing up, she stopped to really observe him. He seemed almost dashing despite his now-dirty cook's whites and sweaty brow. Maybe it was the contrast of his brown skin and his dark hair and eyes with the white of his uniform—or the white cloth jauntily tied about his neck. She almost said yes, then thought of Sam and remembered Ethel's warning.

"I don't think I can make it tonight," she said. Noticing his disappointment she added, "But maybe another time."

He brightened. "Okay. I'll hold you to it."

"I think I just got asked out," she told Adrienne as they ate their dinners.

"By that hunky Rafael?"

She nodded. "He wanted me to go to the after-work party in Bellmore."

"I saw you two talking in the kitchen. So what'd you say?"

"I told him no—maybe some other time."

"You're a nutcase."

"What?"

"Why not go, have a little fun? He can't be any worse than that two-timing Sam, and he's probably better looking."

"Adrienne...I...I'm not ready."

"Ready shmeady. The best way to get ready is to jump right back in. Just don't get involved. Keep it light."

"That's hard for me."

"Gabrielle, you're much too serious," she replied, picking up her plate to take it to the dishwashers. "Come on, let's give our feet a rest and count our tips before the show lets out."

Dressed in their cocktail uniforms, black versions of their dinner ones, the waitresses helped Charlie and Ralph, the second bartender who just arrived, finish the remaining bar setups. Then they all took their stations. As the theater crowd streamed into the tent, Guy Lombardo and his band walked to their places on the stage above the dance floor. In seeming record time, the famous bandmaster lifted his baton and the music began.

Guy Lombardo cut an interesting figure, Gabrielle thought. He was neither tall nor particularly handsome. He was getting on in age and had thinning hair and a few extra pounds about his middle. But he was impeccably dressed and a star with a command of himself and his band that was unquestionable. When he raised his baton, everyone paid attention as his music filled the air and charmed his audience.

As people danced, talked, and laughed, they ordered lots of cocktails. Gabrielle ran constantly from the moment the band started to play until the music stopped hours later.

"A little busy, eh?" Adrienne said to Gabrielle as they stood at the bar grabbing setups as fast as they could.

"Yeah, but the tips are great, much better than dinner."

When the music ended, Guy Lombardo and two blondes in mink stoles left and climbed into his white Cadillac convertible with the license plate that just read "GUY." Soon thereafter,

Adrienne and Gabrielle showered and changed in the locker room with the other waitresses. Several of them were going to the party in Bellmore.

"So how about it?" Adrienne coaxed.

"It's late. I'm exhausted, and my mom will be worried about me. I didn't say anything to her about being out half the night. I'll go another time."

"You'd better. You're a hopeless case you know."

"I know. Hurry up or we'll miss the last bus."

When Gabrielle arrived home, everyone was in bed. She went to the kitchen to catch a quick snack before retiring. There she saw another phone message from Sam that her mother had taped to the refrigerator door. Removing it, she gazed at it for a minute, then crumpled the message and threw it in the trash.

3

The next couple of days went smoother at the restaurant, and they didn't have to be in so early. By late evening, she no longer was so exhausted and acquiesced to party Friday at the Havana Grill with the waitresses, bartenders, and Cuban kitchen crew. She let her mother know she would be home very late.

The two friends arrived there together. "You promise you'll go home with me?" Gabrielle asked.

"You'd think you were going on your first date," Adrienne complained, then noticed her friend's uncertain look. "I'm just kidding—mostly. Don't worry kiddo, I'll protect you." As Gabrielle rolled her eyes in response, her friend put her arm around her and steered her to a table.

No sooner had Gabrielle gotten comfortable and taken a few sips of her cocktail, than Rafael approached and asked her to dance.

"I...I don't...," Gabrielle stammered.

"Of course she will," Adrienne answered, giving her a nudge.

Gabrielle reluctantly took his hand.

"How nice you came," he said, bringing her hand to his lips and kissing it ever so gently. Then he slowly pulled her snugly to him and commenced to dance, leading her skillfully, Gabrielle noted with both admiration and discomfort.

As she tried to pull back a bit, he kept her pressed to him. Eventually she started to relax in his arms and let the dance take her. She didn't know whether it was because of her desire to put Sam behind her, the command Rafael had of the dance, or the Latin music. Or maybe it was the alcohol, his rapt attention to her, his Latin good looks, or the feel of him against her. But she was beginning to be attracted to him.

"You smell wonderful," Rafael complimented her as they drifted into another set. Adrienne was spinning around the floor too—with Ralph. Adrienne gave her best friend a thumbs-up as she twirled off with the second bartender.

"Would you like to sit down for a while?" Rafael asked.

She nodded.

"Where do you go to school, and what do you study?" he inquired as he ordered another round of drinks.

"I go to Oberlin College in Ohio, and I'm thinking about majoring in art. I'd love to take my junior year abroad—not sure where though. Studying and traveling abroad have always been dreams of mine."

"Well if I had the chance to live my dream, I don't think I'd hesitate. But then, at least partially, I'm living mine. I dreamed of coming here from Cuba. Now I dream of going back—but to a Cuba without Castro."

"How did you get here?"

He couldn't tell her the details, he said, but he came to the States six years ago at age nineteen. He had worked for a few years now with Luis and his Cuban friends.

"Is there any danger you could be sent back?"

"No. I've got political asylum."

"How so?"

"Well let's just leave it that I do."

Gabrielle looked at him with curiosity. This was a story she wanted to pursue.

Love that Binds

"Do you have any family here?" she asked.

"An uncle, but he's in California."

"Do you see him?"

"No. Luis and our Cuban friends are my American family now. Do you want to dance the rumba?" he asked, changing the subject as he offered her his hand.

"I don't know how...."

"Then I'll teach you," he responded, pulling her toward him.

When the party wound down and Adrienne already had left with Ralph, Rafael drove her home.

"It's been a lovely evening Gabrielle. Thank you." He took her hand and kissed it. Involuntarily her eyes closed. In that instant he leaned across the front seat and brought his lips to hers. She felt the heat of him. It was a minute before she opened her eyes to see him looking intently at her in the partial light of a nearby streetlamp.

"You really are a beautiful woman," he said.

She felt herself blush in the semi-darkness.

He traced her scar lightly with his finger. "What happened here?"

"Oh, just an accident. No big deal. Good night Rafael."

Opening the car door, she walked quickly to the house, taking care not to look back. Getting out her key, she opened, then closed and leaned against the door for support.

"Holy Mother of God," she whispered.

Sam had stopped leaving messages, and Gabrielle now was seeing Rafael on breaks and every Friday after work.

"I'm glad you're back in the saddle," Adrienne said in the locker room as they suited up for work, "but do you have to be riding bareback? I said go out, not get serious. Is there no in-between for you?"

"I tried Adrienne. I really didn't want to get involved. But I have. He's so impassioned...and persistent."

"And handsome. Let's not forget drop-dead gorgeous. That wouldn't have anything to do with it, would it?"

"It doesn't hurt."
"Good thing you're leaving the country this fall."
Gabrielle didn't respond.
"Why the silence Gabrielle?"
She didn't answer.
"Please tell me you're going."
"I don't know. I'm so confused."
"You've got to be kidding. What are you confused about?" Adrienne looked hard at her. Gabrielle fidgeted and smoothed the wrinkles from her dinner uniform to break her friend's intensity.

"Everything. I know I shouldn't, but I still struggle with leaving the country when so much is happening politically here. I've been corresponding with Rick, and he's been keeping me up to date with what's been going on.

"And there's Jeremy and the other kids at the tutoring center. Maybe I could do something that would make a difference in their lives. All summer I've done nothing for anyone except to write to Jeremy. And even if I were going abroad, I'm not sure where I'd go. I'm definitely not going to Denmark. I've decided that. There's a new program Oberlin just wrote me about, an exchange program with a school in Turkey. But I know so little about the country. And...and...."

"And what?"
"And Rafael asked me to marry him."
"What? What did you say?" She swung to glare at her friend.
"He asked me to marry him."
"No, I mean what did you tell him?"
"I said I'd think about it."
"You've got to be kidding."
"What?" She looked up.
"What about your college education? What kind of a life can he offer you? A summer romance is one thing, but the wife of a cook?"

"I don't care about money," she retorted. "And you know nothing about him. He was so sweet. He got down on his knee and spoke to my heart with kindness and gratitude. It's about more than hormones and physical attraction. He's suffered greatly in his young life and yearns for things you can't even imagine."

"Gabrielle, we're not talking about money, but about a whole way of life. Is this really what you want?" Adrienne softened her voice as her friend's face hardened. "What about all your dreams and ideals? What about changing the world? How are you going to do that married to Rafael?"

Gabrielle said nothing.

Adrienne leaned in toward her to regard her more closely. "Now you're scaring me. Promise me something."

Remaining silent, Gabrielle turned away.

"Promise me!" Adrienne said forcefully as she walked to face and confront her friend with the intensity of her concern.

"What?" Gabrielle responded.

"Promise me that you won't go out with him for at least a week while you think things through. Then tell me what you've decided before you give him an answer."

"Why in heaven's name would I do that?" she snapped.

"Because it's like you're under some kind of spell. And I'm sorry, but I think that spell's hormones. You're not thinking clearly. You have a thing for Hispanic men too. I'll admit they can make my heart race as well. But you have an attraction to them that's beyond that and which I don't fully understand. On top of all that, you're not over Sam and are on the rebound. You're not dealing with what happened to you. And I think I'm partly to blame, encouraging you to date and all."

Angry now, Gabrielle turned to leave.

"Please don't walk away," Adrienne pleaded. "I'm taking a big risk talking to you like this. But you're my best friend, and I don't want to see you make the biggest mistake of your life."

Gabrielle stopped and turned. "What are you talking about?"

"You have so much promise. I really think you could do anything. Just don't get trapped. Not so soon. We were going to fly. Remember?" Adrienne's face sagged, and her voice had grown husky as she implored her friend.

But Gabrielle refused to answer. Furious, she walked into the dining room and with her back to Adrienne, went to work.

4

Before clocking in one day, Gabrielle met Rafael at the marine theater on Zach's Bay. Seating themselves in the stands, they saw only a handful of people scattered around the eighty-two-hundred-seat outdoor theater. The understudies for the characters of Porgy and Bess were preparing for the performance.

"I've wanted all summer to see an opera," she commented, "but when there's a show, we're working."

"I know."

"What a tragic story *Porgy and Bess* is—and what beautiful music Gershwin wrote."

"I don't know the story."

"My mother has the libretto and story line. I read it."

"Libretto?"

"Yes, the words of an opera."

"Oh."

"Essentially the story starts in a Charleston ghetto," she explained, "and it's the tale of a prostitute, Bess, and a disabled beggar, Porgy. Porgy witnesses a murder and offers shelter to Bess, the murderer's woman. Porgy falls in love with her, and they make a life together that includes an orphaned child they take in." Gabrielle stops to pull her hair behind her ears as Rafael watches her.

"All is well until Bess's violent and possessive lover comes back for her. While defending his family, Porgy kills him. The police question him, but they let him go after deciding that a cripple couldn't have committed the crime. Coming back to the ghetto to tell Bess the news, he finds that she was lured away to New York City by a drug dealer. It ends with Porgy vowing to find and bring back the woman he loves."

Love that Binds

At that moment the understudies began their duet, "Bess, You Is My Woman Now." When they finished, Gabrielle wiped tears from her eyes.

"Have you heard anything more beautiful?" she asked, turning toward him as he put his arm around her.

"It was beautiful."

"So full of passion and hope...." She stopped, having something she burned to ask him. This seemed to be the moment. "Rafael, tell me about how you came here from Cuba."

Taking a deep breath, he removed his arm from her shoulder. Gazing at her momentarily as if trying to decide something, he cleared his throat as he looked away and began speaking in a low voice. "Like I told you, it was six years ago. Some terrible things had happened in Cuba. Many people I knew were part of the resistance to Castro's executions. My family was among them. During an encounter with some of Castro's men, my father was killed."

"Rafael..." She reached for his hand.

"I'd just turned nineteen. I was crazy with anger and hatred of Castro. I loved my father. I wanted revenge. I wanted Castro OUT!" His face grew hard and dark. She regarded him with growing concern. "I joined the resistance. I got a gun and for over a year I volunteered for the most dangerous work. I'll spare you the details." She was becoming frightened of what he was telling her.

"Castro's men learned about my involvement and sent them to kill me," he said. "I was tipped off by members of the opposition. I left my home and my family in the middle of the night, with only the clothes I was wearing. People hid me in their homes until the opposition could get me out of the country. Eventually I was brought to the U.S."

"How?"

"On a fishing boat. They took me all the way to Miami. I stayed with people there, found work, and eventually came here. The U.S. granted me asylum, so I don't ever have to go back there—and won't, at least as long as Castro's in power. People who don't know what he's capable of think of him as the savior of the people. But he's ruthless, murdering and imprisoning people in horrible conditions, killing dissent of any kind."

"You once mentioned you had an uncle in California. Why didn't you go there?"

He fell silent, his face further darkening as he answered. "My uncle is a coward!" he snarled. "He did nothing when his brother was killed. He just ran away!"

"Maybe he was afraid."

"He's a coward, and I don't want to talk about him anymore."

"Do you keep in touch with people back home?"

"Yes."

"Your family? The opposition?"

"My family...and I think I've said enough."

Gabrielle's gaze faltered. Then she raised her face to him. "Thank you for telling me. It must have been a very painful time for you."

They sat in silence for a long time, just holding hands as the orchestra and understudies rehearsed. Startled and moved by his story, she also was disturbed by what he had told her—and what he had not. Acknowledging that she didn't really know him very well, she wondered if his secret, violent life was all in the past.

She thought about the opera's tale, about the character of Porgy, a peaceable man turned murderer when the family he loved was threatened. What had Rafael done, she wondered? Who was he really? What awful choices did he have to make at such a young age? She wondered what she would have done if she had been in his situation. She couldn't even imagine.

Her next days were unsettling. While she was drawn to Rafael in ways she didn't fully comprehend, she also was troubled by his past. She understood revolutions. She had joined one. But she believed passionately in nonviolence. Clearly he did not. She wanted to talk to someone about her confusion about him, but she was afraid to tell anyone here his secret. Wishing she could talk to Rick, she knew he would help her make sense of her feelings. But she couldn't bring herself to call or bare this enigma to anyone.

Love that Binds

At home, while she pondered all this as she prepared to leave for work one day, the phone rang.

"Hello?"

"Gabrielle?"

"Is that you Rick?"

"Yes, how *are* you?"

"I can't believe you called."

"Hmmm. Has it been that long?"

"I mean I was just thinking about you."

"I like the sound of that. So how are *you*?"

She almost could see him grinning on the other end of the phone. "Oh fine," she lied. "And you?"

"Just jim-dandy. So tell me about the waitressing job—and your summer."

"Okay, but first I want to hear what you've been up to and how things are going with Jeremy and the tutoring center." She needed to start somewhere safe and wasn't sure she was ready to talk about Rafael and what he had revealed. "I got your letters," she added, "and understand things are going well. But I'd like an update from the horse's mouth."

"Thanks a bunch," he laughed. "But seriously, Jeremy is making real progress with the second-grade reading level."

"That's good to hear. How hard Jeremy must be working."

"His mother says she's never seen him so motivated. You know, Gabrielle, I think those books you gave him made a big impression on him. And the letters you wrote him."

"How do you mean?"

"Your books were a very personal and thoughtful gift. And your letters meant a lot to him."

"I just wanted him to know that I believe in him and hoped that my books would encourage him to keep working on his reading skills."

"Well I think it worked."

"Thanks for telling me. I'm so proud of him. Having a teacher like you is such support, and I know it helped him to see how capable he is. I can't thank you enough."

Rick talked for a half-hour about the center. She could hear his excitement about what the kids and volunteers were accomplishing. "But enough of this," he said. "Tell me about yourself."

"Oh it's been super busy at the restaurant...." Her voice trailed off. She didn't want to just talk about herself or chitchat and wasn't sure she should discuss what was most on her mind.

He waited. "Okay Gabrielle, something's not right. You might as well tell me. Is it Sam?" He knew of her breakup from her letters.

"No...well not really," she said.

"Well then, what?" he prodded her.

While reluctant to bring up Rafael and his proposal, she finally relented and talked about him and his involvement in the Castro resistance. Despite omitting details of his violent past, she couldn't mask the distress in her voice.

Listening, he asked a few judicious questions, then said, "Gabrielle, what does your heart tell you?"

"I'm so confused. I just don't know...."

"You *do*, Gabrielle. You know the answer and need to go deep and listen for what you already know. Give yourself time and space Your friend Adrienne might be right about that. If you do this, you'll have your answer."

Her silence prodded him.

"Is there something you're not telling me?"

"That's all I can say."

He sighed. "I know you'll take care with your life, and you'll figure things out. I'll be thinking about you. You'll do the right thing. I have to go—I'm sorry. Goodbye Gabrielle."

Holding the phone that buzzed now, she knew that he was right about the need to quiet herself and listen to her heart. But she didn't hear that Rick may have been listening to his.

5

As she wrestled with how to respond to Rafael, she began making excuses as to why she couldn't see him as frequently. In time she acknowledged how far apart they were in their values, needs, goals, and perspectives. She had been powerfully drawn to Rafael and their cultural differences, but she knew now that their life together could never satisfy her.

At the end of her last day of work, after she had said goodbye to her fellow workers, turned in her uniforms, and accepted her last paycheck, she coaxed Rafael to walk with her on the beach. Under a sky brilliant with moonlight casting shadows across the seashore and as the surf crashed against the white sand, Gabrielle, with great sensitivity and with pain in her heart, told him that she couldn't marry him.

"What we want is so different…and I have to finish school."

"You could finish it here. And we're not so different," he said softly.

"Yes we are Rafael," she replied, searching in the moonlight for his eyes.

"Because you're born American and I'm from Cuba?"

"No. Because of what we want for our lives and what we're willing to do for them."

He shot her a look. "Is this about what I said to you?"

She lowered her gaze.

"I knew I shouldn't answer you."

"Yes Rafael, you were right to tell me." She raised her head. "We have to know the truth about each other."

"The truth? What *is* that? You know nothing about the things I saw as a child in Cuba."

"No I don't. But I believe that violence only begets violence. I do know *that*."

"You know nothing!" he shouted. The surf crashed beside them. His face grew dark. He waited, then said, "So this is about politics?"

"Not just politics, but what we believe, what we think is right…and what we want for our lives."

"What we want? You know nothing about what I want!"

"I think I do." The ocean seemed to pulsate.

"What then?"

"You want Castro out and to return to Cuba."

"Oh Castro again."

"And you want children—and a wife to stay home and make a family."

"Well at least you understand that."

"But that's not what I want…not yet anyway. I have so much I still want to do. And I'm too young to be having children."

He pulled away from her. "You're a woman. Women from my country marry and have children when they're younger than you."

"But this is America—and I'm not those women! There's so much I want to do, Rafael," she said, lowering her voice and extending her hand to touch him.

"What are you talking about?" he shouted, moving away from her.

"There's so much I have to learn, so many places I want to see. I want to find what I'm meant to do in the world," she said, almost pleading with him now.

"I can tell you what that is," he said, returning to her, taking her hands, and drawing her to him. It was like a dance. A wave slapped beside them. He caught her in his arms. She could feel the force of him as he clasped her to him.

"No Rafael," she said, finding her own strength and pulling away from him now. "You just don't understand…."

"Understand? What's to understand?" he said, grabbing her arm, wrestling to keep physical contact with her. "I love you…you love me. What else is there?" The sea surged.

"It's not that simple," she said, ripping her arm from his grip. Crash! A wave tumbled to shore.

Love that Binds

"It is!" he shouted, jerking back as if slapped.

"No it's not! It's not enough!" she cried. The ocean grew louder.

"Not enough, not enough? You American women have things all mixed up. You don't know what matters!" His voice grew harsher, his face hardened with hurt and anger.

"You don't understand," she said, her voice quieter again.

"No I don't," he said pivoting away, his mood deepening as he fell silent.

She looked at the wall of his back. Pulling in her own emotions, she let in the sadness and betrayal she knew he was feeling. She walked toward him. With tenderness she reached up and laid her hand gently on his shoulder. He pulled away.

"Rafael…," she implored him.

"Go away then, and leave me alone! You're not what I thought you were."

She started.

He stood very still, but for his breathing that grew deeper and quicker. His shadow cast by the moon seemed to throb. Then suddenly he spun toward her. His eyes narrowed with accusation. He met her face squarely. "I thought you loved me," he croaked.

His words cut. The surf cracked against the wet sand sliding back into the advancing water.

"I did," she moaned, feeling lost now. She had used the past tense! He heard it. "Rafael…I'm so sorry…"

He raised his hand as if to strike her, then turned away and growled, "Go!" His arm shot out. "I have nothing more to say to you!" Then he turned back toward her again, his face hardened, his hand tightened in a fist.

In this gesture she heard the rising tide of his rejection and anger and the swelling of her fears. As she backed away from him, she knew this was not how she wanted to end things. She couldn't help but feel his pain. *How could I have let things go so far?* she chastised herself. But she also was careful of him now. He was showing her shadowy places she didn't want to travel. He was terrifying her. *Can we ever really know someone?* she wondered. But she had no answer. She was thinking that she didn't see how she could trust her judgment about anyone ever again.

So she ran from Rafael, the sea, and a summer flooded with heartache. Anxious, she hurried toward the boardwalk and her bus home. As she did so, she began to feel strangely lighter. This summer she had left relationships that had entangled and nearly engulfed her. Suddenly aware of this, she stopped walking. Looking up at the moon, she thought how luminescent it was, lighting her way, guiding her. She felt a certain vague triumph in her actions that she hadn't recognized until now. Her steps quickened in the cool sand, as if she were hurrying toward her future, a future that would be hers and hers alone.

For the first time in her young life she felt truly free. She was seeing that the course she had begun charting when she left home for Oberlin, then Hattiesburg, and now somewhere overseas was a future she was delivering to herself. Feeling a surge of ownership of her actions, she understood that she was passing from the last vestiges of childhood into adulthood. She was making her own decisions and bearing their responsibility. Despite the pain of these months, she felt the liberty her resolutions were delivering. And there in the moonlight, at the edge of land and sea, she grabbed hold of her life and witnessed the birth of a new kind of freedom.

By late August she would be on her way, not to Denmark but to Istanbul, a city that spanned Europe and Asia—a land that would become the bridge between her old life and the future she was running to meet.

~V~
ADVENTURE IN A FOREIGN LAND

1965 – 1966 – Istanbul, Turkey

1

As her airplane flew at thirty-six-thousand feet above the Atlantic Ocean, soon to cross the Mediterranean Sea, Gabrielle gazed out her window at the all-encompassing blackness of the night. Closing her eyes, she tried to sleep. But within hours of touching down in Istanbul, she found herself too excited to rest. She kept thinking about the adventure she was about to begin and about her maiden Great Aunt Etienne who had traveled to scores of exotic places over her lifetime.

Auntie Eti, as the children of her mother's large family affectionately called her, thought that all her nieces, nephews, and their children—Gabrielle and her sister Ruth among them—were special. Most of her adult life she had been a high school mathematics teacher and lived with her spinster older sister Hilda, a domineering and humorless assistant school principal of a Brooklyn high school. Hilda had died by the time Gabrielle was born, so she never knew her Great Aunt Hilda.

Auntie Eti was a tall, substantial woman with a warm and pleasant face, although a not especially handsome one. What she lacked in looks, she made up for in intelligence and pure joy in living. She had a childlike approach to life and a flamboyant sense of adventure. This didn't manifest in her appearance or manners, which were totally conventional. It revealed itself in her ardent interest in and willingness to pursue journeys that even men rarely took in the early 1900s.

She thought nothing of traveling with her sister and their childhood girlfriends by train across the American continent, then hopping a steamer over the vast Pacific to journey to China, Thailand, and Japan. She and Hilda would work the whole school year, then travel abroad with one of their women friends or rent a summer home in another part of the country. In this manner she visited most of Europe, northern Africa, and much of the Far East, hiked in the Alps, rode camels in sight of Egypt's Great Pyramids, and experienced such esoteric cultural adventures as Noh and Kabuki theater in Kyoto.

On a regular basis, Arthur and Kay took Gabrielle and her sister to Brooklyn to see Auntie Eti in her brownstone near Prospect Park. The trips to Brooklyn always were happy ones. The visits not only meant hugs and kisses from Auntie Eti, rich meals of meats, gravies, and lots of sweets, but also trips to what the girls thought was the most special place in their beloved great aunt's house—her attic.

Auntie Eti's garret represented nothing of Ruth and Gabrielle's everyday lives, unless it was their dreams. When they climbed the stairs to it, they ascended into a world apart from anything they had ever known. In their great aunt's attic were birdcages from Thailand, silk kimonos from Japan, figurines from England and Germany, a toy piano from Switzerland, photographs taken in Italy, Africa, and China, coins from Belgium, Spain, and France, and so much more.

Ruth and Gabrielle played in Auntie Eti's loft for hours at a time. They speculated about what certain things were and how they were used or worn. They would parade around in kimonos and pretend they were Japanese princesses. Or they just mused about what it would be like to travel far away, across oceans, mountains, and deserts, to go where so many people looked different, spoke other languages, and lived in places unlike their own.

One picture in particular caught Gabrielle's attention as a child. It was a shot taken in Egypt of her great aunt wearing a long white dress, white shoes and stockings, and a wide bonnet with sheer white netting draped from the brim to her shoulders. Behind

Adventure in a Foreign Land

her and her camel were the Great Pyramid of Giza and two dark-skinned men in long white skirts known as *thoub*. Auntie Eti looked perfectly at ease and totally delighted balanced atop a very tall and regal-looking camel and with one of the Seven Wonders of the Ancient World at her back.

To young Gabrielle this picture represented the essence of the word exotic. She yearned to be sitting beside Auntie Eti on her own camel in the desert, exploring a world so different from hers.

In their great aunt's garret she and Ruth soaked up the strangeness that surrounded them and a blossoming awareness of a world beyond Long Island and their relatives in New England. In this musty attic of their childhood, a curiosity about the world and a deep desire to travel were born in Gabrielle and Ruth. This longing grew with each visit they made to Auntie Eti's Brooklyn brownstone. Every sojourn was a reminder that so much more awaited them.

Finally drifting into sleep, she awoke to the announcement to prepare for touchdown at Istanbul's international airport. Within three hours, she had gone through customs, retrieved her baggage, changed dollars to Turkish lira, and hailed a taxi.

"Oya aşkım çok güzelsin...."

The taxi radio blared. Strings of beads hanging from the rearview mirror rattled and swayed against the windshield. Mosques with their minarets, a long ancient Roman aqueduct, and an endless stream of taxis whizzed by her window. Gabrielle was on her way to her new school, Robert Kolej in the city's Bebek district.

From the moment she left the plane and as she sat watching from the taxi, she felt the press of humanity, the presence of history, the din of the city, and the overwhelming difference from the American culture she had left behind. Despite the newness of everything around her, the language she couldn't understand, the music that hurt her sensibilities with its tinny sound, the dirt, and the ambient noise, Gabrielle grinned. "Well Adrienne," she whispered from the taxi's back seat, "I made it out! And are we flying now?"

Lost again in memories as she watched the evolving scene outside her window, she snapped back to the present when her taxi abruptly came to a halt. All traffic stopped and waited, music blaring, as a man led a donkey loaded with baskets of vegetables across the jammed street. And then the traffic dance began again.

Her taxicab, one of the city's many older Chevys and Fords, followed a road along the European side of the Bosporus strait. Peering out her window at the ships and ferryboats that crisscrossed the wide body of water connecting the Black Sea to the Sea of Marmara, she observed how the Bosporus separated the European and Asian sectors of the city. Soon the cab wove back and forth, dodging other taxis, cars, trucks, and buses, horns blasting and hugging the narrow road along the strait.

Then the taxicab entered Bebek and a line of restaurants and shops before heading up the long winding hill to the American-founded Robert Kolej. She was surprised by how high above the Bosporus the college sat, there in a picturesque spot amid the hills of the city. The taxi stopped as close as the driver could get to the girls' dormitory. Unloading her baggage, he carried it to the entryway. Holding out what Turkish lira she had exchanged, the driver removed what was owed. Not knowing how to say thank you, she just smiled and stuffed the remaining money into her pocket.

"*Merhaba*—hello" a middle-aged woman called, opening the door as she dried her hands on a towel. The matronly housemother introduced herself to Gabrielle as Mrs. Yaktay. Gabrielle reciprocated and extended her hand, which the woman warmly accepted.

"Would you like a little tea?" she asked Gabrielle in her heavy Turkish accent.

"That would be lovely," Gabrielle responded, "but would it be okay if I first clean up a little? It's been a very long trip."

"Of course my dear," she said. "I'll help you to your room. It's on the second floor."

"Thank you."

Her second-floor room was crowded with bunk beds, desks, and the belongings of its occupants.

Adventure in a Foreign Land

"This is your new roommate, Gabrielle Andersen," Mrs. Yaktay said to the three young women in the room as she put down one of Gabrielle's bags. "Gabrielle, this is Azra, Esma, and Zeynep."

"*Merhaba*," they said in unison. "We are happy to meet you. Welcome!"

"I'll leave you girls to get acquainted," the housemother said. "Gabrielle, you don't need to come down for tea now unless you want to. You must be tired and probably wish to get settled. We can do it another time."

"Thank you Mrs. Yaktay," Gabrielle said, relieved. "I would love to come for tea another time."

The woman smiled and nodded in acknowledgment, then turned and descended the stairs to her apartment.

Gabrielle looked at the women now staring unabashedly at her.

"Uh, is this my bed?" Gabrielle asked, looking at an empty bunk on the upper level.

"*Evet*...yes," the woman called Azra said. "And this is your *dolap*, uh, how do you say it? Lamp?"

Esma started to giggle, putting her hand to her mouth.

"I think you mean to say 'closet,' Azra!" Zeynep laughed.

"Of course, 'closet'" Azra corrected herself. "And this is your *masa* or 'desk,'" she said, knowing she had the right English word this time and pointing to a small wooden table with a well-used appearance.

In fact the entire room looked rather worn, terribly crowded, and smelled of old wood and linoleum. Narrow isles ran between the beds and the closets and desks, making it necessary to flatten one's self against the furniture for someone to pass.

"Whose bed is this?" Gabrielle asked, gesturing toward the bunk below hers.

"Mine," Zeynep said. "Where are you from in America?"

"Long Island," Gabrielle started to say, but saw the blank look on Zeynep's face. "Uh, New York."

Zeynep's slender face brightened, and her dark eyes smiled. Clearly she knew of New York.

"Where are you from, Azra is it?" Gabrielle asked.

"Yes. I'm from Balıkesir," she said, adding, "in northwest Turkey, southwest of here." As Azra spoke, a lock of reddish-brown hair fell over her eyes. Unselfconsciously she brushed it back.

"And you?" Gabrielle asked, looking at Esma.

"Esma and I are sisters," Azra quickly added.

"You two look a lot alike," Gabrielle commented. As she observed them, she could tell that Esma was younger than Azra, had the same dark eyes, but darker hair, typical of most people Gabrielle had seen so far in Turkey. "How nice," Gabrielle said. "How lucky that you can be here together."

"Yes," Esma said, smiling at her older sister.

"And you, Zeynep is it?" Gabrielle asked

"Yes. I'm from Ankara—east—the capital," Zeynep said.

"Can we help you unpack?" Esma offered.

"I can do it, but thank you," Gabrielle said. After she answered, though, she wished she hadn't. The women turned away as if rebuffed and started talking in Turkish among themselves. It made Gabrielle feel alone. She was so tired, however, that she didn't have the energy to think about it right now. She really just wanted to take a nap. Having traveled for twenty-two hours between stops, plane changes, and flight times, she had hardly any sleep.

As she started to empty her suitcases, the women decided to go out. "See you later," Zeynep called as they tumbled out of the room.

Gabrielle was relieved to have the room to herself. Removing her outer clothes, she climbed up onto her bunk, pulling the freshly made covers back and crawling under them. In minutes she was asleep.

2

When Gabrielle awoke, sun streamed through the window. Finding her roommates out and about, she retrieved her slippers and bathrobe from one of her suitcases and ventured down the empty hallway in search of a bathroom. Four doors down, she found it.

Walking past the white institutional sinks, she opened the grey wooden door to one of the toilets. Her eyes widened in surprise.

"Damn," she exclaimed.

She thought it was nothing like any toilet she had ever seen. There was a hole in the floor with a footrest on either side. It appeared to be a stand-and-squat affair.

"Damn."

"Tell me about it," a voice rose from behind her.

Gabrielle turned to see a tall young woman grinning at her.

"Hi," she said, "I'm Becky Martin."

"I'm Gabrielle Andersen. You're American?"

"Guilty. There're supposed to be four of us in the dorm this year. The other two haven't arrived yet. When did you get in?" Becky asked, stopping to lean her slim body against the sink.

"Yesterday, but I slept from late afternoon until now. Boy was I tired."

"It's a long trip. What college do you go to?" Becky asked, winding a few strands of her straight hair around her pointer finger.

"Oberlin College."

"I go to Macalester."

"Ah, another Midwestern student," Gabrielle grinned.

"So what are you doing today…after you figure out the Turkish toilet?" Becky laughed.

"So that's what it is," Gabrielle jested. "And I have no idea what I'm doing. Explore a bit I guess, and unpack my stuff."

"I've been here a week. Would you like me to show you around?" she asked, pushing herself away from the washbasin where she leaned.

"I'd love it," Gabrielle responded. She was so glad to be making a friend.

Half an hour later, Gabrielle had cleaned up, dressed, and was out the dormitory door with Becky, an attractive young woman with a slim face and large green eyes. Gabrielle noted her very long blonde hair and collegiate dress that included a knee-length flowered skirt, knee-high socks, and penny loafers. She was not the sort Gabrielle would have expected to see in an exotic city like Istanbul. Becky's appearance reminded Gabrielle of sorority girls she knew who would be more apt to have chosen a college in London or Paris.

"So what brought you to Robert Kolej?" Gabrielle asked.

"My great-grandfather. He did business here long ago, when it was Constantinople."

"Cool," Gabrielle responded.

"My grandfather used to tell me his father's stories about the city and his Oriental rug import business," Becky continued. "Great-grandfather was fascinated with this place. The stories about Istanbul were so enchanting that as a child, I decided I'd find a way to come here someday. Then this program opened up a few months ago between Robert Kolej and Macalester, and I grabbed it."

"The same thing happened to me—the new program opening up I mean. It sounded too good to pass up."

They walked behind the dorm to a rock wall bordering campus and overlooking the Bosporus. Through the trees Gabrielle could see the tops of old stone and wooden structures and a stunning stretch of the vast strait below. Further along their walk, they came upon the ruins of what looked like an old castle and fortress directly below them.

"I don't know too much about this yet," Becky said, "but once this was part of a great medieval fortress—Rumelihisarı—that defended the city from foreign armies."

Adventure in a Foreign Land

"Wow," Gabrielle said. "I'm going to have to look up the history of this place."

Here and there as they continued walking, Gabrielle could see the land that lay on the far side of the Bosporus. "How astonishing," she said.

"What?" Becky asked, turning toward her new friend.

"I just can't get over the fact that...*that*," Gabrielle said, pointing to the other side of the natural strait, "is Asia. We literally are standing in Europe, looking at the continent of Asia."

"Turkey really is the bridge between East and West," Becky said.

"I know. Just standing here and looking at it, though, is amazing. It's one of the things that drew me here," Gabrielle acknowledged.

"What do you mean?"

"I'm fascinated by Eastern cultures, but they're hard for a Westerner to fathom. I thought that Turkey, which has both East and West influences, might make the East easier to understand."

"It's an interesting theory. We'll have to see, won't we?" Becky winked at her.

"I'm curious about the college, Becky. I know it's American founded and run, but are there very many Americans here? I was under the impression that there aren't."

"There are quite a few on the faculty, but not many American students. They're mostly Turks."

"Is this a hard school to get into?"

"*Very* hard. I've been told it's Turkey's most exclusive school. Engineering and business students most want to come here. I understand the best texts on the subjects are in English, and classes at this school all are taught in our language. So students have to be fluent in English, very smart, and highly educated to be accepted."

"This wasn't well explained to me back at Oberlin," she sighed.

"It was the same for me at Macalester. And everyone here wants to practice their English on you, so good luck learning Turkish. But if you can speak even a little, Turks seem to be very forgiving of our butchering their language. They're just grateful when we try."

Walking toward the center of campus, they skirted a big dirt bowl ringed by large stone buildings.

"This massive patch of dirt seems out of place," Gabrielle noted.

"It's where the men play soccer. Turks are crazy for it. And there's the administration building." Becky pointed to a stately building just off the bowl. "It's where you'll go to check in, pick up the course schedule, and register. You might want to do that today to beat the crowd. Let's get you back to the dorm so you can get settled before you check in."

"Right. And thanks Becky. This was fun."

By the time her roommates returned, Gabrielle had unpacked, found the campus café, and ordered something to eat. Having gotten reasonably well-organized, she also had registered with a representative of the Dean of Students Office and picked up a class schedule. She planned to spend the evening reviewing course offerings.

"*Merhaba* Gabrielle, how are you today?" Azra asked as she entered the room with Esma and Zeynep.

"Oh, fine...a whole lot better than yesterday. Boy, was I tired!"

"You looked it," Zeynep said. "So what did you do today?"

Gabrielle filled them in

"So what have you three been up to?"

"Shopping and checking out classes—and boys!" Esma said, covering her mouth with her hand as she giggled.

Gabrielle smiled. Esma was a freshman, Becky had told her, and barely eighteen. "Did you see any cute ones?"

"Cute? How you say, 'cute?'"

"Yes, you've got it. You know, handsome."

"Oh yes...haaandsoooome," Esma repeated, giggling.

"Don't mind her," Zeynep said, "she's never been out with a boy."

"Really?"

"It's not unusual," Azra interjected without elaboration. Then she turned away from Gabrielle and toward Zeynep and Esma as they began talking in Turkish again, occasionally giggling as they glanced at her.

Knowing she was the subject of their conversation, Gabrielle felt shunned. It hurt her, because she very much wanted to make friends with her roommates. Sighing, she acknowledged that she had much to learn about Turks and their culture.

Walking to her desk, she retrieved and opened the course schedule. The background chatter of her roommates' talk in a language she couldn't understand and the derision she felt made her feel very alone. Wanting to engage Becky for support, she checked herself. *I'm going to have to get over this. This isn't the last time I'll be on the outside here. If I look for another American every time I feel lonely or misunderstood, I'll never make Turkish friends.*

So Gabrielle returned to her reading and tried to focus on the task at hand.

3

The next day, when she returned to the administration building, she found a whirlwind of activity. Students were everywhere. When she reached the top of the second-floor stairs, she was looking down and didn't see a student standing there. Accidentally walking into him, she sent his books flying out from under his arm.

"Oh! I'm so sorry," Gabrielle said, immediately bending to retrieve the books.

"No, please. Let me…," a low male voice said.

She watched a pair of tanned hands retrieve the books, then gazed upward into two twinkling, dark brown eyes in a square-chinned, handsome face regarding her with interest.

"How clumsy of me," she said.

"No…no, it's *my* fault. Please don't worry." He tucked his books back under his arm and extended his hand toward her in greeting. "My name is Mehmet Aksoy."

"I'm Gabrielle Andersen."

"Gahbraelllllle…," he mouthed the word as he clasped her hand.

She started as she shook his hand and smiled back at him as he released her.

"You're American?" he asked.

"Yes. And you're Turkish?"

"*Evet*…I mean yes."

"It's very nice to meet you," she said.

"When did you get here?" he asked.

"The day before yesterday."

"Have you seen the city yet?"

"No, I've just walked the area around campus. I've been trying to get settled."

"Well if you like, I can show you the city sometime."

"How nice of you to offer," she said, blushing in surprise.

"When would you like to go?"

"I don't know," Gabrielle said, stalling. She was tempted, but she knew nothing about male-female customs or anything about this young man. "Maybe I should finish getting settled first."

"I can ask you again in a couple of days if you like."

"That might be better."

"Where are you staying? Bebek Hall?"

"Yes," she said, smiling back, "I should be going. It's nice to meet you."

"And nice to meet *you*, Gabrielle."

As she walked to the registration office, she could feel his eyes follow her. Resisting turning to look, she thought, *These men could be a problem. I really don't want to get involved with any man right now.*

* * *

Adventure in a Foreign Land

To satisfy both her interests and Oberlin's requirements for her Bachelor of Arts degree, Gabrielle chose an ambitious mix of first-term courses in Turkish language, Islamic architecture, European art history, and biology. Although she had hoped to take a painting or drawing class, she found that none were offered. This was disappointing, as she was considering a degree in fine art.

Having successfully registered, she headed back to the dorm to see if she could find Becky. On her way up the stairs she spotted her friend coming down. "Becky, just the person I'm looking for. You got a couple of minutes to talk?"

"I was going to run an errand, but I guess it can wait. Let's take a walk.

As they did so, Gabrielle told her about her collision with Mehmet and his offer to show her Istanbul.

"Was he cute?" Becky asked.

"Well yes, quite handsome actually."

"So what's your question?"

"I don't know the proper response—I mean what the socially acceptable thing to do is."

Becky was momentarily silent and gazing at Gabrielle as if she just landed from outer space. "Look. You're a hottie, he's a hottie. If you were home, what would you say?"

"Well... 'that sounds nice,' I guess."

"Uh huh. So what's your problem?"

"Coming to Turkey was such a last-minute decision that I didn't have time to research this country and its culture. So now I'm really trying to understand Turkish mores and what a Turkish woman would do if she was asked out in a similar situation. I don't know anything about this man or Turkish customs."

Becky sighed. "Look, I'm not aware of very many Turkish customs yet, but I know men and women students do go out with each other. Now they may take their sister or brother along...or a friend—I really don't know—but I think you could let him show you the city. It would be in public places after all. These students come from good families or are on scholarships—either way, they're not riffraff. I think you'd be safe. Just no petting on the first date, okay?" she laughed.

"Very funny. I just didn't want to create a *faux pas* by accepting an invitation from a man I don't know."

"Look. We're Americans. By virtue of that alone, they probably all think we're 'easy,' given the way American women are portrayed in movies. So you might as well go out and have some fun. I think maybe I'll go over to registration again and see if I can bump into some cute guy. Clever way to get a hot date Gabrielle."

"Ha ha. And it's not really a date. But I don't suppose you'd want to join us if I decide to go."

"Well I'd love to meet this guy, but no. I have no desire to be a third wheel. Thanks anyway."

"I thought you'd say that."

"Look, I'm sympathetic. Well maybe not all that sympathetic, as some of my desire to come here was to meet handsome men. So maybe I'm not the best person to ask."

"Becky, you're the *only* person I can ask. You're my one friend here so far. My roommates are nice, but I can tell they talk about me behind my back."

"That's something I've already learned. Turkish women seem prone to gossip. So be careful what you tell them. I definitely wouldn't let it slip that you're going on a date with this guy."

"It's not a date Becky. It's a tour by a Turk. I really would like to see this city with the help of someone who knows it. It's a great opportunity. I really am not interested in dating right now."

"Why not?"

Gabrielle sighed. "It's a long story. Suffice it to say, I've had some disappointments, and I don't plan to repeat them here."

"If you say so. When are you going?"

"I don't know. I told him to check back with me in a couple of days, after I get settled."

"Playing hard to get, eh?"

"Oh sure. No, just trying to be cautious."

"Well don't be so cautious. You're only here for a year—nine or ten months actually. So kick up your heels and have the

Adventure in a Foreign Land

time of your life. You may never get to do anything like this again, so make the most of it."

"You're right. Thanks Becky. I just didn't want people to get the wrong impression of me or see me as an Ugly American."

"That doesn't seem to be who you are. Don't worry about it. We'll probably be gossiped about even if we do nothing unusual. So we might as well just do the best we can and try to ignore the rest. Let's not worry so much and have some fun. See you at dinner!"

As she watched Becky turn to leave, she noticed Becky's blonde ponytail swishing side to side as she walked. For some reason that made Gabrielle smile. Then she knew what it was. *It's almost as if she's Adrienne in the body of another woman. What are the odds of finding a friend like Adrienne here?* she mused.

Taking the path behind the dorm, she gazed between the cypresses, horse-chestnut trees, and umbrella pines toward the Bosporus below. Thinking this would make a great picture, she returned to the dorm for her sketchbook and pencils. With her roommates gone, she headed back to the walkway and began sketching.

An hour later she had a detailed drawing of the view from her bench—the granite rock wall, the trees, the concrete pathway, and the more distant glimmering water. It was a perfect late-August day, sunny, with blue sky and no appreciable humidity. As she worked, her spirits soared, much as they had as a child when she played violin in the school orchestra.

It had been a difficult instrument for a child to learn, having started lessons in the fourth grade. But as a high school student, she had reached a point whereby playing the violin had begun to give her more pleasure than pain. In fact, she had been named concertmistress of her high school orchestra. The orchestra conductor, who also was her violin instructor, challenged his students with everything from Liszt's *Hungarian Rapsody No. 2* to Beethoven's *Fifth Symphony*, giving her and the other players a wide range of orchestral experience.

Although she didn't practice as much as she knew she should, she did well enough to make first chair and to be admitted as one of the first violinists to the District Orchestra that showcased the best players from several schools. Furthermore she played violin in her high school's Rodgers and Hammerstein musicals, which always were grand affairs and required months of rehearsals.

In truth she adored performing in all of the orchestras—the big sound, the sense of being part of a team of people giving life and expression to music written by great composers who knew how to elicit from musicians a certain swelling, auditory beauty…even from amateurs. She loved that she knew every note and rest in every piece and which instrument it was that played at any particular time. It gave her the chance to be part of something that took her out of herself and into something larger, eliciting a feeling in her that was at once spiritual and sensual, daring even.

As Gabrielle sketched and thought about the years when music was such a big part of her life, she revisited her decision two years ago to end her violin training. In the end, she had concluded that she didn't love the violin as much as she did playing in a group. *Violin is an unforgiving instrument that can howl like a cat or sing like a bird,* she thought. Too often it sounded more cat than bird, she decided, until she made music with others. Then it sang. *Maybe someday I'll take it back up,* she pondered. *Now I have other things I want to do—study, travel, draw, paint, work for things I care about, learn and experience everything I can.*

With that, she finished her sketch and held it up to appraise it. She was pleased with what she drew. *It's a shame that I probably won't get to paint here. With no classes in creating art and no place to work, painting will have to wait till I get home. But drawing is good—I can work on that.* And with this thought, she felt satisfied, happy even.

Adventure in a Foreign Land

4

On Friday when her roommates had left for the dining hall, Gabrielle showered and dressed in a simple white blouse and dark green skirt that came just below the knee, and slipped on comfortable shoes. Having accepted Mehmet's invitation to see the city, she grabbed a hat and sunglasses and stuffed a light shoulder bag with a comb, a few tissues, her wallet with some Turkish lira and U.S. dollars, her passport and student visa, a camera, and a small sketchbook and pencil. Then she headed to the campus café for a quick lunch.

It was nearly quarter-past one when she reached Mehmet, who stood patiently and calmly by the side of the road just off campus.

"Sorry to be late," she said as she hurried toward him. "I stopped at Kazim's for a quick bite to eat, and it took forever. I'm so sorry."

He smiled as he walked toward her. "Please. It's nothing. In Turkey we all are long accustomed to waiting. You'll see that everything here takes longer than you expect." He laughed, putting her at ease.

"Well then, I should fit right in," she said, smiling now.

"Shall we go? It's a long way down. I hope you have comfortable shoes."

"I do."

"Ah, a woman with a practical side. This is good. When we get to the main road, we'll hail a *dolmuş*, uh, a share-cab I think you would say. I thought we'd start our tour with Süleymaniye. It's a mosque complex and masterwork by one of the world's greatest architects. His name is Sinan, beloved architect of Sultan Süleyman the Magnificent during the Ottoman Empire."

"Sinan. Süleyman the Magnificent. How exciting. I'll love seeing this."

During the rest of their walk down the winding hill, they talked mostly about their upcoming classes. Soon they had reached the bottom, and Mehmet flagged a 1950s yellow Ford *dolmuş*. "Süleymaniye," Mehmet told the driver. A man already sat in back, so Mehmet got in first.

As when she took a taxi from the airport a few days ago, Turkish music rose from the radio and beads that hung from the rear-view mirror slapped in and out of rhythm against the windshield. The share-taxi smelled of cigarette smoke, she noted, and the open windows brought in aromas of dust, automotive exhaust, and now and then the very mildly salty Bosporus sea air.

As they entered different districts, Mehmet named them for her: Arnavutköy, Ortaköy, Beşiktas, Beyoğlu, Eminönü. The road hugged the Bosporus, so views of this great body of water peeked through the spaces between the buildings that crowded along the road.

At one point they drove around a tree growing in the very center of the street. "Why is a tree left here in such a heavy traffic area?" she asked.

"Trees are much loved in Turkey," Mehmet replied. "When Mustafa Kemal Atatürk took leadership of Turkey after World War I, he put in place a program to deal with the country's massive deforestation. Preservation of trees remains important today. It actually is illegal to cut down a tree in Turkey without permission, even on your own land."

"That's amazing. Actually I think it's lovely," Gabrielle responded. "Tell me more about Atatürk."

"You've probably noticed his picture around campus. In fact it's in about every business, building, and home. The father of modern Turkey, he was a great military leader during World War I. He rallied Turkey after the war from being the Sick Man of Europe to become a stronger and more modern society. He required everyone to have a last name. Before then family names were optional and rarely used."

"Having only first names is hard to imagine."

"Yes. In the ten years before he died in the late 1930s, he completely redesigned Turkish society, right down to the language,

Adventure in a Foreign Land

going from an Arabic- to a Latin-based alphabet and altering it to be more purely Turkish."

"In ten years? Remarkable."

"There's so much more," he said. The passenger beside him shifted in his seat. Mehmet lowered his voice. "He westernized the country, outlawed polygamy and the fez—fallbacks to an older and more Eastern culture—and separated religion and state. Islam no longer was the state religion. He created a democratic structure, unlike anything the Middle East had ever seen, stabilized the economy, which was an enormous undertaking after the war, adopted the Western calendar, and created a truly secular state. He brought strength, pride, and respect back to what was a crumbled Ottoman Empire. The people loved him for it. They still do."

"What an amazing and forward-thinking man," Gabrielle responded as quietly as she could. "I can understand why he's revered and why people still are so passionate about him decades after his death. He gave them a new identity, it seems, one they could take pride in and that gave them hope for a better life after the breakup of the Empire and the hardships of war."

Mehmet looked very directly at her. "You understand, don't you? That's remarkable."

She blushed. They were silent for the remainder of the ride, both deep in thought. She was beginning to understand some things about this country that drew her to it in a way she hadn't anticipated. *The culture of this country is very old and intricately layered*, she thought. *I have so much to learn.*

In no time the fellow *dolmuş* passenger was delivered to his destination and shortly thereafter, they to theirs. Süleymaniye stunned Gabrielle. "Oh," she exclaimed when she first saw it, "how terribly beautiful! How huge and elegant it is—and look how slender the minarets are!"

"Sinan is known for that," Mehmet responded. "It was very difficult to make tall minarets so thin and fine. He figured out exactly how to do it."

They stood for several minutes taking in the sight of the most splendid of Istanbul's imperial mosque complexes before

Gabrielle took out her camera and started shooting pictures. Walking to the mosque entrance, they removed their shoes, placing them beside footwear of every type, size, and color. As she put her camera away, Mehmet gave Gabrielle his handkerchief to cover her head before entering. As they did so, a cooler interior air encircled them. Moving in stocking feet onto the persimmon-colored Turkish rugs spread over the vast floor of the mosque, they took great care not to walk in front of the supplicants.

As she absorbed the cadence of the men praying in the main part of the building, she became aware of the women offering up prayers in a separate place behind the men. She noted that a number of the women had light brown skin, and their dark hair was masked.

Watching them, she realized that she blended well with many in this country. For the first time in her life, she didn't worry about people disparaging her because of her skin color. Her observation liberated her in a profound way. Feeling a budding kinship with the women, she wondered where they stood in a hierarchy built by societal norms and ultimately, she surmised, by men. Was their position in this mosque a reflection of this?

"Mehmet," she whispered, "why are the women required to sit behind the men?"

"So they don't distract the men from their prayers," he replied.

She smiled. As she wondered where Mehmet stood on a woman's place in Turkish society, he turned to show her vantage points to more fully explore the majestic structure that was Süleymaniye.

Everything entranced her about this sixteenth century mosque built to glorify the sultan—the breadth and height of the enormous central dome that rose eighty-five feet from where she stood; the semi-domes; the gigantic arches and piers; the stained-glass Ottoman windows; the huge calligraphy panels; the wooden doors, window shutters, and book cabinets, intricately carved and adorned with mother-of-pearl and ivory. "And the tiles with their floral designs—exquisite," she whispered. "I feel so lucky to be able to stand here in this breathtaking space. What an incredible architectural feat this was."

Mehmet nodded. "I especially love the Sinan mosques. Can you believe Sinan lived to be ninety-seven and built almost a hundred and fifty mosques and some three hundred other buildings? Interestingly, he was born a Christian and later converted to Islam, serving in the sultan's elite Janissary Corps before being made responsible for military engineering works. Ultimately he became the sultan's Architect of the Abode of Felicity, a post he held until his death."

"What he accomplished is almost unimaginable, isn't it?" she responded.

"It is."

After surveying the entire complex, Mehmet suggested they walk back streets, eventually in the general direction of the Bosporus where it would be easier to hail a *dolmuş*. "These streets are where you'll see some of the smaller shops and people's homes, giving you a feel for Istanbul neighborhoods," he said.

"I'd love that."

So for the next hour-and-a-half, they strode past stone and wooden buildings that leaned out from the second and third stories. She took in the sounds of children playing and shoppers bargaining for goods, and the smells of coffee houses and old car and truck engines.

Stopping periodically to take photos, she noted how many women's heads were covered by scarfs, while young children had no such constraints. The scarfs, a holdover from a more restrictive time for women, prodded her to want to know more about Turkey's culture and women's place in its society. Soon, however, she let this question go as she took in the exotic nature of this city, so full of history and mystery.

She loved how in some places laundry hung on lines from one side of the street to the other. She observed crumbling walls, family businesses, a fountain here and there long neglected, fig trees, and a man with a donkey loaded high with goods. Then suddenly, they came upon an exquisite, one-minaret mosque.

"Mehmet, what is this?" she half-gasped her question.

"Rüstem Paşa Camii. It's one of Sinan's most beautiful mosques. It's named for Süleyman the Magnificent's Grand Vezier, who was the husband of the sultan's favorite daughter, Princess Mihrimah."

"Grand Vezier?"

"Essentially the sultan's prime minister, his chief officer of state."

"I see. Can we go inside?"

He hesitated. "You'll want to spend time here. We should plan to come back. The ceramic tiles are quite incredible, made in Iznik during the height of Ottoman ceramic art. The tiles have many different geometric and floral designs. You can see some examples here on this porch façade."

She looked closer, while also observing Mehmet. The fact that he was thinking of another outing wasn't lost on her. Smiling, she responded. "I've never seen anything like it. I'd love to come back when we have more time."

Mehmet's dark eyes showed pleasure at her acceptance of his offer. "Come," he said as he proffered his hand as she descended the mosque steps.

His touch sent an electric pulse through her. She blushed. Mehmet seemed to notice as he released her hand gently when they stepped back onto the street.

Continuing past charming Ottoman and Byzantine caravanserais with their arcaded courtyards and down narrow streets with small shops, restaurants, and residents' homes, they finally neared the Bosporus.

"Well, what would you like to do now?" he asked. "Do you want to go straight back to campus, or would you prefer a ferry boat ride back toward Bebek?"

"Oh could we? I'd love to go out on the water! I've been watching boats crisscross the Bosporus. That would be so nice."

"Then a ferry boat it is."

The ferry stop was crowded, but it wasn't long before they boarded a boat that would take them from the European side to the Asian and back as it made its way along the strait.

"Can we sit outside?" she asked.

He nodded and followed her as they walked to the front of the boat and facing the city's European side. Shortly after claiming a place on a bench, the boat left the dock and a breeze hit them, tousling their hair. It made her laugh, which in turn made him smile. "You're not the typical girl," he said as he pushed locks of hair back from his forehead.

"How so?" She observed him, her hair dancing in multiple directions.

"In many ways," he answered, searching for her eyes through her hair. "But in this instance, I'm talking about your lack of concern about your hair." He laughed.

"Does it look too awful?" she asked, suddenly aware that it was everywhere.

He chuckled. "Actually I find it quite charming—and refreshing. Most females seem to worry about messing up their hair."

"Oh that. I gave up long ago trying to control it," she smiled. "And I was a bit of a tomboy growing up."

"A tomboy?"

"Uh, a tomboy is a girl who likes to climb trees and such...like boys do."

"You really were a tomboy?"

"I was—a bit of one anyway," she smiled, then turned back toward the rough, dark sea surrounding them. "This really is an enormous body of water, so much larger than you might imagine when you're on land."

"Yes, it's mighty, treacherous, and very deep. The currents are particularly dangerous."

"Oh, look at the city! The lights are coming up."

He smiled.

"And you can see the hills the city sits on. What a view," she exclaimed.

They were talking somewhat loudly now so they could hear one another over the grind of the motors, the slapping of the water, and the conversation of other passengers. "What's this we're coming into?" she half-shouted.

"Asia—and Üsküdar," he replied as people pushed past them to prepare to disembark. He stood to protect her from the press of them. "It'll be a few minutes until everyone's off the boat and they reload. Do you want to sit inside?"

"If it's okay, I'd like to stay here and watch everything that's going on," she said, turning to look at him. "Earlier you mentioned your father and grandfather. What are they like?"

Looking serious, he hesitated, sat back down, then cleared his throat. "My grandfather Kemal died some years ago, when I was a teenager. He was wonderful—kind, smart, funny, hard-working...and a devoted family man. In the army in the first World War, he sustained a bad leg injury, leaving him with a limp and lifelong pain. But nothing got him down. He always had a smile on his face and a kind word for everyone and was especially attentive to me as the oldest grandson. We were very close."

Seeing Mehmet falter for a moment as pain showed in his eyes, she said more softly, "I'm so sorry. That had to have been a terrible loss for you."

Shaking his head affirmatively, he quickly regained his composure and looked toward the sea. "Recognizing a bent I had toward science, he nurtured it with books, chemical experiments, and mechanical projects we did together from the time I was five."

"How special that was. What did he do for a living?"

"He was a science teacher."

"Ah. I suppose then that you becoming a chemical engineer was the most natural thing in the world."

He smiled. "I suppose. My father would have preferred that I become a surgeon, however, which is what he is."

"Can you tell me a little about him?"

A shadow crossed his face. "He is chief of cardiothoracic surgery at Bursa's preeminent hospital."

"What's he like?" she asked gently, sensing this was a delicate subject for him.

He paused for a minute, continuing to look away from her as the wind played in his hair. He removed cigarettes from his pocket. "Do you mind if I smoke?"

"No."

Adventure in a Foreign Land

After he turned the almost-full pack sideways and hit it against his left hand to dislodge a cig, he pulled a silver lighter from his pocket and dropped the pack back into his trouser. Then he lit the unfiltered cigarette and inhaled deeply, letting a long trail of smoke fill the air away from her. She hadn't realized he was a smoker, which surprised her only a little, given how common she understood it was for Turkish men to imbibe in cigarettes. But the mildly sweet smell of the burning tobacco lingered, despite the wind and his effort to keep it from her.

"My father was gone a lot, given the nature of his work," Mehmet began. "But when he was home, he could be a tough taskmaster." He stopped, taking another puff on his cig, which he then turned on its side and examined before letting it rest naturally in his long fingers. "He was especially hard on me as his older son."

"You have brothers and sisters?" she asked, hoping to lighten what was becoming a dark mood.

"One brother and an older and a younger sister."

"You were saying about your father…"

He exhaled and paused. "Perhaps it's better to talk about something else. You know how it can be between fathers and sons," he said, as if brushing aside something trivial.

"Yes, and mothers and daughters," she added, smiling in an effort to elevate their spirits.

But he said nothing for several minutes, taking drags to fill the space that seemed to widen between them.

As the cigarette burned down in his fore- and middle-fingers, he cast it into the water. With it went his mood, which seemed to soften in the light of her discomfort.

"Enough of this serious talk!" he exclaimed. "It looks like the ferry is fully loaded and ready to depart." With that, the engines revved up, and they watched the boat leave the loading ramp. As Asia receded in their view and the great open waterway took them over, so the shadow cast by his father faded.

They chatted about the architect Sinan and his magnificent structures and took note of the many wooden houses lining the Bosporus on both continents. She especially liked how the upper stories jutted out over the great body of this cold, deep, heavily traveled water. "They must be beautiful inside," she remarked. "Imagine the views they have."

"I've been in a few," he said. "Some are better than others, of course, especially given the age of many of them. But there are fewer now than there used to be, as wooden structures are especially susceptible to fire."

"True. I hadn't thought about that. But they have a very romantic look, don't you think?"

"I hadn't seen them quite that way, but yes, there is a certain nostalgia to them."

It wasn't dark yet, but the day was riding toward dusk. Still mostly hidden by the hills and buildings, the waxing moon was beginning its rise. Lights were coming up on the city's hillsides, and the many ferries on the Bosporus turned on theirs as well, making a kind of luminescent dance across the water. They still could see the buildings on both sides quite well, but the lights stole their attention from the architectural features to the scene's pure lucent effervescence.

"Could anything be more beautiful?" she exclaimed. Her grin widened, then her face reflected surprise as he put his arm around her.

"You looked as if you were cold," he covered, gazing at her.

"Uh…a little," she said. But mostly she just felt the warmth of him. It seemed natural to her to be under his arm, he being a few inches taller than she. But she experienced more than warmth. It was protection and affection…and attraction. They were silent as the lights, the whoosh of the water, the purr of the engines, and the conversation of the passengers filled the air. It was as if she were in a lovely dream from which she never wanted to wake up.

But the ferry was arriving at their destination. A warning horn blast shook the relative quiet. Then the engines reversed, slowing the movement of the boat toward the shore. The water churning below them, foam rising around the propellers, the passengers on deck reached to hold the rails until the ferry docked.

Adventure in a Foreign Land

Then a flood of people disembarked onto the pier. She felt her sense of balance rocked as her body made the transition from floating to walking. But Mehmet caught her as they both stumbled and laughed at the familiar transition from water to land.

After taking a taxi up the hill to campus, they walked along the stone wall overlooking the Bosporus. Stopping to watch the lighted ferries crisscrossing the strait, they listened for the boats' horns.

"This is a magical place," she said sinking without thinking into his sheltering arm. It was just enough to allow him to put both arms around her. She could feel the firmness and heat of his body. Her hands were on his chest. Moving one of his hands to her face, he held her to him with the other. Then he kissed her lips softly, as if seeking an answer. Responding with her parted lips, his kiss grew more confident.

Looking into her eyes, shining under the rising moonlight, he said her name. "Gabrielle. You are like no one I've ever met." He closed his eyes, then opened them and gazed at her astonished face. He stepped back and put his arm around her shoulders again, then continued to walk, this time in silence. Minutes later he noticed a breeze that made her shiver and took her to the dormitory entrance.

"Good evening, Gabrielle. Thank you for a very special day." She only could nod as she stood across from him, his body casting a long shadow beside her under the moonlight and the glow from the dormitory windows. "I hope to see you again soon," he said.

And with that he turned into the night's rising breeze. As the moon bore down upon her, she also turned and climbed the dormitory steps with feelings of both elation and consternation.

"Holy Mother of God," she whispered as she opened the entrance door.

5

Meeting Mehmet began a relationship that Gabrielle couldn't have foreseen. From their first adventure into the city to tour Süleymaniye, she thought that their accidental first encounter was more destiny than chance. It was his knowledge, his enthusiasm for the vision of Atatürk and the architect Sinan, his respect for history and for her, and his gentle humor that spoke to her. It both excited and troubled her, fearing another serious relationship that could end in heartache.

And slowly, Gabrielle believed she was beginning to assimilate into Turkish culture. Her excursions with Mehmet to Süleymaniye, then Rüstem Pasha Mosque, with the promise to tour other Ottoman architectural treasures over time, played a large part in this, as did her Islamic architecture and Turkish language classes. Scholastically, the Islamic architecture and European art history classes were especially influential in deepening her interest in declaring a fine art major. But with no drawing or painting classes offered at the college, she fell back on her sketching to develop her skills until she returned to Oberlin.

It was a warm autumn day when Gabrielle drew as she sat on a campus stone bench overlooking the Bosporus.

"May I see that?"

Gabrielle turned to observe a slight young woman who apparently had been watching her. Gabrielle held up her sketch.

"I like the way you shaded the trees and the shadows on the path. You're a talented sketch artist."

"Thank you. That's very kind of you. You sound like an artist yourself."

"I also like to draw. But I'm being rude. My name is Bilge," she said as she stepped toward Gabrielle by way of introducing herself. Gabrielle smiled, while noting Bilge's dark hair, modest dress, and heavy, black-framed glasses.

"My name is Gabrielle," she responded. "You're a student here?"

"Yes, a senior."

"I'm a junior. Actually I'm on a Junior-Year-Abroad Program from Oberlin College in Ohio."

"I think I've heard of Oberlin, although I don't believe we've had any students from there until now."

"No, this is the first year they've had this program with Robert Kolej. I'm actually from New York. Where are you from?"

"Eskişehir. It's in the western part of Central Anatolia."

"Anatolia?"

"Most of what we call Asian Turkey is on the Anatolian peninsula between the Gulf of Iskenderun on the Mediterranean and Artvin Province on the Black Sea coast. Eskişehir is about three-hundred-thirty kilometers southeast of Istanbul."

"That's interesting," Gabrielle remarked. "Your English is excellent."

"Thanks. I went to boarding schools that only teach in English. So I had no choice but to learn. That always helps."

"I'm sure it does. I worry about how well I'll do with Turkish when everyone at the college speaks such good English."

"That can be a problem. But Turks are so accustomed to foreigners not being able to speak any Turkish at all, that they are very forgiving and appreciative if a person simply tries."

"That's what I've heard. I signed up for a beginning Turkish class, but I must admit that languages aren't my forte."

"I think you'll do fine. Any Turkish you speak will show that you're trying to meet people part way."

"That's true, and a good way to look at it. Thanks for that."

"Well, I better be going. I need to get back to my apartment. I have a lot to do before classes start next week."

"I know what you mean. My full name is Gabrielle Andersen. I'm staying in Bebek Hall. What's your last name, and where do you reside?"

"My last name is Tekin. My apartment is in Emirgan—just up the road from Bebek."

"I haven't even explored Bebek, though it's right down the hill. There's so much to see. If you ever want to look me up at my dorm, I'd love to see you again—and your sketches. Maybe we can draw together sometime."

"That would be fun. I'll keep that in mind. It was nice to meet you."

"And you."

Well that was a pleasant surprise, Gabrielle thought as she watched Bilge leave. *I think I just may have made my first Turkish girlfriend.* Noticing that Bilge had a limp, she wondered about the cause of it. With that she closed her sketchbook, put her pencils in her skirt pocket, and returned to the dormitory.

6

A week later, as she headed for the overlook with her drawing pad and pencils, she came upon Bilge.

Hearing her name, the woman turned. As Bilge looked into the sunlight, she lifted her hand to shade her bespectacled eyes and squinted. "It's Gabrielle. How nice."

"It's good to see you again—and drawing, which is what I was about to do."

"Perfect. Do you want to come and sit by me?" She gestured toward her bench. "Tell me how you've been doing."

"My," Gabrielle began. "In short, I've been doing fine. And you?"

"Fine and busy. Have you been sketching?"

"I'm afraid not," Gabrielle said as she gazed at her closed tablet. "But I did take my first excursions downtown. I saw Süleymaniye and Rüstem Pasha. They were incredible."

Bilge smiled. "They are. I'm so glad you got to see them. After many years, the city still amazes me."

"I can understand. May I see your drawing?"

Surveying her work, she noted, "Bilge, the detail in this is remarkable. I can almost feel the roughness of the stone wall, the smoothness of the bench, and the wind blowing through the trees." Bilge blushed. "You have a talent for bringing a scene to life," Gabrielle said, handing the sketch back. "Do you mind if I watch you work? I think I can learn a lot from you."

"Of course," Bilge said as she recovered her drawing and her comportment. "But you're too kind."

"How long have you been drawing?"

"Oh my—as long as I can remember. Perhaps since I was four or five."

"Do you sketch daily?"

"Most often, yes. It gives me an excuse to go outside. It's my way to relax."

Gabrielle looked admiringly at her. "That takes real commitment. They say practice makes perfect, don't they? Of course God-given talent helps too," Gabrielle said.

"I'd say ninety-eight percent effort and two percent gift," Bilge laughed. "How long have you been sketching?"

"Not long. I took one class at Oberlin before coming to Istanbul and fell in love with artwork. Since I've been here, I've only made the one sketch you saw, and I still need to finish it. It seems I've been distracted by everything since I came here."

Bilge observed her. "From what I observed of that drawing you showed me, I'd say you have far more than two percent gifted talent and that you only need consistent effort to grow it. It helps to set a regular time and make it a priority. If you do, I predict you'll surpass me before you return home."

"Bilge, you flatter me."

"No," she retorted. "I've studied many artists over the years, and I have a good sense of what makes for exceptional art. I saw something in your work when we met. Take your sketch out and let me look again."

Bilge examined it carefully as Gabrielle waited quietly. "Okay, check how you drew the tree branches." She retrieved the tablet, but wasn't sure what Bilge was referencing. "Look again at the actual tree," she coached.

Examining it, Gabrielle was baffled. "Yes, but what do you see?"

"Are the tree branches wavy?"

"Hmmm. I think I get what you mean. My sketch makes the branches wavy, which the real tree isn't."

Bilge had a big smile on her face. "That's known as artistic license."

"And…"

"And that's unusual in a beginning artist. The tendency is to try for technical accuracy, rather than to interpret. You saw movement in the branches and created that experience by giving them an undulating line. It made me feel the wind and life in your tree. The unusual accuracy in the rest of your drawing made your tree seem even more alive. That's not an understanding that a beginning artist typically has. I didn't realize this myself for years. You got this implicitly, even though you don't appear to be conscious of it."

She lowered her gaze as Bilge retrieved the drawing, holding it up so Gabrielle could observe it from a distance.

After a minute, she responded. "I see what you're saying. I wasn't aware of doing this. When I drew the tree, I was in a somewhat subconscious place."

"You see? That's what I'm talking about. A beginner most often is very left brained, trying to figure out proportions and lines and perspective. It's much later in an average artist's development to go to that place of deeper creativity. You have that in you naturally Gabrielle. That's rare. Don't let anyone take that away from you. Be careful with your teachers. Some are too pedestrian to understand this and may fail to fully appreciate the deeper realm of individual interpretation."

Silent for a couple of minutes, Gabrielle studied her drawing. "I don't know what to say. You've opened my eyes and encouraged me with your observations. I've always loved art and have family who are artists, but I never thought this was my talent. The one class I took was great and made me consider majoring in art. More than anything, art speaks to me. Although I think you're being too kind, your words give me hope. I'll do as you say and set aside time to regularly practice sketching."

Her new friend grinned as she handed Gabrielle's tablet back to her. "If you like, we can try to get together weekly to draw."

"I would love that."

So they resolved to meet here on Thursdays after their classes.

"I think I have a lot more to gain from doing this than you do," Gabrielle remarked.

"Don't be so sure," Bilge countered. "You already have a unique style, and you're just beginning. There's much I can learn from you as well. And it's important to have friends who are artists. This is mostly an engineering and business school, so artists are not exactly in abundance."

"Bilge tell me, what is your major?"

"Electrical engineering."

"Really?"

"Really."

"I would have thought you were an art history major."

Bilge laughed. "When you speak of art, you talk about my passion. Electrical engineering is my way to support myself."

"I can understand that."

"So how do *you* plan to support yourself?" Bilge asked. "The term 'starving artist' comes from real-life experience, you know."

Gabrielle smiled. "It does. But my thought is to teach art and eventually be able to support myself with my art alone."

"I think this is possible for you if you commit to regularly practicing it."

"And possible for you as well."

Bilge shook her head. "It's different here. And I'm different. I don't come from a wealthy family like many students here do. I came here on scholarships. And I have medical issues—spinal and hip issues—that require regular medical attention. This is expensive. And you may have noticed I'm not a beauty as you are, and I have a strong personality. Men have very little interest in me, so a suitable husband isn't likely. No, my plan is to make a good living, live alone, and pursue art in my free time."

Gabrielle contemplated this. "I think a man would be lucky to have you as his wife. But I respect what you're saying and applaud your independent thinking. I know you'll make a fine electrical engineer—and artist, whether that be part- or full-time. But Bilge, tell me what are the issues with your spine and hip."

Bilge winced as she shifted in a clear moment of pain. Her gaze became suddenly weary. "I've had this since birth and try not to talk about it. When I do, it just seems to make the hurting worse. Now let's do a little sketching."

Sad to have caused her new friend discomfort, Gabrielle replied with her silence as she removed her pencils from her pocket and worked to finish her last drawing. After some time, she asked Bilge a question she had been pondering about Turkish social structure. "I have the sense that men dominate in Turkish society. Is this correct?"

Bilge stopped her sketching and looked up. "In what respect do you mean?"

After explaining the source of her question being the women who were sequestered behind men in Süleymaniye, Gabrielle asked how this translated to male-female relationships in Turkish society in general and also here at the college.

"There's not a single answer to that," Bilge said. "For one thing, education makes a big difference. An educated woman has a pretty much equal chance of obtaining a professional position as a man. But I would have to say that at home, the male still dominates. For less educated or less fortunate people, male dominance becomes an even greater factor. I would say that most of the men here at the college seem respectful of their female counterparts."

She nodded and thanked Bilge. "This has been much on my mind," Gabrielle admitted.

7

As she lay in bed on Saturday morning, she thought about a conversation she had a few days before with several expatriate women in her beginning Turkish class. All had experienced some barriers to friendship with their Turkish roommates and worried about telling them things that could lead to gossip. *Maybe the Canadian woman is right, that we may be the ones creating this situation. I haven't really reached out to my roommates in the same way I have to my fellow foreign students and to Bilge. Perhaps I'm the one at fault here and need to find ways to relate to them more.*

Being the weekend, she and her roommates were leisurely about getting ready for breakfast. Gabrielle took the opportunity to try a new approach. After their usual good morning greetings, she searched for some photographs she had brought from home and shared them with the women. They in turn offered their family pictures. They asked questions of one another about family members, about customs of their hometowns, about the roommates' chosen areas of study, and even about dating and sex and how their countries were perceived by others.

"Can you tell me more about Turkish customs around dating?" Gabrielle asked.

"It depends very much on where you live and how conservative your family is," Azra said. "Esma and I come from a smaller city, where customs are more traditional—some even have arranged marriages. Our family doesn't practice that, but they are very protective of us and make sure that if a boy wants to date us, they've met and approve of him and his family."

"How about you, Zeynep?"

"There's no one special I really like, but I have dated some. I come from Ankara, a large city and the capital. My parents are more liberal. They like to meet anyone I date, but they trust me to make good decisions."

"Azra and Esma, do your parents require the company of another family member on a first date?" Gabrielle asked with interest.

"Only if they don't know the boy and his family and they don't have the opportunity to meet them," Azra replied.

"What if one of you met someone here you wanted to date?" Gabrielle asked the sisters.

"I think we would go with each other on a first date and watch out for one another," Azra said.

"Zeynep, how about you?"

"I have dated here. I get to know a boy pretty well before I go on a date—or I might take one of my roommates along." Zeynep laughed, looking at her friends.

"I have been curious about this," Gabrielle said. "If someone wanted to date me, I've wondered how you and others would see that. I didn't want to do anything that would be against Turkish customs."

The roommates looked at each other. "We had wondered about American customs. What you see in the movies is…very…how should I say…very…liberal." Azra said.

"I see what you mean. Heavens, it seems liberal to me too."

"I'm glad to hear that," Azra said. "We didn't know what to expect. We didn't know if you…still…virgin."

Gabrielle blushed. "Yes."

"Oh good," she responded. "I didn't know what to think. People expect Americans to be…what you say…very free?"

"Well we're all different," Gabrielle said. "Please don't think badly of Americans. Like you, we're good people. Our customs may be different, but our hearts are good. We American students here have a lot to learn and want very much to fit in and make friends with you all. Thank you for being so open with me."

"Thank *you*," Zeynep said, as Azra and Esma nodded. "We didn't think badly of you. We just thought you weren't very interested in knowing us. You have been mostly with other Americans."

"I guess that's what people do when they're new somewhere and are worried that they're not fitting in. Since I don't speak much Turkish yet, when you talk among yourselves I don't know what you're saying. It's easy to feel excluded."

"We didn't mean to do that," Esma exclaimed. "It's just easier for us to talk Turkish."

"I understand that now," Gabrielle said. "And please don't worry about it, now that I see what's happened. Of course you'll talk together in Turkish. Hopefully before I leave here, I'll have learned enough Turkish to be able to talk to you a little in your own language."

"Speaking of studies," Azra said, "I'd better get going. I have a lot of homework to do this weekend." They all nodded and gathered their books to take to the library.

"I need to get a few things together here," Gabrielle said. "You go on. Thanks so much for taking the time to talk to me, and for helping me to know you better. I enjoyed it and really appreciate it." Gabrielle smiled and waved as they left.

Well I'll be, she thought. *So that was all it took to make friends with these women. They thought I wasn't interested in them! Shyness and uncertainty can look like dismissal. I see that now. I'll have to tell the others. It makes perfect sense.*

8

Exiting the cab in the cool of the early evening, she was struck by the bright lights, the traffic, and the noise. "What a busy place," she exclaimed.

"Yes. Let's walk over to Istiklal Caddesi, which has the latest shops and restaurants. The nightlife here is something you have to see," Mehmet said, adding, "but you may want to take my arm so men don't bother you."

"How would they bother me?"

He hesitated. "Some men might, what do you say, goose you if they think you're foreign and available."

She regarded him. "Really?"

"I'm afraid so. So if I get close behind you in a crowded area, I'm not being forward. I'm just trying to protect you."

"Oh."

They walked in silence for a while, her hand on his arm as she glanced about and took in the scene with its upscale stores, eateries, and crowds of people.

In less than a half-hour, they reached their destination—a fashionable packed restaurant in the heart of Istiklal Caddesi. The maître d' seemed to know Mehmet, bowing slightly to him and speaking in Turkish as he escorted them to a table with a white linen tablecloth, black napkins, gold-edged plates, and sparkling glassware. A lit candle and a bud vase with a single red rose graced the center of the table.

The maître d' pulled out her chair, and Mehmet seated himself across from her. "This is very nice," she commented, looking around at the well-dressed clientele and the well-appointed restaurant. "I'm not sure I'm dressed up enough for this. I wasn't expecting anything so grand," she demurred, looking down at her simple cotton dress and well-worn shoes.

"You look lovely Gabrielle. You have nothing to worry about. I'm proud to bring you here," he responded sincerely as he smiled at her.

Blushing, she asked, "Do you come here often?"

"From time to time," he replied. "The food is excellent, and there's music and dancing Saturday nights. I thought you might enjoy it."

She looked around, noticing a grand piano across the room and a large open area for dancing. "That sounds nice."

A waiter approached them and brought dinner menus, as busboys fluttered about pouring water and bringing warm bread, olive oil, butter, and sesame crackers. Mehmet requested a bottle of white Pinot Noir after checking his choice with Gabrielle.

"I'm afraid I don't know enough Turkish yet to be able to decipher the entrees," she said as she perused the menu. "Can you recommend something?"

"Sure. I like their catch of the day. It's always fresh and delicious. Does that sound good, and maybe eggplant dip for an appetizer?"

"Perfect," she replied.

Returning with the wine, the waiter poured a sample for Mehmet before filling their glasses and taking their food order.

"You know about my week," he said. "How was yours?"

As they sipped wine, she described her sketches of Rüstem Paşa Camii that she just finished and her meetings with Bilge. Then she talked about the papers she wrote for her Islamic architecture and European art history classes and the ideas she explored. He listened closely, never interrupting. Then she apprised him of her night on the town with the other expatriate students, which made him smile. When she finished, he was silent and sipped his wine as the waiter brought the first course, the eggplant dish with warm flatbread.

"This is delicious," she exclaimed as she swallowed her first bite.

"It *is* good," he said. "Gabrielle, it seems to me that you've had a remarkable week. I would love to see your drawings of Rüstem Paşa—and any others you've done—as well as the papers you wrote. I quite agree with your hypotheses, which I think you'll find have been proven to be more than theories. We humans surely want to leave something of ourselves behind and fear being forgotten. We want those that come after us to think well of us, whether it's generations of our families or a people, a nation, other kingdoms, cultures…or historians.

"As you said so well, artistic expression can be for the pure love of art, to express the culture and occupations of an artist's life, or can be an act of revolution, whether political, cultural, or simply artistic. We all want some kind of immortality, whether it's through our children or the accomplishments that grow from our talents—or both. Art certainly is filled with complexity, as are we humans."

As Mehmet offered her more wine and a busboy cleared the appetizer plates and used silverware, Gabrielle asked about his visit with his brother. "Ali is it?"

"Ah, Ali. He's five years younger than I am and goes to the same boarding school I went to in Bursa. Since he's intensively studying English, he's considering applying to Robert Kolej for admission two years from now. He wanted to see the campus and stay with me in the dorm so he could get a taste for the place. I also took him to classes to experience that and understand how good his English has to be to follow the lessons."

The waiter brought their entrees, grilled *levrek*—or sea bass—fillets, lemon wedges, and sautéed vegetables, along with more hot Turkish bread, herb-infused butter, and olive oil.

She took a bite of the fish. "This is delightful," she commented. "But please, tell me more about your brother. Did he like what he saw?"

"He did, but he's struggling with what he wants to do once he graduates."

"It seems he's very young to have to make that decision."

"He is," he said between bites, "but it's necessary to know that you're going to the best school to prepare you for your chosen profession."

"What's he considering?"

Mehmet laughed. "Well of course he's considering the medical profession." He cleared his throat. "But Ali is more interested in business—or possibly teaching—which are not the professions our father would like to see him pursue." His face darkened.

"Will he be allowed to choose what he most wants to study?" Gabrielle looked carefully at him.

"That remains to be seen."

"What did you say to Ali about this?"

"I told him to follow his heart. But I'm not sure he'll defy my father if it comes to that. Ali's a gentler person than I am," he said, looking down. "But let's not spoil a nice meal. I much prefer our discussion of art and human legacies."

She looked quizzically at him. Some deep rift clearly lay between Mehmet and his father. She sensed their conflict and the profound impact he had upon Mehmet and his life choices.

As they finished their dinner, the music began and the hum of conversation in the room lowered. A slender male pianist in a black suit was playing, while an attractive, slightly plump young woman in a floor-length black gown sang in Turkish into the floor microphone.

"Would you like something more to eat—or some dessert, perhaps?" Mehmet asked.

"I'm stuffed," she said, patting her stomach. "I couldn't eat another mouthful."

"Then perhaps you'd like to dance?"

Adventure in a Foreign Land

As she nodded, he rose and took her hand to walk to the dance floor. Facing her, he put his arm around her waist and lightly pulled her toward him. She could feel his warm breath on her face and the heat of his hands. As she tried to talk to him to break the intensity of their closeness, she found it impossible to speak over the music. So she turned her head to the side and let him move her closer until her head rested against his shoulder and she felt his whole body against hers. The music and the gentleness of his holding her swam throughout her body. It was as if they were one person floating along on a wave of lyrical sound.

As the music flowed from one song to another, she was aware of how he danced with grace. It made her remember her own love of dance. When the music grew soft, he pulled back a little. "Gabrielle...." He paused, as if searching for words. "I really like you. You're not like anyone I've ever met."

She blushed and caught her breath.

"You're a serious person, which I like," he said. "But you also can be lighthearted and full of enthusiasm. You think deeply about things and are not afraid to express your thoughts. You're culturally aware and appreciate differences between people. And it hasn't escaped me that you're a very beautiful woman."

"Mehmet, you flatter me. I'm not so special." She tried to look away

"No Gabrielle. You *are*." His words made her gaze back at him.

"You are kind to say these things," she said. Then she grew quiet. She didn't know where he was going with this, which left her unsettled. Then he pulled her toward him, then out to spin her around, making her laugh. "My, you certainly know your way around a dance floor," she exclaimed as he walked her back to their table.

"I don't know much about your family and how you came to Turkey," he said as he pulled her chair out for her before seating himself.

"Well, I grew up on the south shore of Long Island, an hour outside New York City. I have a sister who's four years older than I am. My father is a businessman, and my mother is a housewife, although she's worked for short periods of time to help support my sister's college education."

"Just your sister's?"

"Yes mostly, but only because I won a scholarship and took out student loans. I also put away a good bit of money that I earned working during high school and college. So I didn't need as much help as my sister did."

"That's admirable to be putting yourself through school," he said, looking respectfully at her. "How did you come to study here?"

"I wish I could say that it was the result of long reflection," she said with a laugh. "But the truth is it was a very last-minute and impulsive decision."

"I would have thought it the result of research and much consideration."

She laughed again. "Actually I was set to go to Denmark, the country my grandfather came from. But when a student exchange opened up between Oberlin and Robert Kolej, I found the prospect so exotic, Turkey being the bridge between East and West, that I made the switch.

"And that was all it took to take you away from Denmark and bring you here?"

"Well there's a bit more to it, but we don't need to go into that. In any case, I made the right decision. I love this city and love being able to be here this whole school year. It was tough to leave Oberlin however."

He looked quizzically at her as he sipped his third glass of wine. "What was difficult?"

"I was involved in the Civil Rights Movement...." She paused, then explained her involvement in black voter registration in Hattiesburg, Mississippi, in protests, and in her work helping tutor underprivileged kids. "I felt like I was walking away from work that was unfinished."

Mehmet looked amazed. "How did you get involved in this?"

"I had a friend who was the organizer of Oberlin's students to march for justice and to go south for the voter registration drives. I got involved in both of these when I saw how Southern blacks needed our aid. I knew I had to go. All my life I've had strong feelings about injustice. So much is clearly wrong in American society. Sometimes you just have to do what you know to be right. Black people have died trying to vote—and people died helping them to exercise their rights."

He sat in silence for a couple of minutes, staring at the candle flame that flickered as she spoke. Clearing his throat, he responded. "This is an extraordinary story. I never would have guessed you had done such things." He grew quiet again, then continued. "You are a braver person than I am I fear. I can hardly believe you did these things. It's selfless—and courageous."

She looked intently at him. "I don't know. I didn't really see it that way. I don't think I fully understood what I was getting into when I went to Mississippi. I got swept up in a need that seemed so apparent. I thought I could help, so I went. I'm glad that I did, but I sometimes feel guilty for leaving America in the middle of the Movement. I left to pursue this dream I've had since I was a child—to live and travel abroad. It seemed selfish at times. It still does."

He shook his head. "It can't be selfish to educate yourself and widen your perspective by experiencing more of the world. It will make you a more able person when you start on your career path, whatever that is. You have your whole life to make a difference wherever you can."

She nodded. "I know. That's what I tell myself—and what two close friends told me as well. But it may just be rationalization. I do, however, want as many new experiences as possible to find what I'm meant to do in the world and develop resources for the future, whatever that may hold." She looked away, lost in thought.

He observed her long before responding. "The more I learn about you, the more remarkable you seem. I live a much narrower life than you, Gabrielle. Turkish men, especially those from wealthy families, are spoiled. You put me to shame. I think about politics. But I think more about my life and that of my family's—and those of my friends and classmates—but not very much broader than that. I too hope to travel and expand my knowledge of the world. But so far, I've done that mostly through books. You presently have a much wider view of life than I have. You're a very unusual person." Some of the darkness in him seemed to return.

As he grew silent, she struggled to respond to what he said. She feared that she may have ruined a special evening that he had gone to great trouble and expense to give her.

"I think you sell yourself short Mehmet. You're such a knowledgeable and intelligent person—and have so much understanding of your culture…and of life. You have a way of getting to the heart of things. You see many things very clearly, things that not everyone notices or 'gets'. I may have had some life opportunities that you haven't, but I believe that you're a person of principle—and that you would always try to do the right thing when the choice presented itself. We're young. Who knows what lies ahead? I'm sure that you'll use your life well," she said earnestly.

He studied her. "Thank you for that Gabrielle. I hope you're right." His look spoke uncertainty.

Needing to do something to lift his spirits, she requested one more dance.

"Of course," he said, taking her hand and leading her to the dance floor. There he held her in his arms and danced without speaking.

* * *

After her evening with Mehmet, she lay in bed the next morning, reluctant to rise and interrupt her thoughts. As her roommates bustled about and left for breakfast, she remained in her bunk, recalling how she felt dancing with him and hearing his words of caring. She thought how drawn she was to him.

She remembered as well how friends and acquaintances of Mehmet spoke highly of him and related that he was at the top of his class and from a prominent Bursa family. Fluent in English and German in addition to his native tongue, he demonstrated knowledge of an eclectic mix of subjects, including architecture, history, music, and art. More importantly to her, he showed her his integrity and caring nature—and his gentle sense of humor. But what she couldn't get to fit the rest of this picture was his prevarication whenever she asked about his family, his father in particular.

Inevitably it brought on a change in his mood, which troubled her and led her to believe that his issues with his father were sharper than she previously may have thought. But also, she witnessed a certain sadness and hesitation in him when she revealed a previously unknown side of herself—a willingness and conviction to fight for the cause of civil rights and possibly pay a dear price to do a just thing to help people she didn't know.

Was it that he longed to do such things himself? she wondered. *Or that he saw strength in me that he hadn't been aware of and that now disturbed him?* She couldn't fathom his reaction and what that might mean for their young relationship. All she knew was that his goodnight kiss didn't have the full ardor he had shown on previous occasions. *He's a very complicated man,* she decided.

Heartbroken that she hadn't heard from him all week, she worried that she may have lost not only a romantic partner, but also a treasured friend. Later in the week however, she happened upon him when she was hunting for a book among the library stacks. Catching his eye, she noted his surprise as he walked over to her.

"Hi Gabrielle. How are you doing?" His voice sounded casual, but his face betrayed discomfort.

"I'm doing fine, thank you." She hesitated, noticing that he looked tired. "Are you okay?"

"Yes...yes." He looked away from her, then back. "I'm sorry not to have contacted you the last several days. I've been dealing with a personal issue."

"Do you want to talk about it?"

"I really can't...but thank you." His faraway look refocused on her now. He paused before he cleared his throat and spoke. "I'd like to make it up to you for my being so uncommunicative this past week. I shouldn't have left you hanging like that. Would you consider keeping me company on a cruise to the Princes' Islands this Saturday?"

Watching him, she was unsure what seemed different between them. Sighing as she considered his offer, she concluded that she should allow him time to open up to her. "Where are the islands and how far away are they?"

"They're in the Sea of Marmara. We probably would just take a ferry to Büyükada, the largest island. It's not very far—about eighteen kilometers from the city. We can take a picnic lunch and enjoy a long walk or a horse-drawn carriage ride around the island. I think you'd enjoy it." He smiled and looked hopefully at her, while sensing her reticence.

She paused, then answered gently in the affirmative.

"That's great," he said, sounding more upbeat. "Can we leave at nine o'clock Saturday? It takes a full day for travel and sightseeing. I can pick you up at the dorm." He was all smiles.

"That will be fine."

"Plan to dress very casually, as we'll do a lot of walking and be outdoors the whole time." He seemed to be relaxing now.

"Okay," she said, giving him a tentative smile.

"See you then!" And with that, he turned and was gone.

What was that? she wondered. *What personal issue is troubling him? He's so secretive. I just don't understand. I'm not sure I can deal with his mood swings and furtiveness.* She shook her head and went back to looking for a book. Despite her irritation, she couldn't deny her fascination with him and what she implicitly understood—that she would need to give him time and space to learn to trust her enough to reveal his demons to her. She just hoped it wouldn't take too long and that whatever it was wouldn't further shadow their relationship.

* * *

Gabrielle opened the letters greedily. It had been two months since she had arrived in Turkey. It had taken a long time for her letters to reach her family and friends and for theirs to come back to her. It was the beginning of November already.

Adventure in a Foreign Land

She had a long letter from Rick, full of teasing, but also the latest news on the Civil Rights Movement and the tutoring center. The best news of all was that Jeremy passed his reading tests and had progressed to the next grade. Gabrielle was so excited and proud of him.

As for Adrienne, she waxed poetic about the fun she was having dating Barcelona's Spanish men. And a letter from Gabrielle's mother expressed how much she and Arthur missed their girls. She said she was considering going back to work at the bookstore.

The fourth letter was from Ruth.

September 26, 1965

Gabel, I can hardly believe that you're in exotic Istanbul! I'm so jealous. I haven't managed yet to make my way across the ocean as we promised ourselves as kids. But for now, I'm quite happy here in Boston. How I love this city! So much history and culture. You know how I love that.

As you're well aware, I've been consumed by my graduate studies at Boston University's School of Social Work. I'm learning all kinds of great stuff I can use when I become a social worker. Also, I met a great guy who's in the same program. His name is Harry. I like him a lot—well, more than like him. He's really smart, kind-hearted, and handsome. What more could a gal want? So I may not have made it abroad like you did, but with Harry in my life, I couldn't be happier.

I'm wondering how you're doing and whether you've met anyone special. I know you had some bad experiences with men and hope you find someone more worthy of your affections.

I've been thinking a lot about you and me, Gabel. I recognize that we weren't very close growing up. Between our age difference and the issues created by Dad, causing me to flee the house and leaving you to deal with more things than you should have had to, we never really had the chance to bond as sisters should. I've regretted that. I hope that when you return home, I can see you more and we can get closer. I plan on being there for a week or two this summer and will look forward to hearing all your stories.

Enjoy your year in Turkey. I can hardly wait to hear all about it!

Love, Ruth

Ruth's letter brought Gabrielle to tears. She had long wished for a more intimate relationship with her sister and felt Ruth's love in her statements. *I'll write mom and Ruth soon*, Gabrielle thought, *and let Ruth know that I wish the same.* Sliding her sister's letter back into the envelope, she closed the flap, then kissed it.

It comforted Gabrielle to hear from her family and friends. The letters afforded her a sense of connection with her family and her life in America, a life she greatly valued. It was this life that she left to find something new and challenging that would deepen her education and life experiences.

It's a journey this is, she thought, *a quest even, to find what my life can become. I can't let anything or anyone derail this. I'm young and have my whole life ahead of me. I see possibilities now that I hadn't before. My love of art is growing in me, like my love of people from different cultures and walks of life.*

Human need pulls at me, as I know it does for Ruth. The Civil Rights Movement has marked me and continues its hold. I have to find how I can best make a difference by my life's choices. I know now that art is a calling, and it has marked me as well. Art is something I share with Bilge and Mehmet. Both have artistic spirits. I'll have to see where these relationships take me and if they can help me to grow my better self.

9

Before she knew it, it was Saturday. Having told her roommates that she was dating Mehmet, they were excited and wanted to help her prepare for her excursion to Büyükada Island. They filled her in on what to expect to find there, how to dress, and places she should be sure to see. Since it was rather warm for the beginning of November, they suggested she wear her dark-green cotton skirt, a long-sleeved white cotton blouse, and her black flats--and include a light jacket in her shoulder bag. Walking her to the long mirror in the communal bathroom, they smiled approvingly at the picture they had helped to create.

"Now have a good time," Azra said. "It's almost nine o'clock."

"We'll expect a complete report when you return!" Esma chimed in.

"And be sure to take a horse-and-carriage ride," Zeynep added.

"Thank you," Gabrielle said, smiling broadly at her animated roommates. "I'll see you tonight!"

With that, Gabrielle walked downstairs to wait for Mehmet. She had to smile at her roommates' enthusiasm and how she grew closer to them by letting them be part of her adventure. It was the kind of occasion women loved to share, whether in America, Turkey, or anywhere else, and it felt good to make this connection with her dormmates.

No sooner had Gabrielle reached the bottom of the stairs than the front door opened and Mehmet entered. She thought he looked smashing and smiled at him. For a moment she thought she heard her roommates tittering on the landing above, but when she turned to look, they were gone.

"Are you ready to go?" he asked

She nodded as he opened the door and followed her out.

"What do you have in your string bag?" she asked as they walked across campus.

"Our picnic lunch. But the contents are for me to know and for you to find out," he responded, grinning mischievously.

Gabrielle was pleased with his lighthearted attitude and held great hopes for a pleasant day. "Okay so *that's* how it's going to be," she responded with equal flourish, eliciting a laugh from him.

They caught a *dolmuş* to Kabatas, then the ferry to Büyükada. It was a dazzlingly sunny, balmy day. Since it was a ninety-minute ride, they found seats in the sun, watched the trail of the water taking them along the Bosporus to the Sea of Marmara, and arrived at the big island around noon. Since the ferry was full, it took them longer than expected to disembark.

"What do you say we split and head to a park for lunch," Mehmet suggested after passing through the historic Ottoman ferry terminal and crowded town center with its shops and restaurants and men hawking everything from carriage rides to food.

Soon they walked uphill toward a park Mehmet knew. They passed ornate historic homes and gardens and streets filled with pedestrians, bicycles, and horse-drawn carriages.

"It's nice not to have cars on the island, but these carriages sure can tear down the hill," she noted as one screamed by.

Smiling at her, he took her hand. She thought that her hand fit his perfectly. They both were warm and a little sweaty from the hike, but she didn't mind. Soon they reached a small park with picnic tables overlooking the Marmara.

"Look," she cried. "That beautiful sea!"

He smiled, watching her. "And Istanbul is beyond," he added.

"Let me take your picture in front of this perfect view," she said, fishing in her bag for her camera.

"Only if you let me take one of you."

"Deal. Now stand over there by that tree," she said, motioning him to step to the right. He moved obediently. "Now say cheese," she directed.

"You mean *peynir*?" Saying the Turkish word for cheese produced an odd facial expression, which she photographed.

"Okay wise guy. Now if you don't cooperate, I'll use that picture for blackmail," she quipped.

"Be that way," he joked, then smiled the word "cheese."

"That's better. But I'm still keeping the blackmail picture."

"Okay, your turn." He put the string bag on a picnic table and took three photos of her. "Enough now," he said. "Let's eat."

They sat so they both had a view of the Marmara twinkling under the early afternoon sun. Mehmet pulled from the bag a penknife, a full loaf of *ekmek*, crusty on the outside, soft and yeasty inside, two *domates* the size of grapefruits, a tube of black olive paste, and a large chunk of *beyaz peynir*, all wrapped individually in newspaper. She watched as he cut thick slices of the bread, tomatoes, and white cheese, stacking the contents on the bread slices he smeared with the salty olive paste. Then he covered his creation with a top slice of bread. Placing one sandwich on newspaper for her and one for himself, he took two bottles of water from the bottom of his string bag and handed her one. "This is my favorite picnic lunch. I always bring it when I come here. It's a common Turkish picnic."

"It looks great. Thanks for fixing it."

Grinning, he bit into the tall sandwich as she struggled to open wide enough to eat it. She opted to compress it, then tried again, this time successfully. He laughed and she responded, summarizing her satisfaction with the word "delicious."

When they finished their sandwiches, Mehmet peeled an orange nearly as big as a dessert plate and split the citrus between them.

"Are all fruits and vegetables in Turkey this big?" Gabrielle asked, motioning to the orange and the remaining tomato.

"Pretty much. Are they unusually big?"

"By American standards, yes. I wonder what makes your produce grow so large."

"A combination of the right weather and soil conditions I imagine."

"I guess. And I love how fresh everything is, like it was just made or picked."

"Probably both true. I got the bread hot from the bakery oven this morning. And the fruit gets delivered to shops and stands daily."

"It makes for a real feast."

They sipped their water as they talked. "What do you say we take one of those carriage rides around the island?" he interjected.

"That sounds perfect," she responded. "I was hoping for that."

"Good," he said, packing the remaining items. Helping him clear the table, she stopped and took one last look at this view of the Marmara before heading for the street.

Walking downhill, they came to a group of horse-drawn carriages. She pulled him away from the first one in line. "Look at the horses," she said, gently tugging on the arm of his shirt. "They're very thin and not well taken care of. Let's take the next one, the one with the red fringe on top and the two large black, healthy-looking horses."

"Of course," he answered, seemingly touched by her compassion for the animals. After engaging the driver, Mehmet helped Gabrielle into the carriage. "I've opted for the long carriage ride, which takes about an hour. That way we can see the shore and hills as well as the town. Sound good?"

"Perfect."

And with that, the driver snapped the leather reins and turned the horses out onto the road. The horses clipped and clopped until the carriage with its wooden wheels had cleared the most congested area near Dock Square with its landmark clock tower.

As the horses progressed into a slow trot, the driver began his narration in Turkish of the island's sights, with a little English thrown in here and there. Mehmet translated portions of the narrative for her as she watched the historic homes go by, many Victorian in style including the grand old Splendid Hotel—the *Splandit Oteli*. The shoreline with a few tiny beaches packed with sun worshippers came into view, followed by the five-plus-square-mile-island's two prominent rises, one over five-hundred-feet high, the other over six hundred. From there they had particularly spectacular views of the Marmara.

The carriage made numerous stops in town, by the beaches, and on the hills so Gabrielle could take pictures. This elongated the trip by a good fifteen minutes, despite the fact that the driver had let the horses tear along the road from the top of the last prominence, making for an exciting trip down. Mehmet tipped the driver generously for taking the extra time.

Adventure in a Foreign Land

"Thank you so much Mehmet. That was such fun," she said gleefully, taking hold of his arm and pinching it. "I never traveled before in a surrey with the fringe on top. And certainly not at full gallop!"

Mehmet looked quizzically at her, saying he never heard the carriage called a surrey before, then laughed to see her so happy. "I'm glad you liked it. Let's see...," he looked at his wristwatch, "it's after fifteen hours—uh, three o'clock already. What would you like to do? We probably have three hours before we need to catch the...uh...six-thirty ferry back to the mainland."

"What would you suggest?"

"It might be nice to stretch our legs a bit. Maybe walk about town and look at the houses and shops? Or walk uphill to a Greek Orthodox church or get some tea or coffee and a bite to eat?"

"All good," she said.

Gabrielle took more photos of the houses and shops on their way toward Prinkipo Hagia Yorgi Church, where she pulled our her sketch pad and drew the church's charming interior with its blue, white, and red crystal chandeliers; Romanesque features; and ceilings painted with a sky-blue background dotted with gold-and-white stars highlighting Biblical figures.

But Gabrielle thought the grounds were the best thing about visiting the church. From here they had the most spectacular views of the Marmara, the other islands, and the mainland beyond. She made quick sketches of the landscape and views.

"What an amazing scene," she exclaimed as they walked, "and a lovely church. Are there others like this in and around Istanbul?"

"There are. If you like, we can find them another day."

"That would be nice. But I'd especially like to see more of the Ottoman structures."

"There are lots of those," he chuckled. "You may need to stay here a very long time to even begin to see a fraction of them."

She smiled. "Well," she said noncommittedly, "at least I'll see some." She thought she saw a shadow cross his face. *Does the thought of my leaving sadden him?* she wondered. As she squeezed his arm, he returned to his better-humored self.

"In any case we shall see all that our time together allows," he said. "Speaking of which, we may need to start walking toward the ferry fairly soon. It's a bit of a hike down. So let's grab that bench over there and have the rest of these sandwiches."

As they ate, they took in the view and talked. "I think I mentioned that I'm sketching weekly now with Bilge Tekin," she said.

"I recall that you did."

"She's the first Turkish woman I've really connected with on a deep level, although I've grown quite fond of my roommates. Becoming friends with Bilge makes me happy."

"It's good then. I find it quite interesting that you're a new student of art and that already you seem to display a real talent for it," he said, looking with interest at her and the sketches she started while on the island.

"I'm thinking about declaring it as my major. Working with a seasoned artist like Bilge gives me practice and encouragement. I'll just have to see where this leads."

"I'm impressed. This isn't a talent I have, but I love art and enjoy the study of it."

"That's evident to me in your knowledge of architecture," she replied looking admiringly at him. Smiling she added, "If you decide that chemical engineering isn't for you, I know you could make your way as an extraordinary tour guide."

He laughed. "I'm sure my family would be delighted to have spent an enormous sum to educate me and then have me opt for the tourist trade."

She grinned. "It's always good to have a fallback position."

"Is it?" He studied her.

"Don't you think so?"

"As a general rule, no."

"Why?"

"It can make you timid. I think it's keeping something in reserve that you could use to pursue what you're after."

"Hmm. I never thought of it that way," she said, dropping her gaze in thought, then looking up at him. "But don't you think that sometimes life calls for a chess game approach, where you consider many possible moves before playing—including a fallback position prior to a bold move?"

"Perhaps. I can see the advantage of it in certain circumstances. In general however, I think too much of that can hold you back."

"But if something doesn't feel right, I like to prepare myself to be able to make a swift change."

"That takes courage as well."

Gabrielle nodded in acknowledgment, then breathed in deeply. "I love that I can smell the water from here."

"Amazing you can smell it from this distance."

She laughed. "Maybe it's my active imagination."

He smiled, studying her, then responded, "Better than no imagination."

When they finished eating, he checked his watch. "My, we're running late. Let's catch a carriage down. Our ferry leaves in just over a half-hour."

They rapidly stored their paper and remaining food and water in the string bag and hiked quickly to a surrey. Flying down the hill to the ferry station, they arrived as passengers already were crowding onto the boat and hustling to find seats for the long ride back. Mehmet and Gabrielle were among the last to take theirs, which put them outside and close to the engine noise.

As the sun began to set, their ferry left Büyükada Island. The breeze that intensified as the ferry cut through the surface of the Marmara Sea made Gabrielle shiver.

"You're cold Gabrielle. Here, take my sweater," he offered.

"I have a jacket in my bag, but thank you," she responded, raising her voice to be heard above the engine as she pulled out her wrap. "That's better," she said smiling triumphantly.

Donning his sweater, he reached to take her hand. "Your hand is cold. Are you warm enough with just your light jacket?"

"I think I'm okay…just a little cold," she admitted.

He removed his hand from hers and put his arm around her, pulling her close. In just a few minutes she felt warm again, warm and cared for.

Together they watched the sky transform from golden to orange and pink, then paler pink and a deepening blue. The water transmuted as well, the colors of the sky dancing over the moving sea. They felt no need to talk, enveloped in a canvas that changed minute to minute and in a feeling of closeness and gentle longing. The stars pierced the canvas of the sky. These celestial bodies seemed to throb as the moon arced upward, vibrant and certain in its trajectory.

It wasn't long until the lights of Istanbul twinkled in the advancing night sky, and the beams of other watercraft floated on the same aqueous canvas as they, moving with the pair toward a future yet unknown to them. Two young people from different worlds, joined in something they had yet to define or fully understand, just sat and watched, feeling the warmth and resonance of each other and joy in the glow of what surrounded them in this crystal of a moment.

As they sat, bound by what only could be growing love, Gabrielle felt that his plunges and release from a darkness she didn't understand were something she ought not to probe, at least not now, not tonight. Not unless he was ready to unveil himself to her, and she was ready to receive it. She thought about how she believed in his basic goodness and sensitivity, his honesty and honorable nature. Perhaps that was all she needed from him, she thought.

She realized too that no matter what demons possessed him periodically, they wouldn't change her growing affection for him. For now, she thought, she would savor the pleasure of their day and their delight in each other's company. Turning in the dimming light, she looked fully at him, moving her body further against him. He turned to her and seemed to catch the light in her eyes as he drew his face toward hers and covered her lips with his, kissing her with all the passion and yearning he had stored for just this moment. It was as if he felt from her what he had been waiting for—her acceptance. Baring herself, Gabrielle received him, returning his ardor with her own.

10

Over the months as Gabrielle continued to study and develop her skills and commitment to art, Gabrielle and Mehmet's romance deepened. As their love flourished, they became almost inseparable, enjoying their relationship for all the happiness it offered.

Over their courtship, however, hung the specter of her impending return to America. It now was just a month away. She felt torn between her love for Mehmet and her increasing desire to return home, study painting from teachers who could help her progress in her art, and continue her work for social change. Had it not been for her weekly sessions with Bilge, she would have had no meaningful critiques of her artistic efforts.

She had grown greatly and gained confidence as an artist because of these meetings and because of her trips with Mehmet to places of miraculous artistic and architectural creation. All of this had made her resolute in her devotion to art. But now she required more. She needed teachers with skills far beyond hers. This recognition gnawed at her with a fierceness she couldn't deny.

"Gabrielle," Mehmet said on one of their evening campus walks, "we must talk about your leaving. Would you consider taking your senior year here?"

Hesitant, she asked if they could sit, gesturing toward a nearby stone bench overlooking the Bosporus. Seating themselves, they held hands as she turned toward him. She thought how remarkable and handsome he was, his face strong, his dark eyes speaking hopefulness.

"You know there's nothing I would rather do," she said, "if only Robert Kolej offered art classes. I know for certain that art is my path and that a fine art degree will be required. I'm hungry to dive into it to see what kind of artist I can become. But it tears at me to leave, as leaving here is leaving you. I love you with all my heart. I see no good way to resolve this." Looking long at him, she thought how much she wanted him, how his very touch excited her. Then, as he listened, she saw tears in his eyes.

"I can't bear to lose you Gabrielle. I've never met anyone like you…and never will again. I've come to love you more than I thought I could love anyone. Yet I understand your dilemma. Would it not be possible to study art in your senior year at another school here in Istanbul?"

She heard the anguish in his voice, filling her with sorrow. "I've thought of this too," she said as she watched his face soften with hope. "But my love, I haven't found another college here that can give me what I need for a fine art degree, prepare me for graduate school, and communicate with me in English. My Turkish is just not good enough to converse with instructors in a Turkish-speaking school." She gazed at him and thought how hard their circumstances had become and dove deep in thought. "I don't suppose you'd consider finishing your bachelor's degree in America?"

He shook his head. "I have a scholarship to study at this college and have made a commitment to finish here. I don't see how this is possible."

They both looked down, still holding one another's hands and sitting in silence for several minutes. "Perhaps," he said, breaking their quietude, "I could do my graduate work in your country. We wouldn't see each other for a year, which seems unbearable to me. But maybe we could find a school that could serve both of our requirements and be together then."

"You'd consider this?" She looked up at him, surprise reflected in her expression as he turned to face her directly.

"My parents wouldn't like it," he began, then took a deep breath. His hold on her hands tightened, his face transformed with a look that searched her very soul. "But Gabrielle, I love you and I would do this. What I'm asking, my love, is that you honor me by accepting my proposal of marriage."

She gasped in surprise, rendering her speechless. But her love for this man rose fast and thick from the very core of her. Longing to be held by him, she felt his breath on her face and neck, hot and laden with their desire. But then he spoke. "I'll wait for you as long as you need. Just tell me you'll marry me, and I'll find a way to be with you in a year." As his arms encircled her, he held her reverently as he stroked her hair and sought his answer in their kiss. Passion rose in her. All she wanted at this moment was to remain in his arms forever.

Moved to say yes to the sacrifice he was offering, she hesitated, feeling she needed time to think. His proposal raised many troubling concerns, for which she still had no answers.

Finally she responded, "Mehmet, your proposal means more to me than you can imagine. You know how strong my love is for you and how honored I would be to be your wife. We have a very complicated situation, however, that we should discuss and find answers to before making our plans. Does this make sense to you?"

"Yes of course. What questions do you have?"

She hesitated. "I can't help but wonder what happens after graduate school. Would we stay in America, or would you expect to return here? And what would your parents say? What would mine? One of us would be giving up our families, our country, our whole way of life. Can we ask that of each other?"

"Gabrielle, I can't answer these questions. Not yet. Perhaps we agree to a long engagement until we complete our graduate work in your country. Then we'll know better whether we can make this work and where we can best reside. I only know that I don't want to go through life without you. You are my one true love. Please tell me you'll consider my proposal."

She paused only a moment. "Of course I will. You've surprised and touched me more than I can say. I'll need time to think about all that we've talked about. It's a very big step, full of many unknowns."

"It is, Gabrielle. I realize that." He stood, raising her with him. Pulling her tight against him, he kissed her with an ardor that tore at her defenses, his whole being pressed to hers, the hardness of his body seeking hers, his lips finding her breasts. She felt herself grow weak with desire. *God help me*, was the last thing she thought.

Returning to her dormitory, she found her roommates chatting and readying for bed. They tried to engage her in one of their regular conversations, but she begged off, saying she was tired and not feeling well. Soon the lights went out, and she fell into a restless sleep.

The next morning, with her dormmates at breakfast, she lay in bed, reliving the night and the love she felt for this man. While she had thought often about what might happen when it came time for her to go home, she never could have imagined his marriage proposal. If he wanted to come to America to stay permanently and truly had wanted this for himself, not as a sacrifice for her, she would have accepted his offer this very night. She was more in love with him than she had been with any man. Spending a lifetime with someone so respectful and kind toward her, while being highly educated, intelligent, and endlessly fascinating to her, was a dream she never imagined would come true.

But his proposal was not as straightforward as that. It involved huge commitments, but with a wait-and-see component that left questions of major proportions. How could she plan her future without any idea whether he would fall in love with America or be anxious to return to his beloved Turkey at the end of his graduate work? While she wasn't certain, she believed she might be unhappy living permanently in Turkey. Mehmet already alluded to his parents not favoring his going abroad to study, let alone with the intent ultimately of marrying an American.

While she understood that he and his family weren't practicing Muslims, as an outsider she suspected she still wouldn't be accepted by them. Furthermore she was uncertain she could live happily in a society that might regard her as beneath Mehmet and his family and in a culture so strongly patriarchal. Surely any involvement from her in possible political changes she might wish to support in Turkey would be unwanted and perhaps even disallowed. Would she have freedom to follow her heart's callings, as she believed she could back home?

Adventure in a Foreign Land

And what of Mehmet's happiness if he agreed to stay in America, but became estranged from his family, his childhood and college friends—and his country? What if he lost important pieces of who he was and came to resent the sacrifices he had made? How could they fix this if she couldn't make the same sacrifices for him?

Wrestling with all these questions, she thought she would go mad, feeling torn between her ardor for this man and the whirl of questions that encircled her.

* * *

After her roommates left for breakfast, she rose, threw on her clothes, and walked down the hall to find Becky. Fortunately she still was there and alone.

"Becky, can I talk to you?"

"I'm afraid I have to dash…," Becky started to reply, then turned and looked at Gabrielle. "What the hell happened to you?"

"What?"

"You look terrible."

"Ugh. Becky, Mehmet proposed to me last night."

"What?"

"I said…"

"I know what you said. I don't think the way you look jibes with getting a proposal from the man you love. What gives?"

She explained Mehmet's proposal. "You see my dilemma?"

"Wow. I sure do. Talk about a Catch-22."

"I just don't know what to do or how to respond. How do you make such commitments and plan your life based on so much uncertainty?"

"I don't know Gabrielle. That's a tough one. I know how much you two care about each other and how good you are together. But you've never been tested in the scenario Mehmet's painted. It seems your relationship could be weighed down by the tension of impending sacrifice and uncertainty. You could lose your sense of security in each other. Your choices would become more serious. Do you think your love for one another can overcome all this—and things you can't even imagine now?"

"Oh Becky, I do love him so. But I'm afraid—afraid of all the things you just mentioned and more. I don't honestly know if our love would be enough." Tears filled her eyes.

Becky put her arms around her friend. "Give yourself time," she whispered. "Don't rush to answer him. You'll figure this out and know what the right response is. You just need to give yourself space to think things through. I know you'll do what's best for both of you."

"I just didn't see this coming," Gabrielle sobbed.

11

Two days later Mehmet called saying his roommate would be gone all evening and they could talk there privately. "I know I surprised you with my proposal, Gabrielle, and realize you must have a lot of questions. Please come to my dorm room." Reluctantly she acquiesced, still struggling with her thoughts.

His room was quite different from hers at the women's dorm and had two beds, two desks, chairs, and closets, a couch, and Turkish carpets covering the linoleum floors. Larger than the women's dorm rooms and better appointed, it was lit with lamps softer than the glaring lights in the women's dorm.

"Are you sure it's okay for me to be here?" she asked. "I thought women weren't allowed."

"Yes, but women do at times visit men in their rooms. Please try not to worry. No one saw us come in, and we'll be careful when you leave," he assured her. "But I'm sensing that you're conflicted about my proposal and wanted us to have privacy to talk openly about our concerns."

She nodded as he took her hand gently and drew her to sit beside him on the couch.

"Gabrielle, I realize I shocked you the other night. I'm sorry. I know it's a lot to consider."

"It is," she said quietly

"Please tell me how you're feeling about what I proposed." His eyes wore a look of urgency. It was clear to her how unsettled he was, not knowing how she felt.

"Mehmet, I'm afraid I don't have an answer for you. There are so many unknowns and a great deal to process."

"There *are* Gabrielle, I realize that. Please tell me what troubles you the most." He took her hand.

"I don't know where to begin," she sighed, taking a couple of minutes to gather her thoughts. "First I want you to know how honored I am by your proposal. I hope you know how much I love you. I can hardly imagine my life without you."

Smiling hopefully, he tightened his hand around hers.

"But our situation is complicated, and our relationship is still quite new. The prospect of living apart for a year, then you coming to America for school, which your parents apparently wouldn't like, then finding a graduate school where we both can get the best possible educations in our fields…" she hesitated, her eyes averted in thought, "can be tricky. Then we will be waiting a couple of years to know what country we would live in and have us both satisfied with where we settle. These are terribly difficult issues to resolve and puts our relationship under tremendous stress that we don't yet know we can weather."

Knitting his brows in concentration, he nodded his acknowledgment while holding her hand like a lifeline.

"And how do we plan our futures when we don't know where we'll be and whether we can be happy with our choices?" she asked.

"So your biggest concern is where we ultimately will live?" he probed gently.

"I suppose it is," she looked down, "but it's more complicated than that." She took a deep breath and glanced up, their eyes meeting. "How can we have a chance for our love to grow with so much pressure? How can either of us feel glad if one of us has to sacrifice their homeland and all that goes with it? What chance do we really have to make this work?"

He withdrew his hand, his face pained. "Do you not believe that people from different worlds can marry and make a good life together?"

"Yes Mehmet, I do," she exclaimed. "But I think one of them will give up a great deal. That person would have to want to live in the new country for their own sake, not just for their spouse's. I think that if that doesn't happen, the one who made the sacrifice may become unhappy and grow resentful. I don't think I could bear that." She lowered her eyes so he couldn't read the anguish in them.

He pondered what she said. "Let me ask you this. Do you think you could live happily in Turkey?"

Gabrielle hesitated, then raised her face to his. "I don't know exactly how to answer that. I adore Istanbul. I really don't know anywhere else in Turkey. I could happily spend months at a time here, but make it my permanent home? I honestly don't know—and that's what frightens me. And you can't possibly know if you could live permanently in America until you're there at least through graduate school. What if neither of us can give up our homeland?"

"Tell me this Gabrielle, why do you doubt that you could make a life here if it came to that?"

She faltered but a minute. "My sense is that as a woman, I'd have more freedoms in America than I would here where men dominate so. They do in America too, but I believe that it's more possible there to have a relationship between equal partners. And I worry that your family would look down on me, perhaps shun me even. I'd be leaving my family behind…and would need the support of yours, which I don't feel confident of."

She paused, watching him. "We have our whole lives ahead of us. As we are now, we can go in any direction we wish—be who we want to be, pursue whatever dreams we may have. I'm too young to give that up. And I wouldn't want you to either. I can't see how to make this work so we both are happy. That's what scares me."

Adventure in a Foreign Land

He was silent for several minutes. "I see," he said finally. "It sounds like you've already made your decision." He looked sad and resigned.

She hesitated, putting her hand on the side of her face as if she were struck before reaching for his hand. Gently she answered, "No Mehmet, but I *am* wrestling with this. Can you show me something I'm not seeing correctly or should be considering? If you can, please tell me, as I would love nothing better than to accept your proposal." Her hand tightened on his.

He shook his head. "I've thought the same as you. The difference is that I'm ready to accept all that uncertainty for the chance that we may be able to spend our lives together as husband and wife. From what I'm hearing, it seems to me that you aren't confident that we can see a way to make our marriage work—and you're finding it difficult to accept the years of uncertainty we'll have before we can make our decision. Is there something you'd like to ask me that would make you more confident of our chances of success?"

She pondered his question as she withdrew her hand and shifted on the couch. "Do you believe in equality in the home between a man and a woman?"

"What exactly do you mean by equality?"

"I mean that we each have the permission of the other to follow our dreams, that we make decisions affecting us together, that we both are involved in our home responsibilities, especially if we have children—and if we both wish to work, that we find a way to do that." She looked at him very directly.

He thought a bit. "Yes to following our dreams and both working if we wish. Yes to together making decisions that affect us and our family. As to taking on home responsibilities," he smiled, "I'd be very bad at that, as I have no experience with it. Turkish men can be very spoiled. I can say that I'd try and help as best I could, but I'd hope you'd take leadership in that."

"Fair enough," she said, returning his smile. "How would you see handling the situation with your parents and other family members?"

He searched his thoughts and looked more serious again. "Honestly I don't have an answer for that. In time my mother would accept it, especially if we resided in Turkey. But she would cry for a long time were I to live apart from her for an extended period. My brother and sisters would accept you I think. My father is the problem."

She stared at him, trying to decipher exactly what that meant. "Mehmet, I've been aware for some time that you and your father have a...difficult relationship. Can you explain that to me?"

He let out a sarcastic laugh, then grew solemn before quieting his voice. "It's hard for me to talk about him." Emotional darkness seemed to engulf him as he fell silent.

"Please love," she said, "you can tell me anything. I will keep your confidence. I know you've been harmed in some manner by your father. I've been hurt by my father too. He's an alcoholic. It's important that we know what has wounded us and help one another to heal."

It was minutes before he could respond. Looking away from her and clearing his throat, he commenced. "My father is a brilliant cardiothoracic surgeon, well thought of by the hospital executives, his patients, and the community. He's also highly opinionated and not very tolerant. He has an unbending sense of how things should be. Anyone who disagrees with him inevitably feels his wrath." He looked down, as if gathering strength to continue.

"How does he show it?" she asked, watching his face.

"He's destroyed careers of young interns and doctors who've tested him, to give you a taste for what he is capable."

"How has this affected you?" she asked reaching for his hand.

She watched him draw inward as he hesitated, his face hardening. Finally he cleared his throat. "I'm his older son. From the time I was very young, I showed an ability to learn swiftly and accomplish things that other children my age couldn't. I also carry his name—Mehmet. So in me he put all his expectations for a child to be just like him." He stopped to clear his throat. "That included becoming a surgeon. From the time I was in grammar

Adventure in a Foreign Land

school, I showed special talents in science and mathematics and the practical application of them. My father kept trying to bend me toward biology and medicine, but I didn't want to be him. One day," he began, then seemed to falter. She moved closer, putting her arm around him.

"I was home from boarding school," he said finally. "I was fifteen. He was particularly belligerent with me and on a tirade. Of course I'd heard it all before. Always in the past I met his yelling and demands with silence. But this time he pushed me too far, saying I would be nothing if I didn't do as he said. Then he slapped me on the face and told me to wake up and do as I was told or I would be sorry." Mehmet nearly choked on the memories his words described.

Sitting taller, he pulled away from her encircling arm, but took her hand. Then his hold seemed to tighten as he spoke. "I snapped," he continued, "shouting at him that I never wanted to be him, never would be him, and would become whatever I pleased. As I turned to walk away, he grabbed me and beat me until I was unconscious. I lost a month of school until I could recover well enough to go back and not embarrass him."

"Mehmet!" Gabrielle gasped. "How horrible!"

As he fought back tears, he withdrew his hand from hers, struggling to regain his composure and resume his story. "He's never repented of what he did to me, and I can't forgive him. He may have broken my body, but not my spirit. He threatened to refuse paying for my college education. Fortunately he couldn't withdraw me from boarding school without everyone in town knowing.

So I studied very hard to earn a scholarship to pay my college tuition. My grandfather...," Mehmet stumbled as tears flooded his eyes, "whom I loved very much...left me some money. I'm using that to pay for my college living expenses. There'll be enough remaining to help with some of my future needs. That of course made my father furious, but my grandfather's will prevailed." He stopped, collecting himself. "Now my father is putting the same pressure on Ali as he did on me, since he is his only other son. I know that I need to try to help my brother as soon as I begin earning money. I want to be sure he can have a chance to live his life as he chooses. But he's a gentler person than I am, so I don't know if he ultimately will confront my father." With these words he seemed to deflate. His eyes looked hollow.

"Mehmet, I'm so sorry! I see now why this is so difficult for you," she said gently as her arms encircled him and she kissed his check. Looking into his eyes she continued, "You are so precious to me. Please don't be sad—and know that I love you more than anyone. If there's a way to make a life together, we'll find it."

So that's where the darkness comes from, she thought. *What a horrible thing to do to a child. I don't think I could ever bear to be in his father's presence, knowing now what he did to Mehmet. Oh my love."*

In his pain Mehmet softened into her embrace and acknowledged her, his lips finding hers as he pressed against her. In that moment, she felt the strength of his love and his hurt. He slowly unbuttoned her blouse and kissed her breasts, then lay down, pulling her beside him. Reaching to further dim the light, he cradled her in his arms, speaking his love for her as he sought all that she was. His passion aroused her, now lost in a desire so strong she thought it would consume her. "My God!" she whispered as he muffled her words with his kisses.

12

The remainder of the school year all but vanished in the whirl of classes ending and the start of final exams. Furthermore Gabrielle had to prepare to leave Turkey and all she had come to love.

She and Mehmet saw one another with increased frequency as they continued to discuss their future. Over time she came to accept his proposal to live apart for a year until he came to America for graduate studies. Eventually they would resolve where

Adventure in a Foreign Land

they would live and if they could make their planned marriage work.

Then one evening he sought her at the library and told her it was urgent that he speak with her. Looking questioningly at him, she left her books and notes scattered on the library table where she was preparing for her final exams.

Taking his hand she walked in silence with him out of the building and into the moonlit night. At the back of campus overlooking the Bosporus, he stopped in a cypress tree's partial shadow cast by the moon. As he turned toward her, she watched his face, contorted in grief. She took his hand that was uncharacteristically sweaty. Putting her other hand on his cheek, she asked, "What my love? What has happened?"

He took a deep breath, then seemed to retreat emotionally to steady himself. "My mother called me earlier today to tell me that my father..." he hesitated, "...my father died of a heart attack...suddenly...very early this morning."

"Oh Mehmet!"

"She was frightened and hysterical and kept sobbing," he said, catching his breath as if to dampen his emotions. "I could hardly understand what she was saying. She kept repeating that I had to come home. I told her I'd call her back and phoned my uncle in Bursa. He explained that my father got up as usual this morning, was shaving in the bathroom getting ready for work, when he had a massive heart attack and fell. By the time the ambulance arrived he was long dead. My uncle said he apparently died instantaneously. My mother of course was the one who found him unresponsive on the bathroom floor. She's beside herself and won't be consoled. She says she doesn't know how she'll manage without him."

When he paused, she put her arms around him. "My dear, I'm so sorry." He seemed to sink into her embrace as the tears he was holding back came in great heaving sobs. She held him tighter and cried with him. In a while he grew quiet and wiped his face with his handkerchief.

"I'm sorry, Gabrielle, I didn't think I'd do this."

"Please my love. You've lost your father, and your mother is in crisis. You have nothing to apologize for. I'm just so sorry this has happened. Is there something I can do that might help?"

Looking spent, he shook his head. "I've been on the phone all morning speaking with my uncle, my mother, my brother and older sister. I'm the older son. It's traditional that care of our family falls to the oldest son, who essentially becomes head of household. My mother is devastated and begging me to come home and take care of our family."

Gabrielle was taken aback, not having expected this. "Come sit down. You must tell me what this means and what you plan to do." She took his hand and guided him to the stone bench where they always sat. Releasing his hand, she turned toward him, his face now fully lit by moonlight.

He regarded her solemnly, his face haggard. Though he cleared his throat, his voice seemed to stick. "Gabrielle, this is not good for us and our plans. I'd hoped to come to America for graduate school where we could be together again. I feel that I have no choice now but to go home and take care of my family." He shifted forward on the bench. "You know my father and I have had a troubled relationship, leaving no love between us. But my mother, younger brother, and sisters will need my help for some time to come. I would dishonor myself and bring shame to my family if I failed to accept this moral obligation."

Gabrielle thought she had never seen him look so sad. He stopped speaking as he cleared his throat again. She was about to say something, when he continued. "If things go well, I may be able to return here to finish my degree. If not, I'll have to enroll in a school in Bursa." He hesitated as his words filled her with foreboding.

"I won't be able to go to America. ...I can't imagine you would want to come to Bursa after you graduate. The opportunities for you are far fewer there than in Istanbul." She struggled with the shock of his words. "My dear, I don't know how this can work. It's a situation in which I have very little to offer that would be of value to you. It would be an awkward and formidable situation for you to try to enter into. We wouldn't be

Adventure in a Foreign Land

able to start our marriage on our own, thinking only of each other. We'd be tied to my family for the foreseeable future in very burdensome ways."

Stopping as if to brace himself, he continued, "I can't accept your hand in marriage under such trying circumstances. It would be dreadful for you, which would break my heart. I love you too much to ask such a thing of you. I'm so sorry." He sought her hand. "When I weep it's not for my father, but for *you* and for my family...because this means losing the dearest person I've ever known, the great love of my life," he choked the words. "I'll never feel for anyone what I feel for you my love. You're like an angel to me, come to brighten my life and show me what love can be. Please forgive me Gabrielle...forgive me."

Stunned by all that he was saying, she watched as tears traveled his cheeks. *Could this really be happening? Was it truly ending?* she asked herself. His words had risen like a dagger to her heart. She closed her eyes, seeking to center and protect herself. But she still absorbed his pain, understanding how difficult this decision was for him. He was seeing his life as he knew it come to an abrupt end.

As she gazed at their joined hands, she softened again. "There's nothing to forgive my love," she said, her eyes moist. "My heart is broken. I can't imagine ever loving anyone as I love you. I can see your heart is breaking too. Oh Mehmet, life is too cruel to us this day!"

He nodded in grief.

"Then it's goodbye is it?" she asked, her voice husky.

He reached for her and raised her as he stood. "I must leave tonight...I won't be coming back."

She thought she would collapse.

He caught her as she waivered. She looked hollowly at him.

"Oh my dear, I am broken, having to bring such bitter news. Will you be all right?" he asked, searching her face for an answer. She struggled to reply, but no words came. In shock, she looked at him through tears, falling freely now.

They stumbled, then reached for one another again. He held her hard against him, looking deeply into her eyes as if searching for an answer that somehow would make all this right. Hearing none, he pressed her still closer to him and kissed her in search of all that she was and all that they meant to each other, tearing through any hesitancy that might stand between them to one more time join all the anguish and passion that stirred in their hearts.

Holding one another, they each dreaded to let the other go. "Write to me," she whispered into the air that felt suddenly chill. "Promise you'll stay in touch."

"Yes," he whispered as he inhaled her scent one more time. "I'll love you always."

"And I you," she said, her voice breaking in sobs.

Soon he took his handkerchief and gently dried her eyes. Placing the cloth in her hands, he kissed them. "Thank you, Gabrielle, for loving me." They sought each other one more time. She wanted him so, she thought she would faint. Then he released her and staggered as he exited through patches of moonlight and shadow, soon out of view.

She faltered as she watched her dearest person walk out of her life, not for a stronger love, but for duty. Knowing she had lost her one true love, she experienced an emptiness she never felt before. But as urgent to her was the sorrow she carried for Mehmet and how this terrible event was robbing his young life. Heartbroken, she already was mourning all that they had been and could have been to each other. It was over. No more equivocation. Now all she wanted to do was to go home.

Home to America.

~VI~
COMING HOME

1966 – Istanbul and Merrick

1

The day before she left Turkey, she shared bittersweet partings with her best college friends—Becky and Bilge—and with her roommates, her other expatriate friends, and her professors. Walking the campus alone one last time, she sought to imbed in her heart every building, every person she met, treasured views of the Bosporus and this vibrant, historic city, each place that felt part of the sacred ground of her Turkish experience and her time with her beloved.

On the day of her departure she called a taxi. The driver arrived early in the morning. Bustling about, he loaded her suitcases into the trunk of his Chevy sedan. Riding in silence as the car sped toward the airport, the driver honking his horn and swerving around trees and porters on their way to market, Gabrielle watched, transfixed as the city bore itself to her and tore at her heart.

How lucky was I to see Istanbul through Mehmet's eyes, she acknowledged. *He gave me such a gift.* Still in shock from the turn of events that abruptly ended their romance, she found herself wondering, *Did I dream this?* She shook her head. *And Mehmet…all his hopes and dreams have crashed around him—and he's only twenty-one. How I wish I could have helped him. Fate is too cruel. I love you Mehmet and always will.*

Her taxi took her past views of ferryboats crisscrossing the mighty Bosporus, past majestic mosques and minarets, open-air markets, children playing along the streets. Soon she gazed at the massive remains of a Roman and Byzantine aqueduct with its classical history woven tapestry-like through modern Istanbul. It beguiled her sensibilities and made her think of the remains of ancient cisterns and baths beneath the metropolis, hidden like the ardor engulfing her.

She thought she would die of sorrow as she acknowledged how deeply this complex, noisy city touched her heart and given her the love she just left behind. It was in this very moment that her mind awoke to the full realization of how this place and its people had nurtured and deepened her passion for art and led her to discover her own gifts as an artist. Suddenly she understood that this revelation was the very thing that would sustain her through the seemingly unending pain of her loss.

When they arrived at the airport, however, she struggled to leave the cab. Her limbs grew heavy with resistance and buckled as she swooned with uncertainty. Her legs screamed reluctance to leave her love, this city, this country. Could she really go? Her emotions whirled with the finality of her departure.

As she struggled to keep from falling, she pulled herself up short. It hit her in a flash that the decision never was hers to make. It was his. Owning this steadied her and freed her from further hesitation. Dropping back onto the taxi seat, she gazed at the driver who wore a concerned expression. She managed a small smile as she took the support of his hand and his presence as he walked her to the ticket counter, then carried her bags and thanked her for her generous tip. *"Tanrıyla git,"* he said in parting—"Go with God."

Hours later, as her plane taxied down the runway and lifted into the air, she watched this sprawling city, so full of life and seeming contradictions, grow smaller. Soon it vanished behind clouds enveloping the plane briefly before the aircraft reached its prescribed path to its destination.

Gabrielle felt as if she had left a long dream she entered when she began her journey to Istanbul nearly ten months before. But her presence on this plane seemed only a little more real to her, this vessel suspending her between the exotic land and love she just departed from and her homeland that now seemed strange to her, and very far away. She wondered if she would feel at home again when she reached America. Where she was at this moment, riding in air between continents, was where she now lived. *Will I ever truly be able to say again that one place is my home?*

Shaking her head, she leaned back and closed her eyes. Suddenly she was very tired. All the uncertainty and fervor of the past weeks—and now the turmoil of her and Mehmet's parting—had taken their toll. Thinking of him, she wondered if he felt the same exhaustion of spirit. As she contemplated this, she felt his presence as if he were beside her. She almost could feel her hand in his, his passionate goodbye kiss, the surge of feeling that rose in them at the hard certainty of their parting. Opening her eyes, she sought to quiet her emotions, then shook her head as she reproached herself. *I must stop this, or I'll go mad!*

As she continued to try to rest, the man two seats over from her introduced himself—Roy Cob from New York City. Almost immediately he commenced a long story about his life in the city. Gabrielle just nodded from time to time, lost in her own thoughts. She wished that the man would just be quiet and let her sleep. Finally he stopped. After draining her water glass, she dozed off.

It was a couple of hours before she awoke. Gazing at Roy who was snoring, she was relieved to not have to listen to him. Looking out at the clouds below the plane, she watched the sun fading its rosy colors into the last of the day's light. Soon it would be dark as they headed for Iceland to refuel and change pilots before the last leg of the trip. The Icelandic Airways prop plane still had hours to go before reaching Iceland and far longer before arriving in the United States. She longed to get up and stretch her legs, but she didn't want to disturb Roy and lose the blessed silence she was enjoying. So she just watched the last rays of the day before closing the window shade and drifting toward sleep again.

Gabrielle awoke with a start. As the cabin lights came on, the captain's voice crackled over the loudspeaker. As the static cleared, she heard him direct the stewardesses to prepare the cabin for landing at Reykjavik's airport.

An hour later, the plane left Iceland for its final leg of the trip. As Roy related Act II of his life story, Gabrielle thought she would scream. Excusing herself as she got up, she headed for the restroom. Then she took her time walking up and down the aisle in the hope that Roy would fall asleep before she returned.

Hours later the captain informed them that despite the strong headwinds, they were less than an hour from John F. Kennedy International Airport. Following a rocky landing in heavy winds, passengers gathered their things and said their goodbyes. As Gabrielle walked down the airplane steps and across the tarmac, she watched fellow passengers find family and friends crowded behind the windows and around the terminal door. She looked anxiously for her mother and father. Now inside, she saw them waving as they hurried toward her.

"Gabrielle," her mother exclaimed as she embraced Gabrielle and wiped her eyes. "It's *so* good to see you!"

"You look so grown up," Arthur chimed in.

Gabrielle wanted to tell them how happy she was to be home, but she wasn't entirely sure it was true. Although glad to see her parents, she felt disoriented. Being "home" seemed strangely unreal to her, despite how much she had wanted to be here. So she just smiled.

After getting her bags, they piled into the car. In less than an hour they were home. Gabrielle, however, was experiencing a kind of cultural disorientation. Everyone seemed to be in a hurry—in the terminal, on the road, driving through their town to the family home. She thought it odd to be enduring more culture shock than when she first landed in Istanbul.

Suddenly she felt very tired, longing to crawl into bed and sleep. But Kay and Arthur wanted to hear everything about her Turkish experience. Her mother bustled about, bringing them sandwiches, milk, and cookies as they plied her with questions.

After an hour-and-a-half of conversation and hearing that her sister was doing well and hoped to come home this summer, Gabrielle felt as if her head would burst. "Mom, Dad, would you mind terribly if I got some sleep? I'm *so* tired—it's been such a long trip."

"Oh of course dear," Kay responded, brushing her graying hair back from her forehead and getting up to remove the dishes from the table. "I should have thought of that," Kay continued, worry lines working their way back across her brow. "We're just so anxious to hear everything. But there's time enough for that after you get rested."

"Thanks for understanding, Mom…Dad."

"I've got your bed all made up, and I put out fresh towels for you," Kay said. "Now go on up and get some sleep."

With that, Gabrielle climbed the stairs to her bedroom, relieved that she hadn't needed to reveal her relationship with Mehmet and what had transpired. She also was pleasantly surprised by her father's comportment, showing no signs of alcohol. *I wonder what the story is there,* she reflected, finding hope in her observation.

Stopping at the door to her room, she gazed at the familiar furniture—the desk and vanity she and Mrs. Bealey had refinished, the bed skirt and chair cushions the woman had helped her to sew, and the elegant vanity mirror she had given her. *Dear Mrs. Bealey. What a kind woman to have helped me so much. What would I have done without her as a kid? I should see her soon,* she thought. But despite her memories and the familiarity of her room, she saw all this as her past, a past that now seemed very far away.

2

For Gabrielle the summer was long. Eventually she told her parents about Mehmet but downplayed their relationship. She did, however, confide through letters to her old friend Adrienne who was spending a second year in Spain; Becky who was back home in Minnesota; and her sister who now resided in Boston. But she thought of him every day. She and Mehmet wrote one another two or three times a week the first month. Then the frequency of their letters tapered off. She thought it had become, for both of them, just too painful to share intimate news of each other's lives when they knew their relationship was doomed.

Living at home over the summer, she worked four days a week as a checkout clerk in a nearby grocery store to earn money to return to Oberlin. "I'd have preferred our more lucrative waitressing job at Jones Beach," she wrote to Adrienne, "but I dreaded running into Rafael. And now I have my evenings and three days a week free to do my sketching and think about what I plan to do when I return to Oberlin. I expect to declare art as my major. It's my saving grace now, Adrienne. It's what keeps me from the abyss every time I think of Mehmet and fall into overwhelming sadness."

"My dear friend," Adrienne wrote back, "I can't imagine what you're going through. I hate that you're suffering so and I'm not there to cheer you up. I thank God you have your art to occupy your heart and mind. Hold fast to it. Let it fill you and heal your pain. You're an amazing person Gabrielle. You have so much to give the world. Never forget that. And I know you'll find love again—when you're ready. I love you my friend. Hang tight and stay in touch. I'm glad you'll have the company of your sister this summer."

But Ruth was not able to return home, much to both her and Gabrielle's disappointment. "Gabel," Ruth said during one of their phone calls, "I can't believe no one told me I needed two more required classes to qualify for graduate school courses I have to take this fall. I so wanted to have time with you this summer and to learn about your year in Istanbul. Mom says you look older, more mature. My little sister, the world traveler. We'll just have to make do with phone calls for now. I miss you Gabel."

They did speak by phone every couple of weeks, and Gabrielle felt the bond between them strengthen. Learning that Arthur was attending regular Alcoholics Anonymous meetings, she was able to share with Ruth that their father appeared to be trying to curb his drinking. "Thank God," Ruth responded. "It's about time."

All these things helped Gabrielle to reengage with her home and family and to examine her life and what it was that she most valued.

Her hurt at losing Mehmet, however, lingered. The joy she experienced at first when she received his letters, long ago had grown bitter, reopening wounds that wouldn't heal.

Early on she made progress by reengaging with important people in her life. This included letters to and from Bilge, in which they shared their thoughts about art. Soon however, Gabrielle found herself sinking more and more into solitude, interrupted only by her summer job at the grocery store. At some point Mehmet failed to correspond at all. Then she stopped, realizing that the letters deepened her grief—and her depression. She suspected he was experiencing the same.

This led to her tossing about at night, unable to sleep. When she rose in darkness and turned on the light, she would draw to take her mind off her troubles. Mostly they were fragments of sketches never completed, the subject at times being mosques and minarets that ultimately included the silhouette of a man standing in the shadows. Distraught, she would tear these sketches into tiny pieces, alternately angry and in tears.

Lack of sleep edged dark circles under her eyes. Her room was all but lost in piles of clothing, books, letters, and drawings. Her blinds were lowered more often than not. The only thing breaking her spiral downward was the necessity to show up for her summer job.

Then one late Sunday morning she rose from a particularly agitated sleep. She felt how memories of Mehmet had pulled her into a deep black hole. Sitting on the edge of her bed as she struggled for consciousness, she began to pant, her breath growing progressively more punctuated. She struggled to stand in her darkened room. The sensation of loss, a tornado of suffering, hit her like a bomb. Throwing her head back, she released a cry that rose from her belly as she collapsed, weeping uncontrollably.

Her parents had just returned from church when they heard their daughter's scream. "Gabrielle, talk to me!" Kay exclaimed, panting after running upstairs to her room. "My God, what's happened to you my child?" she asked. Pulling her from the floor to her bed, Kay saw her daughter in crisis. "Enough is enough," she exclaimed, "you can't go on like this. What's happening to you? Something's terribly wrong. Are you becoming ill? I beg you my daughter, talk to me!"

Wiping her eyes and gazing hollow-eyed at her mother, she acknowledged Kay's intensity, but was unsure what she meant. Although her mother had queried her day after day, getting no satisfactory answer, Gabrielle still was surprised by Kay's forceful confrontation. "What?' Gabrielle mumbled.

Kay hesitated briefly, then grabbed her daughter by the arm and dragged her to the full-length mirror in Ruth's bedroom across the stair landing. "Look!" Kay commanded her.

Having dropped her gaze, Gabrielle slowly raised her head. The late morning sunlight bathed the room and struck her face. She raised her arm to shield it from the light. It took a minute for her pupils to adjust. Lowering her arm, she stared into the eyes of a stranger, one that was haggard, older. Staggering backward, she nearly fell as her mother caught her.

Gabrielle put her hands to her face, now trailing tears and sobbing. Frightened for her daughter, Kay put her arms around her, stroking her hair as she cried with her. "Gabrielle, what's happened to you? Come," she said, pulling her away from the mirror and seating them both on Ruth's bed as she kept hold of her daughter's hand. "Tell me what's going on."

In a few minutes, Gabrielle quieted. "I don't know if I can talk about it," she said in a husky voice.

"You must," Kay responded, "or whatever has hurt you will rob you of your health—and your sanity."

Gabrielle closed her eyes to think as she gathered strength to answer.

For the next hour Gabrielle explained her history with Mehmet and how hurt they were by its outcome. "I can't get past the pain, Mom, the grief. I've never loved anyone like I love him. I don't know how to go forward, how to leave this sorrow—to leave *him* behind."

Kay looked long at her. Finally she said, "I too have lost loves, although nothing like what you described. It tears at me to see you distraught. I've never known you to be depressed like this. You've always had an indomitable spirit, rising from any tough circumstance. This one has rocked you to the core. I can see that." Gabrielle lowered her gaze.

Raising her daughter's head, Kay clasped Gabrielle's chin so she could hold her daughter's attention. "My darling girl, you more than anyone I know are a survivor." She paused, not letting Gabrielle's eyes stray from hers. "You are a gentle, sensitive creature, easily hurt." Kay paused. "But you have always lifted yourself up from hard situations, learned from them, and gained strength for your next challenges. Look at you my daughter. You have many gifts—talent, strength of character, compassion for others, courage, intelligence, beauty, drive. I could go on and on. If only I had a fraction of what you have. I'm saddened beyond words for your suffering. But I know that you'll emerge from this and that you'll find love again."

She pulled away from her mother. "You don't understand how much I love this man. This isn't some casual romance. He was leaving his homeland to come to school in this country, which his family wouldn't like. We were going to be married for God's sake! We made promises to each other. You can't imagine how special he is—kind, accomplished, respectful, ardent, faithful.... I could go on and on. No love will ever compare to what I had with Mehmet." She turned away from her mother, whose mouth had dropped open at her daughter's rebuke.

"But he left you."

Gabrielle winced, then spun toward her mother. "You don't understand! So please don't pretend to. I will *never* have another love like this."

Shocked by Gabrielle's rebuke, she rose to leave, then reseated herself when she caught the anguish in her daughter's eyes. Turning toward her, Kay spoke softly. "I can't possibly know the full measure of your pain. But I see how your loss haunts and hurts you. You told me that your relationship is over. I understand that you're in mourning. But your lack of care of yourself threatens your very health and well-being. If this doesn't stop, you may not be able to regain your life as you've known it. Make no mistake Gabrielle. You are in peril. Please don't allow this to happen. Lean on me if I can help you. I beg of you my darling." With this Kay got up and walked downstairs, leaving Gabrielle in Ruth's room.

Sitting in silence for several minutes, Gabrielle rose and returned to her bedroom across the landing. The darkness of the room struck her. She hesitated, then turned the slats in the blinds so just a little sunlight entered the room. Squinting as she looked around, she couldn't remember why she had let her room and herself go for so long. On some level she knew her mother was right. But how to get back to her life given the weight of her sorrow, she couldn't even imagine.

3

With Kay's help, Gabrielle's room was put in order. But healing her life proved a far slower process. Kay encouraged her to sit outside by the flower garden and help with the weeding, and to take long walks and bicycle rides. When Gabrielle wasn't working at the grocery, Kay frequently drove her to Jones Beach where they walked along the water's edge and breathed sea air. Weeks stretched to months, but gradually Gabrielle became more communicative and her body began to regain its healthy aspect.

It was then that she returned to her artwork in earnest. As she did so, the empty spaces in her life filled with a passion that deepened with each day, each drawing. Sometimes it seemed to her as if her pursuit of art almost was becoming an obsession.

Drawing in three mediums—pencil, charcoal, and technical pen—she savored how each lent a different effect to her sketches. Perusing her drawings from Turkey, she redrew them all, using different mediums and from different perspectives. She especially revisited Sinan's mosques, Istanbul street scenes, and views of the Bosporus, emphasizing different elements each time she rendered them. Sometimes the subject matter tugged too dearly. She would think of Mehmet and remember how she felt when he would take her hand and gently pull her to him. When she would start down this tunnel of sorrow, she would pull herself back up by concentrating fiercely on the skills she was exercising, putting as much distance as possible between the emotions her memories engendered and the subject of her artwork. When that failed, she would put the Istanbul drawings away and find something else to render—a tree, a door, the neighbor's yard.

All the while, she followed the national news, with special attention to the Civil Rights Movement. She noted how it had grown stronger in the North during the past year, as had an increasing sense of inevitable militancy. Black Power and critics of nonviolence were becoming louder voices. This now included the Student Nonviolent Coordinating Committee after Stokely Carmichael took over. Just the year before, Malcolm X had been assassinated by members of the Nation of Islam in New York City. She thought how hard it was to know where the violence would end.

During one of her good friend Rick's phone calls, he talked about the Chicago Freedom Movement. "It's making waves Gabrielle. It began as an open housing movement organized by Dr. King and the Southern Christian Leadership Conference. They've been targeting Chicago slums and housing discrimination."

"Yes, I've read about them," she replied. "Aren't they getting into other issues now too?"

"They are, pushing for quality education for all, equal employment and pay opportunities, and a bunch of other life equality issues. Of course they continue to preach passive resistance."

"It seems like the Movement's really spreading," she noted. "But it scares me that militancy's also on the rise."

"I know. But people are frustrated. Passive resistance is a slow process," he said. "I don't condone violence, but I understand the cause of it."

"I understand too, but it makes me sad. If we can just stay the course and have faith in the ultimate effectiveness of nonviolence, I believe anything's possible."

"I share your hope," he said. "We need to support Dr. King and the Movement's other pacifists to keep the more combative factions from taking over the Movement."

"Yes," she said.

For all this, not a day went by without her reliving treasured memories with Mehmet—the first time they danced together and how she felt in his arms...sunset ferry rides, his sheltering arm warming her as the city glowed in pinks and golds...their laughter and pleasure on a horse-and-carriage ride on Büyükada Island...his care to introduce her to the magic of Istanbul and the rugged history of his homeland...the passion with which he took her, fulfilling her own ardent desires...and ultimately his willingness to sacrifice for the chance that they could make their hoped-for marriage work So much sweetness, so much love.

These were the thoughts that drifted her back into sadness. Over time however, her heartache clung in shorter spaces as she learned to lift herself from the abyss through her dedication to her art and social change.

Helpful too were Rick's letters, sent regularly in an effort to keep her updated about Oberlin's part in the Movement. "Instead of going south, Oberlin students are demonstrating closer to home, most often in Chicago," he recently wrote. "I've been to two of them, but I spend most of my time here at the tutoring center. I sure miss you and your help and can't wait for you to get back here. And Jeremy keeps making progress. You'd be so proud of him." Gabrielle was moved to hear this. And day by day her commitment to the Movement and the tutoring center's part in it grew.

The subject matter of her art also took a turn. Coming across crude drawings she started as an Oberlin sophomore, she examined these captured memories of people and events from her civil rights experiences, her voter registration work in Hattiesburg primarily. Then she put away these old pencil drawings and started new ones.

Working to recapture her experiences in the segregated South, she now could draw more skillfully her encounters with racism and the people whom racism robbed. Images of Hattiesburg and of civil rights marches and other demonstrations flooded her mind with an intensity she had to acknowledge. She found herself longing for summer's end, when she would return to Oberlin for her last year to pursue a new chapter in her art and her dedication to social equality.

She came to believe that a fire that had smoldered silently during her adventure to a foreign land had been rekindled now with unanticipated ferocity. This made her wonder if she had been destined to travel to Turkey to discover the importance of art and to prepare her for her return to work in the Movement with renewed passion. Did it take losing her greatest love to burn the weeds of her old life and allow her convictions to grow stronger and more focused?

Injustice always was a hot button for Gabrielle. As she followed the latest news, it dawned on her that she might have an alternative way to counter what she knew to be terrible wrongs.

The full weight of her discovery came on a day when she sorted through sketches she had made over the summer. She realized that her pictures were telling a story—a story about the impact of ignorance, hate, and fear…about segregation and the toll it extracted from human lives and the effects that had on a society's very humanity. The recognition of the story that surfaced from her art and its potential implications startled her. She began to wonder if she could effectively combine her love and practice of art with her political beliefs. Could she create art that might enhance people's awareness of the struggle for justice for all of America's people, even meet them on a profoundly human level to encourage positive action?

Shuffling again through the drawings she assembled, she grew excited as she tore through them one after another. Her eyes widened in astonishment. Through these pictures she realized that she just might have the very vehicle she had been looking for, the perfect means of expressing and sharing her convictions about racism and exclusion. She saw now that it resided in what she held in her hands. It was the product of her passion, now in the form of sketches that bloomed in her hand and in her heart into pictures of rare beauty and purpose. She saw now that these drawings were so much more. They were her statements about the importance of standing against inequities, while affirming all that she saw as good and right in the human heart. In many ways they were the countenance of what she had become and all that she was fighting for, all that she hoped for.

As if thunderstruck, she realized in that moment that she had just found her voice.

And her life's work.

~VII~
DISCOVERIES IN A FAMILIAR LAND

1966 - 1967 – Oberlin and Merrick

1

By the time Gabrielle packed to leave for her senior year at Oberlin College, she had completed some fifty drawings of her civil rights experiences. Placing them carefully between tracing paper and cardboard, she stored them with her best Istanbul sketches at the bottom of each of her three suitcases.

She was set to leave on a Greyhound bus with her suitcases and bus tickets that eventually would deliver her to Oberlin. Driving her to the nearest bus depot after church on the first Sunday in September, her mother hugged her and waved as the bus departed.

As she thought about her parents and how her old life seemed strangely far away, she also no longer felt suspended between worlds. This new journey on which she now embarked was more familiar than the one to Turkey a year ago, but no less exciting. She saw herself speeding toward a destination to which she now felt anchored, a platform from which to rocket toward what she now saw as her destiny. And there, she believed, lay her true creative and spiritual home.

* * *

The day after she arrived in Oberlin she registered for classes in intermediate drawing, beginning watercolor painting, beginning oil painting, and American art history. Then she officially declared fine art as her major.

Excited, she sought out Rick at the tutoring center. Sure enough there he was. Walking up behind him, she put her hands over his eyes. "Guess who," she said.

"Uh...let's see. Joan Baez? I hear she's got the hots for me," he quipped.

"Ha ha. No it's Senator Joseph McCarthy back from the dead."

"Yikes...I'm outta here." With that Rick turned toward Gabrielle, who was bent over laughing "Oh it's just you," he goaded her. "I thought it was somebody important."

"Well that's a lousy welcome home," she said as she grabbed and hugged him. "Can we leave and go somewhere to talk? Maybe get a bite to eat?"

"Oh all right. As long as you're buying," he joked.

"Gulp. Hot dogs maybe?"

"Hmmm. I guess we'd better go Dutch."

"Deal." *Same old Rick*, she thought.

"Let me put my stuff away, and I'll be right with you," he said, picking up his books and papers and carrying them to a filing cabinet in the next room.

She could hear the file drawer open and shut. Looking around the room, she noted that everything looked pretty much the same as before, save for a few more books, an added desk, and some additional chairs. It was a nondescript room, except for book publishers' posters that Rick and the other Oberlin students acquired and tacked to the walls along with charts of the children's progress. Checking her watch, she figured it would be at least three-thirty or four before the kids were out of school and on their way here. *That'll give us time to catch up on our news*, she thought.

"Let me show you something before we go," Rick said, walking toward one of the progress posters. He put his finger on a name. She moved in close. "Wow--here's that B in reading you wrote me about, sending Jeremy to the next grade. Damn that's *huge* for him! You know you couldn't give me a better welcome home gift."

He beamed, then couldn't resist a comeback. "So you think you deserve a gift? Dahling, surely you jest."

Laughing, she whacked him on the arm. "Come on you wicked boy, let's get some chow. I'm starving."

"Hmmm," he responded, pinching her arm. "You hardly look like you're starving...."

"Oh you bad boy, let's go before I say something I'll regret. What do you say we hit the A&W? It's still there, isn't it?"

"Yup. Let's go."

Settled into the A&W after ordering hamburgers, fries, and root beers, Gabrielle put ketchup over all her food before starting on her fries. "So tell me anything you didn't put in your letters," she said. "I want to know everything you've been up to, how you're doing, and what's happening at the tutoring center and with other campus civil rights activities."

"You sure know how to keep a guy from eating," he complained, frowning as he got ready to take the first bite of his hamburger.

She grinned. "Okay. Let's have five minutes of silence, chewing, and swallowing. Then you'll have to just grab a bite here and there between sentences."

"Thanks a lot, ol' girl." After finishing his burger and starting on his fries, he talked about the tutoring center. He told her about his success recruiting a half-dozen more student tutors, thereby increasing the number of kids helped by ten. This made a total of twenty-one children between first and sixth grades currently using the center.

"That's remarkable Rick. You're making a big difference in these kids' lives, as you did with Jeremy. What did he say when he got a B in reading?"

"I never saw a bigger smile on his face than when he brought me his report card at the end of summer school. You'd have thought someone had just given him a million bucks."

"He should be really proud of himself. I can't wait to congratulate him."

"Changing the subject, have you decided about declaring fine art as your major?"

"As a matter of fact, I just did today. Before I tell you about that, tell me more about *you*—aside from your work at the center."

He laughed. "Is there anything besides the center? I'm starting to feel less like a student and more like a manager and instructor. With summer over, I'm going to have to relearn how to balance being a student *and* a volunteer. I frankly don't know how."

Looking at him sympathetically and considering his dilemma, she remarked, "I wonder. Would it be more help if I took on the scheduling and other administrative duties rather than tutoring again?"

"You'd do that?"

"If that would be more help to you and the center…yes, of course."

"Gabrielle, that would be fantastic. I don't know what to say."

She felt his mood lighten, which made her smile. "Just buy me a burger and fries sometime. Geesh, I sure missed these in Turkey—and root beer." Downing the remains of her drink and hamburger, she licked her fingers for emphasis.

"I guess you didn't like your burger," he laughed.

At his request, for the next hour she talked about Bilge and their weekly sketching and critiques, and about how this summer she concentrated on drawings from her activist experiences. "I had a kind of epiphany," she concluded. "I've come to realize how art provides the opportunity to unveil racism we've witnessed and speak to people's hearts. Rick, I believe that with this knowledge I may have found my life's work."

He fell silent before responding. "Wow Gabrielle, I don't know what to say." He studied her, as if realizing that she had moved in a direction he hadn't foreseen. "I'm stunned really," he admitted. "To discover what you believe to be your life's work when you're only twenty is extraordinary. I envy you really. I wish I had your certitude."

She paused as she considered this. "You're as committed to civil rights work as I am and have worked in it longer. I think that you already know what your calling is," she responded. "You just haven't acknowledged it yet."

He looked earnestly at her. "You might be right Gabrielle. I hadn't thought about it that way." They both fell silent. Then as he took his last sip of root beer, he checked his watch. "Geesh," he exclaimed. "The kids will be at the center before we know it. We'd better get hoofing." Opening his wallet, he put a couple of dollars on the table—a habit he had, even in fast-food restaurants—and started back toward campus. "We've been gone a long time, and I haven't heard much about Turkey," he said as they walked. "Just tell me, what was the high point of your time there?"

She thought about it before responding. "I'll make you wait until I can tell you the whole story. Suffice it to say that Istanbul is by far the most amazing place I've ever been. It'll take hours, days maybe, to describe my experience and how it touched me. What I'll say is that parts of it clarified for me the importance of art in my life and gave me confidence that I had enough talent to dedicate myself to it. I didn't know that before."

He looked at her. "That's amazing. I'm so glad you went there, although I'll admit I missed you."

She thought she saw him blush, which surprised her. But she said, "I missed you too. You're the best friend I ever had."

He winced, then laughed. "I have to run. Catch you later." And with that he was gone.

* * *

Her first day of classes included drawing and watercolor painting. Spending the previous two days rounding up the books and supplies needed for the term, she also settled into her living quarters—a room in an off-campus house for female senior students. Occupied by eight women, it was a sprawling, two-story, early-1900s building. While the room itself wasn't less expensive than the dormitory, she could save money by fixing her own meals in a common kitchen and was able to garner a large room and half-bath for herself. With this setup she had space for painting and could come and go as she pleased.

At her first drawing class, Dr. Emil Fondante, an energetic man in his late forties, his brown hair and full beard already starting to grey, spoke quickly and moved about as he talked, gesturing frequently as he looked from student to student. He asked them to bring one of their favorite sketches to class for his and the students' critique. After that he would have the entire class draw a common subject, after which he would review each student's drawing and make comments. Then he showed slides of three subjects he had drawn and his sketches of them, while discussing his techniques.

She found his style interesting. He appeared to have worked quickly, using a soft pencil to make bold lines and a series of crosshatches to render his subjects. While the work lacked any sense of delicacy and used minimal detail, they showed a bald passion of expression that she found energizing.

What followed were a dozen slides of pen and pencil and charcoal drawings by Picasso, Degas, and Rembrandt, ending with the teacher's question. "What do you see that these artists have in common?" A minute of silence ensued. Dr. Emil Fondante frowned as he looked to a male student at the back of the room. "You. What do you see?"

"Uh…great art," the student hesitantly responded.

"Yes, but *why* is it great?" The teacher tapped his foot.

"Because of their command of their art?" the student tried again.

"Well yes," he laughed, "but what specifically is it about all these drawings that makes them great?" Seeing no hands raised, he pointed to Gabrielle.

She thought for a minute. "Because you see not just a skillful drawing of a person or object, but the experience of them," she responded. "It's the feeling you're left with, not just an appreciation of technique."

"Bingo," Fondante said enthusiastically, raising his hand and smiling now as he stroked his beard. "That's what I hope you'll come to see this term when you study drawings of the greats. And I hope that those of you who are truly serious about your art will strive, if you're very hard-working and fortunate, to one day accomplish a modicum of this."

Gabrielle left class reflecting on his challenge. *He's right,* she thought. *Mastery of a skill without also producing feeling is cold, mechanical, empty even. I think Dr. Fondante will be not only entertaining, but helpful as I work to develop my own style and improve my drawing skills.*

Her afternoon class was with watercolor artist Regina Constance, an attractive, tall, buxom blonde who appeared to be in her mid-thirties. Along one classroom wall she had hung dozens of copies of watercolor paintings by the likes of Georgia O'Keeffe, Andrew Wyeth, John Singer Sergeant, and J.M.W. Turner. Gabrielle found the body of work of these greats humbling, overwhelming even. It made her feel very small beside these towering talents.

Assistant Professor Constance watched as Gabrielle and others studied the wall. She began class by discussing the paintings. "Just as it's important to read if you want to become a great writer, so is it important for you to study the work of iconic painters if you wish to excel as a watercolor artist. I put this wall together not to intimidate, but to inspire you and show you what's possible. Their techniques can educate you about the use of color or white space, paper texture, water, line, dry brush, perhaps even mixed media, and give you tools to enhance your paintings."

The instructor began pacing between the wall and a table at the front where she had laid out her art supplies. Over the table a huge slanted mirror was poised to aid students in following her as she painted and demonstrated techniques and artistic principles. Pivoting to face the class, she asked how many had some experience with watercolor painting. Of the class's fifteen students about half raised their hands. Tapping her finger to her cheek, she asked how many had prior instruction. Just four had. "Okay. Most of you seem to be novices, so I'll assume nothing other than that all of you have had drawing instruction as a class prerequisite.

"Later in the term I'll let you draw your own subjects as well as paint them. But to start," she said, "so that we can concentrate on learning to paint and not spend class time drawing as well, I'll give you reference photos of subjects and also line drawings of them. You'll trace the line drawings onto your watercolor paper. Then you'll follow my instructions about methods and colors and use the reference photos to successfully complete your paintings. This way you'll learn different techniques you later can use on your own subjects. The last forty-five minutes of class will include a critique of each of your paintings. Any questions?" No one responded.

"Okay," she nodded. "Then we'll start by creating a color wheel of primary, secondary, and tertiary colors and what we call warm and cool colors. This will accustom you to the paints in your palette and help you learn how to mix them to create other colors." With a satisfied look, she turned to pick up her color wheel outlines and distribute them.

An hour and a half later the students had completed their wheels and left class. Gabrielle was disappointed that they wouldn't get to sketch as well as paint, though she understood why the teacher structured her class this way. But she was excited that soon she would learn how to create her own watercolor art.

In two days she would have her first classes in oil painting and American art history. This concentration in art invigorated her and helped fill the hole in her life left by losing Mehmet. *What is my love doing now?* she would think periodically throughout her days. *How is he managing? Does he think of me often, as I do him? Oh my sweet man, I hope you find comfort. Be well and know that I love you always.*

* * *

Enjoying meeting women in her off-campus house as she made her dinner, she promised to attend the house introductory meeting the following evening. Wanting time to herself to organize her room and optimize her space, she ate her meal in her room before rearranging furniture to create a painting area by her bay window. She had chosen her room not only for its size and half-bath, but also for the window's northern light that offered the best exposure for painting. It excited her to think that soon she would acquire her first easel for oil painting and that this evening she would experiment with the watercolor supplies she had purchased.

Searching the room for her first watercolor subject, she carried five textbooks from her desk to a small table by the north window. She then positioned them on a shawl she had brought with her from home. She displayed in a manner that pleased her, the books and the wool wrap threaded with several shades of green. After pulling over her desk chair and nightstand, she arranged her paint tubes, brushes, and palette, filled a glass with water, selected a sheet of watercolor paper, attached it to a clipboard, and began sketching. In a half-hour she had completed her drawing.

Her class notebook beside her, she extracted her color wheels and began experimenting with combinations to create the shades she wanted for her painting. Finding that the exteriors of her textbooks lacked artistic interest, she decided to imagine her books with leather covers and pages edged in gold.

Deciding to tackle the fabric first, she laid out the paint tubes by warm and cool colors. Opening the tubes and squeezing onto a palette a small amount of pigment of each color, she ordered them to reflect her color wheel.

Dipping her largest round brush into the water, she deposited a puddle at the palette's center, followed by a healthy dab of cool yellow. Then she rinsed her brush in the water glass, took a far smaller dab of cool blue, and mixed it with the yellow. Instantly the colors merged into a pleasing yellowish green. Thinking that would make the right background color for the shawl, she put more of the same pigments into the puddle, mixed them again, then filled her brush with the green concoction.

Knowing nothing at this point about how to work with watercolor paints, she began applying the green as one might employ oil paints and in a manner that gave her control of the placement of it. An unsatisfactory result, however, made her mentally step back and think about what she was doing.

Soon she realized the source of her mistake and began spreading water over the paper where she had drawn the outline of the shawl, letting the green move itself to fill the space circumscribed by her application of water. When the yellow-green covered the intended space, she added more cool blue to the puddle on her palette. This gave her a deeper and bluer green.

As the earlier application barely started to dry, she used the bluer green to create designs on the painted fabric. As she dropped the darker color into the lighter, she watched the mix travel to create other varieties of greens on the wet paper. Fascinated she picked up the paper and played with moving the paint-infused water about, generating even more merging designs.

In doing this she realized that the amount of water she applied affected everything. A spare use of water left the paints thicker and more intense, but also less fluid and less alive. Thus an ample mix of water with pigment created colors that could be thinner and lighter in intensity, but also more subject to merging and creating unexpected results.

When she completed the fabric part of the painting, she studied her color wheel and experimented with mixing browns for the leather book covers. And on it went as she played with the paints and worked to develop her techniques.

After a couple of hours' work she propped up her painting on the window ledge and stepped back to see what she had done. The colors and water play clearly would need a lot more work, but for a first try, she thought the result wasn't too bad. More importantly she learned a great deal by just experimenting.

I love this, Gabrielle acknowledged. *How fun to work with color.* She especially enjoyed the fluidity of the watercolor medium, how it would surprise you, sometimes madden you, often delight. *It seems to me,* she mused, *that you may have only limited control using watercolors. It's a medium full of mystery and seemingly endless discovery. I absolutely am going to love the adventure of this.*

With a big smile on her face and feeling at once exhausted and exhilarated, she tidied up her work area and slipped into bed.

2

Enjoying the women students living at her house, Gabrielle found their evening meeting provided an opportunity to

Discoveries in a Familiar Land

get to know each other and to divide up house chores. Two of them even had prepared food for everyone, giving them more time to interact and decide responsibilities.

Earlier that day Gabrielle had her first class in American art history. The professor was Dr. Karen Ramie, a short, slightly stout brunette who appeared to be in her late forties. Gabrielle was pleased to find that Dr. Ramie was an articulate and animated lecturer with a clear passion for her subject. She found the professor's enthusiasm infectious and relished her teacher's selection of great American art images.

The format of the lectures was much like the ones Gabrielle had experienced in her art history lessons in Turkey—lots of examples, explanations of evolving styles, introductions to a myriad of artists and architects practicing groundbreaking work, and just a pure visual feast. She savored this approach, watched, and listened with a hunger for all that she could take away from the experience and apply to her own evolving craft.

The last of her four classes—an introduction to oil painting—came after lunch. Gabrielle was excited to discover what her experience with this paint medium would be. Would she take to it and would it intrigue her as watercolors did?

Just as she and her classmates settled down in the studio, she saw a dashing, early-thirties man enter the room. He wore a dark-grey scarf flung casually about his neck. The class fell silent as he deposited a backpack on his chair, extracted a notebook, placed the pack under a table, and looked up. Gabrielle thought that his coal-black eyes seemed to pierce them. She registered that he was at least six feet tall, tanned, had a prominent aquiline nose and a mass of dark-brown curly hair. Furthermore, he sported a goatee and a small gold ring in his left ear lobe. Dressed in well-worn blue jeans and a red-and-black-plaid cotton shirt, he broke his gaze as he rolled up his sleeves.

"Well," he began in a deep voice. "I'm Instructor Raymond Ramirez, and this is beginning oil painting. We meet twice a week for two-and-a-half hours. During this time, we'll draw and paint a variety of subjects—objects and human models. How many of you have studied oils previously?" Just two students of the sixteen raised their hands. "How many of you are fine art majors?" Half the class responded.

"Let's move the easels into a circle today," he said. "Leave a large space at the center for the subject of our work. While you all will draw and paint the same object, each of you will have a slightly different angle and perspective on the subject. This will give you practice painting subjects from different viewpoints.

"I'll teach you techniques and critique your work individually. From time to time I'll ask the class as a whole to critique class members' finished pieces. You'll have no textbooks, but I'll give you painting and sometimes drawing assignments at the end of each class. I also will have you review art books I'll put on reserve in the library to expose you to a range of artists' work in our medium. In addition I encourage you to frequent the Allen Memorial Art Museum here on campus. It's one of the best campus art museums in the country."

His voice began to rise in volume as he moved about in front of the class. "I want you to practice, practice, practice! It's the only way to learn to paint. The more you do, the faster you'll learn. And that presumably is why you're here." He spun toward them.

"If on the other hand, you're taking this class because you thought this was an opportunity for a good grade with very little effort, then you may want to think again." He stared meaningfully at each student to punctuate his point. "I intend to work you hard. Only those who truly have earned it will get a pleasing grade. So…," he swung back the other way, then walked toward the front of the room again, his voice harsher now, "…if you're not serious learners, you may want to withdraw *now* before we waste each other's time!"

A gasp rose from a few students. Two of them got up and left. The door slammed shut with the finality of a guillotine. Instructor Ramirez smiled, clearly pleased. "Good," he said, "now we have a smaller class of earnest students, and I'll have a little more time for each of you." Gabrielle couldn't help but smile. He seemed elated that his ploy succeeded.

"So let's get the easels, carts, and stools in a circle and begin our first lesson."

Discoveries in a Familiar Land

During the class Gabrielle learned about the bare basics of what was required to paint with oils. One needed canvasses of different sizes, an assortment of palette knife and brush types and sizes, charcoal, turpentine and other mixing oils, gesso, a small number of oil paints in pigments that could be blended with others to produce a variety of colors, a palette, and a small foldable tabletop easel for home use. Making note of these, she realized this made for a more expensive undertaking than her watercolor supplies. For the first two classes the teacher fortunately had provided what they needed.

Instructor Ramirez then talked about how to draw objects to scale by holding your paint brush out in front of you to estimate the relative sizes of different objects, thus gauging the proportions of one item to another. The subject of their sketch in this case was a circular earthen brown-and-tan baking pot; a big cream-colored pitcher; and a large, dark-blue velvet cloth that draped from the top of a small table to the floor.

"Today we'll concentrate on our drawing and leave painting to another time," he began. "I've provided each of you with charcoal and a gesso-coated canvas. Gesso primes the canvas, keeps the paint from being absorbed into it, thus protecting it from the acids in the oils that will destroy your canvas over time. It also can help the paint to adhere and retain its rich color.

"Before painting, I'll ask you to detail the drawing on the canvas as if you were not going to paint it. I want to gauge your drawing skills and how you indicate values. This also will give us a chance to discuss elements that are important to both sketching and painting."

It seemed a simple enough drawing with which to begin, Gabrielle thought, but she found the shadowing of her subject more challenging than she expected. Previously she had made most of her drawings outdoors. Indoor lighting seemed quite different. She raised her hand.

"Yes," the instructor said, circling toward her. "You have a question?"

"Would you please talk about light and shadow in an indoor, versus outdoor setting, how they affect the subject and how they're best studied and drawn?"

"Ah yes." He stopped and perused her drawing. "You're right to delineate indoor from outdoor lighting. They're quite different. Outdoor lighting generally is cooler. Indoor lighting has a different tonal quality. It's generally warmer. If you were painting it, it would be yellower. Outdoor shadows are not as hard, and they come from a variety of sources. Indoor shadows can be very sharp." He looked again at her sketch.

"I see that your subject is well drawn and that you've begun shading your objects based upon the light cast on one side and shadowed in gradations on the opposite. What does the light on the one side and shadow on the other do to an object?"

Without hesitation she responded, "It gives the object dimension."

"Yes. It gives volume to the object's height and width. Both the pitcher and the pot have rounded edges, so the shadowing is very gradual from light to dark. This is unlike straight-sided items like cubes, which have a sharp separation of light and shadow planes. Are we good so far?"

She nodded.

"Now we've been talking about shadows *on* an object. We also have shadows cast *by* the objects themselves. These are known as 'cast shadows.' They're darkest at their source and progressively less dark as they grade away from the object. The edges of cast shadows can be soft or hard, so you should study this property carefully before you draw and paint them.

"Now," he continued, pulling a small flashlight from his shirt pocket and igniting it, "tell me what happens to the pitcher's cast shadow as I move the light source away from it."

Gabrielle studied the shadow. "It grows softer."

"Yes. And as I move the light closer?"

"It becomes harder."

"Right. Now if I move the light directly in front of the pitcher, the light appears to flatten it. If I move the light to the upper left or upper right of the pitcher, what do you notice?"

She observed carefully. "It looks more three-dimensional."

He shifted the light to the back of the pitcher. "Now what do you see?"

She hesitated. "It seems to flatten the pitcher again, but differently."

"Yes. It creates a more tonal silhouette. Now if I lower the angle of the light," he said, moving the flashlight accordingly, "you'll see that the cast shadow is longer. Likewise if I raise the angle of the light, the cast shadow grows shorter. Be careful, however, in your lighting angle, as a very long cast shadow draws your eye and can become more important than the object itself. Be sure that's your intent. Does this answer your questions?"

"Yes, thank you."

He turned back to the class as a whole. "When you are all done drawing, you'll notice that each of you will have a different picture. Drawing in the round like this not only gives each of you a slightly different arrangement of the items, but it also gives you different shadowing. This of course affects the perceived volume of objects and can also create different moods for your pictures.

"When you've completed your drawings, we'll line them all up. You'll see how perspective changes everything." The instructor smiled and stroked his goatee as he walked around, giving students individual comments on their work.

Near the end of class, everyone got up and walked over to the table where all their drawings lay. Gabrielle found it fascinating how similar some were to each other and how others were quite different. It was more than an angle change. Interpretation of the objects also differed, which she found quite interesting. Some were very precisely drawn. Others were more hurriedly sketched with a rougher, bolder quality. *This will be instructive,* she thought. *I can see that we'll learn from each other as well.*

As she picked up her sketch, Instructor Ramirez was directing them to spend their time between now and the next class acquiring supplies and practicing drawing a single object from a variety of light angles. "Bring all of these to your next class. Remember that we have enough supplies to get you through your second class in the event you don't find everything you need right away. You can take the charcoal with you today and what paper you think you'll need. See you later this week."

* * *

Gabrielle wanted to return to her room and get to work on Instructor Ramirez's assignment. She decided, however, that she would first stop at the tutoring center to check in with Rick.

"Hey ol' girl, I thought you'd abandoned me."

She laughed. "Don't think I didn't consider it."

He mocked being struck in the chest. "You sure know how to wound a guy," he said, rolling his eyes dramatically. "Okay. You ready to start work?"

"I thought we could make a schedule so you'd know when I'd be here, then give me a rundown on what you want me to do."

"Right. How many hours would you have available?" he asked, pulling out his schedule book.

"How many do you need?"

He laughed. "Probably more than you can give. What's your situation?"

"Quite honestly, I'm not sure exactly. The art classes are going to require a lot of homework. Let's see…," she was tallying class time in her head, "classes alone will take up maybe twelve hours a week. I'm going to guess that the assignments will take another twenty to thirty hours."

"It doesn't sound like you'll have much time left," he said, looking discouraged.

"No not at all. That should leave me two full days a week to do whatever you need done. Will that be enough?"

He brightened. "That'd help tremendously, but it doesn't leave you down time. You sure it's not too much?"

She nodded, meeting his eyes. "Look. I came back to Oberlin to do two things—immerse myself in art and the Civil Rights Movement, which includes the center. These are what I'm dedicating myself to. So yes, I absolutely am up for this."

He sighed. "Well you just made my day. What hours should I put you down for?"

"I ought to be able to put in a half-day on Tuesdays, a half-day on Fridays, and a full day on Saturdays. Will that work?"

He nodded. "That sounds great. And we can modify anytime you need to. Let's talk about what you'll do." He put her in charge of scheduling the kids, contacting parents and the kids' teachers, paperwork on each student, including charting their progress, and acquiring books in the kids' areas of interest. "Is this too much?"

"No, whatever you need. But tell me, have you heard anything from Jeremy?"

"Actually I have. You'll be pleased to know that he's not satisfied with his 'B' in summer school reading class and wants to get an 'A' this school year."

"Really?"

"Really."

"Well, I'll be...," she mused. "He's incredible. And you, Rick Dressel, are one fine teacher. I'd love to see him."

"Actually he's coming Friday after school. Will that mesh with your schedule?"

"I was thinking that afternoon on Fridays might work best anyhow. Maybe two to six o'clock? That good?"

"Perfect. Any chance I can buy you dinner tonight?"

"I'd love that, but I've got a lot I need to get done. How about Friday or Saturday after we work here?"

"It's a deal," he said.

3

Friday afternoon came quickly. After Rick went over Gabrielle's new duties, a couple of kids trickled in to meet with their tutors. "As you can imagine," he said, "Friday afternoons aren't favorites with kids who have been in school all week. So it's a perfect time to catch up on paperwork."

She smiled in acknowledgment. As she looked up, she spotted Jeremy in the doorway. She couldn't believe how much he had grown in a year, and he had such a look of confidence about him. "Jeremy," she exclaimed.

A big smile spread across his face. "Miss Andersen," he responded as he walked toward her.

Meeting him, she reached for his hands. He looked straight at her, not down at his feet as he had in the past. She couldn't resist giving him a quick hug, which he didn't seem to mind. "I'm so excited for you--a B in reading in summer school and you a third-grader now. I couldn't be prouder of you." He beamed.

"And I understand that you'll be continuing in reading until you have your A." He nodded. "I have no doubt you'll succeed," she continued. "I'm so pleased and impressed with all the effort you've put into your reading. I just knew you could do it. Are you planning to work with Rick tonight?"

"I'm sorry, I can't ma'am. I'll come back Monday. I just wanted to see you…and to thank you for your letters and the books you gave me." He hesitated. "It meant a lot to me, ma'am. I'm sorry, but I gotta go. My mama's waiting for me. I just wanted to say thanks."

"Oh Jeremy, you're most welcome. I really appreciate your taking the time to come see me. It means a lot to me too. I hope to see more of you over the coming months."

"I'd like that. Thanks ma'am." And with that he turned and exited.

"Well I'll be…," she said, shaking her head. "He seems so grown up. He's not the same boy." She turned to Rick. "You've worked miracles with him."

Rick watched her. "I just facilitated. He was determined to read well enough to advance to the next grade. When he reached that, he wanted more. That's all him—him and the encouragement and attention you gave him. You helped make a huge difference in his life, Gabrielle. You were the one who convinced him he was capable of more."

"Well if I did, I'm thankful. He amazes me. I can't say thank you enough for helping him. You're such a good teacher. Better than I am."

"My pleasure Gabrielle. Should we get down to work?"

"Yes of course."

At six o'clock they and one of the tutors, a sophomore named Susan, closed up shop.

"Where do you want to go for dinner?" he asked Gabrielle as he grabbed the backpack into which he had been stuffing work.

"Wherever you want. I'm not fussy."

"Why don't we drive into town. There's a new Thai restaurant just opened up. You game?"

"Sure."

Being new and a Friday night, the restaurant was crowded. They waited at the bar for a table.

"Rick, tell me more about your plans after Oberlin. Are you still headed for graduate school in poli-sci?"

He took a couple of sips of the beer he ordered. "Probably. Eventually for sure."

She turned toward him. "What are you thinking?"

"I don't know. I'm so damned caught up in this work, it's hard for me to focus on my studies. The tutoring center, these kids, the Movement, they're so damned real to me. My classes feel like an interruption to everything that's meaningful to me right now." He fingered the beer he ordered and took a gulp. "I'm wondering why I should spend my time studying about politics and movements, when I can read about them anytime and instead just *live* them. That's what I really care about."

She looked at his troubled face and thought for a minute. "How many more poli sci credits do you need to graduate?"

"Just one more term after this one, actually just one more class in my major and an English class of some sort. And then there's my honors thesis once I get through this term's four classes of course."

"I wonder. Your final poli sci class would involve your senior honors thesis, wouldn't it?"

"Yes. What are you thinking?"

"And the English class could be essay writing, no?"

"Hmm. I think I see where this is going."

"If you can get through this term's academic load, you might be able to talk your two instructors into making your honors thesis the work of both your required classes. Your thesis could be the tutoring center and how it fits into the Civil Rights Movement, which could include your experiences in Hattiesburg and Chicago too." She looked meaningfully at him.

He took another sip as he gazed at her. "You know, you might be on to something. I've been so bound up in the work I care about that I haven't really taken a good look at my options. And I've been exhausted trying to juggle everything. I even toyed with quitting school."

Gabrielle about choked. "You're kidding."

"No. For real. But I'm so close to graduating, and someday I'll need that degree. Besides, my parents would kill me," he laughed, shaking his head. "But you may have just given me a way out that I hadn't considered. I'm going to look into this Gabrielle. Thanks for thinking of it." He picked up his glass and toasted her.

"I didn't fully realize how stressful this has been for you," she said as he looked down. "I've been so bound up in my own issues, I failed to see what was right in front of me. I'm sorry I couldn't have helped you this last year. I don't know how you managed all this yourself. I can't change that, but I can do more to help now."

"You have nothing to feel sorry about, but I appreciate it. Your support means a lot to me. You really understand what we're trying to do here and why it's so important for these disadvantaged kids to succeed academically. It's key to their future success. Most Oberlin students are too bound up in their own educational demands to consider devoting substantial time to helping these kids. I'll admit it's been a bit lonely without you."

She reached for his hand and held it. "Rick, you're my dearest friend. Please lean on me for a bit. I'm so fired up about all this…and all I'm learning about art. I've got so much energy right now. I'll do everything I can for you—and the Movement. You're really something, you know."

He laughed. She could feel the tension in him release.

Then the hostess tapped Rick on the shoulder and motioned for them to follow her to a table. In a couple of minutes they were seated in a booth and studying the menu. After ordering food and Thai beer, Rick asked her about her time in Turkey.

She exhaled slowly. "Where do I begin?" For the next half-hour Gabrielle told him a little about the college, her roommates, Becky and the other expatriate students, weekly art sessions with Bilge, and a few impressions of the city and Turks in general. Toward the end of her story the waiter arrived with their dinners.

"It sounds fantastic," Rick commented.

"You were right Rick, I gained a new perspective by being in a different country, one that has an ancient and remarkable culture. It's a beautiful place, and Turks are good, hospitable people. I have many wonderful memories of Turkey."

"You didn't mention dating. What was that like?"

She cleared her throat. "I was hoping to not have to talk about that."

"Did something bad happen to you?" he asked, looking concerned.

"No nothing like that. Well at least not like I expect you're thinking." She looked down.

"Someone broke your heart?"

"Yes. Something like that."

"Do you want to talk about it?"

"I don't know. I need to move on in my life, but I don't want any more of these kinds of entanglements with men…not for a long time. We both were in love, but it wasn't meant to be. It probably never would have worked out anyway. We come from two very different cultures…."

"He was Turkish?"

"Yes."

"I'm sorry Gabrielle." He looked sympathetically at her. "But this is your friend here. You can tell me anything."

Looking uncomfortable, she finally replied. "He asked me to marry him."

Rick's jaw dropped in surprise.

"He offered everything I could have wanted in a husband, but for the difficult issue of where we'd live. We made plans for him to come to America for graduate school. And then a catastrophe required that he, as the oldest son, drop out of school and go home to take care of his mother and siblings. Family demands entailed a long-term commitment that created an impossible situation for me to enter into. He said he couldn't put me through that—that it would break his heart."

"Wow. I had no idea." As he looked at her, he watched her bite her lip in a struggle to fight back tears. "I'm so sorry Gabrielle. This had to have made this a very difficult year for you."

She breathed deeply to dampen her emotions. "Much of it was quite wonderful…but not everything is meant to be."

"I suppose not. I know what you mean," he said with a faraway look in his eyes as they gazed at each other. Her thoughts, however, lingered on Mehmet and the circumstances of their parting.

* * *

The school year seemed to Gabrielle to rush by. She poured all her energy into the tutoring center and her art. In no time it was the last term, and she was busy preparing her artwork for submission to the senior fine art show at the campus gallery.

The show permitted each student one piece of his or her choosing in each artistic medium studied. Showing more than one piece of artwork per student per medium came as the result of a competition juried by all art faculty. Although a very uncommon occurrence, the jurors as a group could permit up to three additional art pieces for students per area of study *if* they met a very high standard of artistic quality.

Three weeks before the exhibit was to be mounted, Gabrielle received written notice from the awards committee that faculty had chosen nine of her submissions in addition to the three she chose to represent her work. This meant that an unprecedented twelve of her pieces would hang in the gallery for the senior show. Thrilled, she couldn't wait to tell Rick the news.

"You won't believe this," she half-shouted into the phone after reading the letter to him. "While I'm happy about the two Istanbul drawings, the ten Hattiesburg pieces selected are the most exciting to me. They tell our civil rights story in a very personal way—and it marries my art to my political and social beliefs."

"That's incredible Gabrielle! I'm so proud of you and can hardly wait to see the exhibit. We should go out and celebrate. How about Friday? I'll buy."

"That would be great, but we should go Dutch."

"If you insist, but I'd really love to buy."

"Tell you what, I'll arm wrestle you for the bill."

"Ha ha. Well actually you might win. Boy would that be embarrassing," he said with mock chagrin. "Maybe I'd better concede now."

"Not a chance," she responded. "See you at the center tomorrow. I've got a lot of scheduling to catch up on now that I've finished my academic work."

"See you, Gabs."

4

Ads for the senior show not only were posted all over campus, but also downtown. The local paper and an area TV station answered the college's invitation and said they would be there for the Friday night opening. The art students all were ecstatic about the media coverage and pleased with how different their pictures looked when professionally matted and framed, sculpture mounted on pedestals, and all properly lit.

Gabrielle's twelve pictures took up a third of one long wall and were highlighted with a note about her background and the fact that the volume of her work chosen for the show was unprecedented. The notation embarrassed her, as she thought it unnecessary to demarcate her from her fellow students. But her classmates' congratulatory comments helped her to accept how faculty had distinguished her and the opportunities this might create for her at some future time.

Dressing with care for the opening, she donned her black cocktail dress—the only dress she owned—black flats, the shawl she had used in her first still life painting, her gold hoop earrings, and her grandmother's gold locket. As she brushed her long hair away from her face, she studied herself in the mirror, noting that she looked more grown up than she did just a year ago. With a sigh she turned and exited her off-campus house.

The air was cool for the third week in May. Breathing in the spring aromas of green grasses and early flowerings, she felt a freshness and arousal in the mixture of scents and a breeze that brushed her nostrils and skin. As she exhaled her nervousness over her big night, she couldn't help but wonder what people's reactions would be to her work. Would they recognize the plight of a people and empathize with Edith and Mike and their kids, with Reverend Jonas, and the frightened woman guarding her children on the porch of her tarpaper shack? *Well we'll just have to see*, she thought as she pulled her shawl close about her.

The building's exterior was well lit, revealing a banner heralding the gallery's senior show. It was a full hour before the opening, but the art students had arrived early and already had taken their places beside their respective artwork. Wanting to see her fellow seniors' work, she took a little time to view the quality and subject matter of each piece. *Such a range of subjects, mediums, and techniques*, she thought as she chatted with classmates and admired their creativity. A few minutes before eight, she returned to her prescribed spot and waited as individuals began entering the gallery.

Soon it was nearly filled as people from around campus and town circulated about the room, juggling wine glasses and small plates of fruit, cheese, and crackers. She watched as attendees studied her pictures, often spending considerable time with them, the Hattiesburg series in particular. Many of them congratulated her on her work and asked about the inspiration for her pieces.

One of them was a local newspaper reporter who gave her the opportunity to share what she had witnessed and her passion for issues of equality. Then the area TV station—a CBS affiliate—arrived, represented by a cameraman wearing jeans and a ball cap, along with a middle-aged, blonde-haired woman reporter decked out in high heels and too much jewelry.

After stopping to chat with the gallery director, they headed straight for Gabrielle who was engaged in answering a woman's question. "Hey honey," the TV reporter shouted as she practically pushed the woman aside, "we only gotta few minutes. Can ya move over here a little?" she directed Gabrielle.

"I'm so sorry," Gabrielle said to the inquiring woman as she gestured to the TV crew.

"It's okay dear. I'll come back later."

"Thanks so much," Gabrielle responded as she reluctantly walked to the place the brash reporter had directed her to stand.

"Rudy, get that light on her—and be sure to get the pictures behind her!" she barked to the cameraman. Turning toward Gabrielle, the reporter said as the camera rolled, "Well you must be very proud to be the first student in all the years of the Oberlin College senior art show to have twelve pictures chosen for display." She shoved the microphone in Gabrielle's face.

Gabrielle jerked backward, then settled herself. "Uh...I'm very grateful for the opportunity to have a chance to illuminate a struggle for justice going on in our country."

"Can you explain that?"

"I'm talking about my Hattiesburg, Mississippi, series. It focuses on the black community there and their struggle for equal rights under the law."

"How would *you* know about that?"

"I was there two years ago, working on voter registration issues. I made dozens of sketches after my experience there and was greatly moved by the incredible people I met. Their resolve to gain justice for themselves, their families, and other Negroes, south and north, was indisputable."

"You mean south, don't you?" the reporter prompted her.

"Yes, but the North has its own inequalities. I'm afraid neither the South nor the North can claim to provide the kind of social justice we all seek."

"Well surely the South is much worse, wouldn't you say?" The reporter appeared defensive, huffy even.

"Certainly it's more overt," Gabrielle responded, holding her ground.

"Well!" the reporter chafed as she turned her back to Gabrielle. "Out of the mouth of babes," she said into the microphone. "Rudy," she turned to the cameraman, "pan this girl's pictures, then get a wide shot of the whole room with everyone's work." He nodded as the reporter, now off-camera, turned back to Gabrielle. "What makes you so sure we Northerners are bigots?"

"I didn't say everyone is," Gabrielle tried to explain. "Whether it's segregated housing or education or less opportunity in general, it seems to me we Northerners must bear responsibility for failing to recognize the inequities and to put a stop to them."

"Humph," the reporter snarled. "Spoken like a young person who doesn't know what she's talking about. We certainly don't keep people from voting."

Gabrielle paused, meeting her gaze. "Are you sure about that?"

"Humph," the reporter repeated, then turned and walked away.

It looks like I just blew my big chance at thirty seconds of fame, she thought. Then she heard a familiar voice.

"Well you sure gave it to that poor excuse for a reporter," Rick said. "I'm proud of you, ol' girl!"

Gabrielle grinned. "I'm so glad to see you. I sure bungled that one."

"Not at all. Let me take a look at your pictures," he said, walking over to them. He stood there for some time in silence, seemingly transfixed by the collection of her work, the Hattiesburg series in particular. "Geesh. You sure captured these people and their emotions. I feel as if I'm back there—back in those exact situations, those precise moments."

She paused. "Your telling me that means more to me than anything that reporter says," she responded. "You just made my day." He turned from her paintings to look at her. "It makes me hope," she continued, "that the people viewing my pictures tonight just might go away with a tiny bit deeper understanding of who these people are who are fighting for their rights—and the intensity of what they've suffered in their battle for equality. If that happens, that would mean more to me than any amount of media-generated hoopla."

He leaned over and gave her a big hug. "That's my girl," he said as she blushed.

"Thanks Rick. I needed that."

Before they could say more, the newspaper reporter returned with a few follow-up questions before another round of gallery attendees approached her.

* * *

Exhausted after the opening and the party that followed, she crawled into bed close to midnight. Not having listened to the late-night news or looked at the morning paper, she just lay in bed the next morning, thinking about the evening and her interactions with people. Then she heard a knock on her door.

"Yes?"

"It's me, Gabrielle—Doreen."

"Come in," she said as she rose and stretched.

"Have you seen the morning paper?" Doreen asked, brushing her brown hair back and holding up the paper.

"No. I'm not sure I want to." Gabrielle gave a tired grin as she observed her jeans-wearing, barefoot housemate who seemed too perky for this hour of the morning.

"You've *got* to read this—it's a bloody rave review! And look at how many of your pictures they reproduced in the article."

"Really?"

"And did you see last night's TV coverage?"

"No," Gabrielle said, wincing in anticipation of a negative report.

"Well the reporter was a bit weird, but you spoke well and your pictures looked fantastic."

"That's a surprise. I thought she'd find a way to slam me."

"And the campus newspaper just called and left a message for you that the *Oberlin News-Tribune*'s story about you just moved over the Associated Press wire a little while ago."

"You're kidding."

"Nope. You're a bloody celebrity."

"Well I'll be...." Gabrielle took the newspaper from Doreen and perused the full-page spread covering the entire body of the students' exhibited work. It concentrated, however, on her artwork, the Hattiesburg series in particular. "Damn. I can't believe this."

"Well my dear, you're famous, at least in Oberlin, Ohio." Doreen had a triumphant grin.

Gabrielle smiled and shook her head. "For today. But how nice. It's so much more than I expected."

"It's hard to tell about these reporters, isn't it?"

"It is. I'm just glad the print reporter gave the other students their due. They had really good work there." She scanned the article again and noted the photos the paper used.

"I thought they did," Doreen said, "but it just makes sense that the student who had the most artwork in a juried senior show—the most in the whole history of it—would get the most copy."

"I guess so. In any case it's so great that the paper and the station both covered it. It seems that art doesn't usually get that kind of press attention."

"Well you being the first to have so many of your paintings in the show might have been what brought them out."

"I hadn't thought about that. Then it's good for everyone."

"It is," Doreen agreed. "Come on down. I'll fix you a celebration breakfast."

"How nice of you. Thanks!"

5

The Associated Press story generated calls on Saturday from the *Cleveland Plain Dealer* and *Chicago Tribune.* Journalists from both papers did phone interviews with Gabrielle, focusing on her and her Hattiesburg civil rights experiences. They wanted to send photographers that very day. The Civil Rights Movement was continuing to heat up in the North as well as in the South. The reporters noted that her work provided a fresh angle on the hard news coverage their papers had been giving the Movement.

Gabrielle tried repeatedly to contact the campus communications officer and eventually reached him at home. He assured her he would take care of media access to the gallery. The officer turned out to be not much older than she was and stayed close to her until the photographers had left and she had no more need of him. "Thanks David," she said. "I really appreciate your coming in on your day off. It was a big help."

"That's my job," he said, removing his suit jacket and loosening his tie. "I'll follow up with the papers and find out when the stories will run. I'll get copies for you and the college too."

"Thanks. Now I think I'll go back to my room and collapse," she said with a tired smile.

"Sounds good. I can't wait to take off this tie and get back into jeans. See you around," he said as he breezed out the door.

Four days later David delivered two copies of each paper to her at her off-campus house, smoothing back his curly hair as he remarked, "You're a star Gabrielle."

She looked surprised, then opened the paper to the pages where he placed markers. She was stunned to find most of a page devoted to her story and her artwork in the *Cleveland Plain Dealer* and a half-page in the *Chicago Tribune*. And even more satisfying was that the articles appeared in hard news sections of both papers, beside the latest news of the Civil Rights Movement's activities. "Goodness. Who would've guessed?" was all she could say.

"Good work. Let me know if you want more copies or if you hear from any other news media."

"Two copies will be enough. Thanks. Do you really think this isn't the end of the news media stuff?"

He shrugged. "Who knows? Just call me if you need anything. You've got my number."

* * *

A couple of weeks after the stories appeared in the Cleveland and Chicago papers, she received a wire from Parsons School of Design, one of four institutions she had applied to for fine art graduate studies. Her hand shook as she opened the communication, sliding her finger under the flap. This was her top pick of the four schools to which she had applied.

Desperately wanting to be in New York City for her graduate work, she also was drawn to Parsons for its long history as a progressive institution that champions art-forwarding progressive social values, as well as intellectual and creative practice. Throughout the school's history it had demonstrated the belief that art should be for everyone, not just for the few. Philosophically she felt herself aligned with the historic spirit and practice of the school. Parsons also offered a rigorous, studio-class program for students like her who sought intensive instruction-immersion in a variety of media in addition to independent studio work.

Extracting a two-page letter from the envelope, she paused before unfolding it, aware that she held her future in her hands. Would she get to study with a spectrum of committed fine art teachers in the city known for its support for and the quality of its arts institutions and offerings, its emerging pop art and cutting-edge arts scene, and increasingly multicultural population?

Walking upstairs, she sought to be alone when she read the letter's contents. Sitting on her room's only chair, parked in the bay window where she painted, she let the letter rest unopened on her lap. So much of what she had dreamed about over the past year and tried to envision for herself as a young artist, lay here awaiting her action.

Finally she took a deep breath and unfolded it.

Dear Miss Andersen:

It is with great pleasure that we...

Gabrielle thought she might faint.

...write to inform you that you have been accepted into the Master of Fine Art program at Parsons School of Design, beginning this September. You will be one of a small and diverse group of fine art postgraduate students who were selected for their outstanding potential, based upon a diversity of criteria.

She gasped.

We were impressed with the photocopies of your recent artwork, particularly in light of how little instruction you have had to date. Already you are developing a unique style, which clearly is infused with your passion for social justice. Your letter of application clarified that connection further. The recommendations from your faculty advisor and your art instructors were glowing, as were the articles just published in the Chicago Tribune *and* Cleveland Plain-Dealer.

Gabrielle's heart beat rapidly as she looked up from the letter and whispered, "My God," then continued to read.

We were especially taken with your Hattiesburg series, which we found particularly moving, and your own personal experiences in relation to the Civil Rights Movement. It was this series that prompted us to offer you more than a place at Parsons.

"Oh my God..."

We are prepared to extend an offer to you of a full-tuition scholarship and a modest living stipend that constitutes room and board for the full term of your graduate work here, as we are aware of your financial situation and how much Parsons can offer you to fully develop what clearly is an unusual talent with an uncommon backstory.

We await your decision and look forward to your response. Should you have questions, you may call me at the number on this letterhead.

Sincerely,
Jonathan Marberry, MFA, Ph.D.
Chair, Fine Art Graduate Admissions Faculty
Parsons School of Design

She sat for several minutes with the pages of the letter on her lap. Then she perused the correspondence three more times to assure herself that she read it correctly. Were they really offering her not only admission to Parsons' postgraduate program, but a fully funded education as well? "Can this really be happening?" she said aloud.

Still stunned, she shook her head, trying to shake off a feeling of incredulity. Finally she had to acknowledge that the letter was real—this wasn't a dream—and uttered a prayer of thanks. She thought she would burst if she didn't tell someone the good news. Immediately she thought of Rick.

Folding the letter and inserting it back into the envelope, she rose from her chair and tore down the stairs and across campus to the tutoring center.

6

Rick wasn't there when she arrived, so she tried to get some work done. Too agitated to concentrate on the task at hand, she finally scribbled a note and took a walk to calm herself.

Within the hour Rick found her hugging a mug of tea at the student union. "What's going on?" he asked looking concerned.

"I'm sorry Rick. I didn't mean to worry you." She reached into her pocket and pulled out the envelope as he sat down beside her. "I just got this wire," she said.

He hardly began the letter, when he uttered "Holy shit!" He looked at Gabrielle, who was smiling now, then kept reading. Soon he repeated "Holy shit," then "Damn!" Finishing the letter, he sat for a minute staring at it.

"Gabrielle," he said finally, "this is unbelievably great. All you've envisioned and worked for has come to pass. Acceptance is no less than I would have expected, but the scholarship? Who could have imagined?"

She nodded, having no words to contain her excitement and her disbelief at her good fortune. "Rick, I had to know that this is real and not some mirage I've conjured."

He grabbed her hand and moved closer. "Nothing could be more real. You've done it! I couldn't be more proud of you," he said as his face went from serious to gleeful. "Imagine, you in the big city, studying under seasoned instructors…and not having to worry about supporting yourself. Just think. You can totally devote yourself to your art with nothing to distract you. Could anything be better?"

Absorbing his affirmation of the momentousness of Parsons' offer while her face registered concern, she responded, "I hope I can deserve the gift Parsons is giving me and that I won't disappoint them."

"Gabrielle, this school has very experienced people who don't make offers like this without plenty of proof of a candidate's ability and potential. Take this for the compliment that it is and a statement of belief in you as an artist and as a person. All you have to do is to make every moment there count." Rick beamed.

"You're such a good friend Rick. It didn't seem real till you acknowledged it. Some part of me still can't quite believe this is happening. Ouch! What was *that*?"

He laughed. "Just a pinch to let you know you're not dreaming."

"Okay I got it. This is happening."

"I think we should celebrate. Tonight at that Thai place you liked? And I'm buying—no protest allowed."

She accepted and smiled. This was the happiest she had been since the height of her affair with Mehmet. As she released Rick's hand and without thinking, she kissed his cheek. He started in surprise and reddened in confusion.

Realizing what she had done, she blushed and tried to cover. "Can't a gal just appreciate her best friend?" she laughed and said lightly, "I better get going. Thanks so much for finding me and setting me straight. Where do you want to meet and when?"

Recovering, he answered, "Uh how about six when the tutoring center closes. You want to meet me there?"

"Will do. See you later."

As she left him at the union, she realized that her impulsive gesture had crossed a line. She sensed in that moment that Rick had feelings for her that were more than friendship. It pained her that she had introduced confusion into what was her most important friendship. And she didn't know how to make this right.

* * *

Gabrielle and Rick finished their senior year and graduated without bringing up what had passed between them. She feared the loss of their friendship and suspected he felt the same. So they completed their bachelor's degrees, said their goodbyes, and promised to keep in touch and try to see one another sometime in the coming year.

While her plans were set on Parsons, Rick opted to postpone graduate school and work full time to grow the tutoring center and find capable Oberlin students to continue the center's work. Gabrielle lived at home over the summer and took a sales job at Macy's to earn money to augment the living expenses Parsons pledged to furnish. While the school would provide her with dorm housing and meals at the campus cafeteria, she still would have to buy books and art supplies and pay for any other living expenses.

Summer on Long Island also gave her the chance to exchange with Bilge letters and photos of their artwork, offering each other comments and encouragement, and to spend time with her family, especially her sister who came home from Boston for a couple of weeks.

"Harry's the best. I'm so lucky to have met him," Ruth said to Gabrielle. "Next month we're moving in together and starting our new social work jobs in Boston, me at Massachusetts General and Harry at a big local agency. I'm so excited Gabel. It feels like everything's falling into place. I'm so happy."

Gabrielle reached over and hugged her sister. "I couldn't be more excited for you. You worked so hard to get your master's degree, and now you have both the job and the man you've always wanted. That's wonderful Ruth."

Returning her hug, she remarked, "Look at you. You've traveled to the other side of the world, took the Oberlin art scene by storm, became a media sensation, and now got this incredible scholarship to Parsons. I'm so proud of you little sister."

"Thanks Ruth, but I'm not sure that's all quite accurate or deserved."

"Phooey Gabel. You're special. Admit it."

"Well I don't know about that, but thanks. Hey, would you sit for me to paint your portrait?"

"Really? I'd love it."

During Ruth's sittings, she thought how they shared details of their Boston and Istanbul experiences, their loves, their highs and lows, growing closer with each story, each revelation. She was sad when Ruth had to leave and promised to keep in better touch.

Gabrielle painted numerous portraits during her summer evenings, including that of her longtime friend Adrienne, home from her two academic years in Spain. Her portrait sitting gave them time to talk about their time abroad and of course about falling in love. Adrienne regaled Gabrielle with stories about her many suitors and at least four serious boyfriends in Barcelona.

"My Latin lovers were rockets and fireworks," Adrienne said with a twinkle in her eye. "I had a great time. But in the end they were too demanding. And those endless displays of male dominance… Give me a break. Just imagine me as Little Miss Housewife, will you? No siree. I'm going to medical school."

Gabrielle couldn't help but laugh as she jammed her palette knife into a mixture of oil paints before applying them to the canvas. Her friend was plucky as ever, Gabrielle observed. And now she had a drive to become a doctor. "I think that's fantastic Adrienne," she said, spreading the paint mixture in long strokes over the canvas. "And you got into the Johns Hopkins University School of Medicine. Not many women go there or to any medical school for that matter. I'm so proud of you."

"And you going to Parsons and getting that scholarship. Wow Gabrielle, that's some kind of fabulous."

"It is, but it's also scary. I hope I can measure up."

Adrienne snorted. "You'll blow them away. I've seen your stuff, and I know you. When you commit to something, you don't let anything get in your way. You've got so much talent and drive. I know you'll be a big success."

Gabrielle laughed as she applied to the canvas the last of the paint mixture on her palette and prepared to clean up from the session. "I'll just be happy not to disappoint."

"Speaking of which, have you heard anything from Mehmet?"

Gabrielle shook her head as she screwed the lids onto her paint tubes and grew thoughtful. "I think it's just too painful for us to keep in contact. It's a hopeless situation I'm afraid. He's there and I'm here. And that's not going to change. I just want him to be happy and to find someone who can appreciate him for the special person that he is."

Adrienne saw how sad her friend looked. "Hey Gabrielle, whataya say we go somewhere and put back a couple of shots. And hey, when do I get to look at my portrait?"

Gabrielle laughed. "Not till I'm done." She finished closing up paint tubes and cleaning her brushes.

"Oh shucks, you're no fun," Adrienne retorted, scrunching up her face in distaste.

"Careful, I might decide to paint that look."

"You wouldn't dare…"

~VIII~
NO MOUNTAIN TOO HIGH

1967 – 1971 – New York City

1

And so the summer passed pleasantly enough. As classes at Parsons soon would begin, Gabrielle arrived early to settle into her new dorm room and explore New York City.

She hardly could contain her excitement about being in the big city and totally focused on art. Loving that the school was in lower Manhattan's Greenwich Village, she relished how full of life the city was and how aspiring artists and world-class museums beckoned her.

Seeing that her fellow students came not only from across the U.S., but also from around the world, she thought how well the school reflected the city and its people from every imaginable background. When she walked New York's streets, she heard a myriad of languages that played like music to her. As she acknowledged this, she realized that in every respect, she didn't feel different from everyone else. She was just one of many who moved about in the nation's greatest melting pot. And she found it a delicious stew.

What she knew of Parsons and the city fed her imagination in ways she never envisioned. Parsons' championing of art that demonstrated creative and intellectual rigor and social responsibility nurtured her desire to express her social and political convictions through her painting. Reaching and perhaps even helping to move hearts and minds to change had become her motivation for her growing artistic expression.

The fact that the school emboldened students to discuss and even embrace controversial ideas and practices was freeing to her. Liberating as well, by virtue of New York's museums and galleries, was her exposure to the innovativeness of the world's greatest artists.

For the first time she felt she could experience a myriad of artists' work, not just as photographs in books, but in person. She found it astonishing how small and intimate Vermeer's paintings could be and conversely, how mammoth a Botticelli, for example, might be.

She studied the brushwork, the color palettes, and the play of light in the work of such artists as Rembrandt, Monet, and Van Gogh. She felt the horror of Picasso's massive *Guernica*, the passion of Gauguin, the stretching of credulity of a Salvador Dali. She explored the art of the avant-garde, including pop artists Andy Warhol, Roy Lichtenstein, Jasper Johns, and James Rosenquist. *There's something about confronting the actual painting in person,* she observed, *that's so far beyond experiencing it in the pages of a book. It's a visceral experience. Even more, it's transformative.*

Through first-hand exposure to a wide range of art, she witnessed the progression of styles from ancient times to modern and how artists over the generations had served as pioneers, pushing the boundaries of "acceptable" art. For the first time in her young life, she felt completely free to expand the perimeter of her experience and venture into unknown territory. In short she came to believe that anything was possible in the art world.

More immediately she found that this translated into a freeing of her mind to practice being more loose with her brush applications when the subject warranted it, more tight and precise when she felt the object required it, mix media, expand reality, make visible the subconscious.

Just by observing, she truly came to understand that art had no rights or wrongs. She believed now that the only judgments she needed to apply to her work were that she was working to her potential and that her art represented her personal beliefs and her search for her own artistic truth.

No Mountain Too High

After classes began she still took time to travel to exhibits. A pivotal moment came the day she skipped lunch to take in an exhibition of very large photographs of the murals of famous Mexican painters and some of their original studies for the murals. They included those rendered by Diego Rivera, José Clemente Orozco, and David Alfaro Siqueiros. Gabrielle was stunned by the power of their expression, laden with political and social statements of a people wronged and their fight for freedom and justice.

The work she viewed in the exhibit was rooted in the Mexican Revolution of 1910 – 1920, said to be the first major political, social, and cultural revolution of the twentieth century. It included large photographs of these artists' murals. They would forever remind people entering many government and private buildings, what native people of Mexico had endured and fought against throughout their history. Their original sketches, some no more than doodles, she found particularly fascinating. They were the bones of these artists' magnificent works that generated emotion in the viewer as they chronicled what one came to see as the historical rightness of a people's struggle.

She discovered in the murals a kind of spiritual energy. The work of Diego Rivera most deeply spoke to her. He demonstrated a kind of loving solidity of expression in the way he portrayed a people long oppressed. Their faces, their bodies, sturdy and devotedly drawn and painted, awakened something in her she couldn't explain. It was almost as if their expressions reached out and touched her so fully that she felt them in her very cell structure.

She sat on a bench in the exhibition room and absorbed what the artists whispered—and sometimes shouted—to her in the messages that traveled in their work. A people were oppressed. A people rose up. A people strove to sustain the gains won in blood and sacrifice. Nothing she witnessed in the art world had affected her as this did. She found something of herself in this body of work. And she heard its distant voices.

With unwanted suddenness she found herself sifting the seeds of her childhood. She relived now as she had hundreds of times before, the humiliation she felt as a kindergartener made an example of before a class of first graders. Her presumptive sin was that she ran in the hall to reach the bathroom in time. Her adult self knew that Miss Leaper's victimization of her was less about that than about the color of her skin. The teacher treated her as dirty and ripe for discrimination in an all-white school.

Gabrielle thought of how throughout junior high and high school she wasn't asked to dances or birthday parties and was the subject of name-calling taunts from students she didn't know. Even her own father treated her as less valued than his fair-skinned older daughter. All because she looked different.

She felt a knot in her soul when she relived memories ridden with questions she couldn't unravel. It made her feel empty and wanting, as it had so often since childhood. Who was she really? Why was she different from everyone with whom she grew up? And why did she relate so strongly to these people Rivera painted, moving her in a way she didn't understand.

Suddenly she wanted to know everything about Mexico's native people with their almost Mongolian features and darker skin. Who were they? What was their history? Why did she know them in a way she couldn't explain?

There was something in their features that echoed in her own—different, yet not totally unlike hers—aspects of her hair, her darker skin, the shape of her eyes, her full lips. She felt an affinity with these people that she couldn't define. Was it the injustice they suffered that reminded her of what she witnessed among blacks in America? Or was it something even more specific to her?

She sat there until closing, so absorbed in these artists' work and her thoughts that she lost track of time. Although she missed two of her classes, somehow that seemed of very little importance. Rivera and his fellow muralists had touched her heart in a way that she couldn't fully comprehend. But she felt that something had changed for her after this encounter. What it was, she had yet to learn.

* * *

Gabrielle returned to her classwork with renewed vigor, but Rivera's murals percolated in her mind. She began to wonder why she couldn't tell the Hattiesburg experience in similar form. Although she had nowhere to paint a mural, she asked herself why she couldn't use giant canvases placed side-by-side to emulate one.

She began working on her own, creating sketches for the series she envisioned. She wanted to give an account of a people's oppression—and their dignity, their rising up. This was the story she had witnessed and was in a unique position to tell.

Her dormitory had an art studio where she could paint large subjects. If she could set up there, she could work as long after hours as she wished. At considerable cost to her small savings, she purchased a canvas eight feet high by fifteen wide. Soon it would arrive at the studio where she worked sketching small to-scale studies. They echoed the work she created in Oberlin, but in a new form and with a different approach. The undertaking challenged and enticed her. You could say it obsessed her.

Her idea was to begin by rendering one of the eight canvases. If the first was successful, she would use it and her small studies to make a bid—to whom she wasn't sure yet—to fund completion of the work. The materials needed would cost more than she could afford, even for just the one. She decided upon oil paints as her medium, which carried a ruggedness and history that she wanted for this work.

What she conjured was a series that would connect—physically and artistically as well as thematically—producing the illusion of a mural in an exhibition space. Gabrielle wanted the figures to be large, their humanity reaching out to viewers in a way they couldn't dismiss. She wanted the tenderness in her paintings to speak to people in the way Rivera's had spoken to her.

After much thought, she determined to begin close to the end of the series, showing Reverend Jonas addressing the fervent congregation at The Saving Grace Baptist Church. She wanted people to feel the congregation ascending in their voices and bodies in answer to the Reverend's call to battle for their civil rights. She would make an offering of the faces of suffering and enlightenment, of a people rising to claim their rights at great personal cost. Seeking to have those viewing her work bear witness to the dignity and rightness of blacks' struggle, she ultimately was entreating them to support the fight that hadn't ended with the Voting Rights Act of 1965.

It was almost five o'clock when the canvas arrived and she directed the delivery people to place it against the empty wall. Then she ran to the cafeteria to grab a beverage and sandwich before returning. Her plan was to work as long as she could stay awake.

Hesitating but a moment, she ripped the paper from the canvas. She felt its imposing presence and the enormity of her undertaking. The canvas itself was many times larger than any she had tackled. But what she experienced more keenly was the import of her subject. She hungered to do justice to the people she would render and make them proud to be part of this body of work.

Not seeing how she could stretch this large canvas without help, she paid for an already stretched one. Mindful of her need to create a demonstration panel as soon as she could to gain financial support for her series, she had it delivered already gesso-coated and ready for her to begin drawing. Remembering a teacher's instruction as to how to scale up a small picture to a large one, she blocked out her small-canvas sketch in a grid and numbered each square. Then she grabbed a ladder and began tackling the large canvas.

Starting by measuring off the coordinates of her small-sketch matrix, she multiplied the distances between them to give her the correct markings for the large canvas. It took her over four hours to measure and imprint them with dots and draw pale charcoal lines to connect them. It was another four hours to number the squares and double-check all her grid markings to assure she got everything right. Then she checked them all again.

Looking at her watch for the first time since the delivery men came, she was surprised to see it already was past two o'clock. While she knew that she should turn in and resume work the following night, she felt the canvas draw her to begin. She examined Reverend Jonas on her preliminary study. She knew that he was where she needed to start.

"Don't fail me now Reverend Jonas," she admonished as she moved her ladder to the panel.

Charcoal in hand, she began drawing light contours of the Reverend, taking care to keep his form within the area established in her original. She knew that adhering precisely to the correct markings was her only hope of getting this massive piece right. She imagined how his form loomed above the congregation, his arms outstretched as he called his flock. As she examined what she had outlined, she proceeded to also frame a cone of light that would bathe his form and the open Bible on the podium.

Descending from the ladder, she stepped back twenty feet. The charcoal form matched the prototype she had in her hand. But something was wrong. What was it? His body was meant to be imposing, but it seemed too large. Or was it? Perhaps when she drew the other figures, his would be more proportional. She shook her head. *Am I really ready for this? This is way harder than I'd imagined.* She studied her small sketch again. *The proportions work here. Why do they seem wrong on the big canvas?*

Looking at her watch, she saw it was past four o'clock. Her excitement gave way to exhaustion. The full weight of her challenge was crushing her. *Gabrielle, you've finally bitten off more than you can chew. What was I thinking?* Disheartened, she put away her supplies and turned out the lights, closed the studio door, and returned to her room. *I can't think about this anymore,* she told herself as she put the sketch down, threw herself onto her bed, and immediately fell asleep.

She was falling down a rabbit hole of dreams. She observed people from her past stalking her with suspicion in their eyes and denigration in their souls. As the memory of the Boatmans' jeering invaded her sleeping mind with their dislike of blacks, she saw herself struggling to escape. No sooner had she succeeded, than Miss Leaper rose huge and menacing, grabbing her arm and throwing her to the first graders. Surrounding her, they spit on her and repeatedly shouted, "Stupid darkie!" When they grew tired of her, she witnessed herself crawling into the hall, where junior high kids pelted her with books and racial slurs—Wetback! Beaner! Greaser! One of them stepped on her hand. She screamed, then awoke panting and bathed in sweat, her whole body shaking.

In time she quieted. *What a nightmare! God help me. Why does being different make people so cruel?* She felt a knowing of how some had perceived her and what it must be like to be black or Mexican. She thought how her time in Mississippi showed her that while fear historically was used to keep blacks down, a rightness of spirit still led them to rise up.

Furthermore, her study of the Mexican muralists, who captured the nobility of indigenous people and their culture, paved her way to express through art a similar evolution of blacks' rising up. All this gave her comfort and resolve for the challenges she faced and gradually walked her back from the anguish of her nightmare.

* * *

Woken by the morning light, she stretched, still feeling the lingering shadow of her dream. Glancing at her watch, she returned to the moment, suddenly realizing she was late for oil painting class. "Damn," she muttered, "not again!" Still wearing the previous day's clothes, she grabbed her backpack and charged through the city streets. Opening the classroom door slowly, she hoped to go unnoticed as she slunk to her easel.

"Miss Andersen, how nice of you to join us," Professor Ray admonished her with a wave of his hand and a sour expression.

"I apologize sir," she responded. "It won't happen again."

"I hope not." He pivoted from her to the broader class. "As I was saying, like us, great artists can make terrible mistakes...."

Gabrielle was fully listening now.

"...But through our mistakes we learn. We're most likely to err when we don't know enough, when we're trying too hard, or when we're experimenting or exceeding the limits of our abilities." He stroked his long beard and looked with intention at his students.

"When you venture into the unknown, you need your full awareness. And you need grit. Little of enduring worth comes from what's easy. If it were straightforward, anyone could do it. What's hard is the substance from which greatness grows." He paced the room now, his steps long, as he was a tall man.

"Undertake what seems impossible. Persist. You are here not to be just good artists. Many of you have within you the potential for being more than good. But you must be an adventurer with your imagination and with your brush, your palette knife—and have a purpose for your quest that's worthy of the work it will require."

Gabrielle leaned forward to capture each word as he paused to gauge the reactions of his students. His glance was drawn momentarily to Gabrielle's strongly attentive stare. As her eyes met his, she felt his challenge, one that carried seeds capable of growing change in her and her fellow students' lives.

"I can teach you techniques and critique your efforts," he continued, moving about and surveying the class as a whole. "But it's up to you to preserve a lineage of great art by honoring how you approach your work and what your purpose is as an artist. If fame and fortune are your sole aim, you may achieve them. But your art will be devoid of heart, the passion that makes art great. And if you stay within your cone of safety and convention, you'll fail to entertain the possibilities that have yet to be explored."

He stopped, as if to punctuate what he was about to say. "In these you may find your truth as an artist. If you do, you may have the power to help those who view your art to find *their* truth. Great art is a form of magic. It can transform one who is sensitive to it and enlighten the masses. Art is not some esoteric thing. It's sacred and meant to be available to all." *Yes,* she thought, *this is exactly as I see it. He understands. What a wise and visionary man.*

Pacing again, he gesticulated as he walked. "So think big when you choose your projects. Ask yourself why am I painting this? If your response doesn't challenge you as an aspiring artist, then you're thinking too small. Think big! Break boundaries! Be willing to make big mistakes! Learn from them, and don't give up. In persistence is the secret of accomplishment. Surprise me with the project you've chosen when you return next week."

With that he turned and began gathering up materials for his next class. As the students left, Gabrielle sat in amazement of the professor's oratory. She experienced again the truth of his words and felt as if he knew everything about her and what was on her mind. As she rose to leave, the professor noticed and signaled her. "Miss Andersen, a minute please. You've missed two of my classes in a row. This surprises me, as I took you for a serious student. What's going on?"

His rebuke bit. Clearing her throat, she looked into his clear grey eyes. "I'm terribly sorry professor. I've undertaken a project that's so far beyond me, I don't know how I can pull it off. But I'm haunted by it, driven really. I was up past four this morning working on it and overslept."

Professor Ray stroked his greying beard and frowned in concentration. "I see. Why don't you tell me about this project of yours."

Taking a deep breath, she explained her civil rights experiences and her desire to marry her art to her social and political values. Then she related her introduction to Diego Rivera and the other Mexican muralists and how that had fired her to plan for eight large panels. They would tell the story of what she experienced in Mississippi and her need to bear witness. She would mount the paintings mural-like as a continuous chronicle.

Then she told him of her hope to find funding for the series and that she already had purchased her first canvas. "I began working on it last night in the dorm studio, creating a grid mirroring my mockup, then sketching the outline of the principal figure. But something's wrong with the proportions, though they appear the same as on my small-scale version. I was wrestling with this before I fell asleep. I'm sorry I disrupted your class and missed all that you were saying. It was as if you were speaking to *me*."

The professor, who appeared to be in his early sixties, looked at her solemnly. "My dear Miss Andersen, you instinctively have done the very things I was trying to impart to your classmates. But for the disruption, I would applaud the basis for your tardiness. I suppose, if it would help, I could look at your project and give you my thoughts. I think, however, that you'll learn far more if you solve your problems on your own through trial and error."

Observing her, he continued. "You seem to be a serious and persistent person or you wouldn't undertake such an effort. I suspect that if you persevere with what you've started and accomplish something of artistic and social worth, it's possible you could get your backing.

"If you like, when you've finished sketching the canvas, I might give you my honest opinion of it and the possibility of acquiring funding. It sounds as if you already have your class project with this work of yours—and likely for all of your oil painting classes from now to graduation and beyond." He chuckled. "Keep at it Miss Andersen. Don't be discouraged. Unpleasant surprises are all part of the process."

He smiled as he picked up his notes and walked out with her. He waved goodbye as she thanked him and he peeled off in a different direction, his long grey hair seeming to float behind him.

Gabrielle located a bench and seated herself, unaware of the mill of students and faculty passing her. *I've found my project. He's right,* she thought. *I must figure this out on my own. I'll go back to it tonight and maybe things will look different. If not, I'll work this out. I can... and I will.*

She returned to the studio at the close of the day's classes. Grabbing a chair, she walked back thirty feet, holding her original sketch to compare it to the canvas. The Reverend looked massive in both, but proportionally even more so in the large one.

The only way I'm going to know if this will work, she concluded, *is to sketch the outlines of the other figures and see if I should adjust the minister's.*

Taking a deep breath, she rose and carried the ladder to the right side of the canvas, then drove a nail into the back of the frame. There she secured her sketch so it would hang in ready view as she worked. This small study was her map to the treasure she sought, which was art worthy of its subjects and intent.

It was well past midnight when she had the rough contours of the congregation in place. Although a few other students had come and gone from the studio, they were respectful of her intensity and didn't interrupt. She descended the ladder and stepped back from her work. Although much remained to profile, she was starting to believe that the clergyman's dominance in the picture could work. *I just have to keep going with this,* she told herself. *When all the outlines are drawn, then I'll know for sure.*

She stood there for several minutes, searching for what the canvas might tell her. What she felt was its enormity of purpose, to which she was its devoted servant. *Will this work consume me?* she wondered. But she knew. It already had.

2

For two weeks now she hardly could wait for classes to be over so she could return to her project. On one of these days she grabbed a sandwich and coffee on her way there, but the food sat uneaten for hours before she remembered it. She had most of the figures sketchily outlined, and she knew that the next step would be to do likewise with architectural features—pulpit, pews, windows.

Past midnight on another evening, she completed all the rough outlines. She stepped far back and took it all in. The Reverend still felt too large. But then she thought about how colorful the women's clothes would be and the joyfulness of their hats. It would be easy to lose the force of the preacher in the spiritedness of the congregation.

She sought to have a play between them—the brilliance and solidity of the women and the vibrancy of the men in response to the presence, the magic of the minister and his call. To do this she realized that he had to be overly large, but in synchrony with his ardent parishioners. *Yes, this is it,* she decided. Tomorrow she would begin the more detailed drawings, filling in the positioning outlines with important attributes of real people and objects.

Despite how tired she was and how her body ached from the effort, she was so excited that when she went to bed she couldn't help thinking about her next steps and how she would render the figures.

Sleep finally took her, but left her too early when the alarm buzzed. Dragging herself out of bed, she showered quickly and dressed. She ran out the door, forgetting to comb her hair and barely making it to watercolor class. She had to struggle to concentrate on the subjects the class painted, despite how much she loved the medium. Becoming mechanical in her strokes, she only could think of how she wanted to portray the Reverend.

Although she made it through classes, her heart wasn't in it. She was totally focused on her project and nearly forgot to stop for takeout food. She grabbed a carton of Chinese food and a large coffee before charging into the studio. Two students worked there, but she took no notice of them. Setting down her backpack and food, she stood in front of her canvas. She had thought about the Reverend all day and night, even into her dreams, where she saw exactly how she should draw him.

Closing her eyes, she relived her experience of him at Hattiesburg's Saving Grace Baptist Church. She saw him as if he were an orchestral conductor guiding the emotions and responses of the congregation. With each word, each gesture, he brought them to a fervor. His conviction was theirs, and the presence of the Lord was all around. It was like the swelling of an orchestra, the various instruments joining together to create synchronous sound. Gabrielle had never experienced a church service like this before, and she wanted viewers of her painting to see the devotion she had witnessed.

She began by adjusting some of the sketch lines, erasing them with a damp cloth and drawing new ones. Filling in the lines of the preacher's gown, she then detailed the contours of his arms and hands. She stepped down from the ladder, observed what she did, then climbed back up.

This time she delineated his face, the features yes, but more, his expression, the emotions moving to bloom in his features. It was too soon to get this detailed. She knew this. But she felt the challenge of him. He was a force from which she couldn't turn away.

As she worked she found she was coming to understand what true righteousness was. It had no relation to sanctimoniousness. It was integrity of spirit, honorableness of action, dependent upon faith and faithfulness. Faithfulness was the spirit of the congregation and also of Reverend Jonas.

It was devotion to a belief that was religious, but also to one that called upon the humanity gathered there to bring that rightness of spirit to this earthly place.

It was a calling that he issued in this old wooden building with its peeling paint, the house of worship that emulated those bathed in Psalms and Bible stories thousands of years old, a calling that made the church shake with the desire for freedom, the yearning for equality long ago fought for and now battling for again.

As she sketched she relived her experience of this fellowship so intensely that it brought tears to her eyes. Her sight blurred for a moment as she finished rendering the details of the cleric's countenance. She descended the ladder and visibly deflated as she sat.

"Are you all right?" a voice almost whispered to her.

Gabrielle returned to the moment as she wiped her eyes and looked into the concerned face of a young woman. "Uh...yes...yes..."

The student touched Gabrielle's shoulder.

Shaking herself, she gazed at the earnest woman. "I'm sorry. I got too drawn in by what I was doing."

"You have food here. I think it's cold. Maybe you might want some?"

Gabrielle stared blankly at the overlooked carton she bought hours ago. "My, I'm afraid I forgot all about it." Embarrassed, she shook her head.

"Would you like me to warm it for you in the microwave?"

"Oh… no, I can do it. Thanks, but I'm fine, just a little too wrapped up in this painting." Gabrielle gave the slender young woman a weak smile.

"I've been watching you in this studio the last two nights. It appears you have a very ambitious project ahead of you. It's an enormous canvas."

Gabrielle laughed. "It is, isn't it?"

"May I ask what you're sketching?"

She laughed again. "To be honest, I don't think I can describe it right now. On the face of it, it's a church service in Mississippi."

"Ah, a civil rights thing?"

"You might say that."

"It looks interesting. Are you sure I can't warm this for you?" she asked again.

"No really, I'm fine. Thank you."

"I wish you well with your project."

"Thanks," Gabrielle responded, suddenly feeling weary. After heating her meal, she examined her work as she ate, hardly tasting her food. The student's concern already had passed from her mind.

Looking intently at the Reverend's face, she thought her early rendering of it caught the emotion she was reaching for. Of course her oil paints would be the test. She noted that the lines of his robe had the sway she sought, having worked on this as a vehicle to reinforce the grace and lyricism of the message that his voice delivered. Believing that her work was traveling in the right direction, she decided that tomorrow she would draw his pulpit and the architecture around him in more detail. The congregation would follow.

Picking at her food, she tried to finish the meal. The warmth of it nourished her as much as its substance, but strangely, she wasn't hungry. She thought that she ate more from duty than desire and that it was the work that filled her up. Food seemed of little import, she mused as she glanced at her watch. It was almost midnight again. She wondered how long she had been sitting here.

Shrugging, she gathered up her things and turned out the lights. Returning to her room, she instantly found sleep.

* * *

The sun woke her. She rose with a start. Thinking she was late for class and still wearing yesterday's clothes, she grabbed her backpack and headed for the door. Checking her watch, she saw that it was noon already. Then she remembered. It was Saturday.

Although she felt dazed, she thought the better of going back to bed. Instead she walked down the hall to shower. The warm water comforted her as she washed her body and hair. Emerging from bathing, she buffed a hole in the steam clinging to a mirror.

What she saw shocked her. Circles hung like dark crescent moons beneath her eyes. Blinking several times, she looked again. *God, I look like crap.* As she dried herself, she realized she had been neglecting the needs of her body for weeks now. She had fitful sleep since she started the large canvas and was eating poorly. *This project is consuming me, and I don't know how to stop it. It's all I think about, all I want. I'm slipping in my classes and can't focus on what I'm supposed to be learning.* She touched a face she hardly recognized. *I'm afraid I'll get worse. I can't keep this up.*

Suddenly tired, she forced herself to go to the cafeteria where she filled her tray with food. But she picked at it as she wrestled with her thoughts about her project's next steps. *I'm in trouble,* she finally admitted. *I either have to delay this project or withdraw from school until I finish what I started.*

Either path seemed impossible to her, so she determined how she would spend her weekend instead. She would not go to the studio, but rather devote herself to unfinished class assignments. On Monday she would try to see Professor Ray. Perhaps he would have a solution to an unhealthy situation that seemed on the verge of spiraling out of control.

Deciding this gave her some peace. Finishing her meal and about to tackle another class exercise, she did everything in her power to not think about that enormous canvas and how it called her. At least for a while.

Saturday went passably well, despite the war she waged with her mind. Working in her room on Sunday, she heard a knock on the door and a woman saying she had a call on the floor phone "from a Rick somebody."

Brightening, Gabrielle ran down the hall. "Rick, I can't believe it's you."

"None other. Haven't heard from you in ages. How are you doing Gabrielle?"

Though his voice held concern, she missed it in her joy at hearing from him. "I'm okay. Just tell me, how are *you* doing?"

"I'm fine. I'm home in Delaware after wrapping up work at the tutoring center."

"Wow. Tell me about it."

"It took well into fall quarter to get things in order and see who might take my place."

"Who did you find to do it?"

"You remember Mark Weinstein…."

"Sure, one of our most devoted tutors."

"Well, he agreed to take the post."

"That's fantastic. He would have been my choice. It's an incredible amount of work, especially when you're still in school."

"It is, but he gets the importance of what we've built and the impact it's having on the kids. I know he'll take good care of all we've done there, Gabrielle."

"I'm *so* glad. That's great news. Tell me, did you see Jeremy before you left? Is he still coming to the center and doing well in school?"

Rick laughed. "I knew you'd ask. He's still coming, working more on his reading and writing, but also his math. He's a whole different person from the boy who first came to us. He has so much self-confidence now. You'd be so proud of him and our work with him. You left a real imprint on his life. You made him feel that he must be someone special to have a person like you care about him. But most of all it was Jeremy himself. What a kid! He showed so much perseverance."

"It lifts my spirits to hear what he's achieved."

"How about you Gabrielle?"

"I've been totally obsessed with a project. I'm so in over my head that it's all I can think about. I started slipping in my classes and not eating and sleeping the way I should. The project is all I've wanted to do. I'm afraid I could lose my scholarship if I don't get back on track with my classes."

"That doesn't sound like you. Tell me about this project."

She sighed, then related the whole story. Her description made it apparent that the weight of what she had undertaken and her desire to represent her and Rick's experiences honestly and powerfully were all but crushing her.

He was silent for a minute. "Gabrielle you do have a tough time doing anything in a small way."

She laughed.

"Seriously though, it doesn't sound like you to doubt yourself like this. I understand that what you're doing is a huge undertaking, but think how amazing it'll be if you can pull it off. Imagine if even one person who views your series resolves to help."

"That's what drives me and keeps me up at night. I just can't figure out how to balance my classes with this project. It's a full-time job—and then some."

"Is there a counselor or instructor you can talk to?"

"Interesting you'd suggest that, because I plan to do exactly that tomorrow. I have an oil painting teacher I'm very impressed with and trust to advise me on how to balance all this. I hope to get some time with him after class tomorrow."

"Perfect. It's good you've recognized this before things get completely out of hand. It's always hard to admit when you're in trouble."

"Yes."

"Have you thought about getting all your teachers to let you concentrate on your series for course credit?"

"I have, but of course only drawing and oil painting classes, and perhaps portraiture might qualify. Watercolor class is different. It's a whole different medium."

"Yes. But what if you did a smaller version of one or more of your pictures in watercolor?"

"Hmmm, that would keep me focused on one subject. It's all I can think about anyway. That's a great idea."

"Well I hope it works out."

"Rick tell me what you're thinking you'll do next, now that you're home from Oberlin."

"That's what I've been trying to figure out. I've been just as obsessed with the tutoring center and Civil Rights Movement in general as you have with your panels. But I don't have classes and the threat of losing a scholarship vying for my attention. Right now I just can't see myself sitting in poli sci graduate school classes when so much social change is going on. I'm thinking about working as a community organizer."

"Wow. You know, I can see that. Just look at what you did in Oberlin. That was a form of community organizing."

"In a fashion."

"How do you get a job in this, and can you feed yourself doing it?"

He laughed. "This is a question from a woman who just told me she's lost interest in food."

"Very funny. You know what I'm talking about."

"Well I'll research this to see where the most effective work is happening. I suspect I'll have to go to some big city like Chicago, LA, or New York."

"New York—that would be fantastic!"

"One of many possibilities. Finding training and employment in high-level organizing would be very exciting to me."

"That would be incredible. How lucky they'd be to have you. Let me know how it goes."

"I will. But I'm going to have to sign off for now."

"Sorry to have blabbered on so. I wanted to hear more about *you*."

"Gabrielle, never think like that. You know that your well-being is important to me." She thought she heard his voice break. Then he continued, his voice steady now. "Don't ever hesitate to call or write me. And please let me know when you resolve your issue or if you need help working through it."

She fell silent for a moment. "I've never met anyone like you Rick. You're the truest friend anyone could have. Please let's stay in closer touch. I feel like we're both on some mysterious roller coaster that we can't or don't want to leave. Yet we have to find some way to master its twists and turns to not be thrown by it. It seems that you and I are entering new territory that has big demands, perhaps dangers even. We must remember to take care of ourselves and to help each other."

"Yes." He paused, as if trying to decide if he should say more. "It's been good to talk to you Gabrielle. Take care of yourself."

"You too Rick."

Returning to her room, she thought about all that they said and how easy it was between them. They could tell each other about anything. She felt grateful for his friendship and for the ideas and perspective he gave her. Fervently hoping that he would find what he was looking for, she realized in that moment that she wanted his success as much as she craved her own.

3

The task was to draw and paint the nude male model Professor Ray had commissioned for the class. He challenged his students to work quickly to sketch, determine the color palette and values for the final piece, and complete the underpainting in two hours. Despite the time pressure, she found it a good practice leading to a looser, freer style. As she rendered a partially formed figure, she thought of Leonardo da Vinci's studies of the human body as a kind of North Star for dynamic beauty. Signing hers, she left it in front for the professor's critique before stopping after class to request his counsel.

"Yes Miss Andersen," he responded, turning from notes he was making to give her his attention.

"There's something I need to ask you," she said. "Would you have time now to speak with me?"

He considered her for a moment, his grey eyes narrowing under bushy eyebrows before he glanced at his watch. "I have twenty minutes. Will that be enough?"

"I think so."

Removing his painting apron, he walked to a row of chairs and motioned for her to sit. Depositing his tall, slender body on a chair that he pivoted in her direction, he studied her. "Okay then. What's on your mind?" he asked, brushing wiry, grey curls from his forehead.

Gabrielle took a deep breath and told him as succinctly as she could about the quandary she was in and the impact her undertaking was having upon her academically and physically. "I don't think I'll be able to put this project out of my mind, even for the rest of the term.

"I've considered dropping out of school for a while. Then I thought that if there was a chance of being able to get all of my instructors to agree to use my big project's subject matter for my different assignments, perhaps that could be a solution. If you believe it would be a workable idea, how might you suggest I go about it? Or if it's not a good solution, what alternatives am I not seeing?"

The creases between the professor's eyebrows deepened as he listened. Leaning back in his chair so that the front chair legs left the floor, he rocked back and forth in silence and reflection, stroking his grey beard like some sage, aging wizard. But as she watched him, she thought she might faint if he didn't say something soon.

"I see," he said finally as his front chair legs reengaged the floor. "We cannot have your health and well-being suffering. But neither can we interfere with the strength of this calling you have." He leaned toward her from his chair and looked directly into her eyes.

"You absolutely should not drop out of school, nor should you risk your scholarship. I don't know how the other instructors will respond to your idea, but I'm willing to consider letting all of my assignments outside class be fulfilled with something from this series you describe. I'd first like to see your preliminary studies and perhaps the canvas you've begun. If I'm satisfied with the quality of the project, you'll have my agreement."

"Oh thank you…," Gabrielle began, then stopped as he raised his hand before continuing.

"Convincing your other teachers may not be easy, so you'll need to determine what you'll do if you don't get their consent. But if your project has the merit that I suspect it does, I would consider speaking with them on your behalf if necessary. There's one more thing that you've not brought up. What you'll require to complete your series is costly—the canvases, paints, etc. Have you a plan for this?"

She hesitated, embarrassed. "I'm afraid not."

"That's something you should reflect on. I'll give it some thought as well."

"Professor, I hardly know what to say." She glanced down in an effort to control her emotions. Clearing her throat, she collected herself and asked, "Would you like to come to the dorm studio to see the canvas I'm sketching and the studies I did?"

He looked at her as a father would his daughter. "Yes I can do that. Tomorrow at four-thirty?"

"That would be good."

"Okay then. Four-thirty it is." He looked up and turned toward her as he checked his watch. "I'm afraid I have to run. See you tomorrow." And he was gone before she could thank him again.

Taking a deep breath, she gathered up her things and went to her next class. But all she could think about was that she needed to look critically at the work she had done and determine whether it was ready for review. If not, would she have time to improve it before tomorrow?

It was evening before she returned to the dorm. Gathering up her eight sketches, she laid them on her bed in the order she planned to display them.

The first one illustrated the bus loaded with young civil rights workers from the North observing signs as they crossed into Mississippi. The first read: "Welcome to Mississippi." The second: "Prepare to Meet Thy God."

Her second sketch depicted the busload of terrified students who were attacked by a mob of angry white men at a Mississippi gas station.

The third bridged two scenes. One pictured a night scene at civil rights headquarters in Hattiesburg. There civil rights workers introduced the students to their mission and the voter registration work they would undertake. The adjoining scene depicted local blacks transporting students for safekeeping to homes in their section of town.

The fourth was an intimate portrait of Gabrielle and Rick's experience with their host family, Edith and Mike Brown and their five young children.

The fifth portrayed a brush with death when a carload of whites shot to kill as Gabrielle and Rick and a black man discussed voter registration outside his home.

The sixth witnessed Rick and Gabrielle's shock at the living conditions of an emaciated black woman in rags and her two barefoot children. As the students approached, the family retreated in terror into their shantytown tarpaper shack.

The seventh was the Reverend Jonas canvas.

The eighth depicted frightened blacks standing in line to register to vote as whites taunted and threatened them.

While acceptable at this point in her work, she knew that the sketches still were unfinished and demonstrated nothing of her abilities as a painter. As she contemplated this, she remembered the pictures she had taken of her Hattiesburg paintings exhibited at Oberlin's senior art show. She rummaged through her desk and found the photos and copies of the newspaper articles praising the exhibit and her artwork. Extracting them from their envelopes, she assembled them on the bed along with the sketches.

Together she thought they relayed as well as she could what her plan was and what skills she possessed to execute it. Feeling calmer than she had in days, she decided she was well enough ready for Professor Ray's review. Now she would take a last look at her canvas.

When she arrived at the studio, she saw several students at work this evening. Her artwork loomed, but she felt less intimidated by it. Pleased with her charcoal rendering of Reverend Jonas and her outline of the congregation, she was anxious for Professor Ray's assessment. Before her canvas could lure her away again, she left her sketches, photos, and clippings there and returned to her room to study and extract all the knowledge she could from lecture and class discussion notes.

* * *

The next day was sunny and brisk. Before she knew it, she had finished her classes and run back to the studio before the professor arrived. Fortunately no one was there.

She recovered her photographs, clippings, and eight studies from behind her massive artwork. She laid the sketches on her work table in the exhibition order that she planned. Then she put the photographs of her Oberlin Hattiesburg paintings beside her sketches that had similar subject matter.

No sooner had she done this than the professor entered the studio. "Miss Andersen," he said in his professorial voice. She turned and walked toward him. "Professor Ray, it's so good of you to come."

Nodding in response, he glanced at the canvas before walking far back from it. He stood there for several minutes gazing at it. "Let me see the sketch you're working from," he said, moving back toward her.

"This actually is the seventh of the eight panels I've planned," she said, picking up the appropriate drawing and handing it to him. "It's a little hard to see the sketch clearly, as I had to make a grid on the study to get the placement right on the canvas."

"Yes," he said stroking his beard in thought, then striding back across the room. Holding up the study, he again observed the canvas and gazed several times at what he held in his hand. "Tell me about your plan for the eight panels, what each represents, and why you chose them for your series."

Gabrielle's heartbeat quickened as she began telling him about each planned piece of the eight. He looked thoughtful as she relayed the experiences she sought to capture and what she hoped to accomplish with the series grouped and displayed to look like a continuous mural. When she finished, he nodded deep in thought, then asked her about the photographs. She explained them and why she brought them. Again he just nodded and seemed to be digesting all she was showing him.

Striding back across the room with the seventh study, he again took in the large canvas from thirty feet away, glancing periodically at what he held in his hand. As she observed him, she hardly breathed so as not to disturb him. Realizing suddenly that three students had arrived to pursue their projects, she saw them watch with fascination the unusual occurrence of a faculty member's presence there—and that it was the esteemed Professor Ray. Their attention made Gabrielle anxious.

At last he returned to where she stood, returning the drawing to her. His eyes seemed to pierce her, as if he understood everything about her and her project. His voice was little more than a whisper, as he also had become aware of the students' presence. "This is quite an undertaking," he acknowledged, pausing as he looked at her again. "May I ask how old you are?"

Surprised by his question, she faltered, but answered "twenty-one."

"This is not a situation I've encountered before, especially coming from someone so young." He smiled gently, then pressed on. "My dear Miss Andersen, I see here in just this one large canvas, more than a term's work no matter how many other instructors may accept this for your assignments. This and perhaps another easily could take your entire time here at Parsons. Have you considered this?"

His comment startled her. "No," she responded, "I'm afraid that I haven't." Her gaze moved to the floor as she realized her naiveté.

"I'm going to have to think about this, as I doubt that your situation can be remedied with so simple a solution as we'd entertained," he said in a solemn voice.

She felt herself deflate, having so hoped that her prayers were about to be answered. "Is there anything you've seen that you think might be worthy of further effort?" she asked, looking despondent.

The professor was visibly taken aback. "Miss Andersen, you misunderstand me. I wasn't criticizing what you've begun. To the contrary, I'm moved by what you've shown me. I'm impressed that someone so young has had such experiences—and that despite having only a modest amount of instruction, you have the sagacity to forge ahead with this distillation of what you witnessed.

"To the contrary, I believe that this is an effort that needs to go forward for your advancement as an artist and because it's in service to a worthy cause that you're passionate about. I just don't have a ready solution for you, as this is a project that would daunt seasoned artists who didn't have to split their time between this effort and the obligations of their classes."

As he spoke her hopes rose again as a sparrow from the dust. As she watched this thoughtful man struggle with her dilemma, she could feel him take some of her travail upon his shoulders. Before she could respond he said, "One thing you must address, however, is your need to develop a plan as to how to fluidly knit one panel to the next. It could be by using a consistent color palette or by what you decide regarding tonal values for example. Never forget that the artistry you demonstrate must be paramount if you want your message to deliver its full power.

"I'll need time to consider all that I've seen and all that you've told me," he continued. "Don't despair," he added in a gentler tone, clearly noticing the emotion flushing her face, "we'll find some resolution to this perplexing situation. Just keep up with your classes while I think this through. Okay then?"

She nodded her affirmation. Before she could thank him, he turned and exited the studio, his long coat rippling behind him.

Gabrielle concentrated on her studies as promised, but she couldn't put her series out of her mind. Each time she finished her assignments, she sought the studio and continued drawing on the canvas. In this way she completed preliminary sketching of the congregation, with just the architectural features of the church interior remaining. Upon finishing this, she walked back from her work and noted several adjustments she wanted to make. A few days later she finalized her charcoal drawing.

Examining it, she thought she had reached a good balance between the commanding preacher and the impassioned assembly. She believed that her sketch conveyed how he called his flock and how they rose to respond. The many appeared as one voice calling for freedom and collective action.

With the drawing done, she now had to determine how best to achieve the flow between panels that the professor had described. And then the long road that oil painting represented would begin.

4

As students exited Professor Ray's class, he motioned for her to remain.

"I've given this a great deal of thought," he began. "I decided to go to our department chair and explain your proposed project and your quandary."

Gabrielle felt disquietude rise in her.

"We talked for a long time. He's intrigued with your project, but uncertain about the best course forward. Certainly the funding piece is a challenge, but more troublesome is how your other instructors may respond to your request." He paused, stroking his beard in thought. "You see, there's no precedent for this. Condoning it would set a standard that could prove difficult in the future."

"I see," she replied, looking at her feet. "I'm sorry to cause everyone so much trouble."

He was quick to respond. "But this is Parsons, and unconventional is our middle name." He laughed, causing Gabrielle to break a smile.

"We cannot predict what the other instructors will say," he proceeded, "but we won't know until we ask. The other part of this is the funding. It's difficult to ascertain exactly how much you'll need for your materials, but certainly you'll require some thousands of dollars. If the other instructors go along and the chair's satisfied that you've demonstrated your ability to pull off this large undertaking, he believes you may be able to get the supplies you need from a fund to which he has access."

Gabrielle was startled by this, as she hadn't fully considered the issue of her painting supplies.

"Now you must not get your hopes too high, as considerable work remains to acquire the support you'll need. First you must meet with our chair, Professor Rabinowitz, and give him the same overview you gave me, including having him come to your studio. I'll tag along. If he's satisfied with your approach, we can discuss next steps. Does this suit you?"

Suddenly she was filled with unexpected optimism. "Yes of course. You may want to know that I've finished sketching the canvas. As soon as I work out the flow between the panels that we discussed, this one will be ready to paint."

Professor Ray showed surprise, then smiled. "Well you certainly aren't letting any grass grow under your feet. Let's say four-thirty tomorrow?"

"That will be fine."

"Good," he said as he gathered up his notebooks. "Just tell me, are you keeping up with your studies."

"Yes."

"Okay then, until tomorrow." And with that he left the room.

Before she knew it, it was the next day and she was having difficulty focusing on her classwork. After her last lesson, she ran back to her studio. Soon the men arrived. Gabrielle smoothed her hair behind her ears and walked toward them. "Thank you, Professor Rabinowitz—and Professor Ray—for coming," she said as she shook the chairman's hand and warmly acknowledged her teacher.

"Yes," the chairman responded as he accompanied Professor Ray to the far side of the room to better view the canvas. She noted that the chairman was a few inches shorter and at least a decade younger than her instructor, had a clean-shaven head and a dark brown handlebar mustache. Fingering his whiskers, he contemplated her work. "Tell me about the canvas and your project as a whole," he said as he walked back toward her.

As she related her story and plan, the chairman, missing nothing, listened as he studied all she laid out for him to review. No sooner had she finished than he asked, "What makes you believe that you can carry this off? This is a monster of a project. Eight canvases this size could take years, even for an experienced artist."

Believing that his narrowed black eyes sought to intimidate her, she made up her mind that he wouldn't cow her. Standing tall she responded, "Certainly I'm fully aware of what I'm undertaking. I know exactly what I'll paint and how the panels should look. They represent everything I most passionately believe in. I've lived this series. It fires my daily thoughts and my nightly dreams.

"I can no more not paint this than I can relinquish my quest to grow as an artist and to develop a platform to support justice for all people. Marrying my art to my political and social beliefs is of the greatest importance to me as a person and as an artist. I'll find a way to create the series as I envision it, even if I have to give up my studies at this incredible school. I would hate that, but I cannot put off or abandon this work."

She stopped, seeing a look of surprise on both professors' faces, then took a deep breath to calm herself. "I apologize for being so forthright. This work haunts me. I know that I'm meant to do it. If I turn away now I'll not be true to myself and to what I believe and have fought for over the years. I hope you can understand. Please don't think me ungrateful. I want to continue my studies here more than I can express and am so thankful for the opportunities Parsons gives me every day. I just don't know how I can make this work, if I have to divide myself between many class assignments and the concentrated weight of this series."

The chairman gave ear to her without interruption, then said, "Yes. Well we'll just have to see about all this. Good day Miss Andersen." As he turned and walked to the door, Professor Ray followed, glancing back as he left. His eyes mirrored concern, she thought, sorrow even. They made her catch her breath.

"Damn," she whispered. "Damn."

She hardly slept that night, knowing by her own assessment that she had crossed a line. But she couldn't put aside the work she had started, even if it meant not doing well in her classes or worse, dropping out of school. As she considered this, she understood that if she left Parsons, she would have no means of support and nowhere to work. *I'll never get another opportunity like this school has given me,* she thought. *And how would this affect me as an artist striving to create social impact through art?*

"Damn," she said again as she rose in the middle of the night. Sitting on the side of her bed, her head in her hands, the magnitude of her intransigence with the chairman hit her. *I've alienated the department chairman and surprised Professor Ray. Why can't I learn to keep my mouth shut? I failed both of them—and my cause. How can I make this right? Can I? But how can I not continue this work I've begun?*

Feeling distraught and clumsy in her willfulness, she dressed and walked to her studio at two a.m., switched on the lights, and closed the door. She picked up a chair and carried it across the room to examine the canvas. The longer she studied it, the more absorbed she became. Sensing a power in it that was greater than she, Gabrielle felt the intensity of her experience in that Hattiesburg church at that moment in history. She could hear the Reverend's calls, the swelling response of the congregation, how everyone was in movement, impassioned, attuned to the call. Now it was beckoning her—again. How could she not rise as did Edith and Tom holding their young children, there on the cutting edge of impending violence, hoping for peace but aware that claiming justice could cost them their safety—and their lives. She had to ask: What would she lay down for the cause of justice?

But Gabrielle already knew. She had declared herself. And there was no turning back.

* * *

After her next class with Professor Ray, she stayed afterward to speak with him. "Professor, I'm afraid I may have overstepped in responding to Professor Rabinowitz. Can you tell me if he said anything to indicate how he viewed our meeting?"

He paused as if trying to decide how to reply. "I know that he'd taken an interest in your project, but I think he was surprised by the force of your answers to his questions."

"Oh dear," Gabrielle said, "I should have been more restrained."

He gazed thoughtfully at her. "Well he did speak provocatively to you…and you did let him know that you meant business." He smiled.

"Still I ought to have shown some restraint," she said, her brow knitting. "I so hope that I didn't offend him. It was good of him to take enough interest in my project to come and view it. I don't know if there's a way to make this right."

"Well these things can take time, and he's a busy man," he acknowledged. "He didn't say anything to me that indicated he wouldn't explore what options you might have."

She nodded, looking downcast.

"Try not to worry Miss Andersen. I'll make time to drop by his office and see what I can find out. Just keep up with your classwork."

She nodded. "You're kind," she said. "I don't know how I can begin to thank you for trying to help me."

He shook his head in acknowledgment, gathered up his notebooks, and left for his next appointment. Watching him exit, she knew she had made serious mistakes—and that only time would tell whether they were insurmountable.

A week later she received a message from the chairman to come to his office the following day at twelve-thirty.

Hurrying there after her morning class, she stopped in front of his closed door and struggled to compose herself. At two minutes before twelve-thirty she knocked.

"Come in," he called.

"Good afternoon, Professor Rabinowitz," she said.

He studied her as she seated herself and put her backpack on the floor beside her. Then he spoke. "It's clear to me, Miss Andersen, that this project of yours goes much beyond class assignments." She shifted in her chair as he continued. "It's apparent that this is for you a kind of calling. It also is a mammoth undertaking beyond the capabilities of any reasonable twenty-one-year-old with only a modest degree of art training." He leaned back in his chair and took a hard look at her. She glanced up, meeting his eyes that seemed to have found the anguish and conviction in hers.

"Be that as it may," he said, "with what I've seen of your work and the passion with which you've stated your position, I'm inclined to think you might actually be able to pull this off." She started in surprise.

"It will take some financial support and the cooperation of your instructors," he continued. "You may be able to convince them, as you have Professor Ray and me, but you may not be successful with all of them. You'll have to make a contingency plan, should you not be able to get their approval.

"I'll pursue the financial piece when I know that you've succeeded in the other respect. Under no circumstances do we want to see you withdraw from Parsons and lose the value of your teachers' instruction. While you're unusually accomplished for one so early in your artistic journey, you still have a great deal to learn.

"You must promise to go to all your classes and to take care of your health. This undertaking of yours will require a substantial amount of your time and energy while you're in graduate school—and I feel certain, beyond. So you must learn to pace yourself and stay aware of your body's requirements. It does no one any favors if you make yourself sick."

Watching him with growing excitement, she also was aware that she needed to demonstrate a greater measure of self-control. She would have to show a balance between her passion for her work and her respect for what her instructors were trying to teach her—and for her own self-preservation.

"Yes," she responded. "I understand. You're right of course. I'm so grateful to you for being willing to try to help me. I can't begin to thank you enough." Her voice caught.

He looked solemnly at her with his black eyes that peered from under eyebrows nearly as prominent as his Salvador Dali mustache.

"Do you have any suggestions for me regarding how to approach my professors?" she asked.

He appeared thoughtful as he leaned forward in his chair. "I think speaking to each separately would be best. I would give them the introduction you gave me." He smiled slightly for the first time. "I just wouldn't be confrontational." His smile lingered beneath his whiskers.

She blushed. "No professor, I'll take care with that."

"It's their decision individually to determine if using your project for assignments done out of class will be acceptable to them. I cannot speak for them in this regard, nor should you suggest that I do."

She blushed. "I understand. You're most kind."

He stood, and she followed suit. "I wish you well in your pursuit," he said. "Keep me informed of your progress."

"I will. Thank you."

Good God, she reflected as she left, *I can't believe he's backing me. I thought I'd blown the whole thing.* For the first time since the professors visited her studio, she felt more certain that she would accomplish her goal. Furthermore, she would continue her studies at Parsons and acquire the knowledge she had come here to obtain. In recognizing this she experienced for the first time in weeks, a feeling of unequivocal joy.

* * *

She couldn't wait to give Professor Ray the good news.

"You must have said something that tipped his support further in your direction," he said smiling, his eyes acknowledging pleasure in the outcome. "Now you'll need to convince your other instructors. If you like I can go ahead with speaking to them before you do to lay the groundwork."

"That would be wonderful," she exclaimed.

"I'll try to make time to see them over the next week. You should be prepared to point out which of your canvases will contain the elements they'll be looking for. Be prepared that they well may require you to produce a smaller version of your large work—or a segment from it—in the medium of that class. In any case you'll need to produce these studies to work out your colors, values, and flow from panel to panel."

"Yes I'd thought the same," she acknowledged, "...just so I can stay with the same subjects and not have to wrap my head around something completely different. That would be enough."

"Good. Plan to check periodically with me, and I'll let you know whom I've seen. Then you can contact the instructors yourself."

"I can't thank you enough."

"I trust it will help. We've already determined that you can use your large painting for the required work outside my class," he said thoughtfully, tugging on his long beard. "Of course you'll continue to paint in class along with the other students and submit this work for my and your classmates' review."

"This is what I hoped for."

"Good. Then we each have our charge," he said amiably. "I wish you the best of luck with this."

Her voice broke as she spoke. "I owe you a debt I can never repay."

He looked surprised. "My dear Miss Andersen, your becoming the best artist you can be is my recompense. Students like you are why I continue to teach after all these years. Your passion for marrying your art to political and social causes you not only support, but have lived in your young life, is a rare and precious thing. I'd love nothing better than to see you succeed.

Frankly I can hardly wait to witness the completion of your project, even if it's years after you leave here. I intend to follow your career and will be happy if I can help you even a little along your way." He smiled, his face sincere and kind.

Overcome by his response, she was silent.

"Well my dear," he said finally, "I'm afraid I need to be off to another meeting." As he rose from behind his desk, she took the cue.

"Thank you, professor."

True to his word, Professor Ray met with each of her instructors over the course of the week. Gabrielle had done her part as well. Her drawing teacher, Lukens, agreed as soon as he saw her work. Her watercolor instructor Clooney did likewise, assuming she would produce a small-scale watercolor painting of her panel. Both stipulated that Gabrielle also must keep up with her in-class assignments.

Moskowitz was the sticking point, given he had no photographs with which to compare her portraiture. Despite this, she believed that gaining the agreement of three of her four teachers would reduce the pressure on her sufficiently to keep her in school while pursuing her series.

She informed Professors Ray and Rabinowitz that she believed she had what she needed to advance her project. The chairman responded a week later that the fund he had access to would cover her project's materials costs while she remained a student at Parsons. Elated and grateful, she returned to her studio later that day and began painting a small study of the scene at The Saving Grace Baptist Church of Hattiesburg, this time using oil paints Professor Ray supplied.

She settled on a palette for the series that was rich in earth tones—browns, reds, yellows, oranges, grey-blues, and cool greens—and darker values for the first six panels, becoming brighter for the final two. The Reverend Jonas piece, which was second to the last in the series, would shine with lighter values and brilliant color, joyful, vibrant, warm, exuberant even, while still carrying hints of earth tones. The pigments and values in this panel would mark a turn in coloring and mood from the more somber canvases to those carrying a rising sense of hope for the cause.

A week passed before she could finish the Reverend Jonas study and feel confident about the colors she possessed and mixed numerous times before settling on the final blends. Recording how she derived her colors in her notebook, she then made a list of what she would require for her large canvas and submitted it to Professor Rabinowitz along with her mock-up.

In a week, large boxes arrived with her requested supplies. At the same time, her prototype came back from the chairman's office with a note: "A good start. Keep me informed of your progress."

His note made her smile. Still grinning, she left the boxes unopened behind her large canvas, certain they contained everything she would need. In the fullness of the moment she felt in her gut that a new phase in her life's journey was about to begin.

5

It was early Friday evening, and Gabrielle was alone in the studio. This was the moment for which she had been waiting.

Opening the newly arrived packages she deposited on the long table beside her big canvas, she gazed with expectation at the supplies she had requested. They lay in their boxes like soldiers awaiting her command. Her hand trembled as she removed first the palette knives and brushes of varying sizes, then the mountain of oil paint cans, gesso, the drying and mixing oils. Then she extracted from its box the very large glass mixing palette and smaller ones she would hold when painting.

She never dreamed of being able to have such a selection, made possible by the chairman's willingness to tap a special fund. In that act she understood his and Professor Ray's belief in her as a young artist capable of work that might prove worthy of preservation over the years.

Laying out her supplies, she arranged the cans by color before opening and mixing the first one with its earthy reddish brown. She transferred a portion of the color from the container to a palette, then did likewise with a lemon yellow. Pulling color from different hues, she began blending the warm medium brown that would form the base for the Reverend Jonas's skin. To this she added a small amount of turpentine and combined again.

As she worked with these and other shades, she noted how she was drawn to the beauty of the pigments and luxuriated in their thick, creamy texture. She found this to be a sensory, even a sensual experience, a kind of visual and olfactory awareness that fired her creative spirit.

She saw history in these oils, proven durable over the ages, and sensed the weight of the work she was about to undertake. The subject of her effort was what sat most heavily on her and ultimately called her to lift the smaller palette with the brown mixture and choose her first brush.

As she raised it to begin her undercoating, she paused. A sensation very like that of falling in love rose in her. She knew that her ardor for this work she was beginning was greater than any pursuit she had undertaken, and that the people she was about to render had stolen her heart and placed upon her a fierce sense of purpose. As the oils enveloped her brush, she felt the parishioners draw her in, their brown skin speaking to the lighter brown of hers, a color burned into her experience of what it was to be viewed as different from everyone around her, even her own family. The warmth of the shade she had mixed radiated throughout her body now and wooed her to commence.

Beginning the underpainting, she struggled to not delay. She knew she had to work fast and lean to apply the first layer of pigment to the minister's face, hands, and raised arms.

She moved then to the congregation, which soon would host an array of beautiful browns. She sought the subjects mirroring the minister's pigment, among them Edith and two of her children, whom she painted with special devotion. Seeing nothing else on the canvas that would use this shade as a base, she cleaned her knives and brushes in mineral spirits and recorded in her notebook the quadrant numbers and human figures that bore the tints and how she mixed them. Referencing the time and date, she applied this first layer of oils, knowing she would have to wait until the paint was dry enough to apply the next layer.

It was past midnight by the time she finished cleaning up. Walking far back from the panel, she turned and witnessed the beginnings of life that color gave to her work.

She thought how her skin color coated her life and presented her with a multitude of questions that bore no answers, leaving her unmoored. She clung to her recognition that discovering and working to develop one's talents was an essential part of life. *But without sacrifice for the good of others,* she told herself, *there is no salvation—and self-realization by cultivating one's talents eventually will grow hollow. I believe we know and contribute to the world through the gifts we're given and the skill and good heart with which we learn to use them.* As she assessed her work, she knew it was the barest of starts. But it filled her with joy and a deepening desire to do what she could to help right terrible wrongs.

As the ever-watchful moon made its way across the sky, Gabrielle slept dreaming color. She woke Saturday morning after the sun chased away the moon and streamed through the mostly closed window blinds, traveling her face into wakefulness.

Gazing at her watch, she noted it was nearly mid-morning. Stretching and yawning, she lay in bed for a few minutes, reliving her memory of the previous night. Swinging her legs around, her feet now touching the floor, she rose, showered, and ran for food, carrying it to the studio that hosted just one other woman student. She acknowledged her before turning toward her canvas. Knowing that it was the barest beginning of her vision, she believed it was a good and true start.

Most of the day, stopping only briefly for meals, she continued mixing and spreading the first coat of the remaining flesh colors on the forms of the parishioners, defining color values—lights and darks—as she painted. As she did so, she logged every specific color combination, the numbered quadrants, and when she applied them. By the time she had cleaned up and stored her supplies, it was midnight again.

She allowed herself a moment to sit in the now-empty studio that had hosted all day students coming and going from their artwork. Seated far back from the canvas, she studied it. It jogged thoughts of her own experiences as a person who always was haunted by how different she looked. She knew how the pain and uncertainty of this had marked her.

In Hattiesburg she more fully understood how the physical dissimilarity of the people in the black side of town from those in the white had created an imprint so profound in its heinousness that nothing short of total justice and time could lesson and remove it from people's consciousness. If young children could engage with those of different colored skins without assigning value to color, she wondered if adults might learn to experience a deeper truth in their fellow humans by searching for kindred spirits beneath what ultimately she saw as a largely meaningless veneer.

Sitting very still in her thoughts and memories, she felt as if she were a member of the congregation she was painting, fearful yet hopeful in their mutual commitment to fight for acceptance and their inalienable rights.

As she had created and placed shades of brown on her towering canvas and stretched to reach one figure after another, so she reached as an artist and human being for a life of surrender and free expression, marrying her art to her passion and commitment to social justice. At this moment she realized she was at the juncture of a road that she knew she must travel, but without knowing where it ultimately would lead.

6

Months passed as Gabrielle divided her time between classes and her project. In the second term she reduced her courses from four to three—two in oil painting and one in figure drawing.

And then toward the end of the term, a news bulletin rocked Gabrielle, the nation, and the world. She knew she would always remember this day, April 4, 1968. What had begun as a pleasant spring day shattered under unbearable news. A sniper had shot Dr. Martin Luther King, Jr., as he stood on the second-floor balcony of the Lorraine Motel in Memphis, Tennessee. Rushed to St. Joseph's Hospital, he was pronounced dead an hour later, at 7:05 p.m. Central Time. He was just thirty-nine years old.

One of millions shaken by the news, she called Rick. They cried together and talked about the next day's planned New York City march following a rally in Central Park. Protesting Dr. King's assassination, Gabrielle and many of her fellow students joined thousands who filed down Broadway to City Hall.

On April 6 she learned how rioters burned buildings in Chicago's West Side as looting and shootings brought in the Illinois National Guard. Worse yet was Washington, D.C., where twelve thousand National Guard troops were called up to protect the nation's capital as buildings burned in northeast D.C. Then reports came that some one hundred cities across the country held protests or were the subjects of riots that raged for days.

In response to the assassination, Gabrielle watched as President Lyndon B. Johnson asked the nation for calm. He then urged Congress to pass the Fair Housing Act to support the housing equality regulations Dr. King had long championed.

In record time the bill succeeded and Johnson signed it into law on April 11. Rick and Gabrielle were ecstatic. This was one of the issues that civil rights organizations and local citizens had worked hard to further. It was a day of legislative triumph from the ashes of Dr. King's assassination. Rick and Gabrielle and many others held on to this accomplishment through all the shadows of racial injustices of the past, the present, and what they knew would exist in the future.

Dr. King's assassination and the nation's responses deepened Gabrielle's resolve to complete her project, swearing that nothing would keep her from finishing what she had begun.

In her third term she took just two subjects, one in portrait painting and one in the history of Renaissance and Baroque art. This reduction in classes enabled her to complete her Reverend Jonas canvas. It ultimately would become the seventh in the series of eight. The finished piece shone with emotion and brilliant colors, from sunlight streaming through the church windows to the women's dazzling, Sunday-go-to-meeting hats.

In this painting she demonstrated how she was beginning to integrate into her series more of what she learned in her classes, even the more academic courses. She took special note of how Rembrandt had innovated in and mastered the play of shadow and light. And she absorbed how Leonardo da Vinci's inventiveness and scientific studies led to his introduction of atmospheric perspective and to delivering how human movements can be captured and used to reflect the emotions of the mind.

Four men arrived to transfer her first completed panel from the studio to the fine art department's storage facility. Following this Professor Ray sent a note to Gabrielle. Calling her work "powerful," he quoted Chairman Rabinowitz as saying, "It exceeded my expectations."

By the end of the fourth term she was halfway through what would become the first in the series, in which student volunteers from the North entered Mississippi by bus. Even at this point in her work on it, one could begin to see dread on the students' faces as they passed the sign reading "Prepare to Meet Thy God."

As she worked, she again suffered the trepidation she experienced then, absorbing the warning in her tensed muscles and chilling her very bones. She knew she would need to call on every shred of memory she had of her first exposure to Mississippi, which felt to her like entering the gates of hell.

From this panel forward, she would work sequentially through to the eighth. She completed this first in the series by the close of the next term. Then she began sketching the second, in which angry whites mobbed and rocked the students' bus at a Mississippi filling station. She would have to call on all that she had learned and observed to render the expressions of dread on the students' faces, the hatred and violence of the mob, and the determination of the bus driver who ultimately saved them.

This canvas haunted her as she struggled to render the nightmare that she knew. She held the memory of the horror in her body as she began to paint herself. She recalled how one of the mob, his face distorted by loathing, wielded his fist-covered rock and a bloodcurdling scream before smashing her window and wounding her.

She trembled in the revived fear that had gripped her body, sweat oozing from every pore and mingling with the blood running down her face. She remembered how her voice and heart were squeezed in pain and shock as she tasted their acrid hostility as they worked to tip the bus. She heard again the men's shouts of "Bitch!" "Nigga lovers!" as they surrounded them, swelling in number and intensity until she believed she would die. And just as she resigned herself to her fate, the bus driver found the smallest of openings and rocketed the bus away from the clutches of the mob.

Breathing heavily, her heart racing, she descended the ladder and sunk into a chair, her clothes wet with sweat, her body collapsing under the memory of the terror she felt. Tears traced her face. Suddenly she was exhausted, unable to think, to move. She knew that her experience was unusual only in how it played out. This was a scenario that occurred too often and sometimes with more dire consequences to freedom riders and voter registration workers like herself. She thought how the violence waged against blacks was ongoing and even crueler. In time, as all this traveled her body and mind, she felt the full passion of her resolve to give all she had to expose these dreadful wrongs.

And so it went as she settled further into her routine of dividing her time between classes and the work she held most dear. All seemed to be going well until she met resistance from the teachers of two studio classes, one in advanced watercolor work and the other in advanced oil painting. These teachers were borderline hostile to her proposal to use her series for out-of-class assignments.

Surprised and dismayed, Gabrielle struggled to understand what appeared to be a new animosity toward her. She had become friendly with Emily, a lanky graduate student who regularly worked in the dorm studio and was in the same classes as Gabrielle. She considered Emily to be a casual friend with whom she regularly discussed various painting techniques. So it was only natural that Gabrielle expressed her concern to Emily.

"I don't know," Emily responded, hesitating momentarily, "but I did overhear one of the students in our oil painting class complaining about your getting special treatment. In fact she was quite nasty in her description of you."

Gabrielle was taken aback.

"But I wouldn't pay her any mind," Emily was quick to add as she considered Gabrielle's comportment. "It sounds like simple jealousy to me. From what I've seen of her work, you're a far better artist than she'll ever be. I expect the professor's getting pushback from students like her."

"Who is she?"

Emily hesitated again, pulling at her light-brown hair as her eyes pierced Gabrielle. "I don't really want to tattle on anyone. Don't let this get to you. You really should just forget about it," she concluded, narrowing her eyes as she assessed Gabrielle.

Despite shaking her head affirmatively, Gabrielle couldn't help but feel she had received an affront. Replying she said, "I'll try to put this behind me, though it'll make it harder to complete my project. It's been difficult to find enough time to move the large canvases ahead while also keeping up with classwork."

Emily wore a noncommittal expression.

"Well I'd better get to work," Gabrielle said, feeling bewildered but attempting a smile in the face of her uncertainty about the student's intentions.

"Me too," the woman said, abruptly turning back to her work.

It was Emily's attitude more than her responses that unsettled her. She thought she detected a certain craftiness in her classmate's eyes and in the way she spoke that Gabrielle hadn't noticed before. It troubled her and made it hard for her to cast off her disquietude as she turned toward her painting.

But with the discipline she had reaped by virtue of the heavy load of her series, she took a deep breath as she studied her canvas before mixing colors and continuing her artwork.

*　*　*

The next morning, as she sipped coffee and ate breakfast, she thought about her progress in painting the previous night and about the odd conversation she had with Emily. She began to wonder if this fellow student was the one instigating her professors' refusal to honor her requests. Considering initiating a frank discussion with the two instructors, she decided that she would look for an opportunity to speak with them.

After her next oils class she approached Professor Raoul. "Professor, may I speak with you for a moment?"

He frowned as he responded. "Yes, if it won't take long."

"I wondered if I could get your advice on a problem I'm having with one of the figures in the large canvas I'm working on outside of class."

The professor's craggy face showed surprise. "I thought you had all the answers and no need of our instruction."

Gabrielle visibly recoiled. "Excuse me?"

He looked vehement. "I understand you've been quite brazen in your criticism of the instruction you're getting here. So why would you seek my humble opinion?"

Shaken, Gabrielle took a moment to recover. "Sir, I don't know where you got that idea. Quite the contrary, I'm grateful beyond words for everything I'm learning here. I wouldn't come to you now if I didn't value your teaching and advice. Please tell me what gave you this impression."

His dark eyes seemed to probe her, then soften as he absorbed her troubled demeanor. "On more than one occasion I overheard two of my students decry your arrogance and dismissal of us unworthy professors." He hesitated, looking thoughtful. "Perhaps I was meant to hear their banter—and perhaps I was wrong to believe it. You seem earnest." Pausing again, he observed her squarely. "I'd be willing to try to help you with the problem you've encountered, but we'll need to schedule a time."

"I'd be most grateful," she replied, relieved by the seeming mellowing in his attitude. "When would be convenient for you—

and would you be able to come to the dorm studio where my canvas is? I also could explain the series."

"We probably should do that though I'm crammed for time. I have a show of my own to prepare for. Let's see." He was thumbing through his appointment book impatiently. "Four o'clock the day after tomorrow. I can manage maybe a half-hour."

"Thanks so much."

"I have to run." And with that he quickly gathered up his things and left.

On balance Gabrielle thought that their discussion seemed to have bridged a chasm that had developed between her and her instructor. She hoped that their next meeting would further convince him of her sincerity and resolve. Believing more strongly now that her classmate was not her friend, she thought that Emily likely was the instigator of the problems she was having with her instructors.

7

Two days passed quickly. Gabrielle returned from class to her studio just minutes before Professor Raoul was to arrive. To her dismay she saw Emily setting up to paint in her usual place across the room from her. "Hi," Emily said cheerily. Gabrielle waved, then turned to discourage conversation and to have everything set up.

At exactly four o'clock the professor appeared. "Thank you for coming," she said.

He nodded, already studying her large canvas. "Tell me your problem," he said.

"It's the expression on the bus driver's face. I wanted to show alarm, but also determination. He's the hero, the person who'll deliver the terrified civil rights workers from a vicious mob. As I've detailed him," she said, handing him her small painted study, "I see only fear."

The teacher's chunky hand traveled his square chin as he contemplated her dilemma for several minutes, looking from the study to the large canvas and back again. "I think I'd keep the terror in his eyes, but show resolve in the wrinkles in his brow, the set of his jaw, and the attitude of his arms and shoulders. Don't forget his body. It's as important as the attention you give his face. And in all this you must show the delivery of his action just as it starts to precipitate. This will be the very point where surprise begins to show on the faces of some of the mob. It'll heighten the drama in your picture."

Gabrielle was silent, studying her work and his comments.

"And be sure the attitude of the passengers' bodies and that of the mob's reinforces the expressions on their faces as well," he said.

After a couple of minutes Gabrielle said, "Yes. That's it! I see exactly what you mean. Of course delivering what you rightly diagnose may require having a model to study."

"Hmm," said the professor, "I think I have a solution for that." He pivoted quickly, facing Emily who looked pale and attentive to everything they said. "You will be Miss Andersen's model. I think you owe her that!" He turned abruptly and walked back toward Gabrielle's canvas, leaving Emily red-faced and open-mouthed.

"I'm glad we had this discussion," the professor said. "I most certainly misjudged you. I'm impressed with what you've undertaken and how committed you are to what you describe. I'm willing to work with you on the assignments outside class so you can use what you're doing here to fulfill them. Just give me regular updates. I'll assess your work later in the term. Now if you don't need anything else from me," he said, checking his watch, "I must be going."

"I can't thank you enough. You've helped me a great deal."

"Good. Oh," he said, raising his voice so he could be heard across the room, "and make sure that Emily over there serves as that model you need!"

And with that, her instructor left. Not wanting to deal with Emily, Gabrielle picked up her small studies and exited the room, resolving to return when her classmate was gone. Back in her dorm room she thought briefly of Emily, now caught in her lies—and smiled.

* * *

"You have a call!" came a voice from outside Gabrielle's door.

"Thanks," she said, as she left her classwork and hurried to the hall phone. "Hello?"

"Hey there. Three guesses who."

"Rick! I'm so glad to hear from you. It must be a month since we talked."

"Five weeks, eight hours, and forty-six minutes."

"Very funny. How are you—and where are you?"

"Chicago."

"No. What are you doing there?"

"Well I got a job doing community organizing on the south side of Chicago."

"Fantastic! But it's a tough place."

"Yes parts of it are, but for good reason. There's a lot of poverty and effects of racism."

"Anything like what we saw in Hattiesburg?"

Rick paused. "It's all seeds of the same thing, but it's different here—lots of gang violence among the races. The despair is raw and apparent. So many boys and young men get caught up in these gangs. It seems to be the only thing that gives them a sense of power, of belonging to something that doesn't feel to them like abdication. It's quite terrifying Gabrielle. I don't know how we got here as a country. It's been a long time since the emancipation of slaves. But from what I see, there's very little sense of freedom in how a lot of minorities live."

He fell silent for a moment, a silence cradling the strength of his convictions.

"Such hard work you have ahead of you Rick," she responded. "What specifically are you doing now?"

"I'm working with various groups, including schools and churches, to help organize peaceful demonstrations to support equality in housing and public education. Of course the new fair housing law Johnson signed gives us legal backing for pushing housing parity. Still, in practice, too many people continue to live in squalor, unable to get a decent place to live because of their poverty and their racial or ethnic backgrounds. This leads to inequitable school funding and a substandard education for the children living in these neighborhoods. Ultimately this shows up as unemployment or under-employment. It's a vicious cycle." Rick's voice trailed off.

"It sounds terrible."

"Yes. There's so much work to do. It's worse here than I'd imagined. But tell me about *you*. How's your big series going?"

"Better than I could have hoped," she said before filling him in on the latest happenings.

"Good for you. I'm so glad to hear that things are going well for you. I worried about you after our last talk and am relieved to know you're okay. If you get a chance to take a picture of your Reverend Jonas picture and anything else you want to send me, I'd love it."

"Sure. It's good to have a visual record anyhow. I'll try to get pictures to you in the next couple of weeks."

"I'll look forward to it. Well I'd better go. Take care Gabrielle. You're my bright light in this darkness I'm working in now." He paused. "I miss you."

"I miss you too."

As she hung up she felt the sadness in Rick's voice and the desperation of the people he was trying to help. It made her even more determined to be a witness to what was happening in this country and do all she could to be a force for change.

8

"Miss Andersen, a word please," Professor Ray said as she rose to leave class. "How are you doing?"

"I'm fine, professor. I'm learning a lot and progressing well with my series."

"Are you taking care of yourself? You look tired—and like you've lost weight again," he said, observing her with fatherly concern.

She blushed and responded, "I'm trying to take care to eat and sleep more, but it's hard to keep up with my project and everything I need to do for my classes, even given the professors' leniency with me. But I'm managing."

The professor looked doubtful. "Have you thought about stretching out your time here at Parsons, taking only one class at a time at least for a while? It would give you more independent study time to concentrate on your series and take better care of yourself."

"You mean I actually could do that?"

He smiled. "I imagine it could be arranged."

"But what would that mean to my scholarship—and to the special funding the chairman was able to make available? Elongating my stay here would cost the college a lot. Wouldn't that be an insurmountable problem?"

"We can't know until we ask. How many hours a week are you spending to keep up with your classes?"

"I'm not sure. Maybe twenty-five hours?"

"How much on your series?"

"Wow, not sure. Eighty perhaps?"

"Let's see. There are....one hundred and sixty-eight hours in a week, I believe. If you add twenty-five and eighty you get one hundred and five hours—which I suspect may be a conservative estimate. Subtracting that from one hundred and sixty-eight hours in a week gives you...let's see...," he looked up, calculating mentally, "sixty-three hours a week, which is...let's see...nine hours a day for sleep, eating, exercise, traveling around campus, relationships, relaxation, and general care of yourself. Does that seem sustainable to you?"

Embarrassed, she realized she hadn't thought about her present life this way. "No," was all she could muster.

"No indeed. Miss Andersen, I don't wish to embarrass you, but you can't continue like this."

She looked down, distraught and at a loss as to what to say or how to remedy her situation.

"Please don't despair," he said, sensing her thoughts. "We should have a talk with the chairman and see if my suggestion to lengthen your time here is possible. This would give you more opportunity to complete your instruction *and* your series. We'd request continuing support for both your scholarship and the art supplies grant. You might even ask for a term off to work solely on your series, which could serve as your master's thesis project."

"All that's really possible?"

He smiled again. "As I said, we won't know until we ask. But given the quality of your work on the series and in the classroom, I think you have more than a fair chance of succeeding. Do you realize how powerful your canvases are becoming?"

She shook her head no.

"Well you should. Each piece you complete demonstrates your progress as an artist, while engaging viewers by putting them in the drama of the moment. Your instinct to work in the size that you have was exactly right, although you had no experience and little if any instruction in working on this scale. Your effort to create a flow between panels is working. You've accomplished this beautifully through color and tonal value. And the force of the eight completed panels, when hung together, I believe will be overpowering.

"I've no doubt that you'll complete what you've started and that you'll achieve your desired effect. Don't ever despair. And take the care of yourself that you'll need to finish what you've begun. You must make that a priority. I believe that reducing your load and giving you a semester's sabbatical could make all the difference. Do you want to try for this?"

"Yes…of course," she replied. "I couldn't have imagined such an arrangement."

"We may not succeed, but it's also possible that we might. Shall I make an appointment for us with the chairman in the next couple of days?"

"Certainly. I hardly know what to say. I'm so grateful." She fought to maintain composure.

He observed her, his eyes reflecting her face in the warm light of them. "My dear Miss Andersen, I'm only too happy to try to help. It's what I'm here for. Now I'm afraid I must go. I'll ask the department secretary to call you with our appointment time."

Two days later they sat in Chairman Rabinowitz's office as Professor Ray outlined his idea. The chairman leaned toward them attentively as his colleague spoke. Then he sat back in his chair and stared into the space not occupied by his two supplicants as he fingered his mustache and knitted his prominent eyebrows. He turned to Gabrielle. "Do you understand the import of my colleague's proposal and how much is being asked not only of me, but also of all in my department who also seek support?"

Surprised by his question, she thought for a minute. "I understand that this is a large and probably outrageous request. In fact the very nature of what I've undertaken, especially given my inexperience, could be called preposterous. I've come to see, however, that at times in life a person may be called upon to tackle what no one reasonably would or even should be expected to take on. I believe this is one of those moments. I may be an unseemly candidate to undertake the work I've assumed. I didn't set out to find such a challenge, but rather it found me and demanded I accept it."

She paused, glancing momentarily at Professor Ray, then the chairman. "I don't know what workings of life transpired to send me to Hattiesburg to witness the human suffering that I saw. Nor do I understand what lured me to take my sketchbook and document what I lived through in Mississippi and the civil rights battles in the North. But these things happened. They found me and set me on a journey from which I find there's no retreat, though often it's almost more than I can bear." Looking very directly at the chairman who was watching her intently, she softened her tone.

"Still it troubles me to think that others might be denied help if you decide to further support my effort. I can only present my case and know that you'll weigh it and do what you believe is right. I regret putting you in this position. Please know that I'm deeply appreciative of everything you and Professor Ray and this school are doing for me."

"I'll say that I'm more than pleased with your progress on the series and with your performance in your classes," the chairman responded. "But as you say, I have much to weigh to decide what I think is the best use of our funds. In any case I'll have others to consult as well before a determination can be made. When I know more I'll be in touch."

"Thank you for your time," Professor Ray said. "I assume you'll want us to formalize this request by giving you a written proposal?"

"Yes of course. Can you get it to me by the middle of next week?"

"I believe I can do that," Professor Ray said, standing and shaking the hand of his colleague, who nodded to Gabrielle before returning to a pile of paperwork.

"What do you think?" she asked as they walked down the hall.

"I think he'll do what he can. As he noted, it's not his final say and a lot of obstacles remain. Then there's the issue of a proposal, which he's not given me much time to complete."

"Can I take care of that for you?"

He laughed. "I wish you could my dear, but this is one of those pesky things we academics simply must deal with ourselves. However, you can prepare a statement such as you just made to the chairman and detail your accomplishments at Oberlin, including news media coverage of your artwork. You also should explain your civil rights experiences and how they've formed your political and social beliefs and influenced the direction you now take with your art."

"Would it help to take pictures of my completed canvases and all of my small studies?"

"Yes, but I'll need all this by the first of the week."

"I can make that. Let me know if there's anything else I can do. I can't thank you enough."

"I have to run," he replied. "Take care of yourself, Miss Andersen, and pray for our success."

The week passed quickly as she juggled classwork and her part in the proposal, while struggling to make progress on her current canvas.

Remembering Professor Raoul's suggestions regarding the bus driver, the students, and the mob, she used drawing paper to work and rework her sketch of the driver. After a multitude of attempts, her rejected renderings scattered across the floor, she thought she finally captured the tension and determination harbored in the driver's body, brow, and jaw—and the terror in his eyes.

Then she began sketching the bodies and faces of the mob and the panicked students. She had to fight her feelings of dread and the horror of so much hatred hurled at her and the other northerners now imprisoned in a rising hysteria. Struggling with her memories, she had to step away from her drawings and calm herself.

As she sat thinking, she remembered how difficult it was for her to make the decision to go south. Bloody Sunday had just occurred and it was only months since the bodies of civil rights workers Chaney, Goodman, and Schwerner were found in Neshoba County, Mississippi, not far from Hattiesburg. The brutality of their murders was still raw in her and others' minds, and she relived the turmoil she felt as she wrestled with her fears and ultimately decided she must go.

It took the considerable time to fully work the figures on paper. She modeled them from sketches made in her figure painting class and by observing her own face and body in a mirror as she assumed movements she sought to capture in her painting. By the end of the following week Gabrielle had completed all her final drawings of the driver, mob, and students and was ready to apply them to the big canvas.

Throwing herself into her project, she stopped only for food, classes, homework, and delivering what Professor Ray had requested. It took her two weeks working nights and weekends and any weekday hours that she could, but she finished painting her small-scale color study and accomplished a rough charcoal drawing on the large panel.

As she continued working on the small study, she darkened the colors she had used in the previous panel, following her earlier decision to gradually deepen tonal values before lightening and brightening them in the seventh and eighth canvases. All eight, however, would display unity not only in theme, but also in graduated tonal values and the color palette she had designed.

Luxuriating in the empty studio and glad that Emily still had not returned to it, she stepped far back from the canvas to take in the totality of her massive sketch. The body language and facial expressions required detailing, but the overall composition and subject matter were dramatic. The tension between the mob and those in the bus was palpable. And the lines of the picture all pointed to the bus driver, whom she bathed in light. He was the person upon whom the fate of all in the picture rested.

It was midnight on Thursday. Exhausted and happy she turned out the studio lights and went back to her dorm room. Fully dressed she lay on her bed, pulled the covers around her, and immediately fell asleep. She didn't wake until the sun streamed around the edges of the blinds and across her sleeping face.

9

Three weeks passed and still she hadn't heard from the chairman. She began to think that the news wouldn't be good. After her next class with Professor Ray, she stopped to inquire about their proposal.

"No, nothing," he said as he packed up his gear, his words hanging in air heavy with fresh oil paint and turpentine. "But I hadn't expected hearing this soon. Things move slowly in academia, even in as progressive a place as Parsons." He smiled as he removed his painting apron, which wore every conceivable pigment, and hung it on a hook on the studio wall.

"Do you think it could take as long as another month?"

"Hard to say. I suspect that not having heard anything yet probably is a good sign. If it were rejected outright, we'd have gotten some response by now." He gathered his notes and stuffed them into his briefcase, then turned to look at her.

"There surely are a lot of issues to work through and a lot of egos to soothe. Then there's the question of where the money will come from, not just for art supplies, but more troublesomely for the extension of your scholarship and your attendant living expenses. That would involve other offices of the college and some sticky issues. And then there's the whole precedent-setting thing.

"It's complicated Miss Andersen, so don't worry about it—but also don't depend on it. You may have to continue as you are and finish your project on your own after graduation."

Crestfallen, she searched the wall that held her classmates' artwork, looking for something to uplift her. Observing her more closely, he seemed dismayed as he watched her visibly sag. "But it's much too soon to draw any conclusions," he said. "Just continue as you have and hope for the best. Are you eating better and getting more sleep? You still look very tired."

"I'm sleeping more and making sure I eat three meals a day. But this big project does consume me. I don't seem able to mentally leave it behind in the studio."

"I know what you mean," he replied smiling. "Many times in my painting career I became so drawn by a project that I had trouble sleeping. It would haunt me even into my dreams. But in time I found that whatever problem I was having, I almost always could conjure a solution in the morning. Have you experienced this?"

"You know, I have, although not often."

"You might try this. Consciously place the problem in your mind before you go to bed and be conscientious about not mulling it over when you're trying to sleep. Then the problem can work its way through your subconscious and deliver your answer when you wake. It works almost every time for me."

"Maybe that's what I'm doing wrong. So often I take the problem to bed and wrestle with it while I'm still awake. So my subconscious will take over and solve it for me if I just let it?"

"It may when you develop the discipline to not lose sleep when you have an issue to work out."

"I'll try this."

"Good. I must run. I'll let you know if I hear anything."

Gabrielle explored Professor Ray's technique, finding success often enough to advance her problem-solving as her series progressed. By the end of the term she was well into painting the second in the sequence.

And then, in what seemed a miracle, word came from the chairman that the proposal had succeeded. The decision permitted Gabrielle to remain supported at Parsons through the duration of her project and her studies. This included her series' art supplies and a sabbatical of sorts for her next term. To help fund this, the chairman made application on her behalf for a grant from an arts foundation to which he had a connection. From his discussions with the foundation, he felt confident the grant would be forthcoming.

After the chairman called her and Professor Ray to the meeting to further discuss the outcome, Gabrielle broke down. Tears flooded her cheeks as she struggled to control herself. Wiping them away, she stumbled, "This is so much more than I could have imagined. I don't know how to begin to thank you."

"Just take care of yourself and enjoy the work of finishing what you've begun," the chairman said. "Yours is a scale of effort I haven't seen in my tenure here. You can thank the other members of our department and the Parsons administration for their agreement to add to the foundation's support, if needed, to complete the series."

Wiping her cheeks and blowing her nose, she shook her head in affirmation. "Please give me the names of everyone I should thank. But most of all, it's the two of you...," her voice faltered as she struggled to regain her composure.

The chairman interrupted. "You're most welcome, Miss Andersen. You've earned this support through your dedication to an undertaking that even we, at this stage in our careers, find daunting. Although your humility is laudable, don't underestimate how remarkable you are." He paused, his dark eyes seeming to pierce her.

"Those of us who support you believe that you'll go far as an artist who has greatness in her and who puts mission above personal gain. I don't say these things lightly. I believe you'll not disappoint us. Keep us apprised of your progress, and know that you can come to us whenever you need to."

"Thank you," she said as she stood and reached to shake the professors' hands. "You've helped me more than you can imagine. I'll always be indebted to you and will try to never disappoint." Exiting the chairman's office, she felt overwhelming gratefulness, love even, in the face of the kindness and support from these two extraordinary men.

* * *

Ecstatic, she threw herself into her series, working day and night. If other students came there to work, she wasn't mindful of them. Her painting was her sole focus, letting nothing stand between her and her work.

She completed the second canvas early in her sabbatical, then forged on to the third in the sequence. This one was complicated by the need to seamlessly depict more than one action in the same painting—the students' orientation at the civil rights office of Delta Ministry, COFO, and SNCC and their drive to their Negro host families. As she wrestled with how to make the painting work, she relived the warnings given them and how anxiety rose in them as volunteers took the students in the dead of night to their black families for protection. How to capture these actions came to her when she successfully exercised Professor Ray's technique. When she awoke, she saw the picture exactly as it needed to be in order to flow from one scene to the next while capturing the northerners' trepidation.

When she rose, she dressed quickly and ran to the cafeteria for food. As she dutifully ate it, she stared at her blank canvas. Then she grabbed a large sheet of sketch paper and then another and another as she drew and redrew the images she conjured in her sleep. Four hours later she stepped back from her final sketch. "That's it," she said aloud. "That's the structure that'll make this work." Then she moved to a point-of-interest sketch, then a value sketch.

Save for lunch and dinner, she worked nonstop on drawings incorporating different facets of the piece. When midnight came, she left the studio strewn with her rough sketches, to find the sleep she had promised her mentors. By seven-thirty in the morning, she was up and back at work in the studio. And so it went.

The term seemed to Gabrielle to charge by as she labored over the challenging depiction. The discipline of her schedule and the single focus of her attention yielded nearly finished work on the piece by the end of her sabbatical. After that, taking only one class at a time, she continued making more rapid progress than she or her professors could have imagined.

Months passed as she struggled with the remaining panels. The fourth in the series returned her in memory to her host family of seven. She knew she never would forget the caring solidity of Edith and Mike Brown.

Every night and morning she and Rick witnessed the Browns' generous nature and supportive family. Gabrielle treasured the gift not only of the Browns' protection, but also of the awakening that comes when you travel for a time in the shoes of others. These were people who suffered for their rights and dedicated themselves to giving all they had for the chance for a freer future for their five young children.

As Gabrielle painted with a loving hand the picture of their family life that included Rick and her, she remembered the faces and forms of each treasured person and all they stood for. She relived how Edith sang to her young children to woo them to sleep each night and how cared for Edith's crooning made her feel. Being part of Mike and Edith's family during their time in

Hattiesburg gave her insight into their sacrifices, their poverty, their strength, and their societal struggles.

Reluctantly turning from this experience to another, she began to consider her approach to her next work. The scene she would paint began with her and Rick's interchange with Joe, a brakeman for the B&O Railroad. A man in his thirties, he was sitting on his front porch and speaking about voter registration and his desire for freedom and the chance to move his family north.

Gabrielle shuddered as she recalled what happened next when a carload of whites shouted racial expletives and fired a rifle. Any of the three of them could have died.

As she began sketching, she relived the crack of the gun, a bullet whistling barely above their heads as they sought the ground. She remembered the sharp, bitter taste of fear, the recognition of the tenuousness of their lives, the suffocating presence of prejudice and acrimony. In this moment, she witnessed the full horror of an oppression that tore at the very fabric of a people, of a nation.

Months later, she completed the piece.

With just two more panels to go, she next chronicled her and Rick's encounter with third-world poverty in America. Recollecting their first experience with a shantytown, they had approached a black woman and her barefoot children in rags and near starvation outside their tarpaper shack.

As she sketched, she recalled the stench of the settlement that lacked sewers and fresh running water. She recoiled from her remembrance of the dread that gripped the woman when she saw two white people approach. Gabrielle always would think about how the woman gathered her children and backed away from Rick and her in silence, raising one hand to her face as if warding off a blow. To this day, Gabrielle was thunderstruck that America could harbor such deprivation.

By the end of her twelfth term, she had only her final canvas to complete, the one that followed the Hattiesburg church scene. It was to depict a long line of Hattiesburg's black citizens attempting to register to vote. It was one of her most challenging pieces and represented the climax of the eight panels.

As she considered this, she was cognizant of the need to convey the tension of the blacks seeking registration. But also she sought to capture their hopefulness, their rising up, this claiming of a right once given but summarily coopted through repression and fear.

She needed to show the danger these brave people were in and the anger of whites determined to not let the blacks' actions go unthreatened and unpunished. She wanted people to see these petitioners for the courageous individuals that they were and to witness the intensity of their desire to claim what was rightfully theirs.

Ultimately she yearned for those viewing the series to understand these peoples' resolve and bravery. They were exposing themselves to violence and potentially even death in the quest for the very things white Americans took for granted—equality and specifically the right to vote. This was oxygen to them. It was the prize. And their bodies, if required, were the price.

10

As she worked through the steps of creating her final piece, building one layer of paint upon another, she reflected on how the comments regarding her series made by both faculty and fellow students had helped her. Mostly as part of studio class discussions, but sometimes by chance encounters or during her independent studio work, she found that their remarks suggested solutions to problems she encountered that she otherwise might not have discovered.

She also thought about how the sensory nature of oil painting had taken full hold of her. Laboring on such a large scale, she grew sweaty moving up and down the ladder and across the canvas. As she sketched with chunks of charcoal, the powder quickly coated not just her hands, but her perspiring face and arms. While painting, she always was aware of the smells of the paints, turpentine, and other mixers. And her hands and arms, her clothes, even her face wore the colors she employed.

She came to not just rejoice in the beauty of the colors she explored, but to feel the colors in a very sensuous way—the warmth and earthy nature of browns and yellows, the vibrancy and heat of the reds, the cool allure of blues, the solace of greens. She felt parts of her physical and emotional being remaining on her canvases, onto which she imbued all the fire of her artistry, the strength of her commitment, and the yearnings of her soul.

In truth she had given all that she was to these panels. They were her children, the echoes of her life's longings. Soon she would complete this work. What might lie beyond hadn't even entered her mind.

* * *

By the end of her fourteenth term, she had finished her eighth panel and earned the credits required for her fine art master's degree. It had taken her more than three-and-a-half years, but finally she was done.

Physically exhausted, but emotionally ecstatic to have completed what she set out to do, she now had to await her professors' assessments. Of growing concern to her was the fact that she would leave Parsons soon and would need to determine what to do with her series. Furthermore she realized that she had been so focused on her effort that she had given no thought to her own future. It frightened her now to think that she had no plan as to where or how she would live after graduation.

As all this raced through her mind, she got word that she had a phone call.

"Hey there Gabrielle."

She woke as from a dream. "Rick?"

"The one and only."

"I'm so glad you called!"

"I like the sound of that. How are you doing?"

She filled him in on the last couple of months since they had last spoken.

"I can't believe you finished."

She laughed. "I can't believe it either, but finally it's done. My question now is what am I going to do with it?"

"Won't Parsons or your professors have a plan for it?"

"I don't know yet. I've submitted it as my master's thesis project and am waiting to hear back."

"I can hardly wait to see it Gabrielle. Surely they'll want to mount an exhibit of it at the college."

"That's what I'm hoping. But I have no idea what might happen to it after that. Then there's the whole question of what I'm going to do with my life after Parsons. Can you believe I've been here almost four years?"

He laughed. "I most certainly can believe it's been that long. I've missed you, you know."

"I've missed you too Rick."

There was a long pause.

"That brings me to a thought I have," he said. "When you're done there at Parsons, why don't you come on up to Chicago. There's so much going on here in the Civil Rights Movement and in community organizing in general. I think you'd find a lot of material for merging your painting with your commitment to the cause."

"Hmmm. I'd have to think about that. I don't see how I'd live."

"My guess is you could find a job teaching art at one of the schools here. Or if your series gets the kind of attention I suspect it might, you could get commissions or an arts grant to pursue your work."

"I don't know. It's too soon to have a sense of whether any future work will come from what I've done. I'm going to have to make a living somehow."

"If you want, you can stay with me…at least until you sort out what you want to do and find employment."

"You'd do that? You have the room?"

"It's not a big place, but we could manage."

"But until I find a job, I wouldn't have any money to help with the rent."

"Gabrielle, I neither need nor expect that. I'd be happy to do this."

"Rick, you're too good. I don't deserve you. I'll think about your offer and let you know after I get done with everything here and learn the fate of my series."

"Okay. Just give me a call when things look clearer. And if they mount a show with your work, which I suspect they'll do, let me know quickly so I can put in for vacation. I'd love to come there to see it—and you."

"That would be wonderful! Thanks Rick. You're the best."

"Take care now. I gotta run."

When she hung up, she realized how buoyed up she was by Rick and his care for her. To her chagrin, she realized she hadn't asked him about his life. She felt ashamed to have been so self-absorbed. But she also realized that she loved Rick more than anyone now in her life. She loved him as a friend. But could it be more? she wondered.

After showering she returned to her room and retired for the night. Rick was her last thought as she fell asleep.

* * *

The department assistant sent word to Gabrielle that she and Professor Ray were wanted for a meeting in the morning at the chairman's office. All day she was anxious about what would come of the appointment, suspecting it involved the future of her series.

She arrived early outside the chairman's door. At exactly ten o'clock, she knocked.

"Come in," the chairman responded. He looked serious. His office, always filled with paperwork and now crowded with the three of them, made her feel claustrophobic and uneasy. But then Professor Ray smiled, making her relax a bit.

"We convened a group of studio instructors," the chairman began, "and presented your eight large canvases to them. Seeking their feedback, we asked what further responsibility we as a department and Parsons as an institution should have regarding them. We had one professor—I won't say who—who mounted a vigorous argument against giving any more attention to and promotion of your work." As the chairman hesitated, Gabrielle's blood ran cold. *My God, does this mean that my panels won't be displayed and find a home? Is this what all these years of work have come to?*

Seeing the dismay on Gabrielle's face, he quickly continued. "But ultimately we had robust agreement to mount an exhibit of your Hattiesburg series in our main exhibition space. Furthermore we will invite not only members of our campus to its opening, but the art community at large, particularly staff of the New York galleries and museums, perhaps some media as well." Gabrielle was floored, then elated.

The chairman continued. "Miss Andersen, it's a long time since I've witnessed such strong support by faculty for a student's work and the responsibility we have for it. They used words such as 'stunning,' 'powerful,' 'moving,' 'enlightening.' They were incredulous that you completed this work in the time that you did and with the relatively modest amount of instruction you had before beginning it."

He fingered his mustache, pausing in thought. "They believe that what you've created will stand the test of time and have relevance beyond our current social and political climate. Your instinct to work large and display them together as if one long mural was exactly right, although the size of these works compounded your challenge.

"It's exceedingly rare for one so young in years and in artistic craft to achieve what you have. We're prepared to try to do everything we can to advocate for this body of work, to see that it gets shown not just at Parsons, but elsewhere. I congratulate you Miss Andersen on a job brilliantly well done."

Chairman Rabinowitz smiled broadly now under his handlebar mustache. This was the first time Gabrielle had seen him smile enough to see his teeth. Professor Ray beamed. She was overwhelmed by everything the chairman just said. She couldn't imagine that they were talking about her and her work. After a long pause she replied, "I hardly know what to say. This is so much more than I could have imagined. I'm so grateful for everyone's help, particularly the two of you. I've been struggling with what comes next for my series, and for me as well. Perhaps this will aid me in finding a path for my future as an artist, a plan that I've neglected in my single-minded focus on this effort."

"My dear Miss Andersen," Professor Ray began, "I think you shouldn't worry about your future. I think that your future will find you. This accomplishment of yours is just the beginning," he looked meaningfully at her.

"If you keep to your dedication and your principles—which I know you will—you'll find your path. It will deliver your talent where it's most needed. Art has the power to reach people on a very deep level. With this work, you've shown that you already understand this and know how to use it for good. Congratulations my dear. You've merited a one-woman student show, a rarity for our exhibition hall."

"I'm honored and can't begin to thank you enough," she replied.

"Do you have any questions?" the chairman asked.

"When do you expect the exhibition might be?"

"My best guess is three months to complete our current exhibits, then prepare for, mount, and advertise your work," the chairman said.

Gabrielle paused to think, then responded, "Since school is ending, do you think it will be possible to stay in the dormitory until the exhibit is over?"

"I think that can be arranged," the chairman replied. "And you ought to plan on some time past the exhibit to get everything worked out about the panels and where they'll go from here. We'll be in touch to finalize arrangements soon."

"That would be wonderful. Thank you so much."

And with that the two men stood, as did she.

After closing the chairman's door and alone now, she leaned against the wall and whispered, "Damn! Holy crap! Is this really happening?" She started to shake as the full import of what had occurred washed over her. Then her body swam in emotional release as tears flooded her cheeks.

She couldn't wait to tell Rick the news. Knowing he would be at work, she left a message for him to phone back.

"What a pleasant surprise to get your call," he said. "How are you doing?"

"So well I can hardly believe it," she said.

"Your series pleased your professors?"

"You're not going to believe this," she began, then told him about her good fortune.

"That's fantastic! When will the opening be?"

"They're thinking three months."

"Won't that be hard for you to find somewhere to stay, since you're graduating soon?"

"I thought that too, but they told me I likely can keep my dorm room through the exhibit and until arrangements are made for the panels' future."

"I can see this is a big concern."

"Yes. But the chairman said something surprising."

"Which was?"

"Department faculty were strongly supportive in saying that the college had responsibility to me and the series to preserve and show it beyond Parsons. At least that's what I understood."

"Your work must be spectacular, no less than I would have expected."

"I don't know, but it does appear that they were moved by it and surprised that I was able to pull it off in the time that I did."

"It seems like a long time to me," he said.

"It seems to me long and short at once, if that makes any sense," she replied.

"Yes. So what will you do in the months till the exhibit?"

"Collapse, rest, see the city. When I first came here I thought I'd have all kinds of time to explore New York. But I really haven't seen that much of it, what with classes and the series."

"I can see that would be a good way to spend a month," he noted. "What would you say to come visit me in Chicago for a few weeks?"

"Wow. That would be great. But you'll be working, no?"

"I will, but I also can take off here and there—and then there are evenings and weekends. You've wondered what to do after graduation. Chicago offers a lot too, and you'd have somewhere to live while you decide what you want to do next."

"That's very tempting. I'll try to find out how much they'll need me here. Maybe I can come up when my presence isn't required."

"That would be great," he said.

"Rick, how are *you* doing?"

"I'm doing well. I've settled into this job and like living here. Although it's got its problems, Chicago's a great-hearted town. I think you'll like getting to know it."

"I'm sure I will...especially if you're there."

He hesitated. "Gabrielle, you know how much I care about you."

"And I you," she replied.

"Let me know when you might be free to come up here."

"I will."

"I've got to run," he said. "Congratulations again, Gabrielle."

Everything seems more real when I tell Rick about it, she mused as she hung up the phone. *He's my touchstone, my best friend. I can hardly wait to see him. I do love that man!"*

11

Within a week the chairman apprised her of a September 1 opening for her exhibit and that they wouldn't need her assistance until August 1.

Upon learning this she called Rick, who invited her to come and spend as long as she liked. A week later she stood on the steps to his apartment building, her suitcase and backpack in hand. No sooner had she rung the buzzer than she heard a familiar voice.

"Gabrielle?"

"None other."

"I'll beep you in."

As the buzzer sounded, the door unlatched and she entered the foyer. She could hear Rick running down the stairs. "Gabrielle!"

She looked up to see that impish grin she had always loved, his dark, curly hair long and trailing behind him as he bounded into the foyer. She smiled as he grabbed hold of her and gave her a bear hug. As she started to pull away to look at him, he drew her back in and covered her lips with his. Melting into his kiss, she returned it. When she opened her eyes, she saw the intensity of love in his. It left her breathless. Was this what she had waited for all these years? Had *the one* been there all along? "Rick," was all she could say.

"Come," he said, "let's go upstairs. I made dinner for us."

"I didn't know you cooked," she exclaimed, nonplussed and anxious to cover her surprise at their sudden intimacy.

"Well I wouldn't say dinner will be great, but for a bachelor it's not too bad," he said.

She laughed as he took her suitcase and walked ahead of her up the stairs to his second-floor apartment. It was a small place, but comfortable looking. It had a fair-sized living room hung with pictures of Bob Dylan, Joan Baez, Satchmo, The Stones, and Jimmy Hendrix, and sported a couch, coffee table, two overstuffed lounge chairs, and a large bookcase crammed with books, a TV, radio, records, and stereo equipment. The kitchen had a small dining table, while a good-sized bedroom included a double bed, desk, file cabinet, and bureau drawers. And of course there was a compact full bath.

"This is nice, Rick. And what's that wonderful smell?"

"Pot roast. It's been cooking all day. You hungry?"

"Famished. I may need to use your bathroom though."

"Of course. Feel free to freshen up. There's a clean towel beside the sink. The roast is in a slow cooker in a kind of stew, so it will keep as long as you like. Are you tired?"

"Not very. I'm probably more hungry than tired. Feel free to dish things out. I'll only be a few minutes."

When she emerged from the bathroom, he had dinner served up in large bowls, candles on the table, bread and butter, as well as two glasses of red wine.

"My, this looks lovely. You're full of surprises."

"Pleasant ones I hope."

Her smile said "yes."

He pulled her chair out for her, then seated himself across the table. "Your trip here went smoothly?" he asked as he lit the candles.

"You know how buses can be," she smiled. "But it gave me time to enjoy the scenery and catch a few winks. I've been in such a whirlwind that it's nice to finally slow down a little."

"I can imagine. Did you bring pictures of your panels?"

"I did. I'll get them for you after dinner."

"I can hardly wait."

She took a spoonful of stew. "Oh Rick, this is delicious."

"Here, have some bread with it. It's sourdough."

After they finished eating, she fetched the photos and arranged them in sequence.

Looking slowly at each of the eight, he held them close to the candlelight. "Gabrielle, these are incredible. I don't say this lightly. Your Hattiesburg series in Oberlin was wonderful, but these are miles beyond even those. How large did you say they were?"

He shook his head at her response. "I'm amazed you were able to do this mammoth work while still meeting your class obligations. I absolutely see why the college made the commitment to you that they did, including helping to ensure your panels get the exposure and recognition they deserve." He lifted his wine glass in a toast. "Here's to your greatest feat to date. May you have many more successes!"

She raised her glass to his and said, "And here's to your accomplishments in a terribly challenging environment. May you have many successes!" They clinked glasses, swallowed their wine, and gazed at one another. The light in Rick's eyes carried more than the flicker of the candle's flame. Watching him, she felt a deep sense of joy, an emotion she hadn't experienced with a man since her affair with Mehmet. It had taken her five years to be fully over him. But now she was ready. For the first time she thought that her longtime friend could become her lover.

Perhaps Rick read her thoughts in her eyes. He reached for her across the now-empty dishes and brought her hand to his lips. He kissed her fingers, then turned them to expose her palm, in the very center of which he pressed his lips. With this gesture, he stirred desire in her and the recognition that she always had loved him. She thought in that moment that fate may have been saving them for each other. He looked long at her, then released her hand.

"We have dessert," he said, watching her as he got up, cleared the dishes, and brought back two small plates with a slice of cake on each. "I think I should caution you that this is the first cake I ever made. So be forewarned," he said smiling. "Would you like to risk giving it a try?"

Suddenly she didn't care about eating, but she shook her head "yes." She gazed at the dessert he had made just for her and realized that she was falling in love with her best friend.

* * *

She had arrived on Wednesday. Already it was Friday. Rick had given her his bedroom and slept on the studio couch. She was grateful for the space he gifted her to recover from exhaustion and decompress from the whirlwind that her life had become.

Having rested and had time to settle in, she ventured out in the afternoon and found a neighborhood grocery a few blocks away that had everything she needed to prepare a meal for him. The walk gave her a sense of the neighborhood. It was busy with cars, buses, and people who were more black and brown than white. It seemed to her a neighborhood in transition from the worst poverty to modestly revitalized and decided that in the days ahead she would explore it. Mostly, however, she thought long about Rick and her newfound attraction to him. But as he was her best friend, she worried what might happen if lovemaking disappointed.

When he returned from work that evening, she had a meal ready for them. Bringing him a glass of wine, she returned to the kitchen to dish out dinner. She thought about how she had found a tablecloth and napkins in his linen closet and the pleasure it had given her to set the table and prepare for their dinner together, the first she cooked for him.

As she dished out the food, he stood in the kitchen doorway. Observing her warmly, he answered her questions about his day. Then she carried to the table two plates of pesto on pasta, garnished with fresh parmesan cheese and tomatoes, along with a side dish of green beans. Plates on the table, his wine glass refilled, he talked about the people he had met over the course of the day and the work he had accomplished. She sat quietly, listening with love in her heart for one of the most giving men she had known. It occurred to her that she couldn't think what she ever would have done without him.

As she got up to clear the dishes, he took the plates from her, returned them to the table, and pulled her onto his lap. As he kissed her with passion, she responded with emotion. Then he picked her up and carried her into the dimly lit bedroom without a word passing between them.

Gently, lovingly, he unbuttoned her blouse and slid off his shirt. Unhooking her bra, he pulled back to look at her. "My God," he whispered as he pressed himself to her. As he kissed her face and body, she thought she might faint. His tenderness tore at her. Removing their remaining clothing, he rested her on the bed and reclined beside her.

Gazing long at one another, she felt that they truly saw each other fully for the first time. He placed his hands on her face, cupping it in a gesture of recognition. Stroking her neck, breasts, and abdomen, he soon found her in the place most wanting him. She nearly came as he entered her, holding herself back until he released in her, warm and wet and full of ecstasy. They held one another in climax, locked together in something stronger than pure pleasure. They gazed into each other's eyes with a look that was knowledge. It was love, and she thought for the first time in her young life that nothing would ever change that. Wrapped around one another, he pulled the covers about them and turned out the light. She fell asleep and woke the next morning still in his arms, his breathing warm on her face and heart.

* * *

"How about if I show you the neighborhood?" he asked, smiling at her as he broke eggs into a pan for Saturday breakfast.

"I'd like that," Gabrielle said, turning toward him as she tried to smooth her still-tussled hair. "I got a sense of it yesterday when I was searching for a grocery."

"Was it Di Salvo's Grocery Mart?"

"It was!"

"That Italian grocery's where I usually shop. It's family owned and carries a little bit of everything. What's your impression of the neighborhood?"

"That it's in transition—and we're in the minority."

"Yes. It borders the neighborhoods where I work. I can walk to the office if I want, though usually I wind up taking the bus," he said, turning the eggs in the pan. "My employer found this place for me four years ago when I moved from Delaware. Some of my coworkers live in this general area. You may get to meet some of them while you're here." He flipped the eggs onto two plates that already held buttered toast. "Can you grab our coffee?"

"Sure." Seated now, she was quiet, then said, "Rick, do you believe in destiny?"

He looked at her quizzically as he sipped his black brew. "I'm not sure. Perhaps I do. Do you?"

She shook her head affirmatively. "I think you were destined to do the work that you do and that I was destined to paint."

He was thoughtful as he chewed and swallowed a bite of eggs. "Yes, I suppose. But could it not just be that we're born with talents and once we discover them we explore them—and then they just become what we do?"

She smiled. "I guess you could say that, but I prefer to call it destiny," she said before diving into her eggs. "These are good!"

He laughed. "I love your passion Gabrielle. Even for these sorry little fried eggs."

With that she laughed almost to the point of tears.

After breakfast they walked several blocks in each direction. North and east of them held transitional neighborhoods like Rick's, with north looking more prosperous. South was the arena in which Rick worked—the parts that were poor, often black or brown, strewn with garbage, and rundown. In a city park six blocks south of his place, they met a couple Rick knew. They stopped to talk, the man high-fiving Rick in greeting. The couple wanted information about the next rally for fair housing and better schools in their part of South Chicago.

Continuing their walk, Rick filled Gabrielle in on the local scene. "It'll take a long time to see change. The greatest challenge is to keep residents engaged when so little progress has resulted from all the protests. Civil suits may prove our saving grace," he concluded as a taxi horn blared as they got ready to cross the street.

"How do you keep going when you don't see a lot of results for all the effort?" she asked, stepping up onto the curb on the other side.

He sighed. "I just have to keep reminding myself that radical change generally is a slow-moving train. It's the result of dogged persistence. Dr. King taught us that. I just remember what he said and try to take the long view. Kind of like our tutoring. Great change doesn't happen overnight with an individual or a system, wouldn't you say?"

"I guess, but it can be discouraging," she said studying him.

"Yes, but then we go on." He gave her a resigned smile. She stopped, turned to him, and gave him a hug.

"Hugs do help," he said.

She laughed and reached for him again, then turned serious. "How is it that no woman claimed you in all the time we've been apart?"

"Who said no one did?"

"You never told me you were seeing anyone seriously."

"No. I dated quite a bit here in Chicago, even got serious a couple of times. But I never felt for anyone what I feel for you. I've always loved you, Gabrielle. In truth I suffered every time you lost your heart to another man. I kept telling myself I should pull back from our friendship—self-preservation and all—but I couldn't. You're the love of my life pure and simple. Part of me said I'd wait forever for you if need be. Thank God I didn't have to." He laughed.

Taken aback by his admission, she understood now how much pain she had caused him over the years. "I'm so sorry Rick. You're the last person I would have wanted to hurt. How insensitive of me."

Stopping and turning toward her, he watched concern travel her face as he managed a comforting smile. "You weren't ready for me is all—and maybe on some level I wasn't ready for you either. We know better now who we are, where we're headed, and what we want for our lives. It took a long time, but I think we finally found our way to each other. You were worth the wait Gabrielle. I hope you feel the same."

When they returned to Rick's apartment, Gabrielle responded with her whole being. Their lovemaking brought out in her an ardor that had been long restrained. She had never known such desire, such joy. It was as if Rick knew every sensuous part of her.

But her fulfillment reached deeper than the joys of physical pleasure. It was as if he knew and touched her very soul. In the safety of his arms, she opened herself to him in ways she never had to another person. "Rick," she whispered as she lay beside him. "Thank you for waiting for me." He rolled toward her from his back and gazed at her, her hair tangled about her face and wet from lovemaking, her full lips and breasts beckoning him. He joined himself to her again and answered with his passion.

12

And so the days and weeks passed. She savored walking the Chicago streets, taking pictures with her camera, then coming back to the apartment and sketching from memory or from the photos she had developed. In the first month she already had filled two sketch pads with drawings—city scenes, but mostly people, black, Italian, Asian Indian, Hispanic, young, old.

The evenings and weekends were all with Rick, visiting neighborhoods, markets, museums, galleries, and neighborhood restaurants. They took a boat ride on the Chicago River, gazing up at the city's tall buildings, symbols of wealth and power, alien structures from the rubble of parts of Chicago. Inevitably they talked at great length about the Civil Rights Movement and the inequities that were everywhere apparent. They spoke their hopes and dreams and lay together each night, joined in increasing knowledge and happiness.

And then it was time to return to New York.

Having fallen more in love, they found the thought of parting almost unbearable. Their last night they held each other after lovemaking, gazing into one another's eyes and without speaking. He stroked her hair with his graceful fingers, tracing them along her neck, her arms, her stomach, to that place of deep desire, making love again. When the morning light broke along the edges of the window shutters, they still held one another, not wanting to let go. And then the alarm registered the harsh reality that their time was up, and she would have to leave.

The bus ride back took most of a day and seemed to her like forever. She tried to sleep, but she couldn't stop thinking about Rick and the people she had met and sketched. Rick and his city called her. Ideas for paintings flooded her mind. Pulling out her photographs and sketchbooks from her backpack and thumbing through them, she realized she had another series here, perhaps even large-panel work. But where would she paint after leaving Parsons? How could she afford a studio and the materials to create new artwork? She had so many questions that seemed to have no answers.

Already she was missing Rick more than anyone she had known. It hurt to think of him. She missed his physical presence, their lovemaking, and the insightful, playful, truthful person that he was. *He's the soulmate I saw in Mehmet,* she thought. *But I know now that this is the relationship I've been searching for. For the life of me, I don't know why it took so long.*

The bus was very late getting into New York City. Taking a cab to the dorm, she dropped into bed at two in the morning. Upon waking at noon, she realized she still was in her traveling clothes. Looking in the bathroom mirror at her disheveled hair and clothing, she laughed as she headed for the shower. By one o'clock she was dressed, had eaten lunch, and was on her way across campus to find Professor Ray.

When she arrived at his office and knocked, she found the door locked. Turning and starting back down the hallway, she saw him making his way toward her. He was looking down, his face partially covered by his curly grey hair. Then he glanced up, spotted her, and smiled. She was so happy to see him.

In that moment she realized that she had missed him. He had helped her time and again and been her ally when others weren't. She felt she never could repay all that he had done for her. But now she had to ask him for something again—not just information about how preparations for her exhibit were going, but for his advice on what she saw might be her next major artistic challenge.

"Miss Andersen, how wonderful to see you," he called. "When did you get back?"

"The wee hours of this morning. It's great to see you too."

"I imagine you want to know how your exhibit is going." He unlocked his office door and motioned for her to take a seat as he put down his briefcase and sat across the desk from her. "It's hot out there," he exclaimed, brushing his long hair away from his brow. "August in the city can be brutal."

She smiled and nodded.

He leaned back in his chair as he spoke. "As you know, your opening is the first of September. In your absence and in the interest of time, I took the liberty of designing your invitation. I hope you don't mind."

"No," she said, "I'm delighted that you did."

He opened a desk drawer and extracted the card, then reached across the desk to hand it to her.

The card's cover displayed a photograph of the Reverend Jonas panel. The inside read:

> *You are invited to the opening of*
> *a master's thesis exhibit*
> *and large-canvas series of the*
> *Civil Rights Movement in Hattiesburg, Mississippi,*
> *by an exciting new talent,*
> *Parsons Master of Fine Art Graduate*
> *Gabrielle Andersen.*
> *September 1, 1971, 8 p.m.*
> *Parsons Fine Art Exhibition Hall*
> *RSVP by August 20, 1971*

"Does this meet with your approval?" he asked.

"Yes of course, but you give me too much credit. I love that you chose the Reverend Jonas panel."

"I thought you might."

She smiled. "You know me well."

"The invitations are printed and addressed, so I'm glad you didn't require any changes. They'll go in the mail tomorrow. But I have the feeling that this isn't all you wished to discuss."

She took a deep breath. "I've spent my time away in Chicago with a longtime friend. He's a community organizer and lives in a transitional area in South Chicago. I shot many photos and filled two sketch pads with pictures of people, mostly black or brown, mostly poor. A civil rights war is being waged there in a somewhat different manner than it is in Mississippi. A myriad of inequities are decimating whole communities in Chicago. I believe there's a place for art to shine a light on this and help people to witness the pain their fellow men and women are suffering. I don't know if I'm the one to do this, but I'd like to try." She paused, watching the professor's eyebrows knit in thought.

"I have a place I can live in Chicago, but I have no studio," she said. Her mind swam in her growing awareness that she needed, but had no clear plan for, how to sustain this next part of her life. She continued, "I foresee that I likely will want to stay with the large panels if I'm able to take on this work. That, as you know, is an expensive undertaking. I also will need a modest income to pay my personal expenses. Someone once mentioned National Endowment for the Arts grants. Do you think I'd have a chance of obtaining such a grant, and is it possible it could cover these expenses? And is applying a very long process?"

Professor Ray studied her, then closed his eyes for a minute. He seemed to be concentrating all his energy on his thoughts. When he opened them, a look of mild irritation surfaced on his face as he answered her. "Miss Andersen, you never cease to amaze me. We're readying to open an exhibit of work it took you three-and-a-half years to complete, an effort that would have exhausted anyone. And here you are, after only a short break, itching to run another marathon." Her gaze lowered in embarrassment. The weight of her moxie hung on her like sodden clothing.

Noting her discomfort, he continued. "I don't say this to temper your enthusiasm. I think, however, that you would be wise to wait until after your exhibition and see what comes of it. If I'm right about the reception it may get, we could have answers to your questions that are beyond what I presently can conjure. Although I'd be sorry to see you leave New York, I recognize that Chicago has its own attractions for you. Let's revisit this conversation after the opening of your show and again at its conclusion at the end of the month. It's possible that everything could change by then."

Admonished, she blushed as she grasped the wisdom of his reply. "I guess I need to be patient and let circumstances evolve as they will."

"Yes," he said.

"It's only in the past couple of months that I've come up for air from immersion in the Hattiesburg series," she struggled to explain her feelings. A feeling of terror about all the uncertainties that lay in her immediate path washed over her as she continued. "With that came a sudden awareness that I'd have to move on from both Parsons and New York very soon—and I didn't know what I'd do or how I'd live. That made me think about applying for a fellowship or a grant of some type, but I suspected this could be a long process. If it didn't come through or took a very long time, I realized I might not have the means to live and to work. These had become terribly scary thoughts."

He absorbed her fearfulness, then looked at her very directly. "I can understand what you're thinking, but you underestimate your talent and drive. I'll be surprised indeed if doors don't open for you. If we professors didn't think that this could occur, we never would have undertaken all this effort on your behalf. You must have faith my dear. I don't think that we're wrong to take this gamble."

Startled by what he said and not having thought about the exhibition this way, she felt ashamed, shaking her head in affirmation. "I'm sorry to have asked so much of you, the chairman, and Parsons as a whole." As she spoke, the walls covered with paintings and photographs, manifestations of his long and illustrious career, pushed back against her fears. Noting a look of concern on his face, she gathered herself and pressed on.

"I'm glad that you told me this. You're right of course. I guess I haven't seen myself as you have. It's hard for me to own that description. But I'll be patient…and I am grateful…more than you know." She paused, taking a breath.

"I'll try to have the faith that you seem to have in me. I can't begin to tell you, the chairman, and the others how thankful I am that I came here four years ago, met you all, learned from you, and had support I couldn't have anticipated. Without that, this new Hattiesburg series wouldn't exist, and I would be just another art student at Parsons or somewhere else."

The professor threw his head back as he chuckled. "My dear, I can't imagine you as 'just another art student,' here or anywhere else, but thank you. I'm more pleased than you know to have had the privilege of helping you along your way. Now I must get going if these invitations are to be mailed. It would be a sorry situation to have no one there just because they went out late."

She laughed. "Yes indeed. Thank you."

And with that the professor rose and exited his office, Gabrielle following. She stopped in the hall and just watched her mentor hurrying along on her behalf. She realized that her life would not be where it was, were it not for this wise and caring man. He had been her guide and advocate through difficult times these last years. He had taught her more than how to paint. He had taught her how to live.

13

During the weeks before the opening, Professors Ray and Rabinowitz asked Gabrielle to compose a narrative about the canvases, including her motive for creating them.

She began by telling how she came to be an eyewitness during her voter registration work in Mississippi. Having experienced how racially divided Hattiesburg was, she talked about the poverty and lack of freedoms she observed, the fear that cadres of whites instilled in Negros and civil rights workers, and the bravery of blacks who stood up for themselves and each other to dare to register to vote.

She was shocked to learn that just two years prior to her time there, only twelve of the seven thousand and five hundred voting-aged blacks in Hattiesburg's Forrest County were registered to vote. To give a face to the Negroes who were denied registration, she cited a report that David Robertson, a local teacher at the black segregated high school, was one of many whom the county's circuit clerk deemed "ineligible" to vote. Robertson was a Cornell graduate and National Science Foundation Fellow. He was told he failed the required literacy test.

As an endnote, Gabrielle spoke about the Mexican muralists, Diego Rivera in particular. She told how a photographic record of the muralists' work she viewed soon after arriving in New York City profoundly impacted her. Through them she fully realized both the artistic and storytelling possibilities of art. She recognized as well the effect that murals—even large canvases simulating them—could have, not only as an art form, but also as a social and political statement. She ended by saying that it was her hope that viewers of her work might better understand the plight of America's blacks and find a way to support them and help assuage their suffering as they struggle to secure their rights.

To the narrative, Parsons added a photograph of her and a paragraph about her academic and political background and the fact that she had spent three-and-a-half years creating the series. All these notes would precede the first of the eight panels.

As her canvases went up, one after another, Gabrielle stood in awe of what the staff had put in place. When everything was ready the day before the opening, she sat on a bench in the middle of the exhibition hall and gazed at the series, truly seeing it in its totality for the first time.

The canvases held the experiences of many people's lives. She looked into Edith and Tom's faces and knew that she had done them justice. Whatever did or didn't come from this show, she knew that she had done the right thing in creating this work. Through art she had given Edith, Tom, the Reverend Jonas and his parishioners, the civil rights workers, and numerous others a voice that carried the possibility of touching, enlightening, and perhaps even persuading viewers to action. In this moment, she knew with certainty that these past years of long hours and hard work all had been worth it.

* * *

It was the day of the opening, and she was excited that Rick would be there. She was disappointed, however, that her parents weren't able to attend her big event. Her mother, however, promised that she and perhaps her dad would see her work before the end of the month. Figuring her father was the reason they weren't coming to the opening, she thought how since childhood she had felt his lack of acceptance of how she appeared, looking so unlike the rest of the family. And she never would forget how he voiced his belief that a woman's pursuit of higher education and a career as an artist were frivolous and wasteful aspirations.

As she struggled with her disappointment, Professor Ray raised her spirits when he told her that more than one hundred and fifty people had responded to attend the event. The list included many from New York's arts scene, including artists and gallery owners, even a couple of museum staff members, as well as Parsons donors, faculty, students, and alumni. An art critic from *The New York Times*, a reporter from *The Village Voice*, and staff from the local CBS affiliate also stated their intention to be there.

Eating her lunch dutifully in her dorm room, she tried to ignore how her stomach churned with nerves. She hadn't expected such an auspicious turnout and in truth it frightened her. She almost wished the media hadn't been contacted, especially the *Times* and the *Voice*. She wondered how her youthful work could ever compare to the established artists they were accustomed to covering. Would their criticism keep individuals from coming to see the work for themselves? Would she fail the people and the cause she labored to depict?

Shaking her head, she tried to dispel her doubts. Then she rose, drew herself a hot bath, and immersed herself, resting her head on the back of the tub. *Rick*, she thought, *I wish you were here now. You'd tell me not to worry, stroke my hair, then say something funny—and my anxiety would disappear. I love you Rick, more each day.*

After her bath and back in her room, she laid out her clothes before seeking a nap to calm herself. Around five she had a snack, groomed herself, and dressed with care. It still was warm in the city, so she slid on her short-sleeved, black cocktail dress and donned a colorful lightweight Mexican shawl she bought in Greenwich Village, followed by her trusty black flats. She inserted her gold hoop earrings through her pierced ears, placed her grandmother's gold locket around her neck, and noted with chagrin that her garb mirrored what she wore for her Oberlin exhibit four years ago.

As she walked to a mirror, she noticed a three-inch tear in her dress. It ran down from her armpit and along the side seam of her garment. *Oh no,* she fussed, *I should have looked. It's been months since I wore this. I don't have needle and thread and have no way to hide the tear. My shawl may mask it, but it'll make me hot in no time. But it's too late to fix it—and I have nothing else I can wear. God, I hope no one notices.*

Turning from this new worry, she scrutinized her face and hair in the mirror. Noting that her dark hair had grown long, she brushed it and let it hang naturally over her shoulders. Then she studied her face as she picked up the only makeup she possessed—a tube of red lipstick—and painted her lips.

As she observed herself, she noted the dark circles that had developed under her eyes, remnants of long hours in the studio and too little sleep. She had nothing to mask them, nor did she wish to. Her face spoke truth, with only the artifice of lipstick, a splash of color to knit her face to the brilliant colors of her shawl, creating a little festivity to mark the occasion.

It was about quarter to six. She was due at the hall at six-thirty. Thus adorned, she walked outside and made her way through the eighty-degree heat and humidity to the exhibition hall. She used a handkerchief in her dress pocket to mop her brow and upper lip. Hearing the tinkling of wine glasses with the rattle of dishes that soon would hold finger foods and smelling the aroma of roses that graced the food tables, she turned to see the catering and exhibit staff run about making last-minute adjustments. Nearby were Professors Ray and Rabinowitz conversing with Parsons' communications person, an attractive woman in her mid-thirties.

"I'm so delighted to meet you," the slender, blonde-haired woman said, walking with her hand outstretched toward Gabrielle. "My name's Delores. I'll take care of the media when they arrive and assist with their requests."

"Thanks," Gabrielle responded. "Are you still expecting the *Times* and the *Voice* as well as the local CBS station?"

"Yes, but I wouldn't be surprised if others showed up—or if any who said they were coming wind up with a change of plans. That happens all the time." She smiled.

"Is there anything or anyone I should be concerned about?"

"I don't know who'll be coming from CBS, but the critics from the papers can ask tough questions." Gabrielle looked concerned. Delores continued. "But they know that you're a young artist just out of school. All you need to do is answer their questions honestly."

"Yes," she responded, "of course."

"It's nice to meet you Gabrielle. If you require anything at all, just ask for me."

"Thanks. Oh, one thing," she said. "I forgot to add a special friend to the guest list. His name is Rick Dressel, that's D-R-E-S-S-E-L. Would you add his name please?"

"Of course," she said. "I'll be touching base with you throughout the evening. But remember, if you need anything just look for me."

As Delores left, Gabrielle's professors came to greet her. Professor Ray immediately noted her nervousness. "Don't be anxious. Your paintings are even more extraordinary as a collection filling this big room, don't you think?"

She looked at him gratefully. "I'm happy with how they're displayed. Having them all in one place like this is everything I could have hoped for."

"You should be proud of your accomplishment," Chairman Rabinowitz noted. "It's a body of work I couldn't have imagined a young art student would have created, let alone while still taking classes."

"I couldn't have done this without the two of you," she said. "I just hope that tonight honors the faith you have in me—and does justice to the people who lived the truth I've sought to capture in this work."

"It seems to me that you've already done justice to us all," Professor Ray said. "It's for others to recognize that truth is in your work. They only have to find and accept it. That's not *your* job. It's *theirs*."

"I'll try to remember that," she responded. "Do you have any final words of advice for me?"

He looked at her thoughtfully. "Just be who you are. This is *your* night. So just relax and enjoy."

"We have a few things to attend to," the chairman interjected, a crescent moon of a lower lip surfacing from beneath his ample mustache, "so we'll leave you for now."

As they turned, she checked her watch. Since a little time remained until guests arrived, she walked the exhibition hall before returning to the room's center. Slowly she pivoted to experience the totality of her work. She hardly could believe that she had completed the eight panels and that her one-woman show was about to commence. Taking time to examine each of her paintings, she noted something she and her instructors had missed in the rendering of Edith and Mike Brown's family. The hand of the younger boy was misshapen. How could this have gone undetected? Will the critics notice? Dear oh dear, she whispered, how careless of me.

The full realization of what she would face shortly was frightening her. To reduce her stress, she walked the building's corridors before stepping outside. Although still very warm, the air temperature had begun to cool and a slight breeze had picked up. She forced herself to take a short campus walk before coming back to the building before guests arrived.

When she returned, however, some thirty visitors already were in the hall. The fashionably dressed among them mostly were middle-aged and white, although several were black or brown, the men wearing suits and ties, the women in the latest dresses and pantsuits. Donors to Parsons were met by Parsons staff with glasses of wine and trays of food. Twenty or so students in jeans and sneakers soon filtered in, as did Parsons faculty and local artists in an array of clothing, ages, and ethnicities. Then there were the New York gallery and museum staffers. Gabrielle watched the growing crowd ever more uneasily.

As she walked through the gathering toward her assigned spot before the first panel, she watched guests stop for several minutes to study each of her paintings before moving to the next. This encouraged Gabrielle, who saw this as affirmation of the seriousness of the subject matter.

And then the floodgates opened, and people poured in by the dozens. She drew her shawl tighter to mask the rip in her dress and the perspiration running beneath it, as visitors approached to ask her questions and make comments. Within an hour she guessed she spoke with seventy or more people, mostly in small groups.

Checking the room regularly, she kept hoping to see Rick. Close to nine o'clock the local NBC-TV affiliate arrived and immediately sought her. Soon thereafter Delores brought the *Times* art critic to her, Steven Weintraub, and a little later *Voice* art critic Leon Gander, both of whom had been there awhile studying her paintings and mingling with some of the better-known guests.

The scrutiny of these critics was nerve-wracking, causing her to sweat more, but she dared not remove her shawl and expose her torn dress. Although unsettled by this and the probing of these seasoned critics, she worked hard to answer their questions as best she could, while being aware that she lacked the artistic sophistication to which these critics were accustomed.

Later, a staffer from the Museum of Modern Art asked her what would happen to the series following the exhibition. When she said that she hoped a museum would acquire the work and make it available to other museums around the country, he gave her his card and said to call him if no one came forward. He said he might be able to help. Several gallery representatives queried her, and locally well-known New York painter Pierre Sazar congratulated her on what he saw as the daring and personal nature of her work in content and in format.

Fifteen minutes before the close of the event, the New York CBS-TV affiliate showed up, did a short interview with her, and shot footage of the panels and crowd. Photographers from the *Voice* and the *Times* arrived as well, taking pictures of Gabrielle, her paintings, and some of the more prestigious people in attendance.

Minutes before closing, she looked up and saw Rick across the room. He seemed to be observing her and the crowd. Wearing a navy suit and tie, his long curly hair pulled back neatly in a ponytail, he wore a smile that lit up his face, and now hers. She struggled to satisfy the people around her, when all she wanted to do was to run to him. It was ten-thirty before everyone left and she could feel his arms around her. "Rick," was all she could say. Although hot, exhausted, and still anxious, she took Rick to meet her mentors.

After exchanging introductions and niceties, Professor Ray turned to Gabrielle. "What is your impression of how the exhibition went?"

"It seemed to go well, given what people said to me. The media, however, I'm not sure about, and I didn't hear any offers for the series at this point."

"Well you shouldn't draw any conclusions from that," he said. "Members of the artistic communities I conversed with seemed impressed with you and your canvases. I'll be surprised if you don't get an offer of some kind before the month is over. This of course could be helped or hindered by the media coverage, but I suspect more helped than the latter."

"I hope you're right," she said. "The *Times* and the *Voice* asked especially tough questions. Oh, a staffer from the Museum of Modern Art gave me his card in the event we get no museum offers."

Professor Ray glanced at it. "I don't know him, but the card could be useful. Be sure to hang on to it." He turned to Rick. "If I'm not mistaken, Mr. Dressel, your likeness is in several of these paintings. You accompanied Miss Andersen to Mississippi I presume?"

"I did, although we didn't know each other before the trip. Later we worked together in a tutoring center for local kids on the Oberlin College campus."

"Rick pretty much was the tutoring center for three years," Gabrielle interjected. "Now he's a community organizer in South Chicago."

"Then you're an integral part of Miss Andersen's civil rights experiences," Professor Ray noted, observing Rick with interest. "It's good to see that she's not alone in what she's undertaken."

Rick shook his head affirmatively. "We've been friends for years. I'm glad she's getting the recognition she deserves and am delighted to meet the two of you. Gabrielle has told me how supportive you've been."

"It's been our pleasure," the chairman said before turning to Professor Ray. "I think we should get going. They're trying to close up."

"Thank you again," Gabrielle said. "Have a good night!"

"You too," they called as they exited the hall.

"So that's the famous Professor Ray," Rick said. "He has an intelligent and wise face."

"And a kind heart," she added. "I've learned more from him than you can imagine."

"I had that sense," he said. "Should we go somewhere to celebrate your big night?"

She looked at him through the lens of her exhaustion and told him how concerned she was that the media could disparage her work and the people and cause to which she was committed. "I don't think I could bear it," she said.

Outside in the moonlight, he pulled her to him and kissed her long and hard. She scarcely could catch her breath. When she leaned back to look at him, the moonlight bathed his face and swam in his eyes. "I love you Gabrielle Andersen," he said, his voice hoarse with feeling.

"I love *you* Rick Dressel," she whispered. He put his hands to her face, traced her Mississippi scar with his finger, and drew her lips to his. Then he pulled her close as they walked in silence, daring to hope.

* * *

When she awoke in her dorm room, Rick still was asleep in her arms. She thought of how they made love long and tenderly last night. His breath now was warm on her skin, his dark curls spilling over his shoulders and onto her breasts. She thought she had never been happier and more fulfilled than she was at this moment.

As if sensing her attention, Rick opened his eyes and smiled. He pulled her still closer as he kissed her neck, her brow, her lips, first softly, then passionately. As they rolled over, as if one person, he entered her. Sweaty and breathless, they fell back on the bed.

As he lay on his side next to her, their hearts still racing, he outlined her face with his fingers, stopping at the three-inch line remaining on her right cheek from the mob attack on their bus. "What do you feel," he asked, "when you look at this scar?"

Startled by his question, she felt a quiver take her body. Then she released a long sigh. "Mostly I try not to think about it," she said. "But for years, when I closed my eyes to sleep, I would see the face of the man who smashed my window, threatening, berating, then cutting me. I had nightmares about him for years. I still do sometimes.

"When I painted that panel, I dreaded working on it. It brought everything back. I would have to walk away from it periodically and reach for my objectivity. But at night, it all would descend upon me. The incident with the gun wasn't much different, creating similar feelings when I worked on that painting. But I never really saw the faces of the men in the car, just the barrel of the gun and the sounds—and of course, the threat. The physical mark I wear is a constant reminder that runs deeper than just the scar."

"I had no idea," Rick said. "You never told me this before." He reached to hold her for several minutes in his arms. "Sweetheart," he finally said as he bent and kissed her navel, the nest of hair below, her inner thighs, the back of her knees. She had never known such pleasure, she thought as she succumbed to him. "Rick," she moaned as his lips swallowed her words. Pressing her to him, he kissed her neck and hair, now wet against his face. "Gabrielle," he said, "God, how I've missed you!"

Then she began to cry. All the tension of the past months and years seemed to release in the light of their love. He held her until her tears ceased and the promise of a smile rose gentle on her face. At that moment, she wanted to stay just as they were now...forever.

As they prepared to leave her room, someone knocked on the door. It was Delores.

"I'm sorry to come over without warning," she said, glancing at Rick, "but apparently no one's answering the dorm phone. Have you seen the TV coverage of your show?"

Gabrielle shook her head no.

"Both stations had it on their morning newscasts. The city's NBC-TV had a clip on the evening newscast as well. I taped them. Whenever you want to view them, you can come by my office in the administration building. I'll get them copied for you too, but that may take a little time."

"That would be great," Gabrielle responded. "What did they say exactly?"

Delores took a deep breath. "In a nutshell the CBS affiliate said very little about you and the purpose behind your work, although they had quite a few shots of it in their morning report. The city's NBC-TV, on the other hand, carried a brief report last night and a longer one this morning. They said that the large-canvas story you told was a powerful condemnation of racism in the South and a celebration of black courage and sacrifice in the battle for equality. Both stations noted that the exhibition was well attended, and NBC said it was not to be missed."

"In truth I hadn't expected much from the TV reporters," Gabrielle said. "It seemed as if they weren't there long enough to understand what the paintings were about."

"In NBC's case, they got it," Delores said. "Also, I checked in with *The New York Times* and *Village Voice*. The *Times* review will be in the Sunday paper, and the *Voice* will have one in their next weekly issue. It's possible the *Voice* may wish to interview you further. I'd appreciate if you stay in touch with me in case we have to schedule something else."

"Sure. If I don't hear from you first, I can give you a call every two or three hours until this evening. After that I'll assume it's less likely you'll need to reach me."

Delores pulled a card from her pocket. "Here's my number. If reaching you is urgent, I can try the dorm monitor again too. But it should all work out. I'll be surprised if we don't hear more from the media. I think your show created quite a stir."

Gabrielle smiled. "Thanks Delores. I appreciate all your efforts. I'll be sure to be in touch today."

"Thanks. Have a nice day." And with that, Delores sashayed out the door and down the hall.

Rick grinned. "I'm glad she didn't show up any sooner."

Gabrielle laughed.

After breakfast at a nearby coffee shop, Rick and she stopped by Delores's office and viewed the tape. "The CBS coverage was okay, but the NBC was very positive," Rick said after they left the office." The paintings showed well and you gave great interviews. I think it ought to create a good bit of interest in the exhibit."

"I hope so. I'm still worried about what will happen to the panels after the show."

He put his arm around her. "I'm not concerned and neither should you be. The exhibit is spectacular. The right person will come along and snap it up—you'll see." She smiled, but she wasn't as sure as Rick seemed to be. "And remember," he added, "you still have the *Times* and the *Voice* articles."

She nodded, but without conviction. "Come then, let me show you around campus," she said, changing the subject. "Oh and I forgot to mention that my mother promised to come and see the exhibit—and maybe my dad—but it might not be till late in the month. She said something came up with my dad, which is why she couldn't be here earlier. I would have loved you to meet my mom.

"I wish I could. I had a hard time getting away, even for just this long weekend. I'll have to hope for another chance to meet her. But what about your dad? Is he ill?"

She hesitated. "It's complicated, and I really don't want to talk about it now. Suffice it to say that he thinks that higher education for girls is a waste of money and that getting an art degree makes even less sense."

"Really?"

"Yes, and that's all I'm going to say about it now."

Rick looked at her quizzically, but dropped the subject. Changing direction, he requested the opportunity to look at her paintings again.

Thirty-some visitors were in the exhibition hall. They were absorbed in the paintings and didn't seem to notice them when they entered. This gave Rick the opportunity to examine her work and discuss it uninterrupted. "Gabrielle, these paintings really take me back to our time there. I can feel our apprehension and that of the people we met there—and their conviction." He stopped at the Reverend Jonas picture. "Do you remember how swept up we were with the Reverend's calls and the congregation's responses?"

"Yes. I'd never experienced a service like that before."

"Me neither. It was powerful, a kind of call to arms." He turned then and walked back toward the picture of the black family who hosted them in Hattiesburg. "You captured them so well—Tom, Edith, the kids. Such dear people."

"They are. And you'll never forget Edith's sweet potato pie!"

He laughed, then looked around, embarrassed at breaking the serious mood of the art goers.

"We'd better leave," she said. "Maybe we can come back when no one's here."

"Promise?"

"I'll do my best." She looked at her watch. "We'd better stop and see Delores again."

Back at the administration building, the woman was a flurry of activity. "Thank heavens," Delores exclaimed. "A reporter from *Newsday* is on his way. He wants to interview you. I told him I'd try to reach you and meet him at the hall...," she checked her watch, "...damn, in five minutes! Please say you'll run over there with me. We'll literally have to run."

Complying, they jogged behind Delores who ran amazingly well in high heels. The reporter already was at the hall, and the *Newsday* photographer was shooting pictures.

"I'm sorry to be late, but I have the artist," Delores said between gasps of air.

Glen Frye shook Gabrielle's hand. "Art isn't normally my beat, but our arts critic is out of town. So I got elected." He smiled apologetically. "I've covered civil rights issues, however. Tell me how you came to go to Hattiesburg and what compelled you to paint your experiences."

For the next twenty minutes she told him her story, as Rick took the opportunity to further study her panels. The reporter made copious notes, stopping here and there to ask her to elaborate. She explained her hopes for the exhibit, both for viewers of it and for a museum to own and circulate it.

"That's an enormous ambition for even a well-established artist," he noted. "What gives you the moxie to think your work merits this?"

She blushed. "I know it's a lot to hope for. But it's exactly that, my hope. I don't wish this for myself, but for the people I've painted...and those like them. If this work helps viewers to feel what these people have endured and moves some to take action, then it's done all I could have imagined."

"You're a new master's degree graduate of Parsons?"

"Yes."

"What's next for you?"

She laughed. "Right now I'm waiting to see what comes from the exhibit. But my thought is to paint the faces of the Civil Rights Movement in the North."

"Would this be as dramatic as your experience in Hattiesburg?"

She looked hard at Glen Frye. "When you've covered civil rights in New York or other places in the North, I'm sure you've seen all kinds of inequities. There may not be as many overt voter registration issues, but surely there are serious economic and social issues from equality of education, housing, and work opportunities to conditions leading to violence and incarceration. It's important to put faces to these conditions and know these are people with families, histories, needs, dreams, but often with no means to fulfill them. This weighs heavily on me."

"You've made your point," he remarked before asking several more questions and directing his photographers to get shots of her in front of her paintings.

"It appears that you're of Hispanic heritage," he said, studying her as she posed for the photographer. "Does not being an Anglo make you more sympathetic to blacks?"

She started, caught off guard. "Hispanic? No. Why do you say that?"

"It's your skin color, some of your features," he said.

"I can't explain that," she responded. "What I can tell you, however, is that all my life I felt I looked unlike the people around me. Yet there was no explanation for it—some distant relative perhaps…or just the way God made me I guess. What it's done however, is to make me more sensitive to the plight of people who've been labeled as 'different' or 'less than' someone else. As one who's felt that stigma and was not accepted because of it, yes, that may well have made me more sympathetic to people viewed this way."

Soon the interview concluded, and Delores accompanied the reporter and photographer as they exited.

"I'm glad that's over with," Gabrielle sighed her relief as she turned toward Rick. "What's with that Hispanic comment anyway? Did you hear that?"

Rick nodded and looked at her solemnly. "Gabrielle, you do look Hispanic in many ways. Have you not been told this before?"

She gazed at him for a minute. "I admit I've thought that any number of times. But there's no Hispanic heritage in my family."

"Are you sure about that?"

"That's what my mother told me."

"Would it matter if you were Hispanic?"

"Actually it would be a relief. At last I'd have an answer as to why I look and feel different. But it's quite impossible."

He appeared uncertain, but replied, "Well then, that's that. I don't know about you, but I'm starved. Should we get some lunch?"

After spending the afternoon in Central Park, they crossed Fifth Avenue and located a pay phone to call the PR office.

"I'm so glad you called," Delores exclaimed. "Leon Gander from the *Voice* wants to ask a few more questions. Can you phone him?"

"It's too noisy here," she said. "We'll have to come to your office."

Once there, she called him and answered questions that took some forty-five minutes. "I think I gave Gander everything but my Social Security and checking account numbers," she said as she hung up the phone.

"Sounded to me like he asked a lot of good questions," Rick commented.

"I would have to agree," Delores said. "It's not every day a publication like the *Voice* shows this much interest."

"I'm sure that's true," Gabrielle responded, "but I never thought about how much I'd have to bare myself. I've always been a very private person. I'm not used to people knowing so much about me. It makes me feel naked."

"A lot of people experience that," Delores affirmed, "but in truth, your paintings tell as much about you as your words do. Perhaps more."

Gabrielle scrutinized her. "I see what you mean. I just thought this work would be all about the subjects of my paintings—not all about *me*. I so wanted the focus to be on *them*, on *their* lives, *their* bravery in the face of horrific challenges."

"I understand," Delores said, looking sympathetic. "But *you* are part of the story you depicted. You're the witness who lived this and synthesized it through your unique artistic lens. You need to accept that you now are part of all this. Just as you appear in your paintings, so are you both creator and subject of your work. "

She stared at Delores. Gabrielle had underestimated her. "You're absolutely right. I have to get over this. I see what you're saying. If they focus on me, they also focus on the work and the people illustrated. They are one and the same."

"Exactly," Delores said.

Gabrielle checked her watch. "It's five-thirty…"

"Oh!" Delores interrupted. "We should turn on the TV. The NBC affiliate said they were running another spot on the exhibit. I should record this."

Rick pushed the TV "on" button as Delores fumbled with a tape. Deep into the newscast their story surfaced.

"The art exhibit that opened last night at the Parsons exhibition hall," the reporter began, "highlighted a unique collection of large canvases telling a story about the Civil Rights Movement in Hattiesburg, Mississippi, in 1965. It's a visual story of oppression and action taken by committed black citizens as well as civil rights workers, of which the artist was one.

"The exhibit is exceptional," he continued, "not only for its subject matter and the scale of the artwork, but for the fact that it was accomplished by a young Master of Fine Art graduate while she still was a student at Parsons."

The reporter's interview with Gabrielle followed the introduction. The camera then panned the entire room, showing the panels and the crowd, and took a quick clip with one of the better-known gallery owners. "If I had room for the entirety of this work," he said, "I would mount it in my gallery. Parts of the paintings may appear crude, but the story they tell and how they tell it is original and skillfully assembled. It's not for everyone, but it's a provocative statement and thoroughly worthy of exhibition and study."

The camera swung back to the reporter. "The show is free of charge and continues through the end of this month. David?" And with that, the segment ended.

"You couldn't have asked for more than that," Delores exclaimed triumphantly.

"I agree," Rick echoed.

"Calling some parts of my work crude sure stings. But I'm glad he found it provocative, which is the point."

"We may have more phone calls," Delores cautioned.

Gabrielle sighed and acknowledged that would be to the good. But all she wanted to do right now was to curl up in Rick's arms and shut out the world, even if it was just for a little while.

14

On Sunday Delores showed up at Gabrielle's room only shortly after they had gotten up and dressed. When Gabrielle opened the door, she saw Delores wearing an enormous grin and holding an armful of copies of *The New York Times*.

As Gabrielle opened the Sunday paper to the arts section, she found a half-page of photos of her and her paintings, her interview, and the comments of art critic Steven Weintraub. She skimmed the article.

"Ouch," Gabrielle remarked reading his criticism of her amateur status. But Delores dismissed it and summarized his viewpoint.

"Gabrielle, you should be ecstatic about this. Weintraub's review held you to a standard only far more seasoned artists could meet. Acknowledging this, he seemed impressed that a student could have conceived of and carried out such a massive project and pursued it with such passion and conviction. He picked at aspects of your paintings, but also expressed positives, like the size you chose to work in and how you echoed the muralists that inspired you." Delores looked very directly at her before continuing.

"Noting that while you have a way to travel to fully master your craft, he found it a worthy effort deserving to be seen and understood for the socially and politically significant work that it is. Gabrielle, Weintraub rarely heaps praise on anyone. Those who follow his critiques know this. You couldn't have gotten better from him. You'll find this will be helpful to you and the future of your paintings."

She remained uncertain. "Thanks Delores. I didn't expect a glowing report from the *Times*. It's just hard to see in print that you're a rank amateur, which of course I am."

Delores persevered. "You may be an amateur, in that you're not paid and are continuing to perfect your art, but you're a very good and adventuresome one. That counts for a lot in artistic circles."

"I'll try to remember that."

"I think the article is bully good," Rick said, looking up from scrutinizing the *Times* review. "We should go out and celebrate."

Gabrielle looked from one to the other. "I hope you're right. I should be happy. I am really. I'm just not used to being dissected this way."

"You'll get used to it, "Delores said. "I'm afraid, though, that you may not have much chance to celebrate over the next few days. This article is sure to generate more media calls."

"Then we'd better kick up our heels while we can," Rick said.

"I know when I'm being shown the door," Delores said. "Give me a call in a couple of hours if you can?"

"Sure—and thanks," she said as Delores exited and clicked down the hall in her spike heels.

With that, Rick put his arms around her and kissed her with passion. Then he picked her up and carried her back to bed.

* * *

Gabrielle had a couple of other interviews on Sunday with less-prestigious papers, taking up a good bit of her and Rick's day. Finally she and Rick were alone.

"Where's that picture of your family you were going to show me?" he asked.

"Right." She rummaged through her desk. "I don't know what I did with the more recent one, but here's one that was taken when I was seven and Ruth was eleven."

He scrutinized the photo. "Gabrielle, you look so different from the rest of your family."

"I know. My parents couldn't explain it either."

He nodded, but looked skeptical. "I don't know. Maybe it's worth pursuing again with them."

Her look carried perplexity and a painful sense of loss. She had been down this road so many times, her questioning yielding no gratification. She had no answer for Rick. Her face drooped in sadness and exhaustion.

Seeing this, he pivoted. "Well hopefully I'll get to meet them all sometime soon."

Early Tuesday morning he boarded a bus for Chicago, leaving a crater of a hole in Gabrielle.

In the coming days Delores and Parsons required more of her time for the exhibition and news media. Meanwhile, Gabrielle's anxiety grew as she waited to learn the ultimate fate of her panels. Even more disturbing were the questions about her heritage that *Newsday's* Glen Frye and Rick had raised, feeding her doubts.

And then, in the final three days of the show, Chairman Rabinowitz received a call from the Minneapolis Institute of Art. The curator stated the museum's willingness to pay one-hundred-thousand dollars for the eight panels and communicated their agreement to offer to circulate them to interested museums. As the chairman discussed the offer with Gabrielle and Parsons' faculty and administration, The Velvet Glove, a large and well-known SoHo gallery, came in with a one-hundred-and-twenty-thousand-dollar bid for the last two paintings in the series—the Reverend Jonas and the voter registration canvases. The gallery representative said she already had a buyer for the pair.

Two days remained for the exhibition. She was troubled by the gallery bid, in that she never had imagined the panels being split up or in private hands. She had envisioned them as being available to the public, which always had been the audience for which she had directed her series.

And then there was the lingering sadness of knowing that she soon would be parted from the eight panels she had labored over these past four years. She had given them everything she had. They were her children birthed and raised, now ready to go out into the world. But she knew she would suffer the loss of their presence, for they carried the lessons of her experiences, the longings of her heart, and the beliefs she nurtured in her very soul.

In the midst of the turmoil she was experiencing, a further complication arose. Her mother was due to come to town the next day to see the show before it closed. Gabrielle only had visited her parents a couple of times a year since she moved to the city—and Ruth came home even less often, given she resided in Boston now. Gabrielle was anxious for the chance to see her mother again. She felt badly, however, that her father still refused to acknowledge her success and the worthiness of the art education that enabled her to achieve this.

She was concerned too about the whole issue of her heritage and was worried about how Kay would respond to what the paintings reveal. Her mother always had a tendency to worry. So when Gabrielle returned from Hattiesburg, she explained away the scar on her cheek as the result of a clumsy fall. Now it was just modestly visible. She never told her parents about the attack on her bus that led to her injury or about the shot fired over her head. When Kay saw her work, she would understand the danger her daughter had put herself in by going south. She knew that Kay would be upset.

* * *

Waiting for her mother at an eatery at Penn Station, she felt a chill in this cavernous building with its impatient crowds. Brushing off her apprehension, she soon sighted Kay walking toward her with a big smile on her face. "So this is my famous daughter," Kay said hugging her, then pulling back to get a good look at her, a shadow of concern crossing Kay's face. "You look exhausted dear, but very pretty. I'm so glad to see you."

"Mom, it's good see you too. Do you want to catch some lunch in the Village, or would you rather eat here?"

"I'm terribly anxious to see your exhibit. Could we have lunch later? It's only eleven o'clock."

"Of course Mom, whatever you want. Let's go and catch the subway downtown."

Soon they were on campus and heading for the exhibition hall.

"I haven't seen you in months," Kay said, turning toward her daughter. "I'd hoped that going to school in the city would mean we'd see more of you."

Momentarily irritated by Kay's anticipated comment, she had to acknowledge that her mother had every right to point out her absences from their family life. "I'm sorry about that," Gabrielle mustered. "I've been so occupied with finishing my schoolwork and getting the paintings ready to exhibit—and now dealing with the news media. You can't imagine the time the media takes. They ask so many questions and sometimes get things wrong, which takes even more time. It's been so hectic."

"I understand dear. It's just that I miss seeing my daughters. Ruth gets down here maybe once or twice a year at most. I don't see you much more than that. It's hard to not see my girls."

She looked closely at her mother. Her hair had grown grayer over the last four years, and the worry lines on her brow and around her eyes had deepened. She was a little thinner too. "I know Mom. I'm sorry about that. How's Dad?"

"I'm afraid he wasn't up to coming to your exhibit. He's getting older like the rest of us…and he still drinks too much. It'll be the death of him, Gabrielle. I feel sure of it. But today is about you, not about us older folks and our problems. I saw the article in *The New York Times*. Mrs. Johnson next door brought it over to us. My little girl, all grown up and in the *Times*. Imagine that. I'm so proud of you dear."

"Thanks Mom. Here we are."

When they entered the hall, Kay appeared almost overwhelmed when she viewed the size and number of the panels in person. "Goodness, I had no idea."

"It works best if you start over here Mom. The paintings tell a story, so you'll want to begin at the first one."

When Kay got to the painting depicting the mob attacking the bus, her face paled. "Gabrielle, is this what really happened?"

"Yes. Everything you see here is just how it happened."

"You could have been killed."

"Yes, but I wasn't."

"If your father and I'd had any idea it was this dangerous, we never would have signed those papers giving our permission for you to go down there."

"I know Mom."

Then when they arrived at the panel showing a shot fired over Gabrielle's head, Kay's knees gave way. She would have fallen if her daughter hadn't moved to catch her.

"Gabrielle! How could you have put yourself in such danger? It's a miracle you came home alive. Why would you take such risks?"

Owning her emotions, Gabrielle exhaled slowly, saying nothing as she coaxed her mother toward the next painting.

"Well I understand now why you couldn't come visit your father and me," Kay finally acknowledged after viewing all eight panels. "I don't know how you managed to do all this at the same time you were taking classes. It's really remarkable. And look at all these people here in the middle of the day—must be thirty or forty. I understand now what all the fuss was about. But I have to tell you that what you experienced in Mississippi horrifies me. I don't know what I would have done if you had been badly hurt…or worse."

Absorbing her mother's fears, she sighed and changed the subject. "You must be hungry and a little tired, and it's still quite warm outside. Why don't we catch lunch here in the Village."

Within a half-hour they settled into chairs at a café on Bleecker Street. After ordering salads and beverages and getting caught up on news about Ruth, her dad, Mrs. Bealey, the neighbors, and extended family members, she told Kay about Rick. "So I guess you'd say I've fallen crazy in love with my longtime best friend."

"I'm so glad to hear this. After things didn't work out with that Turkish fellow, you seemed to have sworn off men."

"For a while. But then I got so absorbed in these paintings, I just didn't have time for them."

"Well now you'll have more time. I'm so happy for you. When will I have a chance to meet this young man?" Kay smiled, looking hopeful.

"Believe it or not, you didn't miss him by much. He came down for the exhibit opening, but he had to get back to work in Chicago. He was sorry to miss you. He's a community organizer there."

"That's nice dear. Do you have a picture of him?"

"I do." She dug into her purse and pulled out a photo she shot in Chicago.

Kay studied the snapshot. "He's rather nice-looking, don't you think?"

"I do," she grinned.

"What religion is he?"

"He was brought up Jewish. Mom, I want to ask you something." She studied her mother. "I was showing Rick a picture of you, dad, and Ruth. He remarked that I didn't look at all like any of you. Because of this he seemed skeptical of what I understand my heritage to be. One reporter even asked me if I was Hispanic." She hesitated, noting that Kay appeared uncomfortable.

"All my life I've known that I looked unlike everyone around me—my family, the kids at school, the neighbors—until I came to New York City and was surrounded by such diverse ethnicities. I've thought that I appear more Hispanic than I do Danish, German, English, Dutch, and everything else I'm supposed to be. All my life I've wanted answers to questions about my origins. The older I get, the more important this becomes. If there's anything at all you can think of that would help me to find the reason I look different, it would mean the world to me."

Kay started as she observed her daughter who had seen the look of panic in her mother's eyes. Then the little bread plate Kay had picked up fell from her hand and shattered on the tile floor. After the waiter disposed of the broken plate and its contents, Kay, visibly shaking, struggled to calm herself. As she looked at Gabrielle, she must have seen the pain in her daughter's eyes. It caused her to pull herself together. Growing very still, she took a deep breath and commenced to tell her daughter the whole story of how she became her and Arthur's child.

As her mother spoke, Gabrielle's eyes grew wide in amazement. She couldn't believe what Kay was telling her.

Adopted? From a Catholic orphanage in a small town in southern New Mexico? She had been left in a basket on the steps of an old mission in San Miguel, then saved from a wild dog by the priest who found her? *Why did she never tell me this before?* Gabrielle thought as she fought to control the turmoil raging in her mind. *I've asked her time and again about my heritage. Adopted? I was adopted? Saved from a wild dog?*

Outraged, she demanded Kay give her every detail she could remember. Suddenly Gabrielle knew that she wouldn't rest until she found someone who could connect her to her birth family and her genetic heritage.

As Kay spoke, Gabrielle trembled, growing more and more exasperated. "How could you Mom?" she said, struggling not to raise her voice. "How could you lie to me all these years?"

Kay began to cry as she answered, "When I was growing up, adopted kids were stigmatized. I didn't want you to go through that. I didn't want you to feel different."

"But I *did* feel different! I always felt different!" she said, her voice growing more intense. "Your saying I wasn't was a lie. How could you not tell me this before?" Gabrielle's eyes burned with accusation.

Kay now cried audibly. Everyone in the café was looking at them.

"Mom, we have to go." She dug into her purse and pulled out bills that she knew would more than cover their lunch. Then she got up and left with her mother. They found a park bench away from passers-by. Kay couldn't stop weeping. "I thought I was doing the right thing," she kept saying. "I...I..."

"But when I was grown and off to college, surely you could have told me then."

Kay hung her head. "I was afraid...."

"Afraid of what?"

"...Afraid...I'd lose you if I told you."

"What? And that was more important than telling the truth?"

"At the time...I thought...it was...the right thing to do," Kay gasped.

"For you or for me?" Gabrielle elevated her voice, oblivious to people walking by.

Kay continued to sob.

"Mom I have to go. I can't talk to you anymore right now."

"Can you ever…forgive me?"

Gabrielle was silent. "I'll get you a cab to Penn Station."

Kay tried to wipe the tears from her face as Gabrielle put her in the taxi, paid the driver, then closed the door without uttering another word. As the car pulled away from the curb, she turned her back to it and walked toward her dorm, tears streaming down her face, her hands clenched in anger.

Back in her room, she slammed the door, leaning against it. She breathed deeply, then more rapidly. Grabbing books and shoes, she hurled them against the wall. Her breath grew fast with a rising rage. Shaking, she ran to her desk, pulling at the drawer with such force that it fell to the floor, cracking and scattering its contents. She bent down on her knees. Frantically she sought her family picture. As her hand found it, it seared her heart as if it were fire. Burning, she ripped the photo in half. Gripping the image of her parents, she faltered, then tore it to pieces as a sob rose in her. Shattered, she found herself unable to rise, agony burying her. "How could you, Mom?" she moaned. "How could you?"

15

She dragged through the days following her mother's revelation. Wounded by knowledge coming decades late, she relived times too numerous to count when awareness of her adoption could have altered her life. She might have had answers to questions she pondered, to hurts she didn't understand. She could have had a history rooted in the heritage and circumstances of her birth. The cruelty of school kids would have had a name, not just endless questions she wrestled with as a child. Why don't they like me? Am I ugly? Why do they make fun of me? Why does no one invite me to dances or parties? Why don't I have more friends?

Gabrielle thought that while her mother's rationale may have been protection, she believed it had been her right to know the truth, to own it. As a child, each time she asked her mother about how different she looked from everyone around her, her mother's disavowal denied her strength and ability to handle the truth. Questions begged answers. Not giving them diminished her, she contended. In so doing, she—and her family—lived a lie. The truth matters, she wept. It's the core of connection, the substance of trust in relationships.

Her nights left her swimming in dreams, conjuring circumstances from her childhood and all the confusion and inadequacy she experienced as a young person. In the ether of her dreaming, she felt her angst as an olive-skinned child in an all-white world and how it hurt her to always be on the outside looking in. While acknowledging her family's love, she believed her parents never grasped her need for an identity that was real, whole, and not manufactured to mask her difference. In refusing truth, she concluded, they made her appearance a stigma, made her "less than" others, her life smaller, lacking, something to be ashamed of, hidden from view.

In time she calmed enough to make a pact with herself. *I need to separate for a while from the turmoil created by mom's revelations. My paintings are in jeopardy. I have to keep my attention on them until their fate is determined. When it is, I'll pursue this new knowledge wherever it leads. I have to find my roots, no matter what the cost. I have to know the full truth of who I am!*

When the exhibition ended and no new bids were on the table, the chairman sat down with Gabrielle, Professor Ray, and members of Parsons' administrative team. The paper she had signed when Parsons consented to fund her effort and extend her scholarship, was that Parsons had the right to own the final product of the planned series if it so chose. The administrative staff wanted to enable the school to return any proceeds from the work to a scholarship fund to help other students with special efforts. The chairman and Professor Ray supported the spirit of the pact, but suggested a modest stipend from the sale to provide her with some support while looking for work.

In addition there was the question of which offer to accept. The administration discussed taking the higher bid, but she argued passionately against it. "I would rather you give me nothing than split up the series. Its power is in the whole. Remove the final two pieces, and the first six become aimless. I ask you, *please* don't do that. I would do anything to keep the eight intact."

Then Professor Ray had an idea and turned to the chairman. "Do you think Minneapolis would be willing to sweeten the deal by giving Parsons ten percent of the net proceeds from each installation of the series at another museum?"

The chairman knitted his brow. "I don't know, but it's an interesting thought. I certainly would be willing to give it a try." The administrators consented to let the chairman make his bid, and the meeting ended. When they left, Gabrielle stayed behind with her mentors. "Whatever happens," she said, "I beseech you to please never agree to split up the series. I'm also concerned about selling to private individuals, in that the paintings seem less likely to be viewed by the public in general."

The chairman responded, "Neither Professor Ray nor I want to see that happen. We plan to do everything we can to keep the exhibit intact. Private versus pubic is another matter, as wealthy individuals may loan their private collections to museums. This would of course still split up the series, which we'll argue against. The administrators, however, have the final say, as they provided a significant part of the original funding. But they're good people who understand the artistic impulse behind keeping the series intact. They just have a lot to balance in making their determination."

"I see," she said. "I appreciate your support. Please let me know when you hear back from Minneapolis."

"I will," the chairman said. "I'm afraid I have to be going now."

"I need to as well," Professor Ray echoed as he watched her. "Come and see me anytime. But Miss Andersen, please try not to worry. Things have a way of working themselves out."

Feeling helpless, she shook her head in acknowledgment, but her heart sank. She hadn't thought much about the paper she signed years ago, not realizing that she could lose control over what happened to her work after she graduated. It wasn't the money, although she certainly needed it. It was the integrity of her work that was at stake. She only could hope that in the end, the administrators would embrace this understanding and assure that the series remained complete.

* * *

It was a week before Minneapolis responded. The museum said that they couldn't raise their original bid, which had been a stretch for them in present circumstances. Their dispatch concluded: "We were willing to take a gamble on a young, largely unknown artist, save for recent media articles, because of the importance of her subject matter in today's sociopolitical climate. We also have been willing to try to interest other museums to exhibit the series, not an easy feat given the lack of public knowledge of the artist and the space requirements of the canvases. We still are interested in the series, but only under the terms we outlined in our original bid."

"Well we gave it a try," the chairman said. "Now it's up to the administration to decide which offer to take."

"Is there no other option, should they decide to accept the higher bid?" she asked, a note of desperation in her voice.

"I'm afraid not," the chairman said.

"Professor Ray, what about the man from the Museum of Modern Art, the one who gave me his card at the exhibit opening and that I left with you last week?"

"I already checked with him" he said. "He only had the names of galleries that he thought might be interested in the paintings."

"We really need to find a good caretaker for the panels," the chairman added. "And remember you'll have a chance to argue your case again. Gaining the support of a majority of administrators won't be easy. One has been quite vocal about taking the higher bid. And though we'd like to see you get a modest stipend from the sale of your work, we think that more importantly, it could provide a bargaining chip with the budget custodians."

A meeting of all the parties involved in the decision was set for the following afternoon. She had reviewed the situation at length with Rick and with Professor Ray. Both encouraged her to speak from the heart, but to keep in mind that the administrators were just trying to do the right thing by the college and all its students.

"Before you make your decision about the offers on the table, Miss Andersen would like to say a few words," the chairman said.

Gabrielle stood and struggled to hide her nervousness as she watched this gathering of solemn men and women. "I wanted to thank you for having given me assistance for my Parsons education and for these paintings that are the subject of our discussion. Surely you understand better than administrators anywhere, the importance of preserving artistic integrity.

"Almost four years ago," she said, her voice growing resonant with the strength of her convictions, "I was compelled to undertake this work by the circumstances of my experiences in the Civil Rights Movement in Hattiesburg, Mississippi, and conditions that still exist in one form or another throughout our country today. I felt called to bear witness to the inhumanity of inequality and the humanity of those who suffer under it.

"I always viewed the general public as the audience for this work. Its purpose is to educate and touch people with the Hattiesburg story and perhaps cause discussion and action to support people suffering from repression and retribution—thus working to help counter systemic racism. My understanding has been that this very intention was what originally encouraged you to help fund my work."

Studying the faces of those in attendance, she continued, their show of interest emboldening her. "I certainly can understand why you would consider the higher bid. But accepting it would destroy the story that the eight panels tell as a group—and with it, the ultimate power of the full body of this work and its intention. It would render the paintings incomplete, without form. The intent and impact of producing a mural-like series of large works, works that capture a piece of American history that we forget at our peril, would be lost. The first six pieces mean little without the last two. And the last two alone lack the story that informs their meaning." She looked from one person to another.

"I implore you to *please, please* keep the work intact and let Minneapolis have a chance to offer it to other museums nationwide. As you well know, murals are a *public* art, an art that belongs to the people. I created this work to echo their scale and intent. I am forever grateful for all your support and for allowing me to speak. But I beg of you, please help me to preserve what this work was created to accomplish."

The administrators requested that she leave the room while they deliberated. Pacing back and forth in the hallway, she was terrified that the outcome might not be good. Tense and sweaty, wracked with worry that the purpose of her work could be foiled by six of her panels lying in storage somewhere, she quickened her pace. But try as she might, she couldn't dispel her lingering sense of dread. Nearly an hour later, the chairman opened the door and called her back into the room.

"After much discussion and some division of thought," the group's leader reported, "the majority voted to accept the museum's offer."

Released from the turmoil raging in her mind, she thought she might faint. She had to fight to keep her composure.

He continued. "We also don't want to see the work that we have underwritten over several years dismantled and its ultimate intention interrupted. We do, however, have a responsibility to assist other students with opportunities such as you have enjoyed, which is why this discussion was necessary. Because of our commitment to *all* of our students, we are not in a position to share the proceeds of the sale of your work with you and must add them to a fund to aid other promising students. We hope you can understand that we cannot provide support to you beyond your time here at Parsons."

He paused, looking meaningfully at her and at Chairman Rabinowitz before concluding. "It will be up to you from this point forward to discover how to sustain yourself as an artist, something most of our students also must do. We encourage you to apply for arts grants as soon as possible. You've already had the benefit of one such grant that Chairman Rabinowitz obtained early in your series effort, so you have some familiarity with the process. Professors Rabinowitz and Ray can guide you toward the grantors most likely to be interested in the type of art that you practice. We wish you well in your life going forward, Miss Andersen, and we're glad to have been of help to you these past several years."

"I will be forever grateful for your decision," she responded, her voice laden with emotion. "What was most important to me was that you understood and respected the importance of preserving my work in its entirety and its intention to be available to the public. I'm heartened that other student artists may find assistance similar to what you've granted me over the years. I can't thank you enough for supporting the purpose for which I created this work and for all your help since I came here."

Leaving the administration building, she walked the campus. She was relieved to the point of tears that the museum would purchase and circulate her series. They would be the caretakers she had prayed for. This work carried her soul's longings for acceptance for people of color.

She should have experienced a sense of triumph. But the cloud left by her parents' lifelong betrayal of the truth of her birth and her adoption hung over her with a heaviness that suffocated. How could she ever look at her adoptive parents again without feeling their betrayal? And how, after all these years, would she ever find her birth family? She had so little to go on. But this new awareness of her beginnings stoked a fire within her to find the truth of her birth, wherever it led. This was her mission now. Without knowledge of her true ancestry, she felt unmoored. She sought the truth. She *had* to know.

~IX~
INTO THE UNKNOWN

1971-1972 – Chicago to New Mexico

1

"Gabrielle, I understand your need to find your birth family and how your feelings toward your parents have changed," Rick said, softening his response as he absorbed the pain he heard in her voice.

She was holding the phone and listening to him as if he were her last refuge.

"I just wish you were here now so I could hold you. You have so much happening in your life right now. I think you're at a defining moment as a painter. The *Voice* ran such a great piece about your artwork and the quality of it--and the importance of the subject matter. This really is the time to apply for arts grants and get backing to do what you've dreamed of doing."

"I know, but you can't imagine how I've longed to understand my heritage. It's consuming me, Rick. For Christ's sake, I almost was killed by a wild dog after being abandoned on the steps of a New Mexico mission. How can I not pursue this?"

"I hear you Gabrielle. And of course you must pursue it. I'm only talking about timing. It's possible you may be an Hispanic woman, but you also are a young artist on the verge of an amazing career. Why don't you come back to Chicago, stay with me while you apply for grants—and *then* go?"

"It's hard right now to think about anything other than what my mother told me."

Into the Unknown

"I know. But going there in anger isn't good either. You need to try to make peace with your mother's fears."

"*Her* fears?"

"Yes. You said she first was afraid that the truth would damage your childhood. Then she feared it would change your relationship with her. People's love can be complicated Gabrielle. It's part of being human."

She hesitated. "I hear what you're saying. But there were so many lies, Rick! It's hard for me to forgive that and trust my parents again. And I may have this new knowledge too late. I was born twenty-five years ago. People move someplace else—or die. The longer I wait, the greater chance I have of never finding my birth family. Without that I'll never fully know who I am."

"This is true Gabrielle. I hear the hurt in your voice. Just please consider giving yourself time to digest what's happened these last few weeks before you run off to New Mexico." He stopped, then continued. "But whatever you decide, I'll support you. You're a smart, good person, and I know that you'll do the right thing."

Flushed with emotion she responded. "Thank you Rick. I love you."

"I love you too Gabrielle."

She struggled with what Rick said and the sense that it made. But her feeling of betrayal by her parents and her drive to know her truth burned in her belly with a fire she couldn't extinguish. Wrestling with her path forward, she sought Professor Ray's counsel.

"That's hard news to receive," he responded, leaning forward on his office desk as his hair shifted forward onto his shoulders. "I can only imagine the shock you must have felt when you learned that you'd been adopted. I can understand your sense of betrayal. It would be only natural." He wrinkled his brow in concentration. "I also can imagine the courage it took for your mother to admit the truth after all these years. Owning up to one's failings is not an easy thing, as I'm sure you know. Be that as it may, I also understand your anxiousness to find your true heritage."

She watched him pause, gathering his thoughts and weighing his words, his eyes meeting hers. "Two things occur to me," he said. "One is that you have the rarest of opportunities right now. As a young artist you're riding the crest of a wave fueled by your exhibition and the response of the news media and others in the arts world. Your panels are going to a fine museum and have the potential to circulate to other museums over time. You will not have another opportunity quite like this again, Miss Andersen. So you'll have to think long and hard about walking away from it now, now while so many doors are open to you. People can become forgetful of you if you don't continue to pursue what you've begun."

She looked down in thought, then raised her head to meet his eyes as he continued.

"The second thing is that you have to be exhausted after these last years and the months leading up to the exhibition and its aftermath. The journey to the Southwest that you want to take now will require a great deal of you emotionally and physically. It could take months to follow the threads that arise during your search. You also don't know how you'll be received and how you'll respond to what you learn."

She observed his earnest face and the perceptiveness of his thoughts. "It might be prudent to give yourself time to rest and to level some of the emotion you're experiencing now," he continued. "It will help you to process what you're learning and deal better with whatever comes up. Taking time now to make your grant applications will give you the chance to be fully ready for your journey, while also assuring you'll have the best possible future as an artist to return to.

"I understand your sense of urgency," he acknowledged, shifting in his chair. "But as I age, I see more and more that delaying a little before throwing caution to the wind can be wisdom. You already have waited decades for your answer. Another few months likely will matter very little." He stopped, his eyes probing hers. She diverted her gaze, not knowing what to say.

Into the Unknown

"Just think about it my dear," he said gently. "You'll choose thoughtfully and ultimately, I believe, with compassion as well—toward yourself...and others."

After saying her goodbyes, she packed up and shipped her sketches and photographs, class paintings, art supplies, and books to Rick's apartment. Then she put her remaining belongings in two suitcases and boarded a bus for Chicago to live with Rick and sort out this next phase of her life.

Having a lot of time to ponder on the ride there, she thought about the many times she questioned her mother about her appearance, so different from everyone she knew. She recalled her mother telling her that likely there was an ancestor way back who looked like her. At the time, that made some sense to young Gabrielle. But like all the other times she sought an answer, it was a lie. It was this that she couldn't accept.

Then she reviewed her final talk with Professor Ray and acknowledged why he and the chairman thought she shouldn't delay her grant requests. Shortly after their meeting they sent her their list of granting agencies they recommended she apply to and reiterated their willingness to act as references for her. She couldn't, however, help but acknowledge Professor Ray's implied belief that she should make peace with her parents. Still mired in her memories of the hurts she suffered as a young person, however, she couldn't let go of her belief that the truth could have helped her navigate a childhood filled with rejection and unanswered questions.

Still, knowing that Rick and the professors were right in many respects, she finally resigned herself to delaying traveling to New Mexico. But she couldn't help but be haunted by Kay's actions, her own ire and sorrow, and her drive to pursue her quest for her birth family. This was all she could think about. That...and Rick...and Professor Ray's parting words to her.

* * *

After two months in Chicago where she slept late, worked most of the day on grant proposals, and savored the joy of her relationship with Rick, she came to better understand the sagacity of his and the professor's earlier counseling. She found herself calmer now than she had been in years and even began to release some of the disappointment and acrimony she felt toward her parents.

As she explored Chicago, she sketched city residents and street scenes and studied artwork displayed at the Art Institute of Chicago and city galleries. On weekends and sometimes in the evenings, she and Rick would walk together through different parts of the city. They would laugh and tease one another, uplifting them both at a complicated time in Gabrielle's life.

As her heart lightened, she discovered a growing affinity to Rick's adopted city. She also found that she loved cooking dinner for him and hearing about his day over bites of pasta or chicken. He would tell her about the progress he and his colleagues made, small steps though they might be, and ask about her day. Their lovemaking was passionate and frequent, and the bond between them grew.

As two months stretched to four, however, her drive to explore her roots gnawed at her with increasing urgency. One night, while the candlelight on the dinner table flickered as they finished their meal, she reached for his hand.

"Sweetheart," she began, "these past months have been some of the happiest of my life."

"What do you mean 'some'?" he quipped.

"Oh, you bad boy," she responded slapping his hand and laughing. Then she grew serious. "I've finished all the grant applications the professors urged me to write, and it's likely to be months before I hear the results. Now's the time to travel to San Miguel and search for my birth family."

He studied her. "Yes Gabrielle, I knew this was coming. But you…you've become so much a part of me that the thought of you leaving for a time has grown harder. We've been apart before, but this time it's different. Our love has deepened. I hardly know anymore where you leave off and I begin. It's almost as if we were one person. Does that make any sense?'

She nodded.

"Can't you wait a little longer?" he asked, showing a moment of irritation. "I guess I just hoped it wouldn't be so soon. When are you talking about going?'

"I have some things to put in place, but I'm hoping for a week from Saturday."

"Oh...so soon!"

"I'm sorry!"

They both drifted in silence until he said with resignation, "What's your plan when you get there?"

"First I'll find the orphanage my mom mentioned and see what they can tell me."

"You know that the records you want likely will be sealed."

"That's what I understand. But I have to try. If I can't get any help there, I'll go to the mission where I was found."

"You know the name of it?"

"No, but I'll go to whatever old missions are in San Miguel until I get the information I'm looking for."

"What if nothing surfaces there?"

Looking thoughtful, she responded, "It's possible it might not. I guess I'll try to find if the town newspaper's archives have anything. I'll just have to be there and hope I'll uncover clues."

"I wish I could go with you, but it's quite impossible," he said.

"In any case I really think I need to go alone. People are more apt to open up if fewer others are involved."

She gazed at him, sensing his hurt and longing. She never knew she could love anyone as she did him. "My love...," she said as she stood, drained wineglasses in her hands, her face filled with a tumble of emotions. He rose and reached for her, drawing her to him. As the glasses fell from her hands, shattering on the floor, he kicked them aside as their lips found one another. His fingers sought the curves of her ears, the parting of her lips, the hollow at the base of her neck, the valley between her breasts, the curve of her stomach. Everything seemed to her to spin as passion took them. The candle flickered. And then it went out.

2

She called a travel agent to book a one-way airline ticket, a rental car, and a week's stay at an inexpensive motel in San Miguel. Then she packed a suitcase, including sketching supplies, a notebook, and her camera.

In no time it was Friday night, and she and Rick looked at each other across plates of lasagna. She saw resignation in his eyes and attempted to be cheerful. How quickly they had grown closer than she had ever been with anyone. The prospect of separating, even for just a few weeks, proved more wrenching than she imagined. But the pain that seared her most now was that of not knowing where she came from and the acknowledgment that her childhood had been a lie.

In the morning Rick took her to the airport. His kiss goodbye lingered on her lips as she walked to the plane, the shadow of him at the window, waving to her as she crossed into the unknown she was destined to explore.

In truth her time away could be weeks or months. All she knew for certain was that she wouldn't return until she learned something that tied her to a mother, perhaps a father, and a family that would explain her heritage. Feeling anguish, she saw herself as being not only different, but incomplete. Without finding the source of the very blood that ran in her veins, she believed her life always would have a crucial, missing puzzle piece, leaving the picture of her life wanting.

* * *

As the plane neared Tucson, Arizona, Gabrielle's anticipation of what she would find heightened. Upon landing, she retrieved her rental car, got directions to San Felipe de Jesús, a

Into the Unknown

town a short distance from San Miguel. It looked to be a four- to five-hour drive on Interstate 10 east and then south into the most southwestern part of New Mexico.

Initially she drove into the Sonoran Desert, the road taking her past giant saguaro cactus and scenes of scrub, ranches, farms, and mountains. Although it was early February, the sun beat down brazen and steady. Hours later, she decided to try to locate the Orphanage of Our Blessed Mother before seeking her motel in San Miguel. The sign as she entered San Felipe de Jesús read, "Population 343." Gabrielle thought it was the smallest town she had ever visited. Soon thereafter, she spotted the children's home.

Parking across from it and its white-painted sign, she rolled down the window and turned off the car. She gazed at an old, odd-looking structure, mixing adobe walls with wooden and stone ones, likely later additions. A large front porch wrapped partway around the side. As she watched, the front door of the building opened. A nun walked onto the porch and watered several containers of plants. When the woman looked up, she seemed to glance toward Gabrielle's car, then turned and reentered the building.

Staring at the scene, she felt a rush of excitement. So this was the orphanage where she had remained before Kay came to claim her twenty-six years ago. Of course she was too young then to recall anything. She wondered if anyone still was there who would know her birth parents. Should she leave her car now and cross the street, knock on the door, and ask for the Reverend Mother Juanita? This was the only name Kay was able to recall when she pressed her mother for information.

The more she thought about it, the more nervous she became. Checking her watch she realized it already was late afternoon. She had been up since six o'clock this morning. Suddenly she felt exhausted and fearful. What if no one had any information for her? What would she do next? She shook her head. *I can't think about all this now. I should drive to San Miguel, check into the motel, and get some rest. In the morning I'll call the orphanage and make an appointment. I need to have my wits about me when I return here.*

With this resolve Gabrielle switched on the ignition before turning her head toward the orphanage one last time. What she witnessed moved her to turn off the engine. It was the vision of a young nun wearing spectacles and carrying a baby onto the porch. Watching the nun seat herself on a swing anchored to the porch roof, Gabrielle thought she heard the squeak of the chair as it moved and the low hum of the nun crooning to the infant she held lovingly in her arms. She had been a newborn like this once, she thought. *I wonder if I was as loved as this child appears to be.*

As she restarted the car, her eyes swam with tears. The image of the nun and baby pressed itself into her mind that now filled with imaginings of the orphanage and all the things that may have occurred and comprised precious pieces of her past.

* * *

Sunday morning, as light filtered through the aging Venetian blinds of the motel window, Gabrielle checked the time. It was six-forty-five. It was too early to call for an appointment, so she lay in bed and surveyed her motel room. It seemed somewhat clean, but the bedspreads, curtains, carpets, and fixtures were old and worn and carried smells of tobacco and all the travelers who had been there before her. This was, however, the only motel in San Miguel, a town of just twelve hundred people.

When she drove here yesterday from San Felipe de Jesús, she could see that San Miguel was a poor community with dirt side streets. Between the two towns grew pecan trees and fields with remnants of last year's chili peppers and pumpkins, corn, squash, beans, onion, and potato crops. Shanties dotted the landscape. When she entered the outskirts of town, she saw modest adobe and wooden houses along the main road into San Miguel.

Leaving the motel, she headed for breakfast at the town's only restaurant, the Esperanza Café. She immediately felt an affinity to it, the name of which translated as "hope," the very thing she harbored.

It was a classic greasy spoon, occupied by a variety of people far more Mexican than Anglo and mostly men. She ordered

Into the Unknown

scrambled eggs and biscuits. The eggs were seasoned so heavily with hot sauce that they made her eyes water and her nose run. She had to down two glasses of water and a cup of coffee to get them down. Reaching for paper napkins to wipe her eyes and nose, she noticed several people staring at her, making her self-conscious.

After breakfast she returned to her room and called the orphanage for an appointment with the Reverend Mother. The nun who answered put her on hold. Ten minutes later the nun told her she could come at one-thirty if she had to see the Reverend Mother today. Thanking her, she hung up and immediately called Rick.

"Hello?"

"Hi Sweetie," she said.

"Goodness, what time is it?"

"Eight-thirty your time, I think. You're usually up by now."

"Yeah. I stayed up late last night watching this dumb movie. Can't even remember the name of it. Let me call you back. This is gonna cost you a fortune if I don't. Let me make a cup of coffee too. I'll ring you in twenty minutes. Okay?"

"Sure. Talk to you then."

While she waited she emptied her suitcase, hung up her clothes, put her personal items in the bathroom, and laid her camera, notepad, and sketching supplies on the nightstand.

The phone rang. "Rick?"

"None other. Ah, coffee makes all the difference."

"It was the only way I could get my super-peppered eggs down this morning," she said.

"That's right. You're in chili pepper country. So what are your plans for today?"

"I have my appointment at the orphanage this afternoon."

"That was quick."

"Yes. I thought I'd walk around San Miguel a little this morning, have some lunch, then drive on over."

"Sounds good. Are you nervous about your meeting?"

"I *am*, but I'm also excited. They didn't tell me the person I'll be speaking with. I'm hoping it will be the Reverend Mother Juanita—that she's still there or that I can find her."

"I hope so. I know how much this means to you."

"It's just good to hear your voice. I miss you, Rick."

"I miss you too. I'll call you tonight and hope things go well for you today. Love you."

As she hung up the receiver, she sighed, then grabbed her camera and stuffed it into her shoulder bag before heading out. When she was at the Esperanza Café earlier this morning, she asked the cashier, a short Mexican with a thick mustache and a heavy accent, if the town had a Catholic mission. He mentioned that there was an old one at the end of Mission Street, accessed by heading west on Main Street. It was only ten o'clock, so she decided to walk. If nothing else, she thought that the mission might prove architecturally interesting and give her a little spiritual nourishment for the day ahead.

Outside the motel she felt February's chill breeze, making her glad she brought her warm jacket. Several stores lined Main Street—a general store of sorts, a bakery, three bars, a small hardware store, a grocery, a second-hand shop, and the café. All but the grocery and café were closed on Sunday. Numerous small houses edged the street beyond the shops. Some of them were made of wood, some covered in stucco, others adobe. At last she came to Mission Street.

Walking into the mission's courtyard, she realized she was seeing a piece of New Mexico history—and perhaps a piece of her history as well. She thought that the building had to be over a hundred years old. As she walked up its steps, she believed that this might be where she was found. She shuddered at the thought of her abandonment and rescue from a wild dog. She wondered whether some member of her birth family had attended this church, or even if she might have been baptized here.

Entering the building, she saw a service in progress. Sliding into a pew at the back, she noted mostly Hispanic parishioners and whole families with children and grandparents. Not much older than she was, the priest in his plain cassock was conducting the service in Spanish. The congregation kneeled during prayer and responded as directed. They took communion with a piece of broken bread and a sip from a common cup, while a woman sang as the faithful filed to and from the nave.

She thought that the woman's voice was a touch of beauty in a space that had such simplicity of design and substance that the cross in the sanctuary stood out like a golden light. There were no stained-glass windows, no organ, no tapestries, no adornments of any kind to compete with the brilliance of the cross.

But it was this very simplicity that touched her. For just a moment she felt the way she did as a young child watching from her bedroom window as the light of the moon appeared to grow into a cross in the night sky. That sensation of love that washed over her then filled her now, giving her a sense of comfort from something greater than any human. She said a prayer, asking God to help her through this day. As the woman's singing ended and Gabrielle looked up, it struck her how long it had been since she had prayed.

As the service closed, she rose from her pew and exited this place of worship, this monument to a history that in some manner she felt part of. From the courtyard she saw the parishioners file out of church and wondered if she might be related to any of them. To her, each face represented a chance for a connection and a possible lifeline to her personal history, a past holding the truth of what may have happened here twenty-six years ago.

3

Feeling as if she were in a dream, she left the mission grounds and walked back onto the dirt road. She considered approaching the young priest, but he was busy with his parishioners—and it already was eleven-thirty. Picking up her pace, she realized she would have just two hours to get lunch and prepare for her meeting at the orphanage.

She purchased a turkey sandwich and tomato juice at the grocery store and returned to her motel room. There she reviewed what she wanted to inquire about and how to approach the nun she would meet. At one o'clock she left her motel room, got into her rental car, and drove to San Felipe de Jesús. Having a few minutes to spare, she sat in her car across the street from the orphanage and again went over everything she wanted to ask. Then she shot a picture of the building before raising her window and exiting the vehicle. Shortly she stood on the orphanage porch and rang the doorbell. It took a couple of minutes for a nun to appear.

"Yes?" she asked.

"I'm Gabrielle Andersen. I have an appointment."

"Oh yes, please come in."

Gabrielle thought she recognized the bespectacled nun she had viewed holding the baby the day before. As she followed her down the hallway with its stone floor, plastered walls, and antiseptic smell, she heard babies crying and the squeals and shouts of children playing. Their sounds echoed through the aging hallways and followed them as they walked. When they reached the administration office, the nun gestured for her to be seated. "She shouldn't be long," the Sister said.

"Can you tell me the name of the person I'll be meeting with?"

"Sorry, I thought you'd been told that already. You'll meet with the Reverend Mother Felicia."

"Thank you."

The nun nodded and left, closing the door to the hallway. It suddenly became very quiet in the spartan room that seemed chilly despite the sunlight spilling through the window across from her.

Then a door opened and a hinge creaked. She heard the Reverend Mother's shoes tapping the tiles before she saw her walking toward her.

"Miss Andersen?"

"Yes."

Into the Unknown

Although the aging nun wore glasses, Gabrielle could see that her eyes and her smile were kind, making her relax a little. "I appreciate your seeing me so quickly," she said as the Reverend Mother gestured for her to enter the office and be seated across the desk from her.

"Now what can I do for you?"

Gabrielle tried to settle herself. "I hardly know where to begin." She hesitated. "I actually was an orphan here twenty-six years ago." The nun observed her with a knowing look.

"My adoptive mother came here and brought me back to Long Island when I was four months old. She never told me I was adopted until a few months ago. All my life I've felt different," she began, then told her story. "Now I find it terribly hard to move forward without finding my birth family. Only then will I know my roots and have answers I've searched for since I was a child. Please Reverend Mother, please tell me you can help."

The nun sat back in her chair and looked hard at her. "My dear, your tale is not unique. I fear I've heard this story many times. But let me check something." She rose from her chair and walked to a bookshelf, then extracted a large binder, which she brought back and opened on her desk. Let's see. You say twenty-six years ago?"

"Yes."

"This is 1972. That would be 1946?"

"Yes."

Fingering the tabs till she reached the correct year, the nun opened the section and paged through until she reached the name Andersen. "Would your adoptive mother be Kay Andersen?"

"Yes!" she almost shouted her reply, thinking she might be about to learn her birth parents' names.

"Hmmm," the Reverend Mother responded, running her fingers down the page related to Gabrielle. "It seems you were called Maria when you were brought to the orphanage—and you were perhaps a couple of weeks old."

"I was brought by my birth mother?"

"I'm afraid not. If you were, I wouldn't be able to tell you who that was in any case."

Gabrielle was crestfallen.

"You were delivered to us by Father Martino. It says here that he found you in a basket on the stairs to the old mission in San Miguel."

She started. "I was just there this morning. I wondered if that might be the mission my adoptive mother mentioned."

"It says he brought you here after you were at the mission for a week. He took care of you until a place opened up here. It seems he was the one who named you Maria. Apparently he became quite attached to you, visiting you frequently until your new mother came for you four months later."

Gabrielle's eyes widened in surprise. "Where can I find this Father Martino?"

"I'm not sure," the Reverend Mother replied. "Let's see who was in charge then." She read down through the page. "It was the Reverend Mother Juanita."

"Yes! My mom mentioned her. Is she here?"

"Oh no dear, she hasn't been here for many a year. I'm not quite sure where she is now."

"Oh."

"But I'll check for you and see what I can find out."

"Would you? I would so appreciate that. And Father Martino?"

"Hmmm. I'll ask about him as well. Just give me a few days. Are you from very far away?"

"I came from Chicago."

"Where are you staying?"

"At the motel in San Miguel."

"Ah, then I better see if I can speed up the search."

"I would so appreciate it."

"Give me your number, and I'll call you if I have some information."

Gabrielle took the motel card from her pocket. "Here's the number. Just ask to leave a message for room twelve. I'll phone you back."

Into the Unknown

"Okay. Try not to worry. There are so many like you. You're fortunate that the priest in San Miguel took such an interest in you. This may help you find what you're looking for."

"Thank you Reverend Mother," she said as she rose.

Leaving the office and walking toward the exit, she heard the children again. She knew in that moment that here, in this orphanage, she had found a piece of her past.

* * *

Late the next day she got word from the motel office that the Reverend Mother Felicia had phoned. Returning her call, she was put on hold while the Sister located her.

"Miss Andersen?"

"Yes. Reverend Mother?"

"Yes. I'm afraid I have bad news about the Reverend Mother Juanita."

Gabrielle's heart sank.

"She apparently passed away four-and-a-half months ago."

"Oh no! What happened?"

"I think a combination of her heart and old age."

"I'm so sorry to hear that. And Father Martino?"

"As best I can tell he's still alive, although apparently not in good health."

"Do you know where I might find him? I tried inquiring at the old mission in San Miguel when I returned there, but no one was available to answer my questions."

"No one has lived at the mission for some time now. The priest who gives Sunday services travels about the region, so he may be hard to locate. Someone thought that Father Martino might be in Hachita in an assisted living facility."

"Is that in New Mexico?"

"Yes. It's not too far. You might just want to go to Hachita. I'd be surprised if there's more than one assisted living place there. I hope this helps. If I hear any more about him, I'll let you know. I wish you well with your search my dear."

"Reverend Mother, I can't thank you enough. You've been most kind to take time to help me."

"I hope you find what you're looking for."

When she hung up, she experienced mixed emotions. She mourned not being able to meet Reverend Mother Juanita. *If I'd come down here when I learned the truth about my adoption, I may have been able to see her,* she thought. On the other hand, she found encouragement that Father Martino might still be alive and not far away. She determined she would go to Hachita in the morning. *God willing, I'll find him there,* she told herself, *and he'll know something about my birth family.*

The rest of the day she studied the local telephone directory and made calls to locate the Father. The operator at Hachita's assisted living facility said he was no longer there and suggested she try the Catholic nursing home just outside Hachita. The receptionist there verified that they had a Father Martino in residence, although for privacy reasons they couldn't verify his age or where he came from. Excited, Gabrielle believed this was the man she was looking for. The woman at the home said she could visit in the morning between nine and eleven or between two and four in the afternoon, but she couldn't guarantee he would be awake when she arrived.

"Would you be so kind as to tell him that his 'baby Maria' will be there in the morning to see him?"

"I'll try to do that. Most of our residents sleep a great deal now you know."

"I understand. Thank you. I should be there in the morning between nine and ten."

When Rick called that evening, she told him about her visit with the new Reverend Mother, what had befallen the previous one, and what she had discovered about the old priest and his whereabouts. Rick promised to phone the following night to hear what she learned.

Tossing about as she tried to sleep, she thought how close she might be to gaining clues to her origins. Awaking at five o'clock, just before her alarm went off, she showered and dressed,

Into the Unknown

then placed her camera and notepad in her tote bag before picking up breakfast at the café.

Setting out for Hachita around six o'clock, she arrived at the Nursing Home of the Catholic Sisters of Grant County three-and-a-half hours later. Within fifteen minutes, a nun escorted her down a hallway with its institutional white walls, linoleum floors, and antiseptic smell, to Father Martino's room.

"I'm sorry, but he's asleep. He's not well you know. Did you still wish to stay?" the Sister who had greeted her asked.

"Yes please," Gabrielle responded.

The Sister pulled up a chair beside his bed and gestured for her to be seated.

As the Sister left, Gabrielle turned to the old priest. Observing his mild snore and peaceful demeanor, she looked at a kind face that was weathered and deeply wrinkled. It touched her that he apparently had been very attached to her and visited her often at the orphanage. She thought she could feel his love for her in the slight smile that appeared on his face just before he opened his eyes.

"Father," she said gently, "my name is Gabrielle Andersen. You found me in a basket on your mission stairs twenty-six years ago. You named me Maria."

Father Martino's eyes opened wide in recognition. "Maria!" he said, his voice barely more than a croak. "Please...get the Sister," he whispered.

Gabrielle ran to the young nurse, who now bent low to hear him. Then she turned to Gabrielle. "If you wouldn't mind, would you return to the waiting area? He'd like me to prepare him so he can better speak with you. I need to help him into his wheelchair and give him his medications and something to eat."

"I'll wait there for him. Please don't rush him. I can wait as long as he needs."

It took an hour for him to be ready for her visit. The young Sister escorted her back toward the room. "He had a little breakfast and tea and is anxious to meet with you. You can stay past eleven if you like, since he's awake now and wants to visit."

"Thank you Sister," she said as she reentered his room.

Gabrielle was happy to find him fully awake. "I thought I might never see you again," he said, his voice weak but steady. "Just look at you, all grown up and so beautiful!"

She blushed and smiled. "I understand that you were the one who discovered me all these years ago."

"Yes," he said, breathing heavily as he told in gasps the story of how he found her and saved her from the starving dog. "You were such a peaceful baby," he said, his voice barely more than a whisper. "I never saw a child who could be calm in the face of trauma. I knew at that moment that you were very special."

As she watched and listened to the old priest, she fully felt his love for her. She pulled her chair closer and reached for his hand. Calloused, his was a hand that had worked a lifetime. "I can't begin to thank you for saving me that night," she said, "and for looking after me those months before my adoptive mother came for me."

Father Martino smiled. "Have you had a good life my child? Are you happy?"

"Yes. I've been fortunate in many ways. But the thing that pains me is that I don't know where I came from. I always felt I was different from everyone and didn't know why. I wasn't told that I'd been adopted until a few months ago, although I'd queried my adoptive mother many times. Father, is there anything at all you can tell me about my birth parents? It would mean so much to me!"

"I'm afraid no one ever confessed to leaving you," he said, struggling to clear his throat. "But I do have something that might help. I've kept these with me all my life in case I saw you again. See the desk? If you open the left-hand drawer and look to the very back of it...."

She gently released his hand, walked to the desk, and slid open the drawer.

"...it's wrapped in paper at the back."

She reached for it and extracted something soft.

"Bring it here, child." Receiving it, he peeled back the covering with a shaky hand and offered her the contents.

Into the Unknown

Taking the woven material, she looked questioningly at him.

"You were wrapped in a handmade baby blanket when I rescued you. It has an unusual insignia on it, perhaps a family symbol of some sort? I'm quite sure it's Mexican, Mayan I believe." He winced as he coughed, then continued, his voice husky. "I've kept it all these years. I didn't really think I'd see you again, but if I did, I'd have this for you—something from your past. Perhaps even a key to it?" He coughed again.

Looking concerned, she said, "Father, I'm afraid this is a strain for you. Perhaps I'm asking too much of you."

"Nonsense, my child. If I can help you at all, it would bring me joy."

Fully opening the small, musty-smelling blanket, she gazed long at it. It was embroidered and appliqued with stunningly colored materials overlaying a dark brown background. "It looks like a family insignia or perhaps a map of a place of origin? So intriguing. Do you know anyone who can interpret it?"

The old man sat in thought. "There was a woman in San Miguel—Yatzil Santos. She's Mayan by descent and knows a great deal of Mayan history. She came here as a child from Mexico many years ago. I'd start with her. Perhaps she can help you."

"Do you know where in San Miguel she lives?"

"The last I knew she was with her daughter Martina Sanchez at her house on the outskirts of town. Oh, I almost forgot," he said before coughing and clearing his throat again. "At the back of the drawer you'll find a scarf."

She rose and checked again, then extracted an elegant silken scarf. Looking puzzled she held it up.

"I saw that in the mission courtyard the same morning I found you," he said. "I don't know where this came from or if it has any relevance to your search, but it's possible it might. I wondered if your mother—or whoever it was—could have dropped it when she brought you there."

"It's so different from the woven blanket," she noted as she opened the scarf and checked the label: 100 % silk. Made in Spain. "It appears to be an expensive scarf and a particularly lovely one. Is this the kind of scarf ladies in San Miguel typically wore at that time?"

"Let me think," he said. "I'd say it was unusual for a Mexican woman to have a scarf like this. More likely someone from the Spanish upper class would have a scarf like this. But of course anything's possible."

"Yes of course. You've given me something to go on, which gives me hope that I might find my birth family. Is there anything I can do for you Father?"

He cleared his throat. "Just one thing. Please tell me about your life. I've imagined many times what it might be like. I'd love to hear how it truly is."

She smiled. "How much time do you have?"

"As much time as it takes to tell your story. As you can see, I have nowhere to go." He returned her smile, then began to cough again.

"Are you okay? Can I bring you some water?"

She ran to get some, which seemed to settle him.

For the next hour Gabrielle told the story of her life, concentrating on the last few years.

"I'd love to see something you've painted," he remarked.

Rummaging in her tote bag, she pulled out photos of her eight large canvases.

"So these are the paintings you were telling me about."

"Yes."

He studied them as he adjusted his glasses. When he looked up, he had tears in his eyes. "I knew you were special from the moment I saw you." He paused. "These are extraordinary Maria…I mean Gabrielle. There is something about them that reminds me of the Mexican muralists in the time of Diego Rivera."

"It's funny that you say that Father, as it was their work that inspired me."

"What will happen to these paintings?"

"A museum in Minneapolis has purchased them and hopes to circulate them to other museums around the country."

"That's wonderful. I would hate to see these beautiful pieces languish in storage somewhere. They should be seen." He

Into the Unknown

paused again, drawing a long deep breath. "I'm so proud of you my child, to already have done something great with your young life. I'll pray that you find what you're seeking and that Mother Mary will watch over and guide you on your life's path."

"Thank you Father. That means so much to me. You're kind to say these things and to try to help me. I wish I could do something for you."

"You already have my child."

At that moment the young nurse returned. "I hate to interrupt, but I don't want Father Martino to get too tired. It's almost time for his lunch and next round of medications."

"Oh of course. Would you do something for me? Would you take a picture of the two of us?" she asked as she retrieved the camera from her bag.

"Certainly," the nurse responded as Gabrielle handed her the camera and leaned down beside Father Martino. She thought he smelled of soap and medications and something she couldn't describe.

"Say cheese." the nun said. Gabrielle and the Father obliged, laughing. Then she kissed his cheek as she took his hand. "I'll pray for you too Father," she said. "I hope to visit you again before I return to Chicago."

"I'd love that," he said, "and be sure to let me know what you discover."

"I will." As she took her leave, she pivoted at his doorway and waved. He smiled. Then she thought she saw him wipe a tear from his eye just as the nun turned the Father's chair and wheeled him to another part of the room.

4

Driving back toward San Miguel, she was at once excited and sad—excited that she might have clues to her roots and sad to leave Father Martino. She experienced some distant memory when she looked into his eyes. Or maybe she just imagined it.

Then a vague remembrance of a dream she had as a child resurfaced in her mind, a dream where women in long dresses walked and a man with a nubby robe cradled her and made her feel safe. But what she was certain about was that she knew the Father's heart. He showed it to her today as he had decades ago. She felt love for this man and prayed for him and for the chance to see him again.

The closer she got to San Miguel, the more determined she became to locate Yatzil Santos this very day. Stopping at Esperanza Café for a late lunch, she queried the cashier as to where she might find the woman. Knowing Yatzil and her family, he gave her directions to their house.

Fifteen minutes later she parked across the street from it. It was an older, earth-colored adobe with a bright turquoise door and a yellow mailbox. She was rehearsing what she would say, when the front door opened and a middle-aged woman walked to the letter box. As the woman removed letters, she glanced at Gabrielle. Grabbing her tote bag, Gabrielle immediately exited the car and called, "Martina Sanchez?"

The woman looked at her. "Yes?"

As Gabrielle approached and extended her hand, she introduced herself and mentioned that she used to live in San Miguel.

Gazing at her with uncertainty, Martina declined to take her hand. But when Gabrielle said that Father Martino gave her and her mother's names and suggested that Yatzil might be able to interpret something he gave her, Martina's face softened. "How is he?" she asked as she raised a hand over her eyes to shade them from the sun.

"He's not well," Gabrielle responded, "but we visited for quite a while this morning at the Catholic nursing home outside Hachita."

"I'd heard he was there and understand he's seriously ill. He helped me and my family a lot over the years."

"And me. He saved my life when I was just a baby."

The woman looked puzzled. "How do you mean?"

Into the Unknown

"Would it be okay to answer any questions you have when I meet your mother? The good Father urged me to see her."

Martina hesitated for a moment and looked hard at her. "My mother's getting old, so I hope you won't say anything to upset her."

Gabrielle was surprised. "I'm only looking for information. I certainly wouldn't want to upset anyone."

Following her into the house, Gabrielle heard Martina say, *"Madre, hay alguien aquí para verte!"* to the short, grey-haired woman walking slowly into the living room. *"Madre,"* Martina continued, "Father Martino gave her our names."

"How is the good Father?" Yatzil asked.

"He's not well I'm afraid, but I've just come from his nursing home in Hachita. We had a long talk, so he managed that."

"I'm glad to hear it. What did you want to see me about? Oh, I'm forgetting my manners. Please sit down. Your name is?" Yatzil asked as she gestured toward a frayed, overstuffed sofa that smelled of cigarette smoke and age, while she sat in the recliner beside it. Martina occupied a wooden chair across the room.

"Gabrielle Andersen," she responded to Yatzil's query.

Martina interjected, "Mother, she was telling me that she was born in San Miguel and that Father Martino saved her life when she was a baby."

"Oh my. What happened?" Yatzil asked as her lined, olive-toned forehead furrowed deeper between her thick, graying eyebrows.

"I was newborn when I was left in a basket on the old mission steps. Apparently a dog would have taken me if the Father hadn't confronted it. Later he watched over me for a time."

Yatzil stared at Gabrielle as if truly seeing her for the first time. "How long ago was this?" she asked.

"Twenty-six years ago."

Yatzil glared at Martina before answering. "What was it you wanted to ask me?"

Gabrielle reached into her tote bag and pulled out the small parcel the Father had given her. Unwrapping it, she handed the folded cloth to Yatzil. "I was hoping you might know what the insignia on this baby blanket represents."

Carefully Yatzil opened it flat on her lap. Then she gasped and grew pale. Her hand shook as she held the cloth up to Martina.

"Where did you get this?" Martina asked in an accusatory manner.

"Father Martino gave it to me. Why? Is something wrong?" she asked in an unsteady voice.

"How did he get it?" she demanded.

"He said I was wrapped in it when he found me."

Martina and Yatzil just stared at her. Then the two women began talking excitedly in Spanish. Gabrielle knew a little of the language, but not enough to decipher their rapid-fire speech. It went on for several minutes before Martina spoke to her.

"I think you better go."

"What?" Gabrielle responded in shock.

"You've upset my mother. We can't help you. You need to go." She stood, walked to Yatzil, took the cloth, put it back in the paper, and returned it to Gabrielle.

"But why?" she asked. "Is it something I said?"

"You must go now," Martina said sharply.

Flabbergasted, Gabrielle stared at the two women who were visibly unnerved. "I'm sorry," she responded. "I certainly didn't intend to upset anyone. I've wanted all my life to learn where I came from and who my birth family is. I just thought you could help me decipher what the blanket might tell about them."

"Please!" Martina raised her voice. Yatzil looked as if she might faint.

"Yes I'm going. I'm so sorry." She gathered up her things and exited as the door slapped her from behind, causing her to drop the blanket. Retrieving it, she brushed it off as she walked to the street. She still could hear the women's voices rising and falling.

What could have caused this? she asked herself, troubled now as well. *What did I say that upset them? What was it about the cloth that distressed them? Why wouldn't they talk to me? I just don't understand.*

Into the Unknown

Back in her rental car, she shut the door. Through the open car window the women's voices continued to swell in waves of emotion. Disheartened and confused, she drove back to the motel. *What does all this mean?* she asked herself. *What am I to do now?* She felt that she had come to the end of a road, but she knew she couldn't turn back. With this realization, she decided she just would have to wait and see what tomorrow would bring.

As the day progressed into evening, she couldn't shake the feeling that Yatzil and Martina were part of her story—or at least held clues to it. Clearly they recognized the blanket, and both appeared alarmed when she mentioned Father Martino's discovery of her twenty-six years ago.

When she described her encounter to Rick, he also was perplexed. Like her, however, he seemed certain they possessed information that could help her.

"Have you thought of trying to find public records of Yatzil's family? Maybe there's something there that could explain their behavior."

"I thought about checking old newspaper records," she replied, "but this town is too small to have its own paper. I'll have to look for a county paper, but I'm not sure that will get me very far. Checking county birth and death records, maybe marriage records too, could yield something. That's a good thought Rick. I'll look into it. And it'll give me something to do with my time."

* * *

The next day, after breakfast at the café, she headed north to Lordsburg. It was a much larger town than San Miguel, giving her hope of finding the history she sought. She started with the County Clerk's office. Since she judged Yatzil to be at least in her sixties, she thought she might start by searching birth records from 1905 through 1925. She assumed that Santos was a married name, so she searched for Yatzil in the hope her first name was unusual enough to help her. She found no one, however, with that forename.

Then she went to marriage records, checking five years later. Again nothing. So she searched for Yatzil's daughter, Martina Santos. And there it was—born 1929, Hachita Hospital. The record said: Mother: Yatzil Santos, but listed no father. She found this curious and decided to keep searching. Then she discovered something totally unexpected: Elena Santos, born 1930, Hachita Hospital. Mother: Yatzil Santos. *So Yatzil has another daughter? Martina has a sister? I wonder where she is.*

So she sought marriage records again. She was curious about the younger sister. She started in 1949 when Elena would have been nineteen, and looked through 1961 when she would have been thirty-one. Nothing. Gabrielle went back earlier. And there it was, the marriage of Elena Santos to Ramón Hidalgo in 1948. *That was two years after I was born,* she thought, *so it's unlikely that she was my mother. But wait, Elena only would have been eighteen when she married. It seems young for that, especially since Ramón is recorded as thirty-two. That's a very big age difference.* She didn't know what to make of this. *Why would such a young girl marry a man so much older?* she pondered. *Had something happened to her to make her less valued as a bride? Was she sickly? Or was he a man of some means perhaps, able to interest a very young woman?* Something wasn't adding up.

She decided to check the death records and began looking from the date of Elena's marriage in 1948. Then she found the date of her death: 1950. Cause of death: hemorrhaging during childbirth.

She was stunned. Could this have been her mother? And if so, why was there no mention of an earlier childbirth? Then it hit her. If Elena was her mother, she may have had a baby illegitimately—and possibly not in a hospital. If so she may have been forced to give up the infant as a way to save her and her family's reputation. Or she simply had no way to support the child if the father was not in the picture.

All this was speculation of course, but to her all the pieces fit. It would explain why Yatzil and Martina were so threatened by her questions. As she thought about it, she wondered if perhaps they didn't know about Elena's giving birth to a child at so young an age. But that seemed unlikely. How would she have been able

Into the Unknown

to hide a pregnancy for nine months—and where, but home, would she have birthed the infant if there were no hospital records? None of this made sense. Yet something told her she may have stumbled upon the truth, or at least part of it. But how could she check further if Yatzil and Martina wouldn't talk to her?

She had another thought: to find Martina's records. They showed she had married a José Sanchez in 1952. He was just a year older than Martina. A child was born to them two years later, but died in 1956. No other children were listed. Martina and José were divorced in 1969. It seemed to her unlikely that Martina would have been her mother, but it was possible. Martina, however, exhibited no softening of her expression when Gabrielle told them what she knew of her story. Wouldn't a mother's face demonstrate feeling for her child at the moment of revelation? She shook her head.

The records offices were closing, so she had to leave. The search had exhausted her mentally and emotionally. Had she found the answer she was looking for in Elena? If so, how distressing it would be to learn that Elena had died and at such a young age. And that still left the question of who Gabrielle's father was. Could it be this Ramón Hidalgo? If it was, then it was unlikely they would marry two years later. This seemed improbable. How would she ever find her birth father? She had so many unanswered questions.

As she returned to her car and drove away, the gurgling in her stomach reminded her that she had nothing to eat or drink since breakfast. Although eating seemed the least important thing to her now, she decided to catch dinner in Lordsburg. She saw a restaurant with outdoor seating and parked in front. After sitting among dusty records all day, she found the prospect of fresh air and sunshine welcoming. She pulled her jacket close about her as she stepped from her car into the chill of the day.

As she inhaled the aroma of hot coffee and waited for her meal to arrive, she looked over her notes from the day and decided to record her questions.

Why was no father listed for Martina and Elena's births?
Why had Elena married so young?

Why had she married someone almost twice her age?

Who was this Ramón Hidalgo?

Assuming he still was alive, where could she find him?

Would Father Martino have remembered Elena or her husband?

Would the Father know if Elena had any close friends and if so, how could she locate them?

What could Father Martino tell her about Yatzil and Martina?

Would he know who Yatzil's husband was and why he wouldn't have been listed on the girls' birth certificates?

Could he tell her anything else about Martina and her past that might suggest she had a child out of wedlock?

She wished it weren't too late to stop at the nursing home in Hachita to ask the Father her questions and to fill him in on her search. When she arrived at her motel, she phoned the nursing home to see if she might visit him in the morning. The nun who answered said that she didn't know if he would be up for seeing anyone. He had taken a turn for the worse, drifting in and out of lucidity, she said.

"Oh dear," Gabrielle replied. "I'm so sorry to hear that. Would it be okay if I just came there? I couldn't bear if he passed away without my seeing him again. He hoped I'd return. Please may I come and just sit with him?"

The nun equivocated. "Why don't you call in the morning. We'll see how he's doing."

"Okay. Thank you."

Shaken, she realized that the Father was failing quickly, and she ought to give what comfort she could. *Dear God, please help me to not pester him with questions, but to be one with Father Martino as he was for me when I was newborn.*

* * *

In the morning her call reached another nun, who said that the Father hadn't woken up yet and that his condition remained

Into the Unknown

precarious. But if she wished to see him, the woman offered, she should come soon. Gabrielle grabbed her jacket and tote bag, left her motel room, and headed for her car. "Damn!" she said aloud as she checked her dashboard. "Out of gas!" She knew that every minute she delayed could be the one that kept her from reaching Father Martino in time.

At the station she bought gas, coffee, and a sweet roll. After filling the tank and back in her vehicle, she opened the plastic wrapper with her teeth and put the coffee and roll in the cup holders. As she drove off, she promised herself there would be no more delays.

Three hours later when she reached the nursing home, she found the front door slightly ajar and entered without ringing the bell. Passing a nurse in the hall, Gabrielle explained she was there to see the Father. "He's still sleeping," the nurse said, "but you're welcome to sit with him if you like. We don't know if he'll regain consciousness, but it's possible."

Gabrielle continued walking down the empty hall, the sound of televisions filtering through half-open doors where patients lay in bed or sat in wheelchairs. She heard a moan, the sound of a buzzer calling for help, the click of the steps of nuns and their helpers, the swish of a mop, the smell of bleach.

Tapping lightly, she opened the door that creaked. Stepping into the warm room, she saw the sun stream through a window, while blinds shadowed the one beside the Father's bed. He snored intermittently, his breathing irregular. Pulling up a chair, she sat beside him. It hadn't been long since she saw him last, but he looked strangely older. Examining his heavily wrinkled face, she noted it was drawn in pain, his hardworking hands thick and worn. She thought about how she seemed to carry some memory of his eyes and his kindnesses from when she was a baby, cradled and loved by him.

Moving her chair closer, she took his hand in hers. Despite the warm room, he felt cold as she moved her hands to warm his. Then she spoke softly. "Father Martino, this is Gabrielle, your little Maria. I've come to sit with you. You can sleep if you wish. I just wanted you to know that I'm beside you for as long as they'll let me stay. You're so dear to me Father. I thank you—such an inadequate word—for saving me, and loving me as if you were my own father."

Sitting in silence for a half-hour, she kept hold of his hand. A nurse acknowledged her as she entered, checked his pulse, touched his forehead, watched him for a minute or two, then left. Wondering if he would ever awaken, she started to sing a hymn she remembered from church when she was a child, "Blessed Be the Tie That Binds." Then she thought she saw his eyelids flutter, unveiling his eyes. He just looked at her at first, as if trying to remember something. Then he whispered "Maria."

"Yes Father, it's me."

"You came back," he struggled, his voice weak. Then he coughed repeatedly, his face marked with pain. "Oh Father, I should call the nurse!"

'No," he said, his cough abating. "Just let me look at you. How nice of you to come see this old man."

She regarded his eyes, which had grown moist with affection. She struggled not to cry. "Let me prop up your head for you."

Searching for another pillow, she found one in the closet. "There you go," she said as she raised his head and slid the pillow under it. "Is that better?"

"Yes. A little water please," he whispered.

"Of course." She poured a half a glass from the container beside the bed and held it to his lips, giving him just a small sip so he wouldn't choke.

"How are you feeling?" she asked.

He winced. "Better, now that you're here."

"I worried that I might disturb you."

He coughed, then said in a raspy voice, "You could never disturb me my child. I'm trying to remember…where we left off."

"You gave me the little blanket and scarf and suggested that I might find a clue to the blanket's insignia if I spoke with Yatzil Santos."

"Were you…able to find her?" he asked, struggling to speak and wheezing softly.

Into the Unknown

"I did. You were right about her living with her daughter Martina Sanchez."

"Did they help you?"

She hesitated, not wanting to distress him. "Are you sure you want to talk about this now?"

"Come my dear. Tell me."

She waited a moment, wishing he hadn't urged her to reveal what he wanted to know. But the interest she saw in his eyes urged her to respond. "I'm afraid they became quite upset when they saw the blanket and learned that I was found twenty-six years ago on the mission steps. It seemed to me that they knew something about it, but didn't want to acknowledge it. Martina said I was upsetting her mother and told me to leave."

"That doesn't sound like them," he said, his voice growing more hoarse. "How unfortunate…and puzzling."

"It perplexed me as well. As I meditated on it, however, I thought that it's possible that they might have some connection to my birth mother. Otherwise why would they become so upset?"

The Father listened as he struggled with breathing.

"Father, I think we should stop," she responded, watching his labored breath.

"No my dear…please…continue."

Reluctantly she resumed. "I thought I'd reached a dead end, but then I decided to go to the county seat in Lordsburg and check what records I could find on the Santos family." Explaining what she learned, she added, "I have so many questions. I thought you might have answers to some of them. But I don't want to tire you. Perhaps I've said enough."

"No, my child…. It would mean so much to me… if I could help you… in this search of yours. I see how much… it means to you." He coughed; his face shadowed in pain.

"Father, you should rest!"

"I have…all eternity to rest," he said, his hacking abating as he cleared his throat again, "but only this moment… to be with you. Please… ask me your questions."

Hesitant, she finally continued. "I found no record on Yatzil Santos herself, but I did surface her name on two hospital birth records of her daughters Martina and Elena. Elena would have been sixteen when I was born. The records revealed that when she was just eighteen years old, she married Ramón Hidalgo, who was thirty-two, and that she died in childbirth two years later at the age of twenty. I couldn't understand why this young girl would marry a man twice her age. And...." she hesitated to say what she was thinking.

"And...what my dear?" he probed, his voice barely a whisper,

Seeing his interested look, she soldiered on. "...And wondered if Elena Santos could have been my mother and the girl who left me on your mission steps twenty-six years ago."

Father Martino gasped and then coughed repeatedly, struggling for breath.

"Oh Father! Are you okay?" She sprang from her chair and moved to raise his head and give him a little water. But he started to convulse violently, spitting blood. She saw a cord beside his bed and pulled it. "Please!" she exclaimed, raising her voice. "Dear God please help him!" She shouted, "Help help! Please help!"

A nurse rushed in. She shouted to Gabrielle. "Call the desk. Dial O to get the doctor. NOW!"

Gabrielle hurried to the phone. It kept ringing, but no one answered. "No answer," she yelled. "I'll run up front!"

"Please," she shouted to another nun, "get the doctor immediately! Father Martino is coughing up blood and in great distress. A nurse is with him, but she said to get the doctor NOW!"

The nun ran to find him as Gabrielle tore back to the Father's room. But when she returned, he was no longer choking. He lay still.

Thank heavens he's better, she thought. But then she looked at the nurse, her uniform and hands stained with blood. The nurse just shook her head and closed his eyes.

"No!" Gabrielle cried. "Tell me he's still alive!" She rushed to him and took his hand. She searched for breathing that she saw

Into the Unknown

now had stopped. "Please God...no!" she sobbed, releasing his hand as she fell back onto a chair beside him.

The nurse had gotten damp washcloths and was removing the blood from herself and from his face, chest, and hands. She handed another wet cloth to Gabrielle. "You should get the blood off your hands. Are you all right?" she asked Gabrielle.

Still weeping, Gabrielle looked down at her hands, the Father's blood covering them. She was struck dumb, then became hysterical. "Please calm yourself, my child," the nurse said. "Here, let me clean your hands for you." As she did, Gabrielle gradually quieted.

"I need to go and wash more thoroughly," the nurse finally said. "The doctor should be here soon. Tell him how he died. The time of death is one-o-six."

Devastated, Gabrielle nodded, then stared at the Father's face in disbelief. Unable to think what to do, she sought his hand again and a way to reach him in prayer. *Father Martino, I'm so sorry. I shouldn't have been here. I caused you too much distress. I wanted to soothe you in your last hours. All I did was trouble you. I'm so terribly sorry.*

"What's happened?" the doctor asked as he entered with one of the nuns.

Still in shock, Gabrielle struggled to rise from her anguish and calm herself enough to relay what the nurse had told her to say. After the doctor examined the old priest, he gave orders to the Sister before leaving to prepare the death certificate. The nun turned and began praying aloud for Father Martino's soul. When she finished uttering a litany of Latin words, the Sister stood over him. With her hand, she made the sign of the cross on his forehead and chest before kneeling and praying silently.

Gabrielle watched as she tried to gather herself. She was filled with remorse at her carelessness with what she told the old priest. How could she have forgotten how sick he was? She had been greedy for knowledge, she thought, while he only was eager to help.

Seeing her crushed, the Sister rose from her prayers and walked to her. "My dear," she said, her hand on Gabrielle's shoulder. "Do not grieve for Father Martino. He's with God now. No kinder man lived. He wouldn't want you to suffer so."

In gasps as she battled to control her grief, she blurted out, "It's all my fault. I answered what he asked without realizing how it would distress him. If I'd been more sensitive, he still would be alive. It's all my fault!"

"There there my child, this is nonsense. He wasn't to last the day, the doctor said when he saw him early this morning. He likely was doing what he wished to do. My dear, he's listened to thousands of confessions. Surely whatever you told him when he died was no worse than so many of the stories he heard over the years."

The nun looked sympathetically at her as she patted Gabrielle's shoulder. "Please don't blame yourself. I know that he was excited to see you. He told me how he discovered you as an abandoned child, how he saved you from a wild dog, and how he loved you from the moment he saw you. I can't think of anything he'd have wanted more than to be with you at the end of his life, helping you by listening. He'd hate that you're crying and blaming yourself. Come now. Rejoice that he's relieved of his pain and with the Lord now."

Gabrielle struggled to calm herself. Sitting quietly, she was shaken by all that had transpired and watched now as the Sister prepared Father Martino to be moved. "Please, is it permitted now to tell me his age and what his illness was?" she finally asked.

"Lung cancer my child. He was seventy-six years old. He lived a long and good life—and he died as he lived, helping people he cared about. Be happy for him. He's gone home."

Shaking her head and blowing her nose, Gabrielle struggled to think. Although her hands had been wiped clean, she still felt the memory of his blood there. The sensation held a fire, she thought, destined to burn forever with recollections of the love and selflessness he showed and rooted in her heart.

"This all happened so fast," she whispered.

"Yes, my dear," the nurse responded, "it often is like this. One moment here, the next traveling to God."

Gabrielle fell silent "There will be a service for him?" she finally managed to say.

"Yes."

"When will it be...and where?"

"I expect at his old mission in San Miguel, this weekend if possible. Will you come?"

"Of course."

"Call in a couple of days, and I'll let you know if we have a date."

"Is there anything I can do to help?"

"Just be there if you can. Go now and take care of yourself. Go with God my child."

5

"Rick, it's so good to hear your voice!"

"And yours Gabrielle. Were you able to see Father Martino again?"

She choked back tears as she told him about the Father's last day.

"Gabrielle, you mustn't fault yourself. It just was the Father's time."

"I know, but I wish I could have comforted him, not distressed him."

"I doubt you distressed him. It was his time to go. I know it's sad, but at least you got to be with him one last time."

"Yes."

After a moment of silence he continued. "So where does this leave you?"

"I'll go to the Father's service. After that I just don't know."

"Do you think it's time to come back?"

"Oh Rick, if I leave now, the Father's sacrifices to help me will not be honored. And I'll always live with my brokenness. I *must* find what I came for."

"I miss you," he said.

"I miss you too."

"I understand and will talk to you soon," he said.

"I love you Rick."

"Love you too."

She could feel his affection and how he yearned to be with her. She missed Rick desperately. But her sadness over the good Father's death ran deep. She felt him to be more father to her than anyone she had known. It was so clear to her how much he wanted her to find answers to the questions that had plagued her all her life. His wish made her drive ever more fiercely to find the ancestry that still eluded her. Acknowledging this and with a heavy heart, she dutifully returned to her search and to the questions still begging answers.

* * *

The next day as she paid for breakfast at the café, she asked the cashier if he had ever heard of Elena Santos, or Elena or Ramón Hidalgo.

"Ramón? Sure, I know him. Why do you ask?"

"He might have some information I'm looking for. Can you tell me where to find him?"

"Maybe. Depends on what you want from him."

"Do you know anything about his wife Elena?"

"That's not his wife. Her name's Valeria. Who's this Elena?"

"Oh that doesn't matter. But I may be related. I'm trying to find my family."

"You should have told me that. Sure." He stopped to write down an address on a receipt, tore it off, and handed it to her.

"Thanks Miguel."

"Good luck."

Stepping into the sunlight, she felt the first breath of hope since the Father died. Perhaps Ramón could tell her something that would help. She knew, however, that it would be tricky to probe him without revealing something that Elena or her family might not have told him. *I probably should go after dinner in case he*

Into the Unknown

works. Let's see... She calculated Ramón's probable age and surmised he likely was still working.

Figuring she had at least eight to ten hours to kill until she could approach him, she went back to her hotel room, grabbed her camera, pad, and pencils, and walked about San Miguel, snapping pictures and making rough sketches.

Although it still was winter, the sun bore down on her, making her seek shade and a cool drink at the small grocery in the middle of town. It was past noon when she paid for a soda and chicken sandwich and took them to the porch out front. As she ate, she noticed a man on a bench at the other end. Smoking a cigarette, he wore a flannel shirt, overalls, and a straw hat and appeared to be in his forties. Noticing that she was looking at him, the stocky, dark-skinned man tipped his hat. "Ma'am?" he said.

"Oh sorry. I didn't mean to disturb you."

"You new in town?"

"Visiting."

"We don't get many visitors. Not much to do here."

"Yes."

"What brings you to San Miguel?"

Gabrielle hesitated. "I'm trying to find my family."

The man chuckled and moved to a bench closer to her. "Well if they live here or did anytime in the last forty or so years, I probably know them. Who you lookin' fer?"

She paused again. "I'm afraid that the person I was trying to find has died. So I'm hoping to find someone who knew her well."

"So who's this dead person?"

She vacillated, then relented, "Elena Santos Hidalgo."

The man's eyes widened. He took a drag on his cigarette, then threw it down on the porch floor and stepped on it. He looked hard at her. "Why you wantin' this?"

Startled by how stern the man had become, she wondered if she really wanted to pursue this with him. But she had to try. "I think I may be related to her."

"Related? How?"

She had to think quickly. "Uh, a second- or third-cousin maybe."

The man frowned in disbelief. "Why would someone so removed come here to find her?"

She nearly panicked, having no good answer. Then she blurted out, "It's personal, but I can tell you that I'm working on a family history."

"You come all the way here to this godforsaken place for a damn history?"

"Well yes. And to see family and Father Martino."

The man's visage softened with mention of the Father. "You know him?"

"Yes."

"You seen him?"

"Yes."

"How is he?"

"He just passed away."

"No."

"I'm afraid yes."

They both sat in silence for a couple of minutes. It seemed to Gabrielle like hours before the man spoke again.

"He was a good man," he said finally.

"The best," she said.

"Whatta you wanna know about Elena Santos Hidalgo?"

"Anything you can tell me about her. I'd be so grateful. What is your name?"

"Juan Carlos. You?"

"Gabrielle Andersen."

He looked at her again. "You don't look like no Andersen."

"No, I don't. It's because I wasn't born an Andersen. But I don't want to get into all that."

Juan sighed, removed a crude cigarette from his shirt pocket, tapped and lit it. Taking a drag, he exhaled, then eyed her again. "Well let's see. Elena woulda been born about 1930. Her mother Yatzil was an immigrant from Mexico."

Into the Unknown

I knew that was it, she thought. *So Elena is Yatzil's daughter and Martina's sister! How could they not acknowledge this?*

"Elena was one hot filly," he continued. "Every boy in school woulda given a year of his life for a date with her. But she was well brought up and didn't date until...," he paused as if weighing his words, "...until Mario Santorez, the son of the biggest landowner in these parts, took up with her." Juan halted, then spat as if trying to expunge the boy's name.

She went cold hearing Mario's name and Juan's apparent assessment of him.

"He was a handsome boy...and spoiled. His father was a rich Mexican American, his mother, an uppity Anglo from a rich family in another county."

She hardly could breathe. If there was a chance Elena was her birth mother, could it be that this Mario was her biological father?

"There were rumors that Mario had...taken advantage of her. Someone I knew saw them comin' outa the Santorez fields holdin' hands, grass on their clothes and hair. When they saw him they dropped their hands and went opposite ways."

He inhaled and exhaled from his hand-rolled cigarette, then pressed it between his thumb and forefinger. "Not long after that somethin' happened. Elena kinda fell apart. She'd done real good at school before that, but then her grades fell and she was keepin' more to herself...mostly just saw her best friend Carmen Santiago."

She gasped, then struggled to hide her excitement at hearing the name of Elena's closest friend. Covering, she responded. "I was wondering about any friends she had. Is this Carmen still in San Miguel?"

"No. She married and moved somewhere. Not sure where she ended up."

"Would you know her married name?"

He thought for a minute. "Can't say I do. He was from another town."

"Is her family still in San Miguel?"

"Her mother Maria's just a little ways out of town."

Involuntarily her face registered elation at the prospect of being close to finding Elena's best friend. Reining in her emotions, she continued. "I understand Elena married an older man, a Ramón Hidalgo."

"Yes."

"It seemed strange she'd marry someone so much older than she was," she said.

"Well like I said, a lotta talk buzzed about her after that whole Mario business. Lotsa rumors too. It's a shame, a pretty thing like that. Damaged goods and all." He spat again. "But Hidalgo's not a bad sort. Just a shame she died a couple years later birthin' a child. Baby died too."

She thought she would collapse. Elena's tragedy hung on her with the deadly weight of certainty. A tumble of emotions overwhelmed her. She fought to persevere. Finally she said, "Sad. What about this Mario person. He still around?"

"Oh yeah. His father died and left everything to his aging wife and to Mario, who married an Anglo like his mother."

"Where is the Santorez place?"

Juan snickered. "For as far as the eye can see. Why you wanna know 'bout them?"

"Just curious. Thank you, Mr. Carlos. You've been such a big help. I should get going. Thanks again."

"Best a luck to ya," he said. "Hope you find what you're lookin' fer." He stamped out his cigarette as she left the porch and waved to him.

"Damn," she whispered as she walked away, tears welling in her eyes. "Damn."

6

On reflection, Gabrielle wasn't sure what a conversation with Ramón Hidalgo would yield and was concerned that she might stir up trouble for him. She decided instead to seek out Carmen's mother in the hope of locating her daughter. *Surely*

Into the Unknown

Carmen would know what happened to Elena and whether it was likely she was my mother, she thought.

Finding Maria Santiago's name in the telephone book, she phoned her.

"*Hola!*"

"Hello. Mrs. Santiago?"

"Yes."

"My name is Gabrielle Andersen. I'm here in San Miguel to learn as much as I can about my family. I appear to be related to Elena Santos Hidalgo, who I know passed away some time ago. I've been told that your daughter Carmen was her best friend. I think she might be able to help me, if I could just speak with her. I understand she got married and lives somewhere else now?"

There was a long silence on the other end of the phone.

"Mrs. Santiago?"

"Why you not talk to Elena's mother and sister? They live here too."

"I haven't been able to talk to them, and I'm running out of time. I came here from Chicago where I'm living and will need to get back there soon. I'd hate to have to return with the little information Father Martino was able to give me."

"You see Father Martino?"

"Yes twice. Sadly he passed away."

Maria Santiago was silent again. "Sad to hear that. He a good man."

"The kindest man I've ever known."

Maria appeared to be thinking, then said, "I suppose it do no harm to tell you Carmen's name. Carmen Di Venzi. She live in Lordsburg."

"Can you give me her number?"

Maria sighed, but acquiesced. "I still not see why you don't talk to Elena's family."

"I'll keep trying. Thank you so much, Mrs. Santiago. This means more to me than you can imagine."

Although still struggling with a range of emotions, she held on to the belief that she might be close to learning her origins. Hardly able to contain her excitement, she immediately dialed

Carmen's number. She got a recorded message and decided to call back early that evening.

The rest of the day she continued sketching the town, the mission in particular, and the surrounding countryside as she drove her car several miles in each direction. Most of the land there was agricultural, all or most of which she speculated belonged to Mario Santorez and his mother. She didn't know if he might be her father, but she realized she needed a great deal more information before approaching him. In truth she feared meeting him, given the wealth and position that he occupied and Juan Carlos's clear dislike for him.

Before catching dinner at the café again, she wrote down her questions. It had been several days since her failed meeting with Elena's family. She believed that Carmen was her best hope. *Dear God, please let Carmen talk to me and tell me what I need to know. Please dear God."*

At seven-thirty she dialed Carmen's number again. This time someone picked up. It was a man.

"Hello?"

"Hello. This is Gabrielle Andersen. May I please speak with Carmen Di Venzi?

"Carmen!" he called to his wife. "Just a minute," he told Gabrielle.

It seemed an eternity before Carmen came to the phone. "Hello?"

"Hello. My name's Gabrielle Andersen. I'm here from out of state trying to find family members. I spoke with your mother. I'm so hoping you can help me."

"Oh. Yes. What is it you want?

"I believe I may be related to Elena Santos Hidalgo..."

"She passed away...long time ago... I'm sorry, I'm very busy.

"Please, I need to know about her. You were her best friend."

"How do you know that?"

"Juan Carlos told me."

Silence. "What is it you want?

Into the Unknown

"I...I think...please. I think she is my mother."

Silence.

"Please, Mrs. Di Venzi. I need..."

"Ay Dios mío!"

"Can we meet? Just an hour? Lunch maybe?"

"Your mother?"

"Yes...please."

"I...oh..."

"I hate so to bother you. But I need to know...and there is no one else."

"You shock me. You want to know if Elena is..."

"My mother, yes."

"Dios mío! Elena...let me catch my breath. My beautiful Elena...so close...long ago... so hard. Your name again?"

"Gabrielle Andersen. I recently discovered I'm adopted. I'm desperate to learn about my mother and my birth family. Can we meet?"

Silence. Then, "So long ago. Where are you staying?"

"San Miguel."

"Her family lives there. Why don't you talk to them?"

"I tried, but they turned me away. Mrs. Di Venzi, you're my last hope."

Silence. "How old are you?"

Surprised, Gabrielle hesitated, then realized Carmen was testing her authenticity. "I'm twenty-six. I spoke with Father Martino before he passed. He told me how he found me on the steps of the old mission in San Miguel, named me Maria, and took me to the orphanage in the next town. He didn't know who my mother was. But he gave me the blanket I was wrapped in and a silk scarf he found the next morning. The blanket seems to be Mayan in origin. I have it with me. I don't know if the scarf is connected in some way."

She heard Carmen gasp.

"Mrs. Di Venzi, please!"

Silence, then "Oh, my heart... Yes, yes, I will meet you. Of course you must know. Come now." She gave Gabrielle directions.

Gabrielle grabbed her keys, stumbled against the motel chair, rushed to her car, struggled to get the key in the transmission. Breaking the speed limit, she wiped tears that wouldn't stop as she rushed toward Lordsburg. Seeking to quiet herself, she thought of Father Martino. He would have soothed and encouraged her in this moment. She could feel how much he wanted her to find her roots and a family that would embrace her.

Reaching Carmen's house, she rang the buzzer. No one came. Agitated, she knocked. Then she thought she heard footsteps. Straightening her posture, she struggled to dispel her apprehension. Then the door to the small adobe home opened, revealing a short, plump, middle-aged woman with dark skin and worried eyes. "Gabrielle?"

"Yes." She fought to settle her hair as it blew in all directions, covering her face. Inside, she pulled back her hair.

Carmen just stared at her, her mouth agape.

"Mrs. Di Venzi?"

"…It's just…just…that you remind me of Elena."

Surprised, Gabrielle struggled to control herself. "I look like her?"

Carmen shook her head affirmatively. But her face seemed to battle with emotions stirred by memories of her best friend. "You're taller than Elena," she finally responded as she gathered herself, "and you don't have her eye color. But you have her almond-shaped eyes and high cheek bones, her full lips, that gorgeous, almost-black hair, similar figure and skin. Anyone who knew her well would see the resemblance. Yes Gabrielle, you look much like her. Without a doubt you're my dear friend Elena's daughter."

Choking back tears, Gabrielle felt her throat contract. Seeing her unable to speak, Carmen reached for her hand, enfolding it in hers to soothe her. But Carmen's tenderness only led her to become more emotional.

It was a few minutes before Gabrielle gained control of herself. Blowing her nose she stuffed her handkerchief into her skirt pocket and took a few deep breaths. "I'm sorry Mrs. Di

Venzi, it's just…" Her voice trailed off as she fought to steady herself.

"There, there," Carmen said, patting Gabrielle's hand while observing her eyes. "Let me get some water for us."

Gabrielle waited, wiping her eyes. Shortly, Carmen reappeared, placing the water and a box of tissues on the lamp table between them.

"I'm sorry," Gabrielle repeated, grabbing a tissue. "I've waited so long… "

"What is it you want to know?"

"Everything. Just…everything."

Carmen took a deep breath. "How many days do you have?" She looked long at her. "Talking about Elena still hurts terribly. I loved her like a sister, more than a sister. When she died, part of me died too."

"I'm sorry."

Carmen nodded and took a long breath before beginning the story of who her friend was. She explained the tragedy of Elena's trysts with Mario and how that undid her, ultimately ending in her marriage to Ramón and her death in childbirth. Carmen showed no mercy toward Mario when she told of his betrayal of Elena and their baby. And she still harbored anger toward Elena's family and how they turned their backs on their daughter when rumors of her affair got back to them. Strangely, she noted, they didn't pursue the veracity of a later rumor started by a classmate, that Elena had a child by Mario. Gabrielle looked pained as she struggled to absorb all that the woman was telling her.

"The family listened too much to the gossip. They blamed Elena for giving in to Mario's advances and disgracing them. They threatened to abandon her as the rumors grew. And the stories kept any suitable Catholic man her age from asking for her hand in marriage."

It was then, Carmen said, that Ramón Hidalgo offered himself. Carmen hesitated before describing Ramón as a very fat, slovenly, but seemingly decent man that no woman wanted. "But Elena's family," she continued, "pressured her to accept Ramón.

Elena would rather have been an old maid than marry him. Under threats that her family soon would disown her, Elena finally gave in to her mother's demands. In a strange way I think that Elena also believed that it was her penance for abandoning you and for bringing shame upon her family. Her marriage to Ramón was not a happy one."

"How do you mean?" Gabrielle probed.

Memory shadowed Carmen's face as she released a labored sigh. "Elena dreaded his touch and endless desires, so long denied by women refusing his advances. Then after two years of marriage, she died in childbirth. The baby died too." Carmen fought to calm herself as she persevered. "I have no love for the Santos family…or the high and mighty Santorez family. Be assured, Mario is your father. Elena slept with no one but Mario and Ramón. She was a chaste girl until Mario seduced her, stole her virginity, and later demanded she get an abortion. Elena, as a good Catholic, refused to do it. Then he abandoned her." Carmen's lower lip quivered. Her anger took a long breath.

"Elena was only sixteen when she had you. She was afraid that if she managed to keep and support you, you'd be labeled a bastard and ostracized. Not wanting you to be scorned as she was, she believed you'd have a better chance for a good life if you were adopted. But it about killed her. She loved you so."

"My poor mother," Gabrielle said, smarting. "How she must have suffered."

They both grew quiet. Then Gabrielle asked, "If her mother didn't know about me, how was Elena able to conceal her pregnancy?"

Tension lines creased Carmen's forehead before she released long-held confidences of how they hid Elena's secret and how she helped Elena in her baby's birthing. Gabrielle hardly could imagine what these teenage girls braved and the sorrow and trauma Elena had to endure, having only Carmen to aid and comfort her. Shocked, she now fully realized the toll this took on Carmen as well.

"Your mother was a beautiful, sweet, passionate girl," Carmen continued while visibly struggling not to break down.

Into the Unknown

"She'd have been so happy to know that she bore a child who would become such a lovely young woman, a person who wanted to know everything about her." She paused, as if to collect herself. "Would you like to see a picture of her?"

Gabrielle nodded and wiped her eyes as Carmen left the room. She felt her stomach knot with knowledge of her mother's tragic life and the callousness of Mario and Elena's family. *Now I understand*, she thought. *By abandoning me, she was trying to protect me. My poor mother!*

When her mother's friend returned, she brought a handful of pictures. The first was a close-up of Elena's face as a teenager. Gabrielle's mouth dropped open. She recognized herself in that picture. "Yes," Carmen said. "You see why when I saw your face, I thought my dear friend had walked back into my life."

"Where did my blue eyes come from?"

"Mario. He's got brilliantly blue eyes, just like you do. And he's tall like you...and perhaps his nose resembles yours. But that's all he gave you," she said in disgust.

The next picture showed Elena and Carmen when they were five. They were laughing and had their arms around each other.

"Your mother and I were best friends from as far back as I can remember. For many years we lived just two houses down from each other. We were inseparable, closer than with our own siblings. Even when my family moved outside town, we remained best friends." Carmen had a faraway look in her eyes.

Shaking her head, she continued. "We often talked about becoming teachers someday. Elena was at the top of her class in our school for Mexican kids, with me just behind her. I've often felt sad that she never got the chance I did to teach young children. She would have made a great teacher. She was the best."

Gabrielle started, realizing how her mother's life was not only brief, but tragically unfulfilled in more than love.

The other photos showed the two of them together when they were happy ten-year-old children, then twelve, then fifteen years of age. "Your mother was a dear, lovable, intelligent person with a big heart, right to the end. She didn't deserve what happened to her. You can hardly imagine how she was shunned."

Carmen's voice broke as she dropped her gaze, a brief flare of outrage hovering between her black eyebrows. "Today people are more liberal. Back then, in a conservative Catholic town with strict class divisions, you'd have thought she'd committed a terrible crime by sleeping with a rich boy—and out of wedlock. But no one thought the less of Mario." Her voice rose sharply. "God knows she was too good for the likes of him!" She shook her head and wiped her eyes. "It's hard to talk about all this."

Gabrielle nodded. Watching the pain on this woman's face and absorbing the shock of what had happened, she scarcely knew what to say. Then Carmen unfolded a page from a newspaper. Handing it to her she said, "This is Mario, your father. It's his wedding announcement to his wealthy Anglo from Silver City. I don't know why I kept it. I'm glad now that I did."

Gabrielle took the paper and examined the man Carmen said was her father. She found him undeniably handsome, but he seemed smug and perhaps a bit of a dandy. He apparently was tall—Carmen said six feet—and slender, had dark hair and piercing, light-colored eyes like her own. But she saw no soul, no passion in them—only self-importance and a kind of meaningless superficiality. His fiancé seemed to fit him. She was beautiful but cold-looking, aloof. Shaken by her father's demeanor and at a loss as to what she should feel, Gabrielle struggled to quiet herself. After a long pause, she asked if the couple had children.

"I heard they have two young sons."

"I see," Gabrielle said almost in a whisper as she handed the paper back to Carmen.

"No, you keep it," Carmen said, unaware of Gabrielle's inner conflict "and the close-up of Elena when she was fifteen, taken just before she took up with Mario. Elena was so in love. You can't imagine how she adored that boy. She told me I was wrong about him and really believed that he only abandoned her because his family demanded it. But I never bought it. He didn't deserve her."

Into the Unknown

Carmen's comment about Elena's alternate view of Mario brought her back to the moment. It made her question whether he might have had more feeling for her mother than Carmen believed. While it didn't change the outcome, she yearned for him to have demonstrated some love for Elena.

"I'm afraid that I don't understand why her family wouldn't help her," Gabrielle finally said, changing the conversation's focus in her confusion about her father's intentions toward her mother.

"I don't know either. It seems that Yatzil's need to protect their reputation and the purity of their family history was at the heart of this. Yatzil's mother Maribel and some of the other women in her extended family were legendary in their fight for social justice for Mayan people."

"Oh," Gabrielle said. "That reminds me. There's something I must show you." She pulled out the blanket and scarf from her bag. "Father Martino gave me these. He saved them in case he saw me again and they might be helpful in some way."

Carmen examined them. "I remember them. They were Elena's. The blanket was hers as a child. It was woven and appliquéd by her grandmother Maribel. It has symbols of the family and their region in Mexico. I remember...," Carmen's voice broke, "... that she wrapped you in the blanket before placing you in the basket she wove for you. She said that...since they were made with love, they would keep you in love." She stopped, gathering herself. "The silk scarf was a gift from Mario. It was expensive. Elena was proud of it. It reminded her of how things were when she and Mario were in love. She lost it—and so much more—when she took you to the mission."

Gabrielle fell down a well of silence, unwanted tears etching her face. Carmen gave her back the cloths and took her hand, giving Gabrielle time to recover before pressing on.

"Elena clearly had disappointed Yatzil's family. It's strange that although none of Yatzil's generation were involved in the revolution in Mexico, they believed they'd somehow inherited the standing of their ancestors." Carmen tossed her head as if to expel something odious.

"They took it personally that Elena, who they had high hopes for, would give herself—and her virginity—to this rich boy who was everything they despised. They never could forgive her. From that moment, they wanted her gone.

"For Christ's sake, she was their daughter! Yet they hounded her to accept Ramón, the only one who would have her. Marrying her off gave them a respectable way to separate themselves from her." Her voice lowered. "But after Elena died, I think they realized they'd done wrong. They saw less of their friends and neighbors. They kept mostly to themselves, as if they were the ones doing penance this time. You said you tried to see them?"

"Yes. I actually talked to them briefly. But when they realized who I was, Martina ordered me to leave. She said I was upsetting Yatzil. They never acknowledged that Elena was my mother and that I was one of them. Of course I wasn't aware of our relationship at that point. It all was so strange."

"I'm not surprised," Carmen responded. "I haven't seen them in many years. It's a shame they don't seem to be able to deal with what they did—and now with you. In you was a piece of Elena standing there. You could have been their salvation. How very sad for you, and for them."

Gabrielle nodded, searching her mind for questions that could lead her to something in this family worth holding onto. "When I checked the county birth records for Martina and Elena, it gave Yatzil's name as the mother, but listed no father for either of them. Do you know why?"

"Yes," she said. "Elena's father—your grandfather—was Pablo Rialto."

Immediately Gabrielle grew more attentive, harboring hope of a grandfather who would make her long search for family worth the disappointment she was enduring.

"He and Yatzil were officially married after both girls were born," Carmen was saying, "although Yatzil and her children kept the Santos name. He wasn't listed as the father, though he was, because he was an illegal then. Yatzil got citizenship when she came here from Mexico, because she and her mother were given

Into the Unknown

political asylum. So her children of course were American. Yatzil met Pablo some years after she came here. They lived together for a few years before they married and he became a citizen. That's why he's not on the girls' birth records."

"What happened to my grandfather?" she asked anxiously.

"He was a construction worker. He died on the job when Elena was only ten."

"Oh!" Gabrielle exclaimed, her voice thick with the weight of another loss. "How sad." Silence. "What was he like?" she finally asked.

Carmen's voice warmed as she described Pablo. "A good, solid man and quite handsome. I think Elena got her looks from him, more so than from Yatzil. I believe things might have gone differently for Elena had Pablo been alive when Elena's tragedies occurred."

"How do you mean?"

"He was a kind man who watched over his children and never would abandon them. He was especially fond of Elena. In truth he doted on her. I think Yatzil grew harder after Pablo died. I suppose she needed to, as she became the sole support for her family. She was a domestic, cleaning for rich people. It doesn't pay that much. Growing children have a lot of needs. I suppose she did the best she could."

Gabrielle sighed and nodded, broken by the knowledge of another family death and suddenly feeling depleted. But the mention of Pablo sparked something in her. "Is there anything more you can tell me about my grandfather?"

"He was a hardworking and loving man, and a very good carpenter. Like Maribel and Yatzil, he was from San Cristóbal de las Casas in the Mexican state of Chiapas. Elena adored him and was devastated when he died. It took her a long time to get over his sudden death. I'm afraid that's all I can tell you." Looking apologetic, she glanced at her watch.

"Goodness, it's almost dinnertime. My husband will be home soon. I hope you have the answers you were looking for." Her face sagged as from the burden of unwelcome memories. And her hands clutching her chair arms echoed her need to rise from the hurt she still carried.

"I wish I could have known Maribel and Pablo," Gabrielle said as she got up, looking long at Carmen who was standing now. "I want to thank you for your friendship with my mother and for sharing so much with me. You seem to have been more family to her than anyone. I see that your memories have brought you pain. I'm sorry for that."

Despite her apparent exhaustion, Carmen allowed Gabrielle's request to take a picture of her. Then when Carmen accepted Gabrielle's offered hand before leaving, she pulled Gabrielle in and hugged her. "Your mother would have been so proud of you," she said. "You seem to be a fine young woman. I realize I didn't ask anything about *you*. Are you married? Do you have children? Do you work?"

Gabrielle laughed. "No kids, no husband, though I have a wonderful boyfriend in Chicago. I just finished school. I'm a painter."

"You paint houses?" Carmen looked surprised.

"No," she laughed again, feeling the release this gave her. "I paint pictures, although painting houses might pay better."

Carmen smiled. "That's lovely. Maybe you'll send me one of your paintings sometime."

"I'd be honored to. Thank you for everything, Mrs. Di Venzi. I understand now why you and my mother were best friends."

Carmen gave her a grateful smile.

Stepping outside from the warmth of the house to the chill of the waning day, Gabrielle noticed how the wind had died down and become tranquil. Amid the stillness she pondered Carmen's stories of her mother's ill-fated past. She felt a huge weight of sadness for Elena and sorrow that she herself would never have the chance to know her birth mother—or her grandfather.

She saw now how Elena's was a life that had been short and scarred by tragic entanglements, family and societal rejection, and remorse. Yet she had the clear sense that Elena was a bright, caring person, gentle, steadfast, pure of heart, and scarcely more than a child when she died.

As she drove back to San Miguel, she turned over in her mind what Carmen had told her of her father, her grandmother, and her aunt. She couldn't help but feel disappointment, even some degree of anger toward them. But she still wondered if she should pursue further meeting with them, now that she knew much of the truth of her past. They were her relations after all.

She reflected on this for quite some time. What would she learn that she hadn't already discovered? Were they people she would want to know better or who could in some way enrich her life, or she theirs? In the case of Yatzil and Martina, she felt no kinship. They might, she thought, turn out to be just lines on a family tree that held incomplete answers.

Then she replayed what Carmen had mentioned in passing, that Elena believed Mario's family forced him to abandon her. Perhaps Mario did care about her mother after all. Still, he apparently never tried to find their child—or help Elena. Surely if he truly loved her, he could have conjured a way to ease her situation and make at least some things right. But perhaps he was a victim in his own way. Did he suffer remorse?

She couldn't help but be uncertain about whether her father really was the person Carmen believed him to be. All she knew was that she saw no way to approach him now that wouldn't create a volatile situation for her and for his family. And in truth, her search had emotionally depleted her. *I can write to him when I return to Chicago*, she decided. *If he responds, I'll have my answer. If he doesn't, I'll have my answer.*

7

She waited to depart San Miguel to attend Father Martino's funeral. It was unseasonably warm on this Saturday afternoon. She packed her bags and checked out of the motel, then drove to the street in front of the old mission courtyard.

Arriving early, she was surprised by the size of the crowd already making its way there. She seated herself in the second pew from the front of the nave. Soon she turned to watch a stream of men, women, and children filing in. Seeing how they packed the pews and aisles, she also observed people standing outside the opened doors and windows. She noted how they were from different backgrounds and social strata, but who like her, knew and must revere this humble giant of a man. *Father in Heaven,* she prayed, *I'm so grateful that Father Martino showed me such devotion when I was a baby and again as an adult. I will love and remember him always. Please, Heavenly Father, bless and keep Father Martino in your loving care.*

Just as she looked up, she saw the back of a tall, middle-aged couple dressed in stylish attire. Someone had just escorted them to the pew in front of her. Watching them as they turned to sit, she realized they looked vaguely familiar. Why did she know them? Then it hit her. Could they be the pair in the newspaper Carmen had given her? Was this Mario and his wife?

She broke into a sweat. She thought she might pass out. The service became a blur as she wrestled with questions. *Should I approach him? What if he's not Mario? What would the woman say? Surely it would make a scene, a terrible thing to do at the good Father's funeral. But how can I not talk to this man when he's so close?*

Then an idea hit her. She could write a note and transfer it to him before the pair left their seats. She would request that he alone meet her briefly outside, behind the apse of the church. She wouldn't give her name and would say only that she had information of importance to him.

She opened her bag to remove her sketch pad and pen. Her hand trembled as she struggled to tear off a sheet. But it stuck. As she yanked it, it flipped to the floor. Aghast at her clumsiness and not wanting to draw attention to herself, she tore another piece from the pad, clasping it tight. As she struggled to hide her anxiety and calm herself, she began to write the missive. Her hand shook in fear of mistaking the pair or being rejected. Folding it, she waited until the service neared its end to give it to the person beside her. She whispered her request to pass it along until it reached the tall, elegant man in the pew in front of them.

Into the Unknown

As the service concluded, she watched the folded paper arrive in the hand of the gentleman she hoped was her father. Observing him unfold and read what she had written, she saw him turn to look behind him. Nervously she looked down so he wouldn't discover her.

She hurried to leave the sanctuary, still packed with people. Pressing up against them, she felt she might suffocate. Finally outside, she hurried to the back of the old mission. *Will he recognize me? Will I know him? What will I say? What if he isn't Mario?* Perspiration soaked her. She shifted from one foot to the other and kept checking her watch. The minutes, the seconds crawled with agonizing torpor. She thought she might faint.

Twenty minutes dragged by. The crack of a branch startled her. Then she saw him. Stunned, she acknowledged her own brilliantly blue eyes. His nose so like hers. The slender, tall stature she also carried.

He looked surprised, confused. Then he stiffened, stared hard at her. A seed of recognition bloomed in his eyes. Then shock.

"Who are you? ...What do you want?" his voice quivered.

She couldn't speak.

He glared at her, crossed his arms. "What is it dammit?"

Her voice caught in her throat.

"Well?" he growled.

She sought her courage, took a few steps toward him, nearly falling as her foot snagged a root.

His irritation seemed to rise as he stepped back from her.

"Stop!" she cried. "You are Mario Santorez. And I am...."

"You are...what?" he glowered.

"I am...your and Elena's daughter."

Silence. He studied her. His face twitched. His stare hardened.

"I don't know you," he said, his voice cold, low, accusatory. "What do you want of me? Is it money you're after?" His questions were a wall, a block he threw between him and her.

"That is not what this is about," she said. "I was adopted when I was only four months old. I came here from Chicago to find my birth family. I've been here for weeks and only just learned that you're my father. I have no interest in your money. And I don't wish to cause you trouble. I only want answers to three questions."

He turned away in annoyance. She stared at his back. It was unyielding.

"And then you'll go away and not bother me again?"

"Yes," she said, making him pause, "as long as you answer honestly."

He pivoted quickly on feet dressed in stylishly tooled, white leather boots. Punishing her with a gaze that spoke his loathing and his fear, he tapped his foot petulantly.

"Now you're assaulting my character."

Silence.

"Did you love my mother?"

Hesitant, he bristled, then settled himself. "…Perhaps…I thought I did."

"Did you ever try to find what happened to me?"

"No."

Disappointment crushed her. She battled to steel herself.

"Did you have regrets?"

"For what?"

"For abandoning my mother…and me."

"What difference would that have made?" He raised a smug chin.

"Just please answer the question."

He picked at her through silence as his exasperation grew. "You can't be serious. I come from good breeding and wealth. Do you really think I would marry an inferior person? Elena was very pretty, and she gave me pleasure. But she came from a family of peasants—field workers, domestics. She should have understood this."

"But half my blood is yours!" Her voice broke. "Does this mean nothing to you?"

"…You said three questions."

"Yes…but I need your answer." She clung to the barest of hopes.

Into the Unknown

He smirked. His eyes narrowed. "It means nothing to me. Elena's not the only girl I knocked up." He laughed, his look of disdain trapping her.

His words tore like knives to her heart. She shook in indignation at his coarse dismissiveness and ignoble reply.

As if sensing an opening to wound further, he moved to bring her down. Scowling, he struck. "She should have been more careful."

Gabrielle looked into his eyes and saw no shred of feeling for her or her mother. No remorse. Only ugliness, privilege, and unrelenting guardedness.

"You will not speak to me again. And you will not set foot on my estate or bother my family," he barked. Destroying her dream of connection, he smiled, chilling her. His look was a drawn weapon.

Then he drove for the kill. He cut with a voice cloaked in nonchalance. "You are a bastard. You have no claim on me or my wealth."

With that, he spun on his fashionable boot, annihilating all hope.

Suffering his thrust, her legs buckled. His ostracism and cruelty buried her. A long, low moan rose from her. Racked with sobs, she struggled to stand.

In the pit of her stomach, she felt her father's character. It reeked of callousness and treachery. Falling on her with the weight of boulders, he entombed her with his total disregard for her and her mother.

Shattered, she screamed.

It was more than an hour before she could move. Emotionally exhausted, her spirit battered and in shock, Gabrielle stared blankly at the old mission. At that moment, the memory of Father Martino rose in her. She felt his presence urge her to leave this place. She stumbled to the car. Still in shock and dragging sorrow, she labored to seat herself behind the wheel. Time passed slowly before she started the engine.

As if in a dream, she watched herself leave the town, the place where she, her mother, and Carmen were born, where her grandmother and her aunt lived, where her grandfather Pablo died, where Mario and her mother met, and where Elena fell in love. She felt Elena's sorrow and Mario's betrayal and how, in desperation, she abandoned Gabrielle, knowing Father Martino would find her. It was he who rescued and cared for her. It was he—and her mother—she always would hold most dear.

As the shock she bore began to loosen, she struggled to separate herself from the heinousness of her father's character. But witnessing Mario's malice and how he had ruined Elena's life, she couldn't hide from the reality of his brutality and the cold and arrogant person that he was.

She had hoped his love for Elena was real. Now she saw it only for the self-serving act he had made of it. Wishing he wasn't her biological father, she realized the deep wounds he had inflicted upon Elena—and her. She now had answers she sought. But they were a bitter pill. With no sense of closure and suffering his dismissal, she experienced new depths of sadness for herself and for the sweet, tormented mother she would never know.

Finally she marked that she now knew the hard truth of her birth, her adoption, and her heritage. She understood that this knowledge would change her in ways she couldn't yet imagine. Struggling with her birth father's actions, she felt her brokenness in a darker way. She saw how it stemmed from her birth families' tragedies and in some cases heartlessness, no longer from a lack of awareness of who she was and who her ancestors might have been. Shaken by the brutishness she witnessed, she knew that over time she would have to find ways to move beyond this and mend the fractured parts of herself.

So who was her family, she asked herself as she drove through dry, rocky mining country. She loved her sister Ruth, but had felt estranged from her adoptive parents. Then she remembered Carmen's revelation that Elena wanted to spare her child from the bitter life she saw in their future. This brought her to something she hadn't considered—that the parents she grew up with also may have saved her from a cruel fate.

Into the Unknown

With this understanding and these experiences, she saw now that her harshness with her adoptive mother when they last met was unfair and misplaced. She needed to seek her mother's forgiveness. Acknowledging her own failings, Gabrielle realized how much she loved her adoptive family and longed to reconnect with them. She promised herself she would call them as soon as she returned to Chicago.

Then she considered the whole of her life. How many others had believed in her, even loved her, each in his or her own manner, and helped her to become who she was today? Beyond her immediate family, she found that the list was long. It included her beloved Rick, Father Martino, her childhood mentor Mrs. Bealey, and her adored Great Aunt Etienne. Then came childhood friend Adrienne, past love Mehmet, school chums Bilge and Becky. Finally were her art instructors at Oberlin and her teachers at Parsons, especially Professors Ray and Rabinowitz.

In a very real way she thought that all these people were her family too. When she needed them, they had been there for her. She owed them debts she never could repay. She had come to see her life as a journey, begun in desperation, abandonment, and loss, yet ultimately enriched by the goodwill of wise, caring people.

Long after leaving San Miguel, as she drove toward the airport in Tucson, she watched the moon begin its rise early in the evening winter sky. She thought it was almost as if the moon with its luminous sense of promise urged her as she sped toward a destiny not yet fully revealed to her.

As she pondered her future and her return north, however, she found herself thinking about Chicago. Suddenly she realized that what she most needed at this moment was waiting there for her. Love, purpose, artistic challenge and expression, all of this was there. Home now was where Rick was, where her heart was. He was the love she never thought she would find. She laughed through tears.

She could hardly wait to go home.

Made in the USA
Middletown, DE
08 December 2022